THE IRON BUTTERFLY

A historic novel based on WWII

Oscar Klass

All paper used in the printing of this book has been made from wood grown in managed, sustainable forests.

ISBN 978-1-78003-847-6

Printed and published in the UK

Author Essentials Ltd
4 The Courtyard
South Street
Falmer
BN1 9PQ

A catalogue record of this book is available from the British Library

Cover design by Jacqueline Abromeit

Dedication

To my wife Magdalena, for her patience and tea.

Preface

I was born in Vienna during WW II but made in the Royal Navy. Of a British father and Austrian mother I joined the RN at sixteen, progressed to become a North Sea diver and later, a Deck Officer in the Mercantile Marine.

I decided to write *The Iron Butterfly* from my time at sea and my family experiencing both the Nazi atrocities and the Russian occupation of Austria. The plight of the Cossacks is a story related to me by my father and I trust in telling I have done justice to these proud people.

Oscar Klass

Contents

Continued…

French, German, Japanese, Russian terms
and miscellaneous

Chapter One

U-BOAT BUNKER LORIENT

Death was the survivor – with the raid at its height a Lancaster was in flames. Hit by flak the bomber was transformed, like a fiery comet into a blazing wreck and a Mosquito fighter, caught in the pencil glare of a searchlight projector, made its final approach to target the pen and fire a volley of rockets – as a roof mounted AA battery locked-on to its target.

Kapitänleutnant Kurt Oblitz stood at the entrance of the U-Boat bunker that faced out into the Blavet estuary and gave an involuntary shudder of his broad shoulders as he recalled the events of the night. He reflected on how the structure shook as he dived for cover and the rockets found their mark.

As day dawned on 3 April 1944 at the U-Boat base, Lorient, Kurt dismissed his deliberations as his attention was drawn towards a weather-beaten boat, stripped of its conning tower paint and struggling against the elements to gain access to its pen. Blustery showers had persisted throughout the night whilst further to the north, the rain fell as sleet, but that was after the raid. Now, a watery sun probed the scurrying clouds to filter through and unmask the leaden blanket that hung over the Brittany landscape.

The westerly gale had eased, to settle in the south, but was still gusting at thirty knots as it moaned its way through the bare branches of the nearby trees. The poplars stood like sentinels marking the perimeter of the naval complex, whilst, across the expanse of open water, the only signs of movement were the newcomer and several fishing boats that tugged wildly at their moorings in salute to the short sea.

Below he heard the constant surge of water which beat with impunity against the lock gates and the U-bunker's forbidding structure. His athletic six-foot frame was dwarfed by the cavernous entrance of the building that yawned, dark and menacing in the gathering light. Above him the ceiling culminated in a fifteen-foot thick expansive roof. Constructed with two million tons of steel and concrete, the uninviting structure blended intimately with the clouds and the mud-churned waters of the estuarial river.

The young German U-Boot officer wheeled sharply and turned his back on the brooding dawn and made his way along the bunker's narrow quay towards the far end of the building and its side entrance. He passed a wrecked welding machine and soot-grimed walls as his eyes adjusted to the glaring tungsten lights and the fug from the diesels. The machines created a constant haze and acrid fumes that stung his eyes and irritated his throat and lungs. He coughed involuntarily and cursed the planners for their lack of foresight in not installing an adequate ventilation system.

Away from the entrance, the structure glistened and sweated globules from the heat of the welding torches, numerous arc lamps and the exhausts of running engines. The condensing water, ponding in places as it ran in rivulets down the bunker walls. Nimbly, he sidestepped the pools as he progressed towards the far exit and its steel doors. Annoyingly, the soot-impregnated water would drip, wetting his shoulders and staining his white topped officer's cap. It took him several minutes to reach the end of the bunker; such was the vast size of the pen which at times accommodated two submarines as they returned from their Atlantic patrols.

Passing his boat, he noted with satisfaction the on-going maintenance that was taking place, pausing long enough to watch as the newcomer, of a class similar to his own was being manoeuvred, with fenders rigged, to lie along his port side. On reaching the doors he was greeted by a welcoming draught of air before zigzagging his way past the walls of the blast screen. Once outside, Kurt inhaled deeply and welcomed the morning air into his lungs. The rare tonic triggered an instant spasm of coughing that ended with a lung-wrenching hawk and a gratifying six-foot ejection of the nicotine-stained product. Mentally he cursed the cigarettes as his health was suffering, but then the stale, oxygen-depleted air in a dived 'sardine can', did not help.

Satisfied, and his morning ritual accomplished but still growling heartily to clear his throat, he systematically dipped into his breast pocket for his silver cigarette case and flipped it open with one deft movement of the hand. Nursing the flame with the aid of his uniform jacket he lit up, drew in a rewarding nicotine-enhanced breath and slowly exhaled through distended nostrils. Calmly he slipped the case back and took in the scene before him.

He gritted his teeth and shook his head in disbelief at the ferocity of the raid and the resulting devastation. It was clear the British had

had some success but their targets still stood unscathed in front and behind him. Glancing further afield he noted with satisfaction that the torpedo storage bunkers were also unscathed.

At Lorient the three main bunkers sat imposingly on the low landscape, like giant medieval fortresses, obdurate and built beyond their time. However the unyielding edifices were built to protect submarines and stood challenging for any modern crusader that came by air from the west. To limit blast, the roof area was constructed with a unique explosion-absorbing 'Fangrost' protection of external concrete beams which straddled the roof and incorporated an air gap to absorb impact and bomb penetration. The submarine base consisted of these three major constructions, the pens, (the largest) being ninety feet in height, three hundred feet in length and three hundred in width.

The first two buildings housed the U-Boot pens and repair facilities. The U-pens situated on the estuary were in blocks, seven single pens in one block and five double pens in another with an eight-rail 'transverser' system to the rear. The transverser rails carried the cradle to its selected pen, whereupon a tractor was deployed to haul the boat complete with cradle to safety and repair across a three hundred foot concrete slip. In order to slip the boats, docking cradles were used – the U-pen was partially drained and the tractor then hauled the cradle – from its pen, up to the servicing and repair bunker. The transverse rails allowing the cradle to be moved sideways to the selected pen.

The third building was for administration and living quarters for the Kriegsmarine personnel, together with a hospital and an operating theatre. The structures were constructed by the Nazi Todt organisation using German expertise, the local workforce and gangs of expendable forced labour.

Eyeing the destruction to some out-buildings Kurt began walking up the transverser slipway and towards the administration bunker. He slowed his pace as ahead of him appeared a smoking crater. Continuing warily he stopped short to stare wistfully down into a thirty-foot hole slowly filling with water. Looks like the Tommies have once again left their calling card he mused as he casually drew on his cigarette. Fortunately it had missed the repair bunker and only damaged part of the slip and rails.

Ja, he surmised there was nothing to stop the bombers as he glanced back to the other pens adjacent to his. Other bombs had hit the Fangrost, but failed to penetrate. For once the Führer's planning had withstood the ultimate test and he tacitly thanked him for that.

Pensively he drew on his cigarette, satisfied the Allies had tried but failed once again to destroy the bunkers, however the proof of their invincibility was by now well established – unless of course they came up with something else. He remained at the edge of the crater as he contemplated the war. It had been a game of cat and mouse with new-fangled weapons on both sides. There were his new torpedoes and Schnorchel tube and the Allies had their 'pinging' sonar – sophisticated short-wave radar and the devil only knows what else. But with these thoughts in mind it once again triggered the old enemy within. It was a voice that could not be muted and the curse of every U-Bootman was again gnawing his sentiments. It played on his mind as it calmly suggested that perhaps he, Kurt Oblitz, had already become the mouse.

Ach! Perish the thought; he admonished himself with a shrug. For the time being at least both he and all the other U-Boot crews knew they could sleep, mess and receive medical attention inside that vast bunker citadel and its outlying fifty acre site that comprised the submarine complex at Lorient.

Skirting the crater Kurt finished his cigarette and angrily flicked the dog-end at a smouldering Wehrmacht truck. He thought about Reichmarschall Goering's much vaunted Luftwaffe that was powerless to stop raids like this and the airborne attacks at sea, both on him and the rest of the U-Boot flotilla. Where was the air support from the Luftwaffe that was always promised by the air marshal, so notable by its absence?

It was the steady drone of a low-flying aircraft that now caught his attention as it slowly circled the town some two miles to his right. He was unsure whether it was friendly or that of an Allied recognisance plane but he decided it was German as the Flak batteries to the north remained silent. By now the weather had eased and with mild curiosity he decided to see what else had been destroyed or left standing?

With his bunker behind him he made his way across the rails of the transverser slipway and along the concrete apron that led straight to the main dockyard gate and the road into town. Passing along the side of the repair bunker he made out the open fields and the lower part of the town. On a hill he recognised the taller buildings that were left standing. They stood among the ruins like sightless sentinels overlooking the dockyard, their windows devoid of glass, their skull-like sockets scorched and blackened by fire. It appeared what little remained of the town had not been touched by last night's raid as he could not see any signs of destruction. He felt a sense of relief, as his conscience had troubled him about leaving his fräulein to fend for herself. I think she will have something to say about that, he mused and toying with the idea of seeing her again.

The town itself had been subjected to several heavy raids by the Royal Air Force and, by January of 1943, it had been reduced to piles of rubble, all excepting that part to the north with its small seventeenth-century church and some surrounding cafés at Kerentrech. Fortunately for the German garrison the Allies had missed their chance of destroying the bunkers as they were only then being constructed, however 'Bomber Harris' of the RAF had switched tactics and going for the softer option decimated the town instead. With their houses in ruins it automatically drove the local people out, thus denying the Germans of most of their local labour as well as the comforts of many requisitioned hotels.

Then there was the loss of the renowned Louis XIV Grand Café with its well-stocked cellars of wine and Champagne, a truly historic building and a much-beloved watering hole of both French and Germans alike. However the Bretons did not take too kindly to being bombed out of their homes as they suffered the Boche up to a point and naturally wanted them out but then they were much in favour of the British fighting their war but after several raids and the subsequent loss of life and belongings they despised them for the draconian methods deployed. It was therefore considered by many that in trying to prise out Hitler's occupation forces and wolf pack submarines, the RAF's carpet-bombing was a case of throwing the baby out with the bath water.

For Kurt, still young and single, the raids did not bother him, rather it only delayed matters and he took it all in his stride. As long as a few cafés remained and the local filles de joie were there for company, it was all that mattered.

Cautiously he continued along the road, walking past incendiary devices that lay scattered, some spent and others still burning. By now he was clear of the second bunker and felt relieved as the raid had left little damage as far as he could see. For him the existence of the bunkers was akin to that of a magnet – an attractive force for the bombers, and a must-to destroy. But for now, on this chilly morning it seemed like a weight had lifted from his shoulders. Just like a fox he reasoned, after the hounds had lost the scent and the hunt had moved further afield.

For now he was safe, but it was no secret that the Allies were making a concentrated effort and out-sized bombs to destroy the U-bunkers but here, as elsewhere along the occupied coast of Europe, from France in the south, then Holland, Denmark and Norway, they had up until now failed to destroy a single bunker. Tall Boy bombs as they were known by the Allies but for him and his men, the passive recipients, the ones who sat it out and patiently waited whilst tons of high explosive fell on their heads – they had a less endearing name. The latest were five-ton monsters, constructed in Derbyshire, England; they stood several feet taller than a man and were packed with high explosives, together with a specially designed warhead that would under normal circumstances have penetrated any normal building. However the bunkers were built from a more demanding mould.

Kurt skirted a smaller crater and carried on with his inspection as the drifting smoke from several burning incendiaries momentarily cleared. The small canisters continuously belched a blanket of blinding smoke and burnt with a searing flame but could not have any effect on re-enforced concrete. By now the wind had eased and on the breeze came the sickly and unmistakable smell of burning flesh.

The sweet cloying stench filled his nostrils and wrapped itself like a mantle round him as there to his left and near to the back wall of the Administration Bunker lay the twisted and burnt bodies of several soldiers. As the smoke wafted and cleared, he cautiously approached the bodies and recognised one of the soldiers. His grey, blood-drained features now matched the field-grey of his uniform, while his eyes, wide open in death, stared unseeingly towards him.

'Taschenberg,' Kurt mumbled.

Feldwebbel Taschenberg, a sergeant from the Flak battery and a drinking companion, who often gave the U-Boot men a lift into town in his truck. He now lay before him – lifeless, like a rag doll with limbs akimbo, broken and at a grotesque angle, cast away like a child's spent toy at bedtime. The soldier was not alone in death as his comrades lay close by, maimed and disfigured, some without limbs and stripped naked by the effects of the bombs and blast.

Angrily he stepped up to a body and kicked the burning canister away from the man's side, however the remains of his uniform continued to burn with the deadly phosphorous still charring what remained of his flesh. Kurt cursed under his breath. He cursed the Englander and the bloody war. These men were known to him, some like Taschenberg has a family with grandchildren. Amongst the human carnage lay the remains of their Flak battery, torn from its roof mounting as if by some giant hand and now lay broken and in pieces, its 88mm barrel pointing like an accusing finger to the drizzling sky.

With impotent rage he backed off and distanced himself upwind as grim-faced he recalled the events of the night. It had only been five hours since the raid but it now felt like time had stood still, a world apart as he recalled his nightly sojourn to the local café, its bar and small dance floor. Then he thought about his pleasant evening with Maria, one of the young German nurses.

He recalled the sound of the undulating sirens and the immediate pounding and reverberations of the Flak batteries as the café was plunged into darkness. His hurried departure; leaving the bar and his date and for her to seek the safety of the café's cellar and for him to return through the raid and blackout to the dubious safety of his boat.

Once back at the bunker, he had watched from the pen's entrance the determination of the Lancaster bombers guided by the marker flares of the Mosquito pathfinders. They had singled out and vividly marked their targets as the flares and incendiaries landed on top and around the bunkers. Amongst the pounding of the Flak batteries had come the ear-shattering explosions of the blockbuster bombs as they targeted the bunkers.

He had watched in contented fascination as one of the bombers was hit, plummeting earthwards in a searing fireball of smoke and flames. Its fuselage ablaze from end to end and for some unknown reason he felt glad, even elated, as he saw the parachutes opening and blossoming in the glare of a six foot diameter searchlight projector.

He vividly recalled the fighter, banking to starboard, jinking and weaving in order to escape the probing finger of a searchlight that had found him, singled him out in its radar-guided beam and in that same instant the Mosquito turned towards his pen and fired a volley of rockets as the Flak found its mark. He still visualised the ensuing explosion, the super-nova glare as the aircraft erupted in a ball of flame. He had hurled himself bodily behind a large welding generator as the rockets exploded in the entrance, while shrapnel ricocheted to slam into the machine and pockmark the interior walls around him.

Then as suddenly as they had come, like hailstones in August, it was over as the explosions and the roar of engines ceased. He had picked himself up and saw across the Ter estuary, towards the far bank the bomber was still burning and lighting up the sky in a mass of orange flames but the fighter had vanished. After that came the steady and welcoming wail as the all-clear siren sounded.

By this time he had seen enough. He'd turned his back on the distant blazing pyre and returned to his boat to salvage the last remnants of sleep of what remained of the night.

Here now, in the post-dawn light he saw further afield and the consequences of the raid for there, in a shrapnel-shredded tree hung one of the parachutes. Its occupant blackened and lifeless and still in his harness swayed like a puppet theatre's marionette as the wind stirred the shattered branch that held him. Kurt felt only disgust as he diverted his gaze only to see the others, his companions he assumed as two bodies were lying some fifty yards apart, dressed in flying suits and the leather flying jackets of the Royal Air Force. They lay in their chutes, their bodies partially burnt and not too distant from the soldiers they had come to kill.

Kurt clenched his teeth and gave a derisive grunt as he thought about the futility of their sacrifice, the waste of youth. If only they could realise the irony of it all as they lay together, in death united. Here they were, friend and foe alike, some so burnt and barely recognisable as human beings and previously life-sworn enemies but now lying together in peace at last, but in a foreign field.

He decided for a closer inspection and made his way towards them. He was curious as in four years of conflict he had never met the enemy – except of course at long range, through his periscope or gun-sights, machine against machine – to kill or be killed. Today it was different and nothing he had ever experienced at sea and it was perhaps a stirring within, the humane side of war as he felt a tinge of compassion creeping into his soul.

He stopped short to stare at the nearest corpse and realised that this man, as well as the others, was just an ordinary man like him – the same height and the same flesh and age. As he gazed down at the young airman it suddenly brought to mind his own chances of survival. It could happen to him, only his end might not be as simple as being shot down and laid out on a wet, grassy knoll. Part of his U-Boot's armoury was stealth and surprise, lose that certain element and they would hunt him down. The airman lying here did not have that certain element as the gun crews knew he was coming and were ready for him and all the others on the wing.

Fascinated if not mesmerised Kurt stared at the lifeless body with its swollen and blackened face. He was a brave young man he reflected as he pulled out his cigarette case and selected a Players, methodically tamping it on the case. I wonder, he mused as he lit the comforting tobacco, did this youngster really know why he had to forfeit his life and end up here? Did he, like so many youngsters in the Fatherland proudly sing their youth away – and die?

He recalled his last patrol in the Atlantic where he was pounced upon by a British frigate, HMS *Starling* from what he remembered of her F66 pennant number as she turned and headed in his direction. He had fired two torpedoes at her but missed as the ship rapidly altered course and combed the tell-tale tracks and set off after him in hot pursuit. He was fortunate and managed to elude her but he would not be that reckless again by using the old air-driven torpedoes against a warship. He would not fire unless he was sure of a kill as with experience he knew if he failed to hit a warship, especially a frigate or destroyer and tried to escape they would rain depth charges down on him until he was blown to kingdom come and sent plunging to the ocean floor. He did not fancy being trapped while a million tons of water pressed down and crushed his submarine's hull like an egg-shell in the jaws of Neptune's gigantic vice.

At least, he reasoned, these men had had the open air to breathe their last and the stars above as their final canopy. For the likes of him and his men only the Stygian darkness of a plunging steel tomb and a watery grave beckoned.

But then, what matter? He reasoned and not without a touch of nonchalance. There weren't any degrees to death. The end result was still the same – dead was dead. Whether a Stone Age axe or a modern bullet, one was just as dead from either. But, then was it not the way; not to linger in death or to suffer with pain? The method, perhaps or even a choice of one's demise? Ja, that was it, he reflected. That's the essence in this sort of life, how – when and where to die. Even in this lousy war that element of choice still held sway.

He drew on his cigarette and looked-on, fascinated as the dead airman swung from his harness, like the pendulum on his grandmother's clock. He nodded with gritted teeth at the futility of it all as his morbid thoughts retuned to haunt him. Had he joined up with the army, a soldier with a rifle, death would be by bullet. But here, in the navy it would be by drowning, quite simple. That's how it seemed, so logical and predictable. At least that had been his reasoning just a few years ago, a sort of schoolboy's pocket book outlook on life and beyond.

But that was folly, he knew it now. It just doesn't work out like that as thousands of soldiers had drowned and many more sailors had been shot or even worse, wounded and left to struggle in the water and drown. To die and not to suffer that's the true aspect of the game. But then there's the glory – Valhalla denied with a cow's death or he the warrior and the blazing boat his funeral pyre?

'That's it,' he muttered with conviction. 'Götterdemerung for me anytime but only as a last resort. I want to see this lousy war through, not become another statistic like the others.' He thought about the fallen heroes decorated as U-Boot aces and heroes of the Vaterland; the iron crosses with swords, diamonds and oak leaves awarded to the likes of Prien of Scapa Flow, or Lemp and Schepke with their thousands of tons of shipping sunk, but dead heroes all the same.

Satisfied that he had once again lain to rest this spectre that continued to haunt him he ground the half-smoked cigarette into the soil and left the airmen to lie in peace under the leaden sky from whence they had come.

Upon reaching the far end and entrance of the Administration Bunker he observed with relief the line of vehicles that had stood there the night before still remained intact and the bunker left unscathed. Just like the Englander's Rock of Gibraltar and their St Paul's, he mused, a symbol of defiance for all to see. But better still any damage here would have disrupted the U-boat's turn-round schedules, including that of his own.

About to make his way back he raised an eyebrow in recognition as one of his engineering officers came out of the building. Kurt waved him over.

'Not so bad, Erwin, eh?'

'Nein, Herr Kaleu'nt. We are still standing and better still, my stores have arrived.'

The engineer waved a sheaf of papers and indicated with his head towards the lorries. Kurt nodded with satisfaction as the two men began walking back towards the Ter embankment, where smoke was still billowing and the airman swayed precariously from his branch.

'Looks like he didn't quite make it,' said Kurt with a grin.

'Serves him right,' said the engineer. 'I saw two more in the bunker. They were injured, but should pull through. They put them in the hospital, can you believe it?' He said, raising his tone. 'I heard the interpreter talking to them, saying they would be safe here. What a joke, eh, Herr Kaleu'nt?'

Kurt gave a dissenting snort at the irony of it as they carried on walking in the direction of the embankment and its creek. The masts of several small craft came into view, moored to buoys in the estuary. With the airman hanging close by, the issue of his existence and demise once more invaded his thoughts. These soldiers and airmen were fortunate inasmuch they would have a grave, chronicled and with a headstone and cross. Not so for the likes of him and his crew; there would be no stone to record their ever being on this earth and passing. It would be as if he had never existed, unless some destroyer captain marked his chart, just for the record and location of his kill.

They stopped short as a pall of smoke and flame erupted from the nearby vehicle compound and its garage complex, whereupon a squad of soldiers came running from the building. Kurt with his hands thrust in his jacket pockets looked-on bemused, thumbs turned outwards and twitching nervously, while Erwin began anxiously tapping his rolled-up papers in the palm of his hand. Some of the trucks were now being driven with their canvas tops ablaze, to come to a skidding halt by a nearby static water tank, as others frantically flung buckets of water to douse the flames. Those undamaged were driven away and Kurt glanced in their direction as they passed the main gate and headed in the direction of the town.

It brought to mind the events of the night with his friend Maria and what might have been. Then there was another, Yvonne. She was a local girl who worked as an interpreter and switchboard operator at the Wehrmacht Communications Centre in town. Yvonne was pretty, petite and French and so different in character compared with the other local girls. She cared about him and he liked her easy going attitude, both with himself and about the war. He first met her at the Communications Centre during the spring of 1943 and later saw her again at an officers' garden party at the Château de Porcey. They were mutually attracted to each other over a glass of Champagne and, in a short time had become lovers.

As the main gates closed he thought about her. Would she, a French girl in the final analysis care or weep for him? He thought of his parents, he had last seen them at home in Augsburg, a year ago. He gritted his teeth as he envisaged them and their house now destroyed, out of the picture, killed by those Schweinehund Englander in an air raid over the town.

'Scheiss,' he muttered as Erwin shot him a questioning glance. Kurt scowled un-abashed, shook his head in resignation as he tried to shake off his negative thoughts, and systematically delving for his cigarette case. He didn't care for himself, he reasoned as he handed a cigarette to his engineer and angrily tamping his own as he lit up and inhaled the gratifying Virginia tobacco.

They carried on walking in silence, each with his own thoughts as Kurt reflected on the Allies and their shipping. Just as long as he could get himself and his U-Boot to sea and sink as many of them that had destroyed his family and decimated this town, and all the towns and cities in his homeland, was all that mattered. He would sink or shoot down as many of them that came his way; if it was an enemy warship that crossed his sights and open tubes, so much the better but a fat American or British merchantman was all the same to him.

He had lectured to his crew that every ship sunk meant Germany could fight for another day, but the truth of it was he did not know why he was fighting in the first place and that did trouble him. For him the Nazi ideal had long since faded; a young man's indoctrinated ideal, perhaps with misguided ideas about race and patriotism. He reflected on the night of bonfires and books and the Austrian business – the Anschluss, as the Führer called it. An annexation after the Nazis murdered their chancellor Dolfus and followed by the needless, crazy, land-grabbing attacks on Poland and Russia. Perhaps, he mused, as he shifted his gaze towards the shrapnel-stunted trees, when I've fired my final torpedo in this lousy war, someone would care to enlighten me.

He was jolted back to the present by the shouts from several soldiers as the wind veered, and close to the embankment stood another line of trees where the smoke had momentarily cleared.

'Ein flieger,' said Erwin in marked astonishment. 'We bagged a fighter by the looks of it.'

To Kurt's surprise there in the near distance lay the smouldering remains of an aircraft. His Mosquito he figured with satisfaction, the one that made him dive for the deck last night. Its wooden airframe lay spent and charred but the two bent propellers and engines remained as silent witnesses to its identity and one-time graceful existence.

'Looks like a Mosquito fighter,' said Kurt.

'Ja, ja, Herr Kapitän,' enthused the engineer. 'They've got Rolls Royce engines. Merlins, like the Spitfires.'

Kurt was about to get closer and examine the wrecked plane, perhaps find himself a souvenir when the sound of other raised voices from behind diverted his attention. Several men in field-grey uniforms came into view and at the double from round the side of the Administration Bunker. Guttural German voices gave orders, barking commands and gesticulating to others that followed. French civilians, by the nature of their baggy dress.

The 'charioteers' stopped short; and wheezing like spent horses methodically began running out a solitary rubber hose. A spurt, followed by a pulsating stream of watery foam was the result as they doused the remaining fires which were edging closer to one of the ammunition bunkers and several maimed soldiers. The water came from a handcart incorporating large wooden-spoked wheels and a small, one-cylinder donkey engine complete with bowser.

Three young Wehrmacht medical orderlies with white insignia armbands portraying a Red Cross brought up the rear. They came trotting behind the fire team dutifully carrying a stretcher. As they came upon the burnt and dismembered corpses, the teenagers pulled up short as the stretcher slid slowly from their grasp. Kurt grimaced as he watched the charade and decided he had seen enough for the morning, lit two cigarettes and handed one to his engineer.

'I just hope we will never need those boys,' said Kurt, shooting a derisory glance at the fire and rescue party. He made a mental note about informing the base commander about their late arrival and the fire appliance which would have taken pride of place in any science museum. Leaving the aircraft to burn they carried on back to the safety of their bunker and gaining the entrance Kurt impulsively touched the wall with a finger, it was a fleeting touch but he felt re assurance as he brushed against its cold, unrefined texture. It was akin to a reflex action, gratifying and like holy water in church, a token of faith and blessed assurance. Perhaps a touchstone and a salute to its builders rather than any kind of talisman and like Thomas of old, seeking assurance in its unyielding mass.

'You know something, Erwin?' He turned to the youngster, who dutifully followed his commander at two marching paces to the rear. 'If there ever was a god to concrete, then this place must be his temple. We, the congregation within, should bow to this divinity of Beton as without his walls and protection we would all be sitting ducks. It's the only thing between us and instant oblivion.' The engineer snorted at the absurdity but with a stifled grin, he was still amused by his captain's wit and levity.

'God looks after those that make the effort,' he had often heard his parents say and here certainly their god was a graven image made by the effort of the Todt organisation and their giant cement mixer.

Chapter Two

A DOOR TO THE CITY

After the raid, a heavy silence fell over the mass of humanity that crowded the candle-lit basement of the old museum. The building was of typical Gothic design with its high ceilings, arches and sturdy columns, whilst the floor consisted of grey marble tiles. Granite steps at one end of the building led down and gave access to its basement and the musty vaults below.

Once the bombers had departed, the all-clear sirens wailed mournfully over the stricken city. Their prophetic message and steady wail temporarily drowned the roar of flames and the sound of toppling buildings as the maelstrom of fire took hold. To the remaining inhabitants of Cologne the siren was a welcome sound as it signalled they had survived once more, and their ordeal was temporarily at an end. Released from their living nightmare the local populous emerged from their cellars and shelters whilst at the museum, a subdued stream of humanity re-entered the world above.

Anna Bauer found herself in a column where the old and infirm shuffled, whilst anxious mothers clutched their babies and scant belongings in one hand and pulling frightened and bleary-eyed children along with the other. Others, empty-handed, assisted wherever they could by helping those with children and baggage, as they had already lost everything and had nothing but themselves left to save.

Of medium height, with hazel brown eyes and matching hair, she was an attractive woman and, at twenty-six, in the prime of her adult life. Clutching her four-year-old son in one hand and a leather shopping bag in the other, she followed the moving line of people, past flickering blue-wax candles placed strategically along the wall. Patiently they filed past a warden whose face contrasted in the lambent light etching deep furrows on his sombre features. He indicated the direction to the stairs which lay ahead and repeatedly appealed for the anxious queue to stay calm and keep moving.

Daylight and fresh air filtered down from above as Anna picked up her son to negotiate the stairs. Water now cascaded down the steps and began flooding the basement. Those from behind were anxiously pushing and calling for the ones above to hurry along, otherwise it was an orderly queue and evacuation.

Eduard Bauer was well-wrapped for the occasion as Anna had become a veteran of such raids. She and Eddi, (as he liked to be called) had always taken as much clothing as they could comfortably wear and packets of food, all of which was crammed into the bag. For her and others it had become a routine of such raids, second nature to those that sought survival in the safety of the basements of the Reich. For the fair-haired boy with his father's blue-grey eyes, he always took his prized possession – a field-grey army blanket, a present from his uncle Wilhelm who had been invalided and sent home from the Russian front. Eddi liked to help and carried the blanket for his mother but now had it draped round him for extra warmth in the damp atmosphere of the museum's basement.

After the sudden rush and squeeze Anna found herself back on the ground floor of the museum. However, with the water flowing inches deep, she still had to carry her son as the polished floor was by now quite slippery. There was also the additional hazard of glass and fallen masonry. Sadly she noted the broken figurines of marble and stone, those ancient warriors lying shattered by their toppled plinths, and water gushing from a hydrant, coursing in a steady stream among the fragmented remains.

Eddi was soon asleep; it was the sleep of exhaustion as during the past few weeks the continuous Allied raids, air raid warnings and their staggered and interrupted journey had made routine sleep impossible. Rain was falling into the museum as Anna half covered his face with the blanket, unaware at first that part of the ceiling had fallen and the roof at one corner lay open to the sky. Although not struck directly, the building suffered from the effects of blast as a stick of bombs had missed their target on the Rhine and its shipping and had fallen on the already devastated city. Cries of anguish from the elderly were to be heard, while an old woman wearing a black headscarf began to rant and rave against the Amerikaner air crews.

'These schwarzen, they fly so high, cowards the lot of them. Gott im Himmel help us. *Hilfe! Hilfe!*' she shrieked, imploring the Almighty for Divine intervention and wringing her hands to the heavens as the rain fell softly on her upturned face.

Anna stood patiently waiting for the rubble to be cleared and thought about the tales her husband had related. As an officer's wife of the Kriegsmarine she knew quite well that all this had nothing to do with the Almighty, as she recalled his telling about the bombing

15

of London, Portsmouth and Plymouth. How Goering's Luftwaffe had decimated parts of those cities, indiscriminately bombing with high explosives and incendiaries on civilian targets and the razing of Coventry and its cathedral. He had warned her and always said Britain would one day retaliate and now here it was. It's our turn, she thought bitterly, harvest time.

The museum orderlies were well in evidence now, old men dressed in the dark blue uniform of the Köln Museum with peaked caps to match. They had managed to staunch the flow from the hydrant and assisted the Home Guard to clear a path in the rubble, some even conscientiously salvaging historic pieces and laying them aside as they went. The Heimwehr cleared the fallen masonry with shovels and yard brooms, making a path to the great door and its blocked exit.

One old man came close to Anna and she noticed his dedication as he methodically collected the broken arms of a statue. Painstakingly he picked them out of the rubble and carried them, one in each hand to a pile of similar items on the floor. They met each other's gaze, a fleeting glance, a frozen moment in time and recognition of each other's circumstances.

His weary resigned expression and grey stubbled face said it all, and his eyes – hazel, like hers but red and sore from weariness. They were old eyes, sad and tired eyes, eyes that had taken part in a previous conflict and were now a passive and mute witness to another. They glistened with moisture and as he passed her by she saw the lonely tear that meandered down his hollow cheek to lodge, hidden in his expansive moustache.

Shouts and a command from a warden were heard as it cut into the murmur of the waiting crowd.

'Schnell, schnell!' the man implored. 'You must get out quickly the roof is not safe and the ceiling will fall. Schnell, schnell! Get out!'

Men strained as a host of volunteers removed a final piece of timber and the people surged towards the open space where the doors had once hung. The gigantic bronze portals had been blasted inwards, ripped off their hinges, one of which was now lying at the feet of a statue. 'Adonis' was the inscription on the plinth. Amazingly the statue was still upright, his one arm outstretched, indicating with an open hand towards the door now lying at his feet.

To her the statue of the well-endowed god was saying, 'here you are, have a door,' as a smile crossed her lips and faded as she made her way past the mythological youth and out into the open air and the dubious safety of the street.

All around her buildings were either damaged or in ruins. Some stood burning, while others were on the point of collapse as their gable ends and facades bowed and crumbled. Exposed floors sagged alarmingly, spilling furniture and effects onto the street below. Mercifully the April rain had a dampening effect, both on the fires and the otherwise choking brown cloud of masonry dust which still lingered. Instinctively she glanced with others towards the Dome, as if by a miracle the cathedral, damaged and with its twin spires was still standing.

Perhaps there is a God after all, she mused as she hurried away in the direction of her parents' apartment. All she needed to do was to get there and to see they were safe as they only lived a few blocks from the museum.

Back home in Aachen her street had been bombed and her flat was declared unsafe, therefore she had decided to stay with her parents. She had also brought some needy essentials for them. In her bag she brought Belgian butter, smoked ham, eggs and flour. It was only the raid which had delayed her as she made her way from the railway station, past the cathedral and the old museum. That's when the sirens had sounded and the Allied raid began.

Anna, still carrying her slumbering son, picked her way past mounds of heaped rubble and strewn debris that littered the cobbled street. She threaded her way through the once proud streets as the Heimwehr and fire teams laboured to clear them. With care she skirted the downed power lines, some still live, spitting and hissing menacingly in the wet conditions. She passed a bedraggled line of people whose houses had been bombed. The old men stood staring, angry and with clenched fists, as mothers and grandmothers with headscarves tied at their chins cried to the heavens.

'Mein Gott, Mein Gott bitte hilfe uns,' they wept and pleaded.

The little ones, not understanding stood wide-eyed beside them, some weeping piteously and others holding each other's hands in frightened and confused silence.

Once clear Anna quickened her pace as she crossed the empty market square.

I hope they're safe, she kept saying to herself. Please God, let them be safe, as dense smoke was seen to be rising from the direction in which she was heading. Like her they would have been sheltering in the cellar she reasoned, as they always did once the sirens sounded. Although elderly and living on the fifth floor they would have had ample time to reach the safety of their cellar with its solid construction and a designated air raid shelter.

By now an amber glow had appeared a short distance ahead followed by the sound of raised voices and muffled screams. Instinctively Anna knew that something terrible had happened. Anxious seconds later she rounded the corner of the last block and into the street where her parents lived. She was immediately shocked by the horrific scene that confronted her. It was like an enactment from Dante's Inferno as fierce currents of air were being sucked towards a row of buildings engulfed in a maelstrom of roaring and all-consuming flames. Firemen, with their king-sized black and silver helmets, police and old men from the Heimwehr were already active in preventing people from approaching as they had sealed off the street.

Even from a distance, Anna felt the intense heat and saw with consternation the glowing skeleton of the steel supports as the masonry began to crumble. Like a film in slow motion the tortured girders began to yield and sag and she could only look-on in horror and disbelief as the whole seven-storey building began to sway, buckle and like a child's house of cards, collapse onto itself. In that single moment time stood still for her as her fears became reality and the last vestiges of hope were cruelly stripped away.

'Bitte, is there nothing you can do!?' she pleaded with a nearby fireman, desperately trying to make herself heard above the roar of the flames. 'My parents, they're in that building, they're in the cellar. Please, you must do something!'

The fireman turned to face her. He was an elderly man with a flowing white moustache, his head all but concealed under his great fireman's helmet. With a grim face he took her arm and led her back round the corner of the block in order to escape the heat.

'Bitte Frau,' he pleaded with her. 'You cannot remain here. There is nothing left and it is dangerous for yourself and the child.'

'Nein!' cried Anna, wrenching herself free. 'You don't understand. My parents are somewhere in there, down in the cellar. You must get them out.'

'Ja, lady,' he replied. 'I do understand, but I'm sorry, there is nothing we can do. There will be others trapped and with no air to breathe. It's the fire, you see. It has consumed all the air. Please, go now,' he pleaded. 'Go now and leave this place. We will do all we can for them later.'

Once again he took her arm and gently but firmly sent her walking back in the direction of the market. Others, sobbing and shaking their heads joined her as wardens and police systematically cleared the street. With the fireman's words still uppermost in her mind, she clutched Eddi even tighter to herself and decided to find shelter for them both and return later in the day for any news of her parents.

Chapter Three

SHIPMATES

Having returned along the quay to their submarine, Erwin negotiated the gangway and stepped onboard, while Kurt remained on the quay to make a cursory inspection of his command. He observed his crew as they worked on deck and felt like an Admiral on parade inspecting his men for a smart turnout, only this time it was for real. It was an inspection and evaluation on progress and the advanced fighting capability of his command, a matter of life and death where spit and polish had no place and was the last thing on his mind.

He observed the dockyard workers busy refitting and modifying the hull in readiness for his next patrol, the majority were French and local labour. He always had mixed feelings about that as sabotage was not unknown and recently on the increase. Although handpicked men that were allowed into the base and received special privileges of food, clothing and petrol, which together with their pay was their price for 'loyalty' to the Reich. However, they still had to be watched by all concerned and not left unsupervised by their German masters.

It was an unfortunate situation as the German war machine had become labour-intensive on one side and depleted of fighting men on the other. As a result the Reich was desperately short of skilled and semi-skilled labour. For the fighting men it was an unhappy situation as they eyed the French with justified suspicion but as long as the Germans paid up, the symbiotic stand-off of cat, cheese and mouse flourished and was allowed by all to continue.

Kurt reached for a cigarette, cupping the dancing flame with his hand, lit-up and made his way to the entrance of the pen. Once there he could see along the bunker's width and the remaining pens and observed as the lock-gates opened in the adjoining pen, allowing a replenished boat to sail out and proceed. He watched pensively as a cats-paw of wind whipped up wavelets against its black, freshly-painted hull and observed the gunners readying their quadruple anti-aircraft cannons together with boxes of ready-use ammunition. He pondered the question as oft times before and never came to a conclusion as to why the Englanders were so persistent, so dedicated in fighting Germany. They had their Empire, their rat-infested island and white bread – what more did they want?

Here at the bunkers he had their RAF to contend with, while at sea it was their Royal Navy, sometimes even both as they patrolled the Atlantic. Both services seemed hell bent on hounding him relentlessly and as the weeks went by it hadn't got any better. Calmly he drew on his cigarette and thought about the immense firepower of the British and their American allies and how best to thwart them if he were to survive the war. He suspected that somewhere the Kriegsmarine was making mistakes, as so many U-Booten never returned but the reasons for this eluded him. It couldn't just be the radar beams that detected the boats as to his knowledge they had limited range, uncannily they always seemed to be waiting for him in his field of operations as he surfaced, but why, how did they do it?

He was distracted as patches of oil whipped up by the departing U-boat's propellers made rainbow patterns on the water. He watched fascinated, a memory from childhood days until dispersed by the boat's churning wake brought him back to reality. How was it all going to turn out for Germany, and especially for him? Ever since the Americans had entered the war, things in the Fatherland had gone from bad to worse. Germany only had its fortress Europe left but that was being bombed and decimated as the weeks rolled by – the high-flying Americans by day and the more accurate low-level British by night. Still, he reasoned with conviction, it has a wall of steel as the Führer along with Rommel had put a lot of effort into it and was by now quite impregnable as he had seen for himself the large-calibre guns facing out into the Atlantic and the extensive mine-laying in coastal waters. If he could hang on and survive long enough for Germany to produce these Wunderwaffen the Führer had promised they would win the war. Hitler had announced on the radio to the German people soon he would unleash these special weapons and he, like the rest of his countrymen had to take him at his word.

His thoughts turned to the east, to the Russian front and its associated convoys. It was up to the U-Booten, men like him to stop the Russkies and buy the Führer time. All they had to do was sink the Murmansk convoys which in turn would stop the Russian advance and sort out the Englanders with the new weapons.

'Ja, that's got to be the answer,' he muttered as satisfied with his brief assessment, reasoning and strategy he took a final drag on his gratuitous Players and deftly flicked the dog-end into a high trajectory, to land amongst the rainbow patterns in the water.

'Seven-fifty,' he mumbled as he checked his watch and thinking of the sweet, black coffee with freshly-baked rolls waiting on-board. Taking a final glance at the scudding clouds and the distant boat he wished them good hunting and made his way back to his command.

***

His was now the second submarine lying inside the pen as the newcomer had been made fast alongside. Approaching the vessels, he shielded his eyes from the glare of the overhead lights and the constant flashes of the welding torches that were in the process of tacking a second AA mounting abaft his conning tower bridge.

Arriving at the gangway which led from the quay to his boat he noted bemused that his boat no longer had an identity as its number had been obliterated but its outlines were still visible. They might alter the emblem, but for him it was still the lucky U-835, a type IX D-2 Unterseeboot, ocean-going with the capacity to globe-trot and return without having to refuel. It gave him a fighting edge as he could more or less proceed at full speed without having to constantly watch his gauges.

Kurt walked slowly back and forth along the vessel's 295-foot length to examine progress as welding torches struck blinding arcs, momentarily occulting the light from the tungsten lamps. Mesmerizingly the blue flashes cast dancing shadows along the glistening walls, bathing the pen in their cold, eerie light.

He looked-on as the second sponson was being offered up with the help of an overhead crane and being fitted to augment the existing Flak defences, but the cannon was only 1.5cm rather than the existing 2cm quadruple mounting. Not much of a punch, he mused but it would fire faster rounds, these mixed with tracer will have an unnerving effect on any nosy aircraft that fancied its chances. The deck gun was a 10.5cm affair which was being serviced with a new barrel and greased up by his gunners. Progress looks encouraging, he mused and noted the hole cut in the starboard side of the conning tower bridge where the innovative Schnorchel tube was still to be fitted.

'Alles gut,' he murmured as he retraced his steps back to the gangway and as an afterthought allowed himself a wry smile. Instead of my U-Boot number perhaps this time they will give me a name (and suppressed a chuckle), something like Seewolf or Attila – that should strike fear and alarm into the toughest Tommy and make him crap his pants?

Kurt snorted at his own joke as he watched with satisfaction the dockyard workers applying a black, rubberised compound to the topside and conning tower. It was the latest in wartime technology, Germany's answer to the Allied radar threat and the detection of surfaced U-boats. Negotiating the steep gangway he made his way along his cluttered deck, treading warily on the rubberised compound, and thought about its effectiveness against the searching fingers of a Radar or Sonar pulsed device. Time will tell he surmised, as of yet it had still to be proven.

Eying the cut hole, he had heard about the limited success of the Schnorchel tube for semi-submerged use of the main engines and recharging batteries. This was to be achieved with only the top of the tube and its flapper valve proud of the sea. It had had mixed results but most comments were favourable. He looked forward to its deployment, as it gave him another 'edge' in his fight to engage the enemy and survive.

Observing the dockyard workers the words Sonder Meldung came to mind. He had received notification some special orders were being drafted for his next patrol. This was to be discussed shortly in the Administration Bunker but the word 'mission' had also come to light. What was that all about? He could only think about a commando-type raid on the British as they prepared their invasion fleet. Southampton or Plymouth, right on their Navy's doorstep, which did not excite him one little bit.

It had made him ponder the question and the high category risk such a raid would entail. So far all he knew was that he was to take part in a secret mission. It was all Geheim, top secret and he and his boat had been selected and modifications were to be made prior to sailing. But sail to where? What did the Führer and his Admiral Doenitz, have in store for him?

'Guten morgen, Herr Kaleu'nt.' It was Wenzel, one of the gunners, who greeted him as he and his mate manhandled a box of ammunition on board. Kurt returned their greeting with a cursory nod. He noted several of the new arrivals with the stores party were mere boys and sprung to attention as he passed, while his old crew just nodded in acknowledgement and carried on. Some of my best men are gone, mused Kurt. Gone to other boats to replace the losses, now we have to train these young recruits and fight a war. As he stood and observed the newcomers a sobering thought came to mind. I must look like an old sea dog to them, Gott im Himmel some of them haven't even started shaving yet. Subconsciously he raked a hand across his dark morning stubble which served to enhance his awareness of the lack of sleep and how tired he was. Last night's events were beginning to catch up on him and fast. As a U-Bootman he recognised and acknowledged this all-too-common condition. Fatigue and lack of sleep was just another enemy to contend with, silent but deadly all the same.

He stifled a yawn and adjusted his cap to an authoritative angle as he recalled the long tedious hours of waiting for orders, and his sojourn to the café which, coupled with the raid and subsequent lack of sleep had left him drained. He recalled his gaunt expression in the mirror only this morning as he left the boat, together with the appearance of several etched lines at the corners of his mouth. They told their own story. Added to this was his dark brown hair which was already greying at the temples, belying his age of twenty-six.

To his crew all this premature ageing was the real insignia and trademark of a U-Bootman. For here it was teenage boys became men overnight once they had been 'pinged' by enemy Asdic and hounded relentlessly by a destroyer along with being subjected to an all-too-common treat of a twenty-four hour dose of depth charging. After that sort of harassment and slinking away on tenterhooks in a cramped, cold and leaking submarine was not a tonic for one's health. However, it did have a positive side to it as it brought even the most arrogant of louts that came from the Hitler Youth into line and better still served to puncture their over-inflated egos of National Socialism and self-righteous invincibility.

In Kurt's case, he'd been drafted from destroyers and had only had eighteen months of active submarine service. But then the surface ships of the Kriegsmarine had had their trials, tribulations and heavy losses and had taxed both ships and men to the limits of their endurance. He had been active in the Norwegian campaign and stationed there. Now, with most of the capital ships sunk and the remainder either mothballed or sheltering in fjords, men like him had been drafted to replace the ever-mounting submarine losses.

Gone were those halcyon days when boats came back victorious from the multiple sinking of merchantmen. Now it was a game of bunkers, wits and technology, and a life expectancy as U-Bootmen could be counted in months. Nein, he contradicted himself, not months, perhaps just this next mission.

Lost in thought he stood and stared vacantly at the conning tower as more of the compound was applied and recounted the marine bands waiting on the quay, playing Wagner's Tannhauser at his triumphant return. The makeshift pennants proudly fluttering from whip aerials displaying his kills of Allied shipping. Most of all for him, a single man, there were the nurses – those pretty nurses, both French and German lining the quay and waving bunches of flowers in greeting. They stood, wearing starched uniforms and smelling wholesomely of carbolic, its pungent coal tar scent wafting along the quay as heaving lines sailed through the air and his boat made fast alongside. Others, those off-duty, clad prettily in their summer dresses and smelling sweetly of scented soap and heady French perfume.

As heroes he and his men would step ashore to be greeted with rosettes and warm embraces, the perfumes masking their own of L' Air du Diesel which emanated from both him and his crew. Gone were those glorious and rewarding days, long gone and now just a distant memory as, too, were the men and their boats. All but a few remained; the rest lay forever entombed in the depths of hostile seas.

The vision faded as a riveting gun stuttered into life, its staccato hammering jolting him back to the present and the harsh reality of his command. Shrugging off the mantle of nostalgia, Kurt made his way towards a forward opening in the hull and was about to descend when a familiar shout and the sound of his old academy nickname commanded his attention.

'Obi, Obi, over here!' Again, the echoing shouts. Kurt swivelled round, gripping the stair-rail stanchion to steady himself and glanced up at the quay. Immediately he broke into a welcoming grin as silhouetted against the light was his long-time friend from Naval Academy days. As the officer stood on the quay Kurt straightened up and, tired as he was, gestured with a wave for his friend to come down to join him.

'Franz, come on down!' he yelled, as he tried to make himself heard above the din and rattle of the hammers. The man raised an arm in acknowledgement and picked his way across a tangle of electric cables and snaking hoses as he headed towards the gangway. Kurt was there to greet him as the two men shook hands and slapped each other heartily on the back in an act of revived camaraderie and friendship.

'It's good to see you again you old sea dog,' said Franz with a welcoming grin and sporting a few days stubble. 'I heard you were in town and now by coincidence we share the same berth.' He adjusted the jaunty rake of his cap, revealing a thatch of blond hair and with blood-shot eyes to match. However the faint tell-tale lines across his young features needed no explanation.

Kapitänleutnant Franz Bauer, he too wore that unmistakeable badge of courage, the natural and unbestowed badge of belonging to the Kriegsmarine's U-Booten Flottille and Corps de Elite. Notwithstanding their mutual fatigue, some of which self-inflicted, they were both elated and somewhat revitalised in spirit at seeing each other again. Franz gestured with an impish and knowing wink towards the deck opening. 'Have you still got some of the real Kaffee down there?'

'Ja, but of course,' replied Kurt with a grin. 'Real Nestles Kaffee from America and not that Schwarzblut they serve up in Berlin.' They both laughed with added humour as this was a standing joke amongst the U-Boot crews. It was no secret submarine crews were the only ones that received extra rations, which at times included real coffee and not the roasted wheat, or acorns, known as 'ersatz', that was the wartime substitute for the deprived German nation.

'So, Kognak-Kaffee it is,' said Kurt with a grin. He gestured to his friend with a nod and disappeared through the hatch and was eagerly followed by Franz, who negotiated the steep angle of the stairs in the same well-honed U-Boot manner. With a veteran's ease, he slid his agile six-foot frame through the deck hatch opening and using his hands as a brake, skittered down the rail to land with practised ease on the deck plates below.

Chapter Four

SOVIET ENCOUNTERS

On the Eastern Front, the Russian army was pushing back the German war machine. The winter of 1942/3 had been one of the coldest in living memory, which culminated in the starvation and surrender of the Wehrmacht at Stalingrad.

Thousands of German soldiers had died in their attempt to take the city and on 31 January 1943, the starved remnants of Von Paulus' Sixth Army surrendered and were made 'guests' of Papa Stalin. It was a similar situation at Leningrad as, by late January 1944, the German 980-day siege was broken and another section of the German army was led into the labour camps of Siberia.

With the onset of another spring, the Russian winter slowly released its icy grip on the frozen landscape and so began the Soviet Spring Offensive of 1944.

Now with fanatical orders emanating from Hitler that the army was not to retreat another step, the German generals could only wait for the Red onslaught which was to seal their fate. For the Soviets it was a time of fortune and plenty as the Allied convoys to Murmansk and Archangel had given them the tools, equipment and the vital supplies of food to fight the enemy on the second front. But still the Wehrmacht would sell itself dearly, which would eventually account for some six million dead in the ranks of the Soviet armed forces, together with a further nineteen million civilian lives.

Major Yuri Konstantin's last battle had been the defence of Stalingrad. Here, and for many months previous, he had been engaged in artillery duels and hand-to-hand fighting as his men fought for the possession of the city and by this time he was a seasoned veteran of the war. However, from its onset he had been attached as a Red Army Captain to an anti-aircraft unit stationed on the outskirts of Minsk, the capital city in the heartland of Belorussia, some four hundred miles in a south-westerly direction of Moscow.

Here it was he had his first encounter with the German forces. After several weeks of ground and aerial attack, Yuri found himself to the raised rank of Major and in command of several guns of an

AA battery. At thirty years of age he was young to hold a major's rank but the exigencies of war often made for swift promotions. Prior to his new rank, Stalin had not utilised the ranking system of the Tsars, however once again Russia found itself accepting the order and rankings of the old empire.

Of peasant stock Yuri had a clean-shaven appearance, with the ruddy complexion of his peasant forebears. He was of a stout build and a hearty laugh to match. His shock of dark hair and piercing blue eyes gave him an advantage with the ladies and at the age of nineteen he married a local collective farmer's daughter. It might have been an uneventful military life for him had it not been for the 1941 invasion of his country, when Yuri suddenly found himself catapulted into the midst of the early fighting.

Compromised by an impoverished military and facing a highly mechanised German advance, the Soviets were soon forced to withdraw before the uneven onslaught. Heinkel bombers using fragmentation bombs and incendiaries decimated the city, whilst Stuka dive-bombers laid waste to its rail and fuel installations. In the aftermath and over the fertile plains rumbled the vanguard of General Guderian's 2nd Panzer Gruppe.

Yuri's battery kept up a fierce barrage of anti-aircraft fire, scoring hits and downing several bombers but the contest was soon at an end as orders came for him to withdraw. On a sweltering summer's day and with German artillery rounds screaming overhead Yuri gave the command to cease fire as on 9 of July, the battle for the city was lost. From his hillock vantage he watched in alarm and dismay as the German infantrymen in their half-tracked vehicles laid waste to his country, looting and burning the small wooden houses of his village and scattering their inhabitants. He observed through his binoculars as the villagers fled, panic-stricken from their homes and knew only too well Valentina his wife, Irena and Georgii, his children were somewhere there amongst them.

Visibly calm before his men, he hoped desperately Valentina might have left their house and had taken shelter but with the constant bombing that might not have been an option. Days before they had decided between themselves it would be safer out where their house and collective farm was situated, as the bombers would only seek strategic targets. But like all of Russia they had been overtaken by events as the Wehrmacht swept all before them.

Powerless, he could only watch the destruction before him as his anti-aircraft guns spat their last rounds of defiance at a wing of bombers sweeping in from the west. Orders were he was to spend his ammunition and retreat with his unit towards Moscow and to assist in a final line of defence against the Nazi hordes.

As the city burnt and with no aerial targets in sight, the Flak battery began a hasty withdrawal. Yuri anxiously focused his glasses and in the shimmering distance made out the yellow and green of his brightly-painted Dacha together with its corals and outbuildings. German soldiers could be seen scurrying like ants and systematically burning, looting and slaughtering his oxen and those of his collective neighbours. Grim-faced he witnessed the inhabitants of his village herded like cattle into a clearing and surrounded by aggressive soldiers. Instinctively he knew that his wife and children would be down there somewhere and felt anger and frustration at his inability to come to their aid.

With his frustration mounting, he knew only too well as a soldier he had his duty, as did his men, who also had their homes in and around the burning city. They too had voiced their fears and concern as with alarm several others that lived in the village saw what was happening less than two miles distant but were militarily powerless to come to their aid.

Yuri raged inwardly, cursing the Fascists from the west when a desperate plan of action sprang to mind. Rapidly he swept the plain and sky with his glasses and noted with satisfaction the German artillery had stopped firing. There was a lull and the sky for once was clear of aircraft.

'Serge,' he called to his lieutenant. 'We're pulling out. How much ammunition have you left for your gun?'

'Five rounds, comrade Major,' came the crisp reply. 'The others have all expended theirs. I'll have them put in the transport,' he added as an after-thought.

'Niet Serge, niet. Depress your gun and shell the village.'

'Shell the village, comrade Major?' the lieutenant replied with a puzzled frown.

'Da, da, shell the village. Here, look through my glasses.' Angrily Yuri strode across and thrust his binoculars at the man. 'Range in on the Fashisti soldiers and their transports. There, look to the right of the clearing. We'll account for a few before we leave.'

Still puzzled the young officer surveyed the goings-on in the village as a mass of field-grey uniforms were in evidence around the houses. He saw several stationary Panzers and the ubiquitous half-tracked army personnel carriers, some discharged and stationary whilst others were still arriving from behind a woodland. It was then that he witnessed the plight of the villagers, old men, women and children being herded together in a roped-off compound and awaiting their fate. He witnessed soldiers moving equipment into the larger buildings and others systematically setting fire to the rows of flimsy wooden houses.

'The gun will only depress so far, comrade Major,' said the lieutenant with consternation. 'Shall we reset the fuses and fire over their heads?'

Yuri shook his head. 'Niet Serge, niet. Use the sand bags and build a ramp and with the rest, stop the recoil. Place them all behind the gun to weigh it down.'

The lieutenant saw his meaning but was not too sure it would work. Rapidly he gave commands to his men who, needing no further orders, immediately spun the gun round and began to build a modified ramp. With the rear section elevated they placed several layers of sandbags under and over it. It would help to absorb some of the recoil Serge told his men and hastened them to place the remaining bags on top of the limber and around the wheels. With its muzzle depressed the men reset the proximity fuses and fired a ranging shot at their own village.

The gun leapt with the recoil but remained in position as Yuri watched with grim satisfaction as the round exploded close to a vehicle and a group of soldiers. With the 76mm shell screaming over their heads and detonating in a scything hail of shrapnel it caused instant mayhem amongst them. Completely taken by surprise they ran for cover behind the stationary Panzers, whilst others remained writhing in shock and agony where they fell.

'Boshe Moi!' cried Yuri, his spirits lifted as he witnessed the confusion and yelled to his men to continue firing at will. With the Germans pinned down he watched with satisfaction as the villagers fled towards the nearby woodland and his gunners continued firing. One shell scored a direct hit on a Panzer, the high velocity anti-aircraft projectile penetrating the base of the turret; seconds later the Mk III brewed up in a fireball of fuel and exploding ammunition. Minutes later and with their ammunition spent, the brazen shelling came to an end. Yuri looked on gratified at the burning tank along with several blazing personnel carriers and their sprawled occupants. Reluctantly he gave the order to move out as the surprised Germans had by now gathered their wits and spotted his position. Tanks started to move and soon the first 75mm Panzer round screamed overhead to land with a dull, explosive crump nearby.

'Time to pull out Serge. *Bystza, davai, davai!*' he yelled, with a frantic sweep of his arm as more shells screamed overhead. Grimly he levelled his glasses one more time and with animated glee observed most of the villagers that could, had fled. As the drone of returning aircraft was heard and further shells kicked up plumes of earth close by, Yuri dropped the glasses to his neck and gritting his teeth tore himself away. He was satisfied at seeing the villagers gain their freedom with the knowledge his wife and children were amongst them but anger still boiled within at having to abandon them to their fate.

With a heavy heart he hurriedly clambered into the back of the already moving transport and grasped a stanchion to steady himself, his knuckles showing white, and the veins on his neck bulging with impotent rage. As the lorry with its AA gun in tow gathered speed, iron tears welled to overflowing as Yuri watched his village receding behind the grassy knoll and its bastion mound of abandoned sandbags.

Like him, his men were morosely silent harbouring their innermost thoughts as they, too, were seen to be running and leaving their homes and loved ones to the mercy of the invading Hun. But sometimes things happen for a reason and it was there, in the dusty confines of that jolting truck and with Valentina, Irena and Georgii on his conscience he swore a silent oath. He would make good his escape and one day would exact revenge on these merciless savages that came from the west.

For the remainder of that eventful day Yuri's battery followed in the wake of a stream of army vehicles heading towards the north, whilst others were ordered east, away from the stricken city and the advancing foe. They passed the burning railway sidings where tankers of fuel had long since melted in a bleve of intense heat. Steam locomotives and wagons lay tossed aside, like sandpit toys as tracks lay useless and cratered, their once straight and gleaming lines now lying buckled, bent and broken.

To the north of the city and away from the German advance a steady stream of refugees with horse-drawn wagons, hand-carts and cycles made their exit. Progress on the crowded road was slow as the Luftwaffe continuously harassed the retreating army convoys. But the civilians suffered the most as old men, women and children perished in their thousands, while aircraft indiscriminately bombed and strafed the un-metalled roads, ditches and surrounding fields. Families stopped to bury their dead only to be killed in turn alongside the makeshift graves. Others fled empty-handed, leaving their loved ones dead and unburied, only to be maimed or killed hours later as the German advance progressed.

In such disorder they continued to flee, hiding in woodlands and forests and travelling by night as the columns of spent humanity distanced themselves from the carnage and the city they had left behind. Others, like Yuri's column would go on towards Moscow and its immediate defence, whilst more units were ordered to defend Leningrad and Stalingrad.

Desperately short of rations, lacking good leadership and modern equipment, the bulk of the Soviet army dispersed to lick its wounds and fight again. At Minsk, they left behind four thousand prisoners, with as many wounded and killed, together with three thousand tanks and nineteen hundred field guns. Yuri and his men were to take stock of the Blitzkrieg that had surprised and overwhelmed them and in time to re-group and re-equip in the vast hinterland that was after all, their Little Mother, Russia.

Chapter Five

SAYONARA

Captain Itachi Hideki of His Imperial Majesty's Navy stood motionless at the dock-side. In one hand he carried a black leather attaché case, in the other a small bundle tied with frayed ribbons of red and black silk. He stood stiffly, surveying his new command lying alongside her berth in the docks of the Kure shipyard. Her 350-foot grey-painted hull stood out in stark contrast to the oil and paint-spattered quay, her snub nose tugging gently at her lines and dipping in the slight swell, as if to salute and greet her new master.

She was of the Otsu-Gata type, a development of ocean-going submarine of the 1938 era, but built during 1942. Nevertheless, it was a direct descendant of Japan's own cruiser-style sub-surface vessels. Nodding with satisfaction he reflected on his mission. Speed and timing would be of the essence as British and American warships were systematically closing a net of steel around Japan.

I-59 had engines that would deliver 5,000 horse power which moved her 2,560-ton bulk at a surface speed of 17.5 knots, together with an operational radius of 20,000 miles. This type of vessel was ideally suited for patrols in the Pacific arena and the task which now lay ahead. *I-59* was not a new build, as the boat had been damaged at her launch by American bombing; however after a two-year period of lay-up and refit she was finally ready for her maiden voyage in the theatre of war.

Apart from the AA cannons, other modifications were to her spacious aircraft hangar. This had been altered in order to carry several Kaiten but the suicide subs would not be carried on her first mission. The submarine retained her 5.5-inch deck gun but as additional armament *I-59* carried two extra AA cannons to supplement the existing two already mounted abaft the tower. Her six torpedo tubes remained, together with her capability of firing nineteen standard torpedoes, however only ten were left onboard as the submarine would be required to carry a special cargo.

As he stood and pondered both his and his submarine's destiny, he recalled recent events at a meeting with his admiral. He had been singled out with the Divine Emperor's approval and blessing to carry out this vital mission. All of Japan's hopes for an all-out victory, a gigantic body blow against the Americans now rested on his shoulders. His training, steadfast attitude and determination both at the Etajima-Japanese Imperial Naval Academy and as a martial artist would now be put to the test. Like in any Kendo contest and now here in the theatre of war, a level head under attack was paramount, determination to win was vital but above all things; to surrender was the act of a coward. This ideology was now to be sorely tested as he recalled his Kendo fighting days and with the success of this mission the dojo's bamboo sword would be transformed into a blazing weapon of mass destruction.

Itachi's gaze shifted with the arrival of his transport. Swiftly the sailors carried his baggage across the gangway and down through a hatch into the hull's interior. They cast furtive glances in his direction, to judge the calibre of their new captain and master, albeit from a distance. He would have stood out in any crowd, especially in Japan. His five-foot-eleven height and powerful athletic build portrayed a man of substance and of noble ancestors. Appearing older than his thirty-two years the bouts of interrupted sleep, strain of active patrols and the loneliness of command had taken their toll. Now he had the added stress of an ultra-secret mission, the success of which would win the war for Japan.

After weighing up the boat's air defences and assessing another quadruple mounting would not have gone amiss, Itachi crossed the gangway and stepping on board was greeted by the duty officers who saluted him and bowed respectfully as the deck watch of sailors stood stiffly to attention. Itachi acknowledged their salute and bowed in return as a steward came forward to take the cherished bundle.

With due resolve Itachi faced aft to where the flag of the Rising Sun hung idly in the morning air and saluted his country, its emblem and Emperor. It was a new flag, he noted, and a good omen for his new command.

Barked guttural orders dismissed the ratings and sent them scurrying to their normal duties and a junior officer hurriedly relieved him of his attaché case. With his presence on-board established he automatically breathed new life into the submarine as news of his arrival spread rapidly throughout the boat and anticipation ran high that their departure was imminent.

The sound of footsteps and a faint cough from behind drew his attention. Turning he faced a beaming officer who saluted smartly and with a bow welcomed his old school friend.

'O Hayo gozai-masu, Hideki San. I heard you'd been given this command. Congratulations and welcome on board.' The two officers bowed with due courtesy and shook hands.

'Watanabe San, good to see you again,' replied Itachi. 'When was the last time we met? Before the war at the Kodokan, I believe?'

'Hai, Hideki San,' replied the beaming First Officer. 'You're right. It was our first Dan grading, in thirty-nine, at the old Tokyo dojo. You remember the split nose?'

'Yes, I remember,' said Itachi gritting his teeth and sizing up his former opponent. 'I still bear the mark. Look.' He pointed to his nose in proud memory. Watanabe mustered an apologetic smile.

'I saw in my orders you've been given this command, here let me show you to your cabin.' He gestured with a wave and led the way below, passing a myriad of pipes, valves and gauges, through 'clipped' water-tight doors and bulkheads and on through the control room, finally arriving at the captain's quarters. This was sited close to the operations room, allowing him immediate access for control of his command.

Itachi stepped past the green vanity curtain of the open door and into the modest cabin that was to be his home-from-home for the months ahead. His baggage had already been unpacked by his steward who poured out green-leafed tea into two china cups. A warmed porcelain pot of Sake with six tiny glasses stood invitingly on the low table in the centre of the cabin. The young steward hovered hesitantly in the background, clasping a flask of hot water. Itachi took the flask and dismissed the sailor and waved for Watanabe to be seated. He poured out two measures of the rice spirit and handed one to his friend.

'Here's to our ship and our mission, Takayuki.' Watanabe felt honoured that even as a senior captain, Itachi had called him by his first name.

'And to old times, Itachi,' he replied. 'I guess it's still permissible to call you by your first name, Captain?' He beamed as he emphasised his friend's promotion.

'Yes to both, Takayuki. Especially at rare times like these,' replied Itachi. 'Here's to us,' he added and still holding his raised glass; 'the boat, old times and everything else. Does that satisfy you?'

'Hai,' came Takayuki's reply as together they drained their glasses of the warm rice spirit. Itachi recharged their glasses and watched in amusement as his old friend played host and delicately poured out the dark green liquid. Like himself, he was of heavy build, but stocky, more muscular. Strong as an ox and almost immovable on the mats, he reflected and now he was gently pouring tea and in dire need of a haircut.

'You would have made a good Geisha,' said Itachi with a grin.

'It's the navy,' Takayuki replied with a shrug. 'It teaches you everything. I play mother hen here to half this crew. Raw recruits, still wet behind the ears, you'll see.'

Itachi nodded and felt he might have touched a nerve, as the nation was short of trained able-bodied seamen and technicians. He cast a sympathetic smile at his First Lieutenant and finished his wine. Takayuki, his brown eyes glinting fervently, took out a packet of cigarettes and offered one to his friend. 'Just like old times, only without the music, eh?'

'Hai, without the music,' Itachi replied and nodded melancholically as he lit his cigarette and pushed the lighter across the mahogany table.

'You remember our Kendo fighting and Judo, then off to cool down in that communal bath?' asked Takayuki. 'The one with the two topless Korean girls. Twins they were and you could only tell them apart by their breasts.' Itachi smiled at his friend and reflected on the girls who attended to the needs of the bathers. 'And that German Beer Keller, with those big glasses, and we all sang those German drinking songs…'

'Hai, I remember, those days are long gone now, I think we had better drink our tea and stick to that, eh?'

Takayuki flashed a row of strong white teeth and nodded as he watched his friend remove several items from his attaché case and place some papers into a bulkhead safe. He un-wrapped a photograph with its silver frame and wedged it by his bedside locker.

'I see you've brought the family,' said Takayuki, making his way across the cabin to examine the snapshot.

'Hai, in a way,' replied Itachi with a resigned shrug and carried on emptying his case. 'That picture is more than nine months old. I've not been home since then. Don't think the kids will remember me now.'

'Iie, don't think like that, kids are very good with faces, just as long as Kaiko does.' Itachi raised a smile at his friend's concern and how he still remembered his wife's name.

'Are you still at the same place?' asked Takayuki.

'No, unfortunately not, I liked that place and its nightlife. We moved away from Yokohama during my last leave. The Americans are after the industry there but they bomb anything that crosses their sights. We moved back to my parents' place on Sado Shima. Have you heard of it?'

'Yes, I believe I know it, somewhere up the west coast of Honshu, right?'

'Right first time. They have a farm up there, ideal for the kids. How about yourself?'

Takayuki drained his cup and swallowed hard. 'Got myself married last year,' he replied. 'We moved in with her parents as our house was set on fire by incendiaries. Hiroshima is a prime target, same as this place here. It was a pity, as I could get home some evenings and the odd weekend as the house was not too far, but with the heavy raids we decided to move out into the country. Anyway, *sir*,' he said with a grin, 'I have to go. I'll leave you to settle in. I'll talk to you later and show you around, if you feel a list, it's the torpedoes and stores. We're discharging some of them, a little bit odd but those were my orders from headquarters.' He cast a quizzical glance at his captain, who remained inscrutable.

'Very well, Takayuki. See you at eleven-thirty for lunch. I'll settle in and have a look around later. I'll give the officers a briefing at fifteen-hundred. It will give me a chance to get acquainted; you can spread the word we expect to sail shortly, before April is out. That's all I can say for the moment.'

'Hai, very well, see you at lunch.' With the cordial spell broken it was back to the business of duty and the prosecution of the war, as the FO made a slight bow and excused himself.

Alone and with a few precious moments to himself Itachi sat and poured out the remainder of the tea and stared in solitude at the picture of Kaiko and his two children.

Perhaps absence does make the heart grow fonder, he mused. But all the same he had always loved them and just wanted to be with them once more. It was a stab of sudden pain that brought him back to the present as he quickly stubbed out the remnants of his cigarette and examined his fingers. He was annoyed with himself at his lapse of concentration. Family or not, he had a war to fight and had to shelve his daydreams for another time.

Needled with himself he finished his tea as he gazed round the austere cabin. He reflected about his time ashore, with regular meals and congenial company as the crushing hand of solitude gripped his shoulder. Somehow the feeling of confinement was always there, it

37

never left him. Every time he joined a ship a feeling of melancholy and loneliness would creep and settle to occupy his mind. He was certain others must feel the same but as the commanding officer he had a duty, both to himself and his ship and to banish these morose thoughts and accept the loneliness of command.

Snapping out of his melancholy he went to check his wardrobe where the steward had already placed his second uniform. He needed to unpack the remainder and settle in, for that was a therapy in itself. Picking up the bundle, Itachi untied its discoloured silk ribbons and meticulously unfolded the aged linen wrap. The faded colours of the red, black and gold-painted scabbards were scuffed from wear but still showed the design and markings of an earlier age. He pulled out the larger of the swords to reveal its gleaming blade and artistic design and felt honoured to hold such a symbolic weapon. Slowly and systematically he executed a two-handed cutting thrust and satisfied with the ancient technique returned the noble steel into its keeper.

The swords were a family heirloom and a present from his aged father, a former soldier. They had been handed down from past generations who had been Samurai warriors to the feudal emperors of old Japan. He felt touched and honoured when he had received them as a symbol of his captain's rank and as a ceremonial gift for a soldier going into battle. His father had mentioned he was saddened that he had not carried on in the family tradition, as a soldier and warrior of Japan and the Emperor. He recalled his conciliatory answer, and his father's contented smile as he explained to the old man that he was still a warrior and Samurai, only now a Samurai of the waves.

Itachi placed the cloth and ribbons in a drawer and hung both swords on the bulkhead facing the door, beneath a picture of the emperor, Hirohito. It would do well for his crew to know their captain was a warrior and son of the Bushido tradition.

That afternoon he met his officers and with the formalities of introduction accomplished he briefed them on sailing orders. He would enlarge on the subject once at sea.

***

Days of loading stores and sea-route planning passed quickly and with restricted shore leave the men were keen to get away. So it was, with his cargo of tin and copper ingots loaded on the evening of 5 May 1944, as the sun's upper limb dipped below the western horizon, *I-59* slipped her moorings, to proceed with stealth her ultimate weapon towards the channel and the open sea. The bombers, if they came, would arrive in the early hours and sailing at this time would give them a head start to reach the open water of the Bungo Suido channel. In addition, American submarines also lurked in the seas around Japan; therefore night-time sailings were the only way to elude their increasing patrols.

Once clear of the dockyard and the outer harbour, Itachi set a course at slow speed for a pre-determined position some 95 miles south of Kure. First however, his vessel would have to steam on a northerly course, pass the ancient city of Hiroshima to starboard and clear several small islands as it made its passage along the southern Honshu coastline. Two new-build Akizuki class destroyers were her escorts and led the way in the gathering dusk, their dimmed navigation lights being the only visible guide and indication of their presence. At a reduced speed the three vessels proceeded past numerous wrecks, some with their masts protruding like warning fingers for the unwary in the mined waters of the navigable channel.

Hours later, both submarine and escorts changed to a southerly course and the open waters of the Iyo Sea. Itachi and his duty officer watched satisfied, as a stuttering Morse lamp from the lead destroyer signalled the end of their anti-submarine sweep and *I-59's* signalman acknowledged with a 'dot-dash' reply. With textbook precision their escorts picked up speed, turned 180 degrees and in a welter of propeller wash and blazing phosphorescence steamed off into the night.

Itachi de-clutched his diesels and watched from the open conning tower bridge as the way came off his boat. He gave orders for the diesels to be stopped and to manoeuvre on battery-powered motors and listen out with hydrophones for any underwater activities. In the stillness of the night the only sounds to be heard were the whine and thrum of the departing destroyers' turbines and the constant lapping of the sea as the waves played gently against the hull. Lying in the sheltered waters of the Iyo Sea, in the coolness of what remained of the night they drifted, kept watch and listened. Above them the heavens revealed a spangled canopy of stars which seemed so tantalisingly close one felt compelled to reach out and touch them. To the south an arm of the Milky Way glowed with a million suns, lending a ghostly ambience to the tranquil scene below.

Itachi, satisfied with events, left the bridge to his watch-keeping officer and three look-outs and went below. Four pairs of eyes now kept vigil, peering steadfastly through their night glasses into the velvet curtain of the night.

An hour before dawn and in the southern reaches of the Iyo Sea, captain Itachi called a meeting of his senior officers.

'Gentlemen,' he addressed the six present. 'Please be seated.' Obediently, they took their places round the table. 'As we are now at sea, I have been instructed to inform you of the mission in hand, its intended purpose and its possible outcome.'

Still standing, Itachi swept the table with a cursory glance, gauging their reaction to the word 'mission' and noted several raised eyebrows as the steward entered to serve tea. Their cups filled with the green liquid, the steward made a waist-deep bow and excused himself to exit the cabin. Itachi acknowledged with a benign nod, and seated himself at the oval table.

'As you might be aware,' he continued, 'Japan is no longer fighting a war. On the contrary, gentlemen, it is fighting for its existence as a nation and that of our Emperor. Our armies have been decimated, cut off and isolated, and most of our capital ships and carriers now lie at the bottom of the Pacific. The Americans along with their allies are slowly placing a stranglehold round us with the intended purpose of starving Japan into submission. We are an island nation and we need our merchant ships to bring us the raw materials and the vital oil to survive. Not only to survive but to survive and carry on the fight. This was a fact before the war; in effect it was these material restrictions which triggered this war. Now, with most of our ships of commerce lost, it will lose us the war.'

Itachi paused, sipped his tea and watched for any adverse reactions. He noted with satisfaction their combined nods of acceptance to his interpretation of Japan's plight.

'I would like you all to know we have been chosen to carry out a mission that could, with one stroke, win the war for Japan.' Again he paused and saw with satisfaction that if they were inattentive before, he had their undivided attention now. He sipped his tea and continued.

'You might have heard of previous cargo transfers with German vessels and voyages to their bases in Europe. This time it is us who have been chosen, along with our consort *I-51*. We are to proceed and rendezvous with their submarines in order to transfer vital materials of war, new weapons and the blueprints of their latest achievements and scientific technology.'

40

He paused as silence reigned. 'Some of you might have been to Lorient in your submarines and have seen the German technology. They now have torpedoes which can follow the sound of engines. We in Japan have fallen behind and are now limited in this technology, especially with Radar, which we all know the Americans are using to detect our ships. We have our own Radar, you might say. True, but ours is inferior to that of the Americans and British. We have already utilised the German breathing tube, their Schnorchel, however their latest technology is in the field of rocketry.' He paused to pass round a photograph of a V1 winged bomb in flight.

'They have developed and will shortly launch hundreds of these rocket bombs on London and are working on a long-range missile that will fly at many more times the speed of sound.' Murmurs of astonishment drifted round the table as Itachi continued. 'This weapon will be the ultimate, especially for us to use and launch from our submarines, being our submarines are much larger. By using this weapon, we will be able to strike at the heart of America.'

This time there was a surge of elation from the small gathering. Some banged their fists on the table in triumph as others congratulated Hitachi for being chosen by the Emperor for what must be nothing less than a divine mission.

He stilled them with a raised hand.

'Our scientists are working with theirs at this very moment in order to build a special submarine capable of twice our underwater speed. It also mentions here about another weapon, a super type of bomb, but does not enlarge further.'

The steward returned with more tea and a black-lacquered plate with its hand-painted red Shinto designs and piled high with an assortment of coloured rice cakes. Itachi glanced at his fellow officer, eyeing them with satisfaction for the task that lay ahead. However, once tea was served he had a bombshell to drop in their midst.

'Gentlemen, one more thing and I promise I will not keep you.' He glanced down at his papers and at his watch. 'Convey this to your men, as I want every man to do his utmost for the successful outcome of this mission. We have not come to sea to fight, but to avoid all action if at all possible.' The cabin stilled as a murmur of confused discontent rippled round the table. Itachi had expected a negative reaction and was not disappointed. He rose from his chair as he would now have to convince them in order to press home the strategy of such inaction.

'Ask yourselves,' he said with a wagging finger. 'If we stop to fight and are sunk or damaged, the purpose of our mission would be lost. If we fought and triumphed, our whereabouts would be known to the enemy and we would be hunted and have to abandon our mission. My orders are clear. We are to proceed to our point of rendezvous with the German vessels, without detection and not to compromise them, our consort *I-51* or ourselves.' He paused to give his officers time to consider what their orders actually implied, to mull it over and let it penetrate. He could understand those who wanted to fight; he sympathised with their attitude and their sullenness, as many had lost their homes and loved ones. They wanted to avenge and to strike back at their enemy.

'Gentlemen,' he went on, 'before you go there is one further point I must bring to your attention. As you are all aware, we have off-loaded some of our usual stores and most of our torpedoes; this was done in order to save weight and space. We, therefore, cannot fight with limited weapons, as we would be at an immediate disadvantage.' This was greeted with nods of approval and understanding as they had already discussed this amongst themselves and the remainder of the crew. Itachi continued.

'Further to this we and our consort are carrying a consignment of bullion and copper – the gold in order to assist our allies and the copper in exchange for a large consignment of mercury. With the gold, our German allies will be able to continue their fight and thereby assist Japan in winning this war, the mercury we need for our munitions. Gentlemen, that is all.'

Itachi seated himself and gazed round the table. He noted their change of attitude, a climb-down where common sense now prevailed. Being briefed and now fully in the picture, they rose and with one accord, stood and applauded.

***

At 0515 hours, the hydrophone operator reported the high-pitched sound of propellers. Alarm bells clanged and a whistle shrilled as *I-59* went to action stations. The bridge watch was doubled and gunners closed up; below the forward torpedo tubes were made ready, two bow-caps swinging open. On the bridge Itachi checked his watch and grunted to himself as the control room reported distance and bearing of a surfaced vessel.

If it was a lone enemy submarine he would, without hesitation, sink her as they were still very much in home waters and dead men tell no tales, or lost submarines for that matter. An enemy surface ship, even if crippled would be able to alert others and would be a problem. His immediate dilemma was that Japanese vessels were known to be in these waters, and if he submerged now he would at one stroke become vulnerable and any miscalculations fatal.

Agonising seconds passed as the weight of command rested heavily on Itachi's shoulders as distance and bearing was continually relayed to the bridge. Soon they heard the distinct throb of a surfaced submarine's diesels. Re-checking his watch, Itachi nodded to Yamato, his gunnery officer; eerily and less than 2000 yards distant, a familiar shape with a creaming bow wave materialised. Suddenly a dimmed Morse beam stabbed the early mist as the lamp stuttered into life. A sigh of relief drifted round the bridge at the welcome challenge as *I-59* rapidly replied with her own 'dit-dah-dah' coded recognition signal.

Satisfied the mission was going to plan, Itachi cleared his bridge as the E-motors took the strain, sea valves opened and seconds later the metal leviathan submerged to glide effortlessly into the depths. Above her the eastern sky grew pale as her consort passed with a whine of propellers overhead, on her mission south.

Chapter Six

A TALE OF ONIONS

Franz Bauer joined Kurt in his cabin. It was hardly big enough for them both, but good enough to suit the occasion. Kurt swept several dog-eared charts off his table and stowed them in a drawer under his bunk. From a second drawer he produced a bottle of Cognac and a tin of Players and delving in his bedside locker emitted a satisfied grunt as he produced two Châteaux-crested crystal tumblers.

'Sit yourself down,' he gestured to his colleague, pointing casually to the bulkhead seat. 'Make yourself at home.' Franz squeezed himself past his friend and the bolted-down table as Kurt found himself a folding chair. 'Sorry about the lack of creature comforts but Adolf built this one for third class only.'

They both chuckled at the standing joke, as all German submarines were notoriously tight on space with their non-existent home comforts. 'But not to worry, my friend,' continued Kurt with a grin as he poured out two good measures of the golden liquid. 'The Cognac and the cigarettes will make up for it.' He handed a drink to Franz and sat down. Leaning back, he swept aside the green vanity curtain. 'Kaffee Hans, Mach's schnell!' he called to the cook.

From the galley came a muffled reply. 'Jawohl, Herr Kaleu'nt!' Seconds later the cook appeared with two chipped mugs and a steaming pot of coffee and placed them on the table. The rich aroma of the Brazilian blend permeated the cabin as the cook placed a box of sugar cubes on the table with a distinctive Canadian label.

'Tell me, Kurt, are you sure this boat is victualed by our navy?' said Franz as he helped himself to coffee. Kurt gave a chuckle and an impish grin.

'So you would rather have your acorn and wheat blend, eh? Ersatz and saccharin, just like home, Ja?'

'Nein, my friend, only joking, you're living like the old Kaiser here. However did you manage this lot?'

'It's a long story,' replied Kurt. 'Here, drink up.' He topped up their glasses, took a gulp of scalding black coffee and settled back in his chair, casually resting his feet on his bunk. 'You know, it's said sometimes truth can be stranger than fiction, well, I've got to tell you this story which happened during my last patrol.' Congenially, he tapped out a cigarette from a round tin of Players Navy Cut, lit up and pushed the tin across to Franz. 'As I was saying, I was on patrol off the west coast of Shetland and happened to stop this old tramp, a rust bucket if ever there was. A Swedish freighter and flying his neutral flag. So I sent my boarding party across and the old boy was very helpful. Showed them his papers, Bills of Lading and all that. He declared a hold full of onions along with some general cargo, all bound for a neutral port and loaded in Sweden. But my boarding party smelt a rat...'

'You mean onions,' interrupted Franz with a grin.

'Ha, you could say that. They went to check his hold as they don't grow a lot of onions in Sweden, ja? They found the onions all right. There was a thin layer of them for camouflage and aroma but prodding and delving underneath they found several tons of ball and roller bearings. You know, the type used in gun mountings, tanks and aero engines. These were not mentioned on the lading documents.'

'Contraband,' remarked Franz. 'So you got his coffee and sent him to do some vertical navigation.'

'Nein, nein, nothing like that,' replied Kurt. 'I made a deal with him. Listen to this.' He poured himself more coffee, lit up another cigarette, exhaled contentedly through distended nostrils and continued. 'He also had a consignment of these extra-large ball bearings. There were fifteen tons of them and all the size of Spanish onions. What's more, the top layer was actually painted a golden yellow colour to resemble them.' Kurt drew on his cigarette and burst out in stitches as he mimicked his signalman's face and expressions. 'The boarding officer sent a message across in Morse to our signalman. Can you imagine our poor signalman over here, young Heinrich straight out of cadet school...?' He burst out laughing again.

'"Herr Kaleu'nt," he said to me, "they're sending a signal about the Swedish captain having onion balls and to arrest him and sink his ship!"'

'We all tried to keep a straight face on the bridge as young Heinrich made his report, but I was intrigued by this time. I edged the boat closer and got them to transfer the papers across with a heaving line. It turned out his papers were forged. He'd loaded in Sweden all right but his papers had an English watermark and to top it all it stated he was heading for Spain! Can you imagine taking Swedish onions to Spain? It's like what the Englander say about carrying coals to Newcastle, a joke on us from the Tommies, eh? They must think we're stupid. I told my men to search the captain's cabin and they found his real papers stuffed under his bunk. Heading for Liverpool he was and a little bit off his course for Spain. Anyway, he only had these ball bearings onboard and the rest was foodstuff and paper, great rolls of it. He was a nice old boy and getting a good price for his cargo from the Englander for the high grade bearings.'

Kurt nodded to himself in reminiscence and held up his glass in salute. 'Ja, he actually came out onto his bridge wing and waved his cap at me. I told him he could keep his ship but was to sail it to Le Havre. That's when the old-timer exploded and started to give me a verbal broadside but I told him that if he didn't like it he could take to his leaking lifeboat and row it back home. After that he agreed to co-operate and I gave him a course to steer and told him I would be keeping an eye on him. I mentioned I would also inform the other U-boats and the Luftwaffe. Before he took off he insisted I have some of his dry stores.' Kurt waved his hand across the table in a sweeping gesture, 'So we now have our coffee, sugar and cigarettes, et voilà, gut ja?'

'Bit of a tall story that,' said Franz. 'But the coffee tastes good all the same. Did he make it to port though, through the English blockade? Surely the Tommies would have rumbled him changing course like that and not going for the Mersey?'

'Ja, ja, he made it all right,' replied Kurt. 'Lucky for us there was low cloud and the Sunderlands didn't pick him up. Mind you, neither did the Luftwaffe. It was lousy weather for us all and the limited daylight helped. Apparently he just appeared one fine day off Le Havre and requested further instructions. He told the guard-boat that I, U-Boot Kapitän Oblitz had sent him! Can you believe it?' Kurt burst out laughing as he finished the tale.

'Ja, ja, he told them the Harbour Master was expecting his ship on my orders. I learnt afterwards they sent him and his crew back home minus his ship as it was carrying contraband. Ja, apparently the local SS Gruppenführer had asked him a few polite questions. After that I heard the old boy got the SS to sign him an IOU for his ship. Quoted something from the Geneva Convention of 1907!' Kurt doubled up once more with laughter as a crazy thought struck him. 'Can you imagine Himmler getting an IOU for an old rust bucket and a load of balls and showing it to his mate Hitler? He'd do his Austrian nut!'

They laughed at that as Kurt, empty once again re-charged their glasses. 'If I didn't tell you myself you could call it fantasy,' he said. 'But it's all true. It even made headlines in the papers back home. Here, have some more coffee, it's free courtesy of old captain Sven from Sweden.'

'Danke, good for you,' said Franz. 'A nice manoeuvre that, right past the noses of the Tommies.' He raised his glass and added, 'Here's to you and the old Swede. We'd better drink to his health, ja?'

'Prost Gesundheit to the old boy,' said Kurt and still chortling from the yarn and pleased at having met up again, to spin a few more. Franz finished his drink and helped himself to the last of the pot. He glanced at Kurt and cleared his throat.

'Listen, I have a slight problem.' Kurt eyed his friend and nodded as he lit another cigarette.

'So what's bothering you,' he asked. 'It can't just be lack of sleep?'

'Nein, nein, nothing like that,' responded Franz with a grimace at the well-worn joke.

'Okay Franz, out with it, what's her name?' He said with a knowing wink. Franz glanced at him and sombrely shook his head and not surprised by his lack of understanding.

'It's my wife Anna and the boy, I've not heard from them for six weeks, just a letter dated the last week in February. It mentioned she would go and see her folks in Köln. Her mother had had a fall in the blackout and she would take them some food. She reckoned it would be safer there as there were no large industrial targets left as they were all bombed out and it's close to the cathedral. You know the one with its twin spires? After that, nothing. I've tried to get through to the local police station there but the phone lines are all dead, it's either the bombing or the local bandits here that sabotage the lines.'

Kurt glanced at his friend, picked up the tin and thoughtfully extracted another cigarette as Franz offered him a light. Kurt nodded with understanding as he'd weighed up the situation having heard similar stories from his crew.

'Two things,' said Kurt as he picked up his glass. 'Here's to you and the boy – I didn't know you were a father.' Franz was taken aback by his friend's congenial attitude. It snapped him out of his melancholy as he raised his glass and accepted his friend's gesture, realising he should have told him about his son.

'Jawohl, I'm a dad now, sorry I completely forgot to mention it as this business about Anna has been clouding my mind.'

'Ja, I can well imagine, but don't worry, I'm sure they're all right, otherwise you would have heard different. You know the usual telegram…' Franz nodded as he glanced with gratitude at his friend.

'I'll tell you what we'll do,' Kurt continued, as Franz toyed nervously with his glass. 'I have a little date tonight. You know a rendezvous, as they say around here. But it's sort of a loose arrangement… we'll go to see some other girls who work in the Wehrmacht communications centre. I know it's the army but the girls are only too willing to help us sailors – unofficially of course,' he added with a wink. Kurt noted with satisfaction seeing his plan had taken root as it eased his friend's worried features.

'Ja gut,' replied Franz. 'I knew you would come up with something. I'd better be going back to my boat before they send out a search party. By the way, what time is our date?'

'Seven o'clock. See you at our concrete front door unless the Tommies have other ideas, and here…' Kurt reached under his bunk. 'You had better take some of these along with you tonight.' He handed Franz two packets of sugar, along with two tins of cigarettes. 'To keep the ladies sweet, ja?' With another wink and a Cheshire cat grin Kurt handed him the booty as Franz pushed the tins into his jacket pockets. 'There are some bags of coffee and other things here for you as well. Get a couple of your men to come across and see the cook.'

'Danke,' said Franz with a nod and left the cabin. Behind him he heard his friend calling after him in a lilting voice and smiled to himself as he recognised the popular tune, only his words were slightly modified.

'Underneath the lantern, by the bunker's gate,
See you at seven or we'll miss our date…!'

That guy doesn't change, mused Franz as in a better frame of mind he made his way back across the gangway that separated the two boats. However he could not help the anxiety which again welled up and threatened to blot out everything as he thought about the whereabouts of his wife and son. Stepping back onto his boat he pushed these matters to the back of his mind as his duty lay with his command and the fifty-seven souls that relied on him for their well-being and ultimate survival against the ever-increasing odds.

Chapter Seven

IN THE SHADOW OF THE CATHEDRAL

Eddi Bauer was crying. He was disturbed by the sound of aircraft and was also hungry.

Anna took them as friendly, at least they did not drop any bombs but just circled the stricken city and flew off towards the south. Heading in that direction she assumed them to be Luftwaffe recognisance as there were no sirens or Flack batteries in action. Besides, her child was crying as the boy was hungry and this was now her uppermost concern.

Desperate for shelter and with nowhere else to go, she decided to head back in amongst the narrow winding streets around the cathedral that were reasonably clear of debris. To stop his tears she hugged him, promising him once they got home she would make him his favourite semolina pudding. 'With a sprinkling of sugar and cinnamon, you like that, don't you, Eddi?' she cajoled with a whisper.

By this time the drizzle had stopped as Anna passed by a row of bomb-damaged shops, their convoluted shutters bulging and misshapen from the effects of rubble and blast. Tired from her recent ordeal and still carrying her son she came across a park bench and set both Eddi and the bag down. Here she was in the shadow of the shrapnel-scarred walls of the Dom Kirche, that great medieval edifice with its twin spires rising majestically to the heavens. With the aid of a cloth she wiped the bench clear of the wet masonry dust and using the blanket, took a seat. She put Eddi onto her lap but he wriggled free and began to play with some stones in the cobbled street.

Deep in thought she looked on, as he amused himself in the deserted street and tried to relax as she took stock of her situation. With her parents' safety and survival still uppermost in her mind she knew full well she had a greater responsibility, both to herself and her son, especially as the poor boy had not had his breakfast. She would have to find shelter for them both, make a meal and find out about her parents later. With her mind made up it was from a passer-by she learnt the trains were once again running.

So the Bahnhof is still standing, she mused, and that was welcome news. Perhaps she should go back home she reasoned, back to Aachen now that she had the chance. But then she had to find out about her parents, otherwise she would never forgive herself, especially if they had been injured and needed her assistance.

Her thoughts turned to her husband. She had not heard from Franz for many months and her last letter to him was seven weeks ago. During his last leave she recalled him saying his U-Boot would be stationed somewhere in France, perhaps Dieppe or further south – La Pallice, or Lorient – but he was not sure as he was also listed to attend a torpedo course at Kiel.

If he had been captured or killed then the Kriegsmarine would have notified her, just like everyone else. Families of U-Boot officers were at one time given the courtesy of a personal visit from a 'Brown Shirt' bearing the news of their loved one's demise, but most of these men from Hitler's private army had been posted to the Eastern Front. Now it was the usual blunt telegram, which she had read so many times before from the trembling hands of her friends.

'*The Kriegsmarine regrets –*'

Her phone had ceased to function since early 1944 and then came the raid on 11 April which had destroyed most of what remained of Aachen, so now there wasn't even any mail service. That's when she had packed her bag, as a large crack had appeared in one wall of the house, and opted to stay with her parents. There were too many loose ends she realised and nothing tangible to tie them with.

Anna sat and pondered her next move with the ancient walls and spires lending her spiritual support as she thought about the men who had built this wonderful cathedral to the glory of God. But then there was doubt of His very existence. Where was He now? Her God, her merciful God, the God she always prayed to. How could He let all these things happen? The killing and suffering of children – why doesn't He come down to this earth right now and stop it? She gazed up at the spires, they were so majestic and timeless; whilst above them the leaden clouds scurried as if to distance themselves from what they had witnessed below. With a deep sigh she lowered her upward gaze and reminded herself, as always, the heavens remained schtum.

Agonisingly she turned her thoughts back to her parents. If they had survived she would take them with her back to Aachen as her house was still standing but only deemed as unsafe. She would manage as neighbours had already shored up the sides with balks of timber. Besides she had nowhere else to go and all of her possessions were still there. She regretted not coming sooner, but then it struck her that had she arrived before the raid she and Eddi would have ended up in the same inferno as them. Perhaps God, along with her guardian angel had spared them both from that fate after all?

With an involuntary shudder, Anna pushed her morbid thoughts to one side as she decided to concentrate on the present. She watched her son with concern as he picked up a bright object from the far side of the cobbles. She was about to warn him not to pick things up but he proudly ran to her side and showed her what, to her relief turned out to be a toy bus. It looked brand new, probably from one of the shops she reasoned and told him he could play with it. It would serve to keep his mind off his breakfast but felt pangs of discontent for thinking like that. As a mother it hurt knowing she was unable to feed and nourish her child but then he could hold out a little longer until they found a safe shelter and she would use the food from her bag.

Feeling rested Anna decided she was able to face the world once more. She picked up her bag and beckoned for Eddi to follow as she planned to seek shelter at one of the Luftschutz bunkers and perhaps find a soup kitchen or make-shift goulashkannone. Eddi happily followed, pushing his yellow toy along the deserted pavement.

Anna rounded the last block of houses where the station was now in sight. However her attention was suddenly drawn by the wild shouts and gesticulations of a uniformed Luftschutz warden. Firemen came running from a damaged building and seconds later there was a blinding flash, then darkness—

***

Children were screaming from a long way off. It was a dream but the dream did not fade and the screams became louder. Anna felt only pain and a throbbing to the side of her head as she stirred and regained her senses. Opening her eyes she was greeted by a stab of pain and closed her eyelids as the infant noises faded to a whimper. In the background came the soothing tones of women's voices. I'm alive, she mused as she tried to unscramble her muddled thoughts. Where am I? What happened? Again the background murmur of voices. Old voices and occasionally the muffled cry of a child. It was puzzling as was the throbbing pain that added to her confusion.

It was the piercing wail of a baby's hungry cry which triggered a response to her maternal instincts. It obliterated all else, save the thought and wave of panic that now engulfed her. He was not there and her distressed mind screamed out in loss and fear, *Eddi...!*

In desperation Anna summoned all her strength and ignoring the pain let the light flood into her eyes as she sat bolt upright, frantically peering through the inherent gloom of her dimly-lit surroundings for any sign of her son. As her eyes adjusted and grew accustomed she recalled the panic-driven shouts of the air raid warden. Like an incoming tide it washed over her as she recalled the moment.

'Zeitzünder!' Ja, that's what he had shouted and recalled the flash. Yes, that was it, a time bomb had run its time and exploded. She had survived she reasoned as her thoughts returned to her son. 'Please God,' she whispered, 'I'm sorry I doubted you. Let him be alive.'

Anxiously she sat up trying to make out people in the restricted light and beside herself with worry and fear. She was about to stand and search for him when hearing a familiar voice glanced over her shoulder. It hurt her head but she sank back with relief as suddenly there he was, unharmed and with an impish grin standing right behind her and holding his yellow toy bus.

Relieved, Anna lay on her makeshift bed as a dam of pent-up emotion burst and cried enough to water heaven with her grateful tears. With a vengeance the throbbing pain returned but it did not matter anymore as she had her son, all safe and well. Through a veil of spent tears she tried to make out her surroundings but the sparse lighting made recognition difficult as even the vault of the ceiling was lost in the light that prevailed. Tired and with her wound still tender she rested her head as the comforting shadow of Hypnos brushed her senses and soon fell into a dreamless sleep.

Again, it was the voices of children that roused her. Anna felt rested as she sat up from her stuffed straw mattress and took stock of her situation. Her bag was missing so food was out of the question but she was hungry and remembered her boy had not eaten. She peered round for him at the same time trying to tidy her hair but not having a brush or comb she used her fingers and was surprised to find her left ear was covered with a bandage. That explained the throbbing pain as gingerly she began to explore the dressing. It hurt if she pressed it but that was all. She must have fallen and received a cut and realised it could have been worse.

'Mama,' came Eddi's voice, as he approached from out of the gloom. Gently, as it hurt her head she picked him up and sat him on her lap.

'We'll get you something to eat in a while,' she said. 'But see, we are safe here. Just be a good boy and wait.' He told her that he didn't want anything as he wasn't hungry and happily carried on playing with his toy. That's odd, thought Anna, as he should have been ravenously hungry by now. She felt his forehead for a temperature but it was normal, glancing down at her watch she assumed it was night-time as it said eight-thirty. But then many hours had passed since the explosion and there was no telling how long she had been here, even what day it might be.

The light increased as candles were lit, together with a hurricane lamp. In its radiance realisation dawned she was bedded down with some two hundred others inside a church. She thought perhaps it might be the cathedral; in that case she hadn't come far.

It was only then she became aware of the old woman who sat close to where Eddi had been playing. The mellow light accentuated her malnourished features and fragile frame which was clad in several layers of clothing. Her crowning glory was a red and black headscarf tied with an elaborate bow under her chin. A countrywoman, Anna assumed. As their eyes met, the old woman gave her an endearing toothless smile.

'Essen,' she said in a hardly discernible dialect and pointed to her mouth. 'I gave him some bread with marmalade and some chocolate.'

Anna nodded gratefully as the reason for Eddi's abstinence became clear. In the near distance she made out the stripped altar where all of the saintly statues had been removed. Only a large wooden cross remained, devoid of its tenant but still with its Latin header and inscription, 'INRI'.

She noted it was a large church but it was difficult to make out much detail except that most of the pews had been stacked against a wall and a sea of straw-filled mattresses had been laid out in their place. However, somewhere in the back of her mind she felt a sense of belonging and was quite contented to be here under the circumstances.

Having satisfied herself of her surroundings, Anna side-glanced the old woman and realised she had unselfishly deprived herself of food and given the much-needed sustenance to Eddie. Wide awake now she caught her eye and leant towards her.

'Vielen Dank,' she whispered. The old woman nodded her understanding and said something incomprehensible in her Sudetenland dialect. 'Vielen Dank,' Anna repeated, 'for looking after us both and for the food and chocolate. My head is still hurting but I will be alright in a while,' and indicated to the bandage. The old woman's dark eyes twinkled in response and with a non-committal shrug pointed at an elderly-looking man making his way across the floor, picking his way through the strewn humanity.

'Mein Mann,' she rasped proudly. 'It was he who brought you here. He has an ambulance.' Anna nodded, bemused by her comments and the thought of the old man driving an ambulance through the rubble-strewn city. The woman chuckled to herself. 'It's drawn by horses,' she added and burst into cackling laughter.

Inquisitive heads turned in her direction as the man approached and admonished his wife. He clutched a Tyrolean hat and waved it in greeting as he turned his attention to Anna.

'Guten Abend,' he said jovially as the capercaillie feathers on his hat shimmered brown and gold in the lambent light.

'Guten Abend,' replied Anna with a painful smile, recognising the same hollow features as that of his spouse. His grey farmer's coat with its faded green lapels hung from once broad shoulders and accentuated his stoop as he sat down beside his wife. Malnutrition seems to be our lot, mused Anna as she thought about her own situation.

Ignoring the pangs, she sat there thinking about her circumstances and what might be her next move. Inadvertently she had found shelter but now with the onset of night the bombers might return and church or no church, they certainly weren't selective. She recalled something her husband had mentioned about the Americans starting daylight bombing raids, whereas the Englander only flew by night. It raised a laugh at the time as he stressed that no pun was intended but it was a fact. Now, with their heavily fortified Liberators, the US air force could stretch right down into Southern Germany and release their deadly cargo from high altitude. It was well-known the Amerikaner would bomb from a great height, whereas the Englander were rather more selective.

Franz had said it was because the Englander could not afford to be wasteful as Herr Churchill had put the country on a tight budget. They were at a party and everyone laughed, it was a joke of course, as Germany was beginning to resemble a moonscape – courtesy of the RAF. Selective or not, she reasoned with misgivings as Köln had been attacked the previous May with over a thousand bombers. It made history, all those aircraft and the resulting fire storm as the local rubber factory and the docks went up in flames, along with five thousand acres of real estate in and around the city.

With her husband's words and his hollow chortling laughter still ringing in her ears Anna toyed with the idea of leaving before midnight. She would try to find an underground shelter and make her way home the next day. Without her bag she had nothing left except the clothes they both were wearing and decided to use the market in the morning but panic crept in as she thought about her purse? Her keys? Frantically she felt in her overcoat pockets. To her intense relief her purse was still there, together with her rail vouchers and keys. All she needed now was to find her parents and get away from here as fast as she could.

Incredibly as if in answer to her deliberations the air-raid sirens began their dreaded wail. The eerie sinusoidal lament never failed to make her flesh creep and now that fate had once again taken a hand she could only wait in exposed circumstances for another night of terror to unfold.

Children round her, disturbed from their slumber immediately began to wail and compete with the sirens as the adults tried to hush and calm them, only to sit and wait in fear and apprehension for the conclusion of their fate.

Anna, a veteran of many raids considered it odd as there was no prelude to this particular raid, being the Flak batteries down at the docks remained silent. Perhaps it was a false alarm she reasoned, as the wailing of the sirens slowly died. Absolute silence followed and a short while later came their answer as the dull distinctive drone of heavy aircraft engines permeated the building. They were felt more than heard as the building began to resonate, along with the stained glass windows that soon thrummed in sympathy in their leaded frames. To everyone's intense relief there was neither Flak nor the whistle of bombs – for the moment at least as the AA guns, the heralds of any raid, remained silent.

A low murmur of voices began to fill the void as people prayed for their deliverance but as prayer is sustenance for the soul, many did not go spiritually hungry that night. Anna along with the majority of the women had long since put her hands together to pray fervently to heaven for their Erlösung. Their utterings now drowned the diminishing noise of the over-flying aircraft as a murmur of supplicant voices transcended all else in their hour of need.

Minutes later, silence reigned once more except for the keening and sobs of several grandmothers who, if not before, were now close to their wits end.

'It has to stop,' cried one.

'Dear God, let the war end, come down and help us,' cried another.

'They will murder us all,' lamented others.

For Anna, however it was now the third Apocalyptic Horseman's turn to ride her down. She did her best to ignore the gnawing pangs of hunger as she carried on listening for any ulterior sounds, whilst resting on her palliasse and cradling her frightened son. Tired and hungry she was about to lie down herself when the sound of a softly-spoken male voice demanded her attention.

'Frau! Frau! Bitte the lady with the head bandage!' She glanced round and peered into the gloom. In the sparse light, she made out the silhouette of the old man still holding his Tyrolian hat and another, a taller man in a long dark frock. It's the priest, this must be his church, she reasoned. Wonder what he wants?

'Ja, bitte,' said Anna in a whisper of acknowledgement and looked on as the two men picked their way towards her. Perhaps he has news of my parents she mused, but immediately dismissed the thought. He doesn't know me from Adam, she reminded herself as the two men threaded their way past the final mattress. It was then she noticed the priest carried something in one hand and raised the other in a Christian manner of greeting.

'Guten Abend,' he said in a conciliatory tone. 'I'm Petrus, welcome to my church.' Taken slightly aback at being singled out from one in a crowd she felt like an intruder as the majority here were local people. Nervously Anna cleared her throat.

'Guten Abend, Herr Kaplan,' she replied in a hoarse whisper.

The priest gave her a welcoming smile as he joined her. Anna could not but notice the youthful sparkle and vitality in his dark eyes. She judged him to be in his early thirties, his cassock making him look taller than he really was. The soft candlelight accentuated his serenity and toyed mischievously with his shock of dark curls. He had an aura about him which seemed familiar as he stooped to be by her side.

'This is for you and your child,' he said and offered a small parcel wrapped in brown paper. 'Please take it,' he said with devout sincerity as he sensed her reluctance to accept such charity.

Anna was lost for words, feeling somewhat shamed as she had always been led to believe the Catholic Church never gave, only received. The priest sensing her doubt and reticence went down on one knee and gently placed the parcel by her side. 'Take this,' he said. 'It's for you and the little one. Please take it and may God bless you both.'

Reluctantly and with great humility Anna picked up the parcel. 'Bitte, Herr Kaplan. Vielen Dank,' was all she could think to say. She tried to choke back her thankful tears which soon blurred her vision of the kindly priest. Standing, Petrus lightly touched her forehead in blessing and re-joined the old man patiently waiting nearby.

As soon as they had departed Anna eagerly opened the gift. She felt like a child at Christmas once Saint Nikolaus had been and left a present from his sack. Only this was for real, she reminded herself. Inside and wrapped in greaseproof paper were several slices of rye bread, four thick slices of yellow potato bread, together with four hard-boiled eggs. In another wrapper was a homemade jar of marmalade, toffee sweets and a most welcome bar of chocolate. The chocolate with its white wrapper was printed in English. Confused, she read; Produce of Canada and the word Nestle. There was also a yellow tin of KLIM milk powder, another labelled Butter and stamped with a tiny red cross, and two bars of red soap with the word Lifebuoy, deeply imprinted.

Gently, Anna placed her sleeping son beside her and wiping grateful tears peeled one of the eggs, opened the tin of butter with its attached key and taking a slice of bread slowly began to eat her first meal of the day. As she savoured her Spartan meal, she took in her surroundings once more and her wandering gaze fell on the oil lamp that hung in one corner from the vaulted ceiling. The familiar lamp, with its ruby-coloured glass and guttering flame softly radiated its divine message as the words and memories from her childhood came flooding back. 'Hail Mary full of grace…' She stopped her whispered prayer as in the distance the welcoming wail of the all-clear siren permeated the building.

Chapter Eight

CAFÉ DEL MARE

Darkness came early that night as a light rain began to fall. Kurt and Franz left the confines of the U-bunker and made their way across the cratered and rubble-strewn dockyard as they headed towards the army motor pound. For Franz this was his first time out on the town – or what was left of it, apart from an official visit to U-Boot Command on his first visit to the port in January. He strode jauntily alongside his companion and once more felt the blood-rush of his earlier years as a cadet on his first visit to a foreign port. He acknowledged it was different for Kurt as he had been in dock for the past two weeks with his ongoing re-fit. His friend was single and unattached which made him a magnet for the nurses round the base and town.

'Hallo, Georg!' Kurt called to one of the army drivers about to alight his transport. 'Not going our way by any chance?' he said with a grin and jerking a thumb towards the town.

'Guten Abend, Herr Kapitän,' replied the corporal. 'Jawohl, I'm just leaving.' The soldier crossed to the other side and opened the cab door for them. 'I take it it's to the usual place, Herr Kapitän?'

'Not tonight, Georg, could you drop us by your communications building?'

'Ach nicht das Kaffeehaus! You're not drinking tonight?'

Kurt grinned at the man and chuckled to himself about his reputation and held out the customary five cigarettes.

'Sorry they're English,' he said with a mischievous grin.

'That's fine by me, Herr Kapitän,' replied the soldier. 'Smoking this local tobacco must be De Gaulle's ultimate revenge, his reprisal weapon on our lungs.'

They all laughed with wry amusement, as it was a standing joke only a desperate man or a German soldier would touch the French tobacco, with its distinctive tang and the reek of a sweat-laden sock. The driver lit up and placed the remainder in his glove box as he engaged the clutch and started in the direction of the main gate.

'You submariners are lucky, Herr Kapitän,' said Georg as he turned and headed uphill towards Kerentrech. 'But Herr Kapitän, if you like, I can lay my hands on some vintage Champagne. Perhaps we could do an army-type, navy exchange?'

'Aha, so you are a business man as well as a soldier?' quipped Kurt. 'Perhaps I will see you before I sail. Only don't say too much, we must keep our secrets secret. Isn't that so?' He elbowed Franz in the ribs and chuckled at his own wit, while the driver nodded with a grin. Thirty minutes later the driver halted the lorry by a large blacked-out building near the railway station. Fortunately it was the only part of Lorient which was still left reasonably unscathed.

'I have to drop you here, Herr Kapitän, as I'm heading to the Château.'

'That's fine,' said Kurt, 'Danke.' They both jumped from the cab and the truck sped off, to be swallowed up in an instant by the blackout.

'Just up this little side road and we're there,' said Kurt leading the way through the empty streets. Rounding a corner they made their way past the old church that was still in possession of its spire and down the hill towards the communications complex.

Two soldiers stood guard at the entrance and instantly sprang to attention as they saw the officers approaching. Franz and Kurt returned their salute and noted with amusement their questioning gaze as this was not a place frequented by naval personnel. One soldier opened the heavy wooden door and reminded them about the blackout curtain beyond and closed the portal with a reverberating bang.

As the final echoes died Kurt and Franz made their way along a well-lit, flag-stoned corridor and stopped by a door marked TELEFON ABTEILUNG. Kurt nodded to Franz and with a reassuring grin, turned the handle.

Immediately a cacophony of sound, together with a pot-pouri of perfume scents invaded their senses. Typewriters chattered and tele-printers clicked incessantly to vie with the military jargon of the switchboard operators together with the piquant patter of the girls working amongst the chaff of military correspondence. Above it all the dominant fug of cigarette smoke cast its blue veil across the room, its nicotine blend mixing with the subtle fragrances and perfumes of the girls and their alluring, heady scents. Heads swivelled in their direction as they entered and typewriters slowed audibly as by some primeval instinct the females scented a free night on the town.

Kurt grinned and waved to the girls and some acknowledged with smiles but Franz froze visibly as he took in his surroundings. He felt his pulse quicken as all eyes seemed focused on him. Rapidly he assessed the situation – the hunter had become the hunted as thirty doe-eyed fräuleins considered their chances of conquest. The majority of girls were in their twenties and regarded him as the new face in town and fair game for 'le rendez-vous l'amour' constituting a wine and dine and a visit to the back seat of the Wehrmacht cinema for dessert.

From behind the cover of their desks they peered at Franz as a prize to be taken. The term 'over open gun sights' came to mind as he felt all eyes were locked-on in his direction as these Lorelei maidens unashamedly ranged their sights on him. With the absence of his friend and moral support he felt foolish at having invaded this female bastion of gossip, powder and paint. Franz suppressed it as best he could, as showing any signs of a bashful nature would have heralded instant defeat. He decided like at sea, attack was the best form of defence and began to weigh them up in turn.

Allowing them the courtesy of a nervous smile he glanced tentatively round the room. In a buttock-clenching gaze he surveyed the scene as his adrenalin levels rose and his fight or flight senses screamed for the latter option. Better to face the raging Atlantic and an attack from an enemy destroyer than all these shameless sirens who had him so mercilessly in their lovelorn sights.

Seconds passed which seemed like eternity as slowly, in ones and twos, they melted. Smiling they mouthed their greetings, some wriggling their fingers to reveal the latest warpaint from Paris. Others conversed in loud whispers and he could only look on, bemused as they broke into giggles and smiled whimsically in his direction.

Shells of want and desire continued to scream overhead as they gazed wistfully at the smart naval officer sporting the three gold rings of his rank on his sleeves. To his relief the majority, their curiosities quelled, turned and bowed their heads to continue with the tap-tapping of their keys and the systematic ratcheting returns of the rollers.

After long agonising minutes Kurt returned, nudged his side and indicated with a nod in the direction of a raven-haired girl in a flowery dress. She had swivelled round to succinctly wave in their direction and Kurt returned the gesture as she gave him an enticing, pleased-to-see-you smile. Through pouting cherry-ripe lips, she seductively mouthed the words 'allo, mon chéri.'

'That's Yvonne,' he said with a wink and a tug on Franz's sleeve as he pulled his bashful friend in the direction of the only girl present in a naval uniform. Her dark blue jacket was draped over the back of her chair and upon giving it some scrutiny Franz noticed it sported a single gold 'pip' and two sleeve rings depicting her rank as that of an Oberleutnant zur See.

The officer had a headset firmly clamped over her ears and was busily engaged at the switchboard and had not heard or noticed them. As Kurt approached her desk she half turned her head and a frown of mild curiosity gave way to broad recognition and a cheery and welcoming smile.

'Kurt, you're back!' she enthused as she pushed the phones back, however her eyes remained cool and in contrast to her warm welcome. 'You arrived today, ja?'

'Ja, that's right, Lilli,' he answered with a sheepish grin as he guessed by her insincere expression she would have known all along which boats had arrived from where and when. Kurt mulled it over to what he should say as Yvonne would have mentioned him to all and sundry, one could bet on that.

'I mean… nein, not really Lilli,' he stammered. 'It's just I've been busy.' He nodded vigorously to emphasise the point and with a shrug smiled sheepishly into a penetrating pool of sceptical blue eyes. 'Come on Lilli, you know how it is. I have a submarine to attend to.'

Lilli nodded and wrinkling her pert little nose in a parody of disgust shook her head and sighed with resigned acceptance and decided to let Kurt stew as she shifted her attention to Franz – the handsome stranger. Relieved by her distraction Kurt felt he was now off the proverbial hook as he clasped his friend's shoulder.

'Lilli this is Franz, a good and trusted colleague of mine.' Franz smiled politely and held out his hand in greeting.

'It's nice to meet you,' was all he could think of saying as their eyes met. She held his flustered gaze as demurely she reached across the balustrade to place her hand in his, as her lips parted in a warm and welcoming smile.

'Nice to meet you too, Herr Kapitän. Welcome to Lorient,' she replied with a distinctive northern Rhineland accent. Alluringly she held his gaze, her blue eyes twinkling in the tungsten light as Franz, spellbound, stared shamelessly at her unsophisticated beauty. Lilli knew she could turn heads but now felt a flush rise to her cheeks by this man's undivided attention, welcome though it was. Deftly releasing his hand as an unexplained feeling crept into her body and quickly busied herself with removing her headphones.

The enticing spell broken, Franz looked on in amusement as she fought to untangle herself from the cumbersome device. With several pulls and tugs wisps of honey-blonde hair became stranded from a firmly-tied bun as Lilli, a little flustered by now attempted to extricate herself.

'Sorry about this,' she said with annoyance. 'It always happens when I have visitors. I must look a right mess?' She leant her head to one side and continued to pull and struggle.

'Ja, but a lovely mess,' quipped Kurt as he leant across the railing to assist. 'Here, let me help,' he volunteered, only too glad to make amends as he took the headset from her.

'Thank you, my dear. Perhaps you should come here more often,' she said tartly with a smile to match as the last strands finally pulled free. Kurt dismissed the sarcastic jibe and could only grin at her petulance as he handed back the phones. Under the circumstances he accepted it as a woman's right he reasoned, however it was only a broken date and ruffled feathers – nothing too serious as far as he was concerned.

'I'm sorry Lilli,' he replied. 'I can take a hint. I know I promised to take you out but other things cropped up. You know how it is.'

'But of course my dear, I understand,' she said with a touch of mock sympathy in her tone. 'Yvonne told me all about it. Shall I continue?'

In benign resignation Kurt shook his head and decided to examine his shoes. The game was up, he mused as he cast her a sheepish glance and switched to checking out the ceiling and its gyrating fans. Women he mused, why can't they ever keep secrets? He turned to Franz for moral support but his friend just shrugged and volunteered a roguish grin of mutual understanding.

'Please Lilli, listen,' Kurt pleaded. 'I've come to ask for a little favour.'

'Ach so, a favour now,' she replied, her tone rising an octave and once more putting on a feigned and hurt expression. 'So you have not come to visit your little Lilli?' Kurt was well and truly stumped. He had really put his foot in it now, he mused. Must stop digging, his senses screamed, but he needed her help and co-operation.

'Ja, but of course I have,' he stammered, 'I'm here now Lilli, only for you.' It sounded lame and he never expected her to accept it as she gave him a knowing look.

By now amused giggles and titters could be heard as he cast a furtive glance round the exchange. To his chagrin and intense discomfort the girls seemed to be enjoying the show as they waited eagerly for his next excuse. Then he saw her, Yvonne the mother of his torment sitting on top of her desk and casually filing her nails. Occasionally lifting her head to glance with an alluring pout in his direction and like her colleagues was enjoying every minute.

'Bitte Lilli,' he continued. 'It's not for me, but for Franz here. He needs to telephone home urgently.'

Franz saw his opportunity to bail out his friend as he quickly stepped forward. Into the proverbial breach, came to mind and nodded in agreement. If not for him, Kurt would not have to be dealing with his jilted date. Hell hath no such fury than a girl with a broken date, he mused as he met her tentative gaze and self-consciously shifting his weight to the other foot.

Together they waited for her to mellow, like rumbled truants up before the headmaster as Lilli, growing tired of her charade, smiled in triumph and savoured the moment. She had put Kurt on the spot for two-timing her and had satisfied herself by filling his cup of misery to the brim. She would help, of course but first she would pay back the love-rat for standing her up, and his shipmate could bear witness. She would show him what delights he had let slip through his fingers while, for his friend, it would be something to remember on a lonely Atlantic patrol.

She let them wait as she reached for her handbag and set a mirror on her desk before untying her regulation bun. Casting them both the ghost of a smile she shook and tossed her head as the knot fell away. Tantalisingly it caught the light as an alluring stream of honey blonde hair cascaded down to rest past her shoulders. Even with her hair disarranged, Lilli presented a startling figure as she turned to face them. Her top two buttons had mysteriously become undone and leaning forward gravity took hold as she displayed the canyons of an ample cleavage, together with two restraining Chantilly cups – allowing a peek of pale breasts that beauty could not tame.

'So, Herr Kapitän, what I can I do for you?' she cooed, gazing at Franz with a saucy smile as she straightened her poise and smoothed her skirt.

Was zum Teufel, he mused, as confusion and desire engulfed his senses. She's got the looks and body of an angel, and looks like Kurt missed out here he reflected, as he met her more than innocent gaze. He straightened his tie with the one hand whilst holding onto his cap and sanity with the other. He swallowed hard and with a cough and a growl, attempted to clear his wondering mind and throat.

'Ja, I'm sorry to bother you like this,' he began, 'but I need to contact my wife. Lilli please, it's rather urgent.' Lilli gave him an encouraging smile and nodded her willingness to help.

'But of course, Herr Kapitän, what is the number?' Her expression and manner changed as a more official tone crept into her voice. Gone the idle banter and saucy display of femininity as Lilli resumed the ugly business of war. She had already guessed the nature of his visit once Kurt had mentioned favours, but now at least she understood, alas this handsome man was spoken for.

'I'll leave the two of you for a moment,' said Kurt, pausing momentarily for her reaction.

However she played it cool, giving him a glance of mock disdain as he excused himself. Again she smiled reassuringly at Franz as she reached for her note-pad. During the past months she had done the same for other U-Boot officers who had come to her to enquire about their families. It was an open secret, an accepted thing ever since the increase in Allied bombings as the German public telephone system was by now virtually non-existent. It was only the military and exchanges such as this particular one at Lorient that had connections, so here was the only way of contacting their homeland. 'This will be to your home town, Franz?' she said, dropping the formality.

'Ja, that's right,' he answered, trying not to sound too demanding or anxious. 'It's actually to her parents' place in Köln. Their name is Wagner, here…' He fished about in his jacket pocket and handed her a scrap of paper. Lilli scrutinised it and systematically reached for her headset.

'Ein moment, bitte,' she said as she busied herself and methodically inserted several jacks into the switchboard. Frowning, she tried several times at dialling and sadly shook her head as she unplugged the leads. She gazed up at him with sad pools of blue and handed back the paper. 'I'm sorry Herr Kapitän, it's unobtainable.'

She noted the unspoken fear which lurked in his eyes which only moments before had sparred with hers now moistened with emotion as he swallowed hard and slowly crumpled the paper with his fist. Nodding his gratitude, he returned the scrap to his pocket and turned to leave. She felt for him and awkwardly brushed at her skirt as she witnessed his anguish. However she hit upon an idea and with a hint of a smile, caught his eye.

'Herr Kapitän? Bitte, what is the name of the street? I will try another way; here, let me have that address again.'

Dejectedly he reached into his pocket and handed her the crumpled note. In a tremulous voice he confirmed the address.

'Domstrasse, Haus number...'

'It does not matter about the number, Franz, I only need the area and the name of a street.'

Once more she busied herself with her headset and inserted several more jacks and dialled a number. His spirits rose as he heard her speaking to an operator – it sounded like a woman by the nature of the conversation. He caught snatches of the dialogue and knew she was through to Köln. After having exchanged pleasantries, he heard the names of Bauer and Wagner mentioned.

'Ach so,' she said suddenly. 'Ja, but of course. I will inform him, Vielen dank, Wiedersehen.'

Apprehension filled his soul as he watched this honey-blonde angel methodically pull out the connecting pieces of switchboard hardware and severing the Köln connection. Patiently he waited; his nerves on tenterhooks as she slowly turned in her seat. Lilli picked up the paper and handed it back as he tried to read her face for an answer. Once more their eyes met, his questioning in anticipation, whilst hers, too expressive to be blue, were pools of sadness.

'Franz, I managed to get through but I have some disturbing news about the city.' She paused to choose her words and removing her headset met his questioning gaze. 'There was a big air raid on the river and the factories. Some parts of the city were badly damaged.'

'Were they able to tell you which part? Which street?' he asked anxiously. Lilli shook her head as dewdrop tears began to roll past pale cheeks. Franz, a leader of men knew instinctively she was withholding something and there was more to come. Lilli produced a lace hanky and dabbed her face.

'Please forgive me, I'll be all right in a minute,' she said amidst more tears and sniffles. 'The city was badly damaged eight days ago. That's all the operator was allowed to tell me. Apparently she witnessed the bombing and the subsequent firestorm that followed. The police and the Heimwehr are doing the best they can to sort out the mess as there were many hundreds of people killed and injured.'

'Heimwehr?' he queried. 'What have the Home Guard got to do with it?'

'Ja, Franz, they are compiling lists of all casualties and also of the injured. It is still too soon as many are just old men trying to help.' Her tears turned to sobs and disturbed the others as Franz stood transfixed by the news. Unconsciously he screwed up the paper as Kurt returned from chatting with Yvonne. He went to Lilli's side and calmed the distraught girl who, between sobs, kept repeating, 'Those poor people, those poor people.' He glanced at Franz and indicated with a nod for a timely exit as several of the girls now came to Lilli's aid.

Kurt patted her shoulder, leaving Lilli to sniff into her handkerchief as both men made their exit and out into the welcoming night air.

***

Café Del Mare was a ten-minute walk from the exchange and the communications dormitory. Even with the blackout in force a pencil of light would occasionally escape from its entrance as clientele came and went. But the general attitude by now was there being nothing left to bomb in town, why bother as the town of Kerentrech was no longer worth a tuppenny banger to the RAF.

Strains of music and peals of laughter permeated from its doors as the occasional stab of light acted like a homing beacon to all and sundry. The two U-Boot commanders made their way uphill, guided by the occulting beam from the café's door. On passing through the blackout curtain they were greeted by an atmosphere of cigarette smoke which lingered in blue, stale layers and the friendly chat of soldiers and sailors of differing ranks. Peering round they accustomed themselves to the fug as a jovial booming French voice rang out above the general hubbub at the bar and the merry chink of glasses at the tables.

'Bonsoir messieurs, I will get you a table, non?' It was the voice of their host who hurried himself from behind the bar and quickly ushered the two officers to an empty table, wiping it with a deft swish of his blue apron as they took their seats.

The man was the typical Breton host, of stout build with a fleshy wine blossom nose set in a long jovial face. His cheeks were large, ruddy and drooped like worn saddlebags and were complemented by a three-day growth of stubble. To complete the image he wore a black Breton beret set at a rakish angle, concealing most of the remaining strands of his grey hair.

'Bonsoir Jacques, mon ami,' said Kurt. They had become friends ever since Kurt had come to be stationed at Lorient and it had been many a night the old Frenchman had swept up round him after the wine and Cognac had taken their toll. It was dependable old Jacques who always managed to flag down a passing truck in order for Kurt to regain his boat.

'Monsieur, que voulez-vous boire?' said Jacques with a jovial grin.

'Une bouteille vin rouge, s'il vous plaît,' Kurt replied. Jacques nodded and pointed a sausage-sized finger at Franz.

'Une bouteille Cognac avec glace,' replied Franz in broken French and with a testing grin to match.

'This is Franz, Jacques,' said Kurt. 'He is a good friend of mine.' Jacques nodded pleasantly at Franz and grunted something inaudibly in his Breton dialect before shuffling between tables and making his way back to the bar.

'That's a tall order,' said Kurt, raising an eyebrow.

'I know,' Franz replied with a grin. 'I just don't know the French for two glasses, so you'll have to help me with the bottle.' Their laughter was spontaneous which added to the general bonhomie and congenial atmosphere of the café.

Waiting for their order, Kurt raised his hand to acknowledge shouts and greetings from various tables. Franz took in the atmosphere and gave a cursory glance round the room. An elderly accordion player sat in the far right corner by the bar and in between playing local melodies, played requests for his German guests. Wearing the familiar Breton beret he was not as bulky as the proprietor but seemed to Franz more in the mould of a fisherman than anything else. A Gauloise hung loosely from his lower lip and now, after several cries from a table of soldiers, the strains of Lilli Marlene wheezed from his battered instrument.

Still gazing round, Franz noted with satisfaction he sat facing the door and only two other Frenchmen were in the room – they were young and sitting close to the accordion player along with five local girls, gossiping and sipping their drinks by the bar. Having heard stories he imagined them, like the two men to be part of the Maquis set-up, however he dismissed the thought as the girls at least, seemed very familiar with the troops. Must be the local whores about their usual business, he mused, just as several of his own crew came marching in. He acknowledged their noisy greeting as they made a beeline for the bar. The girls were suddenly re-vitalised as they quickly made room and dragged some bar stools in a well-honed fashion to sit with them.

The remaining clientele were a cluster of soldiers and sailors of various ranks with a smattering of German, off-duty nurses and ancillary hospital staff who, with many empty bottles to their credit, chimed in to the chorus of the ballad with its zeitgeist lyrics and haunting melody.

Jacques returned with a loaded tray of drinks, glasses and a silver bucket filled with ice. He set them down and wished them a pleasant evening.

'How long would Monsieur le Commandant be staying for, this time?' he asked casually. Franz gave Kurt a questioning glance as Kurt answered cordially, whilst filling their glasses.

'Not long enough Jacques. You know how it is, but I hope to finish my wine, oui?'

Jacques nodded without a trace of emotion as the two friends laughed at the evasive answer and wit. Once again, Jacques grunted something inaudible and shuffled away to serve another table.

They sat with their drinks and enjoying the atmosphere as the girls chatted and danced with the new arrivals. Seeing them enjoying themselves, Franz became silent as once again he was plagued by the spectre of the whereabouts of Anna and his son. Kurt, reading his mind flashed his cigarette case and offered one to his friend.

'Sorry to hear about Köln,' he said as he lit up, 'but I'm sure they are safe as otherwise you would have heard different. She might not even have gone there for all you know. Here, drink up and drink to their health.' Franz nodded, lighting his cigarette and draining his glass melancholically pushed it across the table for a refill.

'Ja, guess you're right,' he replied in resignation. 'Changing the subject, this sure is a great little watering hole but you have to watch it with that barman. I see you and him are great friends?'

'Ach, him? Ja, I know him, he's harmless. Thinks he's part of the resistance by wearing that beret. I leave him to suffer the illusion, besides, it gets me free drinks.'

'As long as you don't have one too many, eh?' he replied with a cautionary wink. 'Anyway, thanks for helping me out this evening, I was sorry to upset the girl as that business in Köln is down to me. Now I know what the problem is I might be able to get some compassionate leave. They owe me a couple of months as it is.'

Kurt nodded in agreement and was happy to see his friend talk about his problem and was glad he wasn't married, especially at this stage of the war. Carefree and single, that's me, he reflected as he recharged their glasses with the smooth, Napoleon liquid.

'I've been thinking,' said Kurt. 'Tomorrow we'll go back and see Lilli. They might have more information by then and Lilli can get in touch.'

Franz knitted his brow. 'You sure?' he said with a frown. 'Sounds like you want second helpings from her. She really went for you. Are you playing hard to get or something?

Kurt picked up his glass and held it in salute, 'Here's to Lilli, she's a gem. I've known her for some time, but never a date. I then get involved with her friend, Yvonne. She was away for a few days, so I thought I'd take Lilli out. Yvonne came back early and I had to break the date. But being a typical female Yvonne had to tell the whole world what she did the night before...' He made a gun with his fingers. 'Bang, I was dead.'

'You'll be dead if you show your face there again,' said Franz with a chuckle. 'Anyway, thanks again for taking me there. I hope she doesn't get into hot water with her department. It's against regulations and you know how prickly those army types can get.'

'Ach Lilli can handle it, she's done it all before. As long as we don't abuse the system, anyway,' he said with a shrug, 'she's Kriegsmarine, one of us.' He glanced across at his still troubled friend. 'Look, Franz, in the final analysis it's people like you that can help turn this war around. You give your men the peace of mind that installs confidence and in turn assists the war effort. There's nothing more to say.' He glanced across the small table and was pleased to see him nod in understanding.

'Another thing,' he continued, you know damn well nobody will get compassionate leave. Others in the same situation are just told to get on with it. It's the same the world over, not just us in the Kriegsmarine. I don't think the Englander sends Jolly Jack home after we've bombed his house. No way – he's just got to grin and bear it, like we all do.'

Franz nursed his drink for a while and replied with an air of resignation. 'I guess you're right, but it's my problem. Thanks anyway.'

He had already decided to drop the matter for the time being and wait for results from the base welfare as they were checking out both his home address and that of his parents-in-law. It would not do him any good to brood like this, he reasoned, especially after meeting up with his old friend on such a rare occasion. Willingly he would sail out now with this new equipment they had been promised and carry on with fighting his boat to end the war.

Snapping out of his mood he topped up their wine, 'Here's to us meeting up like this, and thanks again.'

'Prost,' said Kurt as they chinked glasses. 'It's great to meet up again. What do you think of the place?'

'Looks like a single sailor's dream,' replied Franz with a grin. 'Those lads over there are some of my crew. Guess they'll all have hangovers in the morning.'

They looked-on and commented on the girls as they danced on the space allocated as a dance floor, close by the accordion player. The night was yet young as they reached the halfway mark on the Cognac, with the wine bottle dead and upside down in the bucket.

As ever, the attentive Jacques was pulling a cork from the second bottle when the blackout curtain parted and in walked two radiant, beaming girls. Heads turned as the two stunners savoured the moment. Kurt, ever the gentleman, was already on his feet and attracted their attention. Jacques nonchalantly raised a bushy eyebrow as he uncorked the wine and found two more chairs before shuffling away and fetching more glasses.

Yvonne and Lilli attracted wolf whistles as they joined Kurt and Franz. Yvonne sat next to Kurt, who kissed her in greeting on both cheeks. Franz surrendered his chair to Lilli, but she remained standing until Kurt realised his oversight at having forgotten to introduce his girl.

'Sorry Franz, I thought you'd met. This is Yvonne, the fräulein – or should I say, mademoiselle – at the exchange.' Yvonne, on cue smiled sweetly and blew him a pouting kiss across the table.

'Bonsoir, Monsieur le Commandant, welcome to our little café, it is nice, non?' For the second time that day Franz felt like a fish out of water and scrunched his toes until it hurt as Yvonne's pouting cherry lips parted in a sensuous smile, while dark eyes twinkled alluringly from under long jet lashes. He was attracted by the raven colour of her hair with its enticing permanent waves being the haute couture of the day. Then there were those eyes, ebony eyes to match her hair as in the glitter of the chandeliers they flashed and shone like diamonds as she met his inquisitive gaze.

'Bonsoir, mademoiselle,' he volunteered, swallowing hard and regaining his composure under the flirtatious onslaught. 'Oui, mademoiselle, c'est bon.'

It was Lilli who came to his rescue and offered her hand.

'Hallo Franz, how are you?' she asked with an encouraging smile. 'I think I could do with a drink.'

'Guten Abend again, Lilli,' he replied. 'Please forgive me; I'm trying to practise my French, here may I take your coat?' Relieved and without waiting for a reply he assisted her in removing the coat and hung it on the back of a bentwood chair. Franz lifted another chair from the next table as they both sat and watched intrigued as

Lilli began to hand-brush the texture of the coat with the back of her hand.

'Danke,' she replied. 'I have to spread it like this for it to breathe. It doesn't like the rain. Only a shower but it can affect the fur.' He nodded, as he never knew that and poured her drink.

'I would like to thank you for your efforts Lilli, sorry I had to drag you into my problems like this.'

'Ach, it was nothing, really. I've done the same for several of the other boats. Besides, you are his friend.' Her eyes narrowed as she said it and indicated with a barbed pout at Kurt sitting across the table. 'Bitte accept my apologies for my actions this evening, I've never done anything like that before, please believe me.' Franz felt like saying *my pleasure*, but stifled the thought and let her continue.

'I just wanted to let him know I too, have feelings.' Listening, his eyes started to drift as Lilli self-consciously placed an arm across her low cut dress. 'Yvonne's my friend but she just flaunts herself and makes…' She paused, casting a furtive glance across at her and Kurt, whispering sweet nothings and enamoured with each other's company. 'Well, you know… that's the sort of thing he likes.' Some feathers ruffled here, mused Franz as she sipped her drink and morning dew tears began to glisten.

'Jawohl Lilli, I think I understand,' said Franz as her tears made him feel ill at ease and reached for his handkerchief, gently pressing it into her hand.

'Danke, Herr Kapitän, for understanding,' she replied with a sniff.

'Call me Franz, Lilli. Please, we're all off duty now,' he said with an encouraging smile as she contemplated him with tearful, guileless eyes and he recognised the loneliness that lurked in their depths.

'I came with her as she said you might be here.' She paused, to glance across at the engrossed couple and shook her head. 'Well she said he would be here, so I took the chance that I might find you too.'

'Ach so,' said Franz with a nervous chuckle. 'Did I forget something?'

'Nein, nothing like that, please, I had to come because of your family.' He glanced at her and preoccupied himself with lighting a cigarette. He tried to reason what all this was leading to, especially as she was now talking about his family.

'Sorry Lilli, I must apologise for my lapse of manners, do you smoke?' He offered his open case and she shook her head. 'So, you were saying?' said Franz, now keen to hear the rest.

'I feel that at this moment, I am the only person that can help trace your family. No one here cares. They have all become dehumanised in this war, so uncaring.'

Her voice was strained as she tugged at the bestowed handkerchief. Franz glanced at her bowed head as warning bells sounded. The last thing I need is charity, he mused. She means well but I don't need all this emotional stuff.

Lilli raised her head and saw the doubt in his eyes 'I don't wish to intrude, Franz, please believe me as I came here for two reasons. It was the Köln operator, she called me back. Nothing much really, just to say the Heimwehr and police were still compiling casualty lists and so far your wife's name had not been mentioned.'

He startled her as he suddenly leant forward. Gone in an instant were his suspicions as he stuttered an apology.

'I had no idea, Lilli, I'm sorry... I misunderstood.' Lilli reached out her hand and gently placed it over his, still resting on the table and felt his tension subside.

'It's all right, Franz,' she said with a whisper. 'I'll do my best to find them for you.'

He nodded and felt good by her touch but was distracted by the antics of the sailors across the room. He felt resentful at seeing all the happy youngsters that danced, sang and drank the night away. Damn them all he mused, clenching his fist, as Lilli felt his turmoil. Damn the Nazis and their Austrian warmonger. Damn him of all people for this stupid war. Gloomily he recharged his glass as Kurt and Yvonne got up and indicated for Franz to join them on the dance floor. Lilli took the glass from his hand and standing, left him no choice but to follow.

'Come on Franz,' she said with a beckoning smile. 'It's a waltz. We'll join them, ja?'

She was of medium height and they seemed the ideal couple as sheepishly he led her across to the dance floor. They were well-suited – he the naval officer in uniform and Lilli, wearing her spring dress with a flower and leaf motif, the latest in Paris fashion which did justice to her feminine curves.

They danced to the music of the accordion and it made him feel proud and masculine to have this elegant woman in his arms. He felt young again as they danced and swayed and for a fleeting moment, forgot all that was bad in his life, until the music slowed and they held each other close.

With her young body pressed against him, the heady allure of her perfume invaded his senses and triggered a twinge of moralistic conscience. However the jealous fingers of guilt now crept into his soul as an inner voice reminded him of Anna. He dismissed the thought as the wine assisted to cushion his senses and Lilli squeezed his hand in reassuring release.

He led the way back to their table and pulled a chair for her to be seated. They sat each silent and lost in their own world, one a trifle conscience-stricken and the other still savouring the moment in her summer dress.

'I'm not a good dancer,' he said, breaking the silence and invading her thoughts.

'Oh, you are, I enjoyed it,' she replied with a happy smile. 'It's me, I'm out of practice. I used to take lessons, ballet and that sort of thing, but since the war I've not had the opportunity. In fact you are my first war-time dance.' He frowned at that – 'No, really Franz, it's true.'

He cast her doubtful smile and gazed at her in mock suspicion, not too sure if she was as innocent as she made out to be. Lilli giggled and felt like a teenager again and her eyes twinkled mischievously over the rim of her glass, as he found himself ever more attracted to her easy-going nature.

'I suppose you know Kurt quite well?' he said, changing the subject and selecting a cigarette from its case and flicking the wheel of its integral lighter. She turned her head in the direction of the dance floor and shook her head.

'We met on several occasions,' she replied. 'He came to the exchange – you know, like yourself – and I accommodated him. He's a ladies' man, just look at him.' She paused as they both watched the couple. 'Last week it was that girl at the bar, over there in the red dress. He likes the French girls as they...' She paused and swallowed hard. 'He's promised to take me out for a meal at the Château, but just look at him now – he's all over her. Well, he's never going to get the chance again. I'm not that sort of girl, anyway.' With a trembling hand, she picked up her wine and sought solace in its depths.

So his friend was a cad, a love-rat but then he, like all men was never sure with the ladies when this sort of cap fitted. Was it anger, jealousy or just female frustration? Such feelings, these sinews of the soul, if left to fester could maim the mind.

He stubbed his cigarette before making any comment about his friend. One never could tell with the fairer sex, he reasoned. They were an enigma, even to themselves. Why they do it and torture themselves, God only knows, like lemmings diving over a cliff?

73

'Sorry Lilli, I didn't mean to pry,' said Franz, pouring oil on troubled waters as obviously he had touched a nerve. 'Only I haven't seen him for at least two years. When I saw you both in the exchange I thought you knew each other quite well.'

'That was just horseplay; I knew he'd been in port for several days now.' She leant towards him and whispered. 'It's my job. I know when you all arrive and also when you…' She paused in mid-sentence, not daring to breathe another word as she remembered the latest U-Boot losses.

'Sorry about that, Franz. But what I meant to say was that I knew through the grapevine that he had been two-timing me. I was just trying to make him feel a chauvinistic heel, as Yvonne is my best friend. He knew her before he ever whispered sweet nothings in my ear.' She finished her wine with a gulp and felt better for being able to talk to another person about it. One that understood, she reasoned, like her priest in the confessional.

'Well, Lilli, it's his loss,' he added with a sympathetic nod. 'I'm sure you'll find yourself another date. There must be hundreds of lads around here.' It sounded hollow, patronising and he knew it, but there was nothing else for him to say.

'Yvonne can have him.' So saying, she raised her glass to her friend still on the dance floor. Franz nodded with a consoling smile as Aesop's grapes came to mind.

'He told me that you're from Aachen,' said Franz, diplomatically changing the subject. Lilli nodded as she finished dabbing her eyes. 'Then you must speak some French? Are you close to the border?'

'Oui, Monsieur le Commandant,' she replied with a congenial smile. 'That's how I received this posting to the exchange. Belgium is only a short distance. I used to go shopping there in the local markets.'

'Ja, I know the markets,' replied Franz. 'Anna and I used to go there sometimes…' He stopped in mid-sentence as two things happened – Lilli's eyes, like a startled cat at midnight, widened at the mention of his wife's name while Kurt, back from the dance floor kicked his foot under the table and signalled with a wink.

'Better finish our drinks, boys and girls,' he said, draining his glass. 'We have a busy day ahead of us.' Franz took the hint and ostentatiously checked his watch.

'Ja, you're right,' he replied. 'It's getting late and the ladies should be in bed.' They sniggered at their joke as the girls; having heard it all before sighed in unison and demurely picked up their things.

Others were also leaving as they filed in an orderly manner through the blackout curtain and out into the street.

'I'm staying at the hotel tonight,' said Kurt in a loud whisper. 'Care to join me?'

'Some other time,' said Franz shaking his head. 'I'd like to get back to my boat. Besides, I don't wish to cramp your style.' Kurt nodded with a grin and taking Yvonne's arm made his way back towards his hotel.

Franz walked Lilli back to her compound. In the stillness of the night only the distant cries and chants of the sailors could be heard as they made their bawdy way back to their ships and stopping anything on wheels that came their way. Occasionally a shrill female voice and laughter would pierce the night air, otherwise the town had gone to sleep.

They walked in silence, each with their thoughts as Lilli modestly crooked her arm in his. Minutes later they were through the main gate of the compound, and with the dormitory insight across the parade ground they were nearly home. On reaching the two-storey building they stopped at its entrance. He felt awkward now, like a cadet on his first date.

Self-consciously he stood there with his 'date' and recalling his first courtship but together they had been much younger then as now, here he was, a married man and caught in a web of circumstances. What on earth was he supposed to do next? To compound matters a sentry with his Mauser machine pistol now appeared from the shadows and stood watch by the door. After what seemed an eternity Franz plucked up courage and took her hand and sensed that the wretched man was watching his every move.

Gazing into her eyes he felt a gnawing fire take hold. 'I'll try and see you tomorrow,' was all he could think of to say and still holding her hand, raised and self-consciously kissed it.

'Gute Nacht Franz, danke for a pleasant evening.' She wanted to say so much more to this troubled man but words washed over her. Perhaps it was the wine that made her feel glowing and flushed as a burning desire for something more welled from deep within.

'Gute Nacht Lilli, and we'll see each other again,' he said awkwardly as once more her perfume invaded his senses. However he felt something else now stirred and was awakened and quite naturally, it was devoid of conscience. He cursed inwardly as he had become a victim of his own making, but nonetheless, it did feel good...

'Aufwiedersehen Franz,' Lilli whispered. He released her hand and with a laden heart and a maimed conscience left her gazing after him as he made his way back across the empty parade ground to be swallowed up by the mantle of the night.

Chapter Nine

SECRETS TO A STRANGER

Trains left the station at no particular time as schedules on the German railway system had ceased to exist. In fact they now ran to a timetable scheduled by the Allied air force. It was already well after dawn as the locomotive with its bullet-scarred casing, stood hissing and building up steam. It remained motionless as the sweating fireman hastily shovelled coal and the driver systematically tapped his gauges. Finally, with commanding guttural shouts from along the platform, accompanied by the sounds of slamming carriage doors and a guard's shrilling whistle, the train began to move.

Anna was grateful she had managed to get onboard and was able to find herself a seat. With the train gathering speed she and the others in her compartment stared out of the blue-tinted window. In silent disbelief they witnessed the devastation which presented itself as the train rolled on by. The once proud and majestic buildings of the early nineteenth century now lay in rubble and ruins. Bomb craters proliferated and it was miraculous the station had escaped major damage. Adjacent lines lay in grotesque and twisted shapes, whilst engines and wagons lay toppled, burnt and derelict. Others stood cannibalised of their useful parts and were left standing, stripped and rusting. Pools of oil-streaked water dominated the majority of the craters, whilst the latest additions were slowly filling and making the whole scenario resemble a lunar landscape.

With the train running at speed, the monotonous sound of the wheels had Eddi closing his eyes and was soon fast asleep on Anna's lap. Fortunately for her she had managed to catch a few hours' sleep herself before waking at dawn and hurrying down to the station. She had been warned by the old man in the church to get there early as people were anxious to get away from the city.

Now with Köln and her ordeal behind her she thought once more about her parents and the feeling she was running out on them, leaving them to their fate but the old man had informed her that in that block and others in the vicinity there had not been any survivors. With that in mind and now in mitigation she was able to console herself as she justified her actions being that her immediate duty was towards herself and her child. She recounted her lucky escape as she fingered the wound where the bandage had been removed and thought about the priest and his church and his kindness towards her. Wearily she closed her eyes in silent prayer, it felt good to talk to someone and God was always a good listener. She shared her ordeal with Him and thanked Him for her deliverance as she too succumbed to the rhythm of the wheels and the oblivion of merciful slumber.

It was the jolt of the train and the sudden screech of metal on metal as the brakes were applied. It roused her and at first there was silence, then came a series of authoritative shouts and other raised voices, followed by the sound of slamming doors and venting steam. Fully awake now she collected her thoughts. Eddi was still asleep and her new canvas bag was by her feet.

Satisfied, she along with the others in her compartment now gazed expectantly out of the window. From her position in the middle of the compartment she could see nothing but empty fields and trees that were barely in leaf. We're in the middle of nowhere, she mused as the shouts from outside continued and more raised voices joined them from along the corridor.

For the first time she allowed herself a furtive glance round her compartment and taking stock of her travelling companions. Four soldiers sat by the window. The one sitting next to her she took as a Feldwebel as he had an army sergeant's epaulettes and carried a side arm, the others had their single 'V' stripes. Gefreiter she assumed, just soldiers with their platoon sergeant. Above her in the rack she noted their kitbags along with three rifles.

Immediately opposite sat two sailors and sitting next to her, on her right was a clean-shaven man in his thirties, who wore a full-length black leather coat with a matching attaché case that he rested on his lap. The soldiers were playing cards and quite indifferent to the shouts and commotion from further along the line.

The two sailors were mere boys in their late teens and wore the square, blue-grey patches denoting ordinary seamen. However, her heart skipped a beat as she recognised their metal insignias pinned to their chests as members of the Submarine Service. It was the same insignia as worn by her husband, heralding a submarine, Swastika with oak leaves and a spread eagle on top.

Her heart went out to them as she identified herself with them and immediately felt a sense of camaraderie and belonging. In a flash an idea came to mind. What if they were going to join his boat?

Anna closed her eyes and told herself not to be so silly, such romantic nonsense only happened in books and on the silver screen, while this here was the real thing. She stifled the thought and side-glanced the man sitting next to her, whom she assessed to be a government official. He seemed an oddball – distant, as he sat in stony silence and either gazed out into the corridor or stared sullenly down at his highly-polished shoes.

Moments later the train gave a jolt and started to move again. Soon news filtered through that the train would not be heading north towards Essen and Hanover but on towards Magdeburg and Berlin. The soldiers stopped their noisy game of Skat and celebrated their good fortune from a stone bottle of home-made Schnapps as the diversion would give them extra days' leave before joining their unit.

The man next to Anna fixed them with beady eyes and shuffled his feet in annoyance at their unpatriotic stance, whilst the two sailors spoke in loud whispers of their fear of being punished for missing their boat.

'I hope they'll wait for us,' she heard one remark. 'They'll need us to fire the torpedoes.' His shipmate nodded as he nervously folded and unfolded his leave pass. Anna smiled inwardly. The innocence of youth, she mused. But they had mentioned torpedoes, so they must be joining an operational boat.

'They'll have to wait,' said the second lad. 'There are eight of us here.'

It was then that one of the soldiers offered them a drink from two battered aluminium mugs. The youngsters shook their heads and politely refused, but the soldier persisted, being egged on by his mates. Two mugs were handed to them and against their better judgement and with the bravado of youth, both took a gulp of the fiery corn liquid.

In an instant the compartment erupted in an explosion of gagging and choking coughs as the over-proof spirit collided with their senses. One youngster dropped his mug and the remaining liquid splashed over the official man's highly-polished shoes. The man stared balefully at the youngsters; his wan features turned crimson as he began grinding his jaw, the veins on his temples and neck pulsating angrily. The youngsters, having somewhat recovered glanced apologetically at him whilst the soldiers shook their heads and howled with glee and heinous laughter. Eddi awoke with a start and began to cry as Anna tried to soothe him and whispered for him to be good and turned her attention on the braying soldiers.

'*Idiots!*' she hissed, 'look what you've done, leave the lads alone.'

To her surprise they stopped their guffaws and with sheepish grins at their victims and the occasional snigger, resumed their game. The man examined the drying stains that had dulled the shine on his footwear, sniffed audibly in consternation and commenced agitatedly drumming his fingers on his attaché case. Anna gave a motherly glance across at the two youngsters and saw with satisfaction apart from brimming tears and crimson faces her 'children' had come to no apparent harm.

She managed to soothe Eddi back to sleep as the soldiers, in an effort to make amends, offered everyone a cigarette. Anna shook her head while the man next to her ignored them, however the sailors readily accepted and the incident between the army and the navy was thus closed in amiable and passing clouds of friendship.

Still seething at the soldiers' stupidity and concerned about her parents' fate, Anna sat nervously tapping her foot without realising she was doing so. It was only the official man's irate fidgeting and his occasional irritating head-turning motions that made her aware of it. With an apologetic shuffle of her feet she cast him a conciliatory glance as he sniffed in vexation and re-aligned his already straighter than straight tie.

The Schnapps incident behind them, the travelling companions settled down once more as the train sped on through the peaceful Saxony countryside. Eddi was awake now and watched the sailors opposite as they peered and made funny faces at him. One of them leant across and handed him a sweet in a wrapper.

'I hope it's alright with you, lady?' he said. 'It's a Bon-Bon from France. My uncle is there and he sends them to us.'

'Danke,' Anna replied with a nod and a grateful smile and un-wrapped it for him. It was the U-boat insignias which once again began to inspire and concentrate her thoughts. Apprehensively she glanced across at them and with her mind made up decided to apply the maxim of desperate people doing desperate things.

'You're in the U-Boot service, ja?' She pointed at their insignia as the youngsters nodded with pride. 'My husband is a submariner,' she said in a loud whisper and leaning across towards them, added, 'ein Kapitän.'

They frowned with mounting suspicion. However, not wishing to be impolite nodded in acknowledgement as the elder of the two gave her a wary smile. She sensed their unease but knew it might be her only chance of getting a message to her husband. Against her better judgement she threw caution to the wind and carried on with her plan.

'Bitte perhaps you can help me. I wrote to him a few weeks ago.' She leant across once more, and whispered, 'That was in France.'

'Ach, so,' said the younger lad.

'Hunger, Mama, hunger,' came Eddi's sudden cry. Anna reached down to her bag as the two sailors conversed in low tones and cast furtive glances in her direction. She un-wrapped a slice of the yellow potato bread and handed it to him, as she considered her next move.

As Eddi sat munching his bread, she tried to figure out where they might be heading. To the north there was Bergen in Norway but they would not be on this train, then Kiel, Bremen and Hamburg, but they were not so much in use now as fighting bases as the ones along the coasts of the occupied countries. It would have to be somewhere along the west coast, Rotterdam, otherwise, there remained the French ports.

She reasoned perhaps they were on this northbound train because it was the only train that had been available. It was a simple choice – travel to the north and get another connection. A second thought then crossed her mind. Perhaps the navy would fly them to their destination?

Eddi had finished his bread and as a treat, Anna un-wrapped the bar of chocolate and broke off a square. She noticed the two youngsters watching her as she handed Eddi his treat. Feeling guilty she offered them a square each, which they eagerly accepted. It seemed they had not seen or tasted chocolate for a long time as chocolate was a rare commodity in war-torn Germany. There again, neither had she.

She was about to continue her one-sided conversation when one of them fished in his pocket and produced a whistle. He put it to his lips and blew it slowly, making a low sound. Eddi had been watching his every move and was thrilled when the youngster handed it to him.

'This is for you,' the sailor said, 'only blow it outside, Ja?'

Eddi nodded and took it, immediately he blew it as loudly as his little lungs could muster. In an instant the compartment erupted as the soldiers, quietly dozing after their Schnapps recoiled and with a reflex action, leapt to their feet – with the sergeant fumbling for his pistol. With relief and mutterings they cursed the boy under their breath and the Feldwebel, replacing his gun wagged a cautionary finger in his direction.

Anna, immensely embarrassed could only apologise to them and the man sitting next to her. He said nothing as the muscles of his jaw tightened and once more began drumming his fingers on his attaché case. It was now the sailors' turn to chuckle as they were now even with the soldiers but indicated with fingers to their lips as Eddi, with a giggle, was about to repeat the performance.

'Here Eddi,' said Anna taking the offending toy from him. 'We'll put it in your pocket so you won't lose it. You can play with it outside once we are off the train, ja?' He nodded with a smile and soon was back asleep.

'Are you travelling far, or just to the north?' said Anna, addressing both of the youngsters. Once more they became wary of her questioning. Here was this pretty woman giving them chocolate, when there were limited supplies in the country and then asking all these sensitive questions. They had been warned about people like her, about women offering sweets and favours for any information, except that her eyes reflected her deep anxiety along with their accompanying dark blushes of underlying fatigue.

'I'm sorry, lady,' replied the older lad. 'But we can't answer that sort of thing. Please, you understand, ja?' Anna nodded and realised she had perhaps overstepped the mark. It was wartime and as an officer's wife, she of all people should have known better. She should never have asked and chided herself in annoyance at her own folly.

'I'm awfully sorry,' pleaded Anna. 'But you are my only chance of getting news to my husband. I thought perhaps you are going to one of the U-Boot bases.' Uncomfortable with this stranger's questioning they shook their heads in sympathy and left Anna with her thoughts.

Tears of desperation began to show as the countryside gave way to buildings, whereupon the train would soon reach its next stop. Anna was desperate as they were the only ones that could help, when another idea blossomed. She delved into her bag and ripping off a piece of chocolate wrapper, scribbled a few lines as the train began to jolt and slow.

'Here,' she said and thrust the scrap of wrapper into the older lad's hand. 'That's my name, Anna Bauer. My husband is Kapitänleutnant Franz Bauer. I'm sure that Lorient is his base. Please, I beg you; see if you can somehow contact him. Tell him that I'm going back to Aachen after being in Köln. He will understand. I don't want to know anything about your movements. Please, help me if you can.'

The sailor glanced down at the wrapper and, tight-lipped, handed it to his chum to read. With a metal-grinding screech the train came to a halt. Raised voices and the clamour of people on the move, as doors opened and banged to herald their arrival.

Shouts of 'Schnell, schnell!' from the station master filled the air, hurrying them along as the carriages emptied. The engine took on water and coal and soon chuffed its way back down the line. With military precision a convoy of waiting lorries took the servicemen away and civilians crossed over a makeshift wooden bridge for their next connection. There were no names on the station and a line of bomb craters straddled the shunting yard as Anna, carrying her slumbering child, followed the line of people over the bridge.

In the rush, she failed to pay any heed to the two men suddenly walking close behind her until once over the bridge one of them tapped her on the shoulder. Turning she came face to face with two burly military officers in black uniforms. They had the charismatic silver rune flashes on their lapels and on their peaked caps wore the unmistakable death's head insignia of the Waffen SS.

'Kommen Sie mit uns,' one of the officers said brusquely as Anna froze and instinctively drew Eddi closer to her.

'We'll go this way,' said the other, indicating a way off the crowded platform and falling in beside her.

'What's all this about?' said Anna angrily. 'Where are you taking me? I shall miss my train.'

Ignoring her plea and now flanked by the two men Anna was quickly escorted off the platform and taken towards a large building across the station square. They passed a lorry and she recognised her two sailors seated in the back, along with their draft. They sat and watched with concerned expressions having witnessed the events on the platform after their own brief encounter with the authorities just a short while ago.

Anna managed a wan smile in their direction as one of the SS men held her arm and led her into an old, mustard coloured building. Inside it was damp and dark and after walking down a hallway she was ushered into a room. It had a bench along one wall and a small window that looked out onto the cobblestoned square. At the far end stood a solitary desk with a telephone, ashtray, and several chairs.

Confused and with Eddi dozing in her arms, Anna sat herself down on the bench as she tried to weigh up her situation. Why were the SS suddenly interested in her? She had no business with Hitler's private army and surely, as the wife of a naval officer they had no business with her. Had something happened to Franz? But then how did they know who she was and even her whereabouts?

Tired, she sat and waited and gazed tediously at the Nazi posters which adorned the otherwise bare walls as two SS soldiers stood guard by the door, occasionally casting a questioning glance in her direction.

Satisfied with her inspection, one of the posters caught her eye just as a recessed door opened and in strode an Obersturmbannführer of the Waffen SS. He looked resplendent in black breeches, matching riding boots and silver braid insignia and was closely followed by the two arresting officers that had escorted her from the station.

He sat down and was handed a file by one of the flanking officers. He clicked on the desk lamp and motioned for Anna to come forward and sit down in front of him. Slowly he read the hastily-typed document and nodded several times in understanding, and with deliberation gave Anna a cursory glance.

Having seated herself by the desk Anna was confronted by the poster immediately behind the officer. *Careless talk costs lives it read*, with its picture of Churchill wearing a tin helmet and listening intently through a wall. She assumed this was what it was all about and the two sailors must have reported her. That must be it, she reasoned.

It was then that Eddi awoke and became restless, she put him down and he stood clinging to her skirt and peering from behind her chair at the three stern-faced men. Having re-read the document, the senior officer met Anna's anxious gaze.

'Frau Bauer, you are Frau Anna Bauer, I presume?'

'Ja, but of course,' she replied with a nervous tremor in her voice. My name, he knows my name as the thought flashed through her befuddled mind. Ja, but of course, the boys must have told him, she reasoned.

'My name is Herzog, Obersturm Helmut Herzog. I am here to investigate certain irregularities. Perhaps you already know why you are here, Ja?' He removed his cap to reveal a head of grey, short-cropped hair.

'No, I do not,' snapped Anna. 'I don't know how you know my name but please if I can help you I will. As you can see both of us are very tired and we must get back home to Aachen as soon as we can.'

'Frau Bauer,' Herzog continued in his unmistakeable Bavarian accent. 'We don't play games. You have been brought here for questioning concerning the security of the Reich.' He paused for effect and stared at her with an intimidating gaze as he held the scrap of paper up for her perusal. 'I take it that you have seen this before and know what it is, ja?' Anna froze as she recognised the note that she had given to the sailors. But then, so what? It only had her and her husband's name on it and the word Lorient.

Once again the recessed door opened. Anna glanced at the man now entering and a chill ran down her spine as she recognised him as the man that had sat next to her on the train. It now became clear in her mind as the last pieces of the jigsaw fell into place. Again, she reasoned, so they know who I am and that I'm the wife of a Kriegsmarine officer. Now they are duty bound to show me some respect.

'Herr Oberst, I would like to have a glass of water please,' she said with as much bearing as she could muster. Her request seemed to catch him off guard, as he raised his bushy brows and disparagingly glared in her direction and with a wry smile; he beckoned for one of the SS men guarding the door to grant her request.

'Ja, but of course,' he replied. 'How remiss of me but tell me Frau Bauer why are you writing messages to young sailors about military matters, and in a railway carriage?' A glass of water appeared and she took a sip as the man in the long black coat bent and whispered to Herzog.

'I wrote it because my family's house was bombed and it seemed the most logical way for me to get in touch with my husband,' Anna responded. 'They could pass it on or something. They might even be going to the same port where he's stationed. On the other hand, he could be a prisoner, or worse. I have not been in contact with him for many weeks now and he must be concerned about his family too.' She glanced at each officer in turn, but they remained grim-faced and unresponsive.

'That might be so,' said Herzog, 'but I am given to understand that you also asked the sailors about their destination.' Her mind raced. Did she?

'I cannot remember that, I only asked about them travelling to the west. If that was the case then there would be a good chance of them meeting up with my husband's flotilla, and look,' she said in annoyance. 'I put Lorient. That's where his last letter came from. I assumed that's where he would be.'

'Ja, ja, I can see that,' Herzog replied in his Bavarian drawl, which annoyed her even more. 'However, writing messages like this in wartime is strictly forbidden. Especially...' He paused to methodically tap the scrap of paper; 'Especially – on – English – chocolate – wrapping – paper, Frau Bauer!' A deafening silence filled the room as his words sunk in and she realised the gravity of her situation.

'I don't understand. It's just a wrapper to me,' Anna snapped defensively. 'I was too tired when I received it. All I can tell you is that it was given to me by a priest. His name is Petrus and his church is near the cathedral in Köln,' and nodded to emphasise her words. 'As you can see, Herr Oberst, it's a plain white wrapper with some foreign words on one side. I did not take that much notice of it. Besides, I had just escaped from being blown to pieces. Here, look at my ear.' She turned her head to reveal a blotch of purple and a healing wound.

'Ja, we see that, it's just a bruise,' he said bluntly and tapping the paper with a long, bony finger added, 'this is very interesting. I can tell you that this wrapper is from Canada, perhaps some kind of code…'

Herzog signalled to one of the soldiers who took her bag and methodically began to empty its contents onto the desk. It was the final straw for Anna, as hackles rose. This being the height of humility and impertinence to an officer's wife. She leapt up and snatched back her bag. It prompted a knee jerk reaction from the two SS officers who pulled the bag out of her grasp and unceremoniously pushed her back into her seat. Alarmed and frightened, Eddi began to cry as Anna, short of breath picked him up and sat him soothingly on her lap. She looked-on with silent rage as they systematically examined the contents of her bag. With the aid of a magnifying glass they examined the sweets and the wrappers.

'Mmm, Kanada, by the looks of things,' said one officer.

'Here we have two bars of soap,' said the other. 'Looks like an Englischer name to me. Ja, 'Leifpoy.' He placed it on the desk as the Oberstum examined it and wrote down LIFEBUOY. He then took out his penknife and cut the bar in half. To his chagrin, the red bar of medicated soap yielded nothing. He glanced suspiciously at the other, but left it.

'KLIM, "milch pauder",' read the officer and handed the yellow tin to Herzog, who wrote down KLIM MILK POWDER, then copied the printed instructions written in large print, in English, however left out the smaller print written in French and Arabic. He then opened the sealed tin with its soldered-on key attachment and sniffed at the white powder and decided to tip its content on the table. Again, and to his annoyance there was only the powdered milk. Once again, the arresting officer picked up the offending chocolate with the remains of its white wrapper.

'Ja, Schokolade und Nestle, Herr Oberst,' said the SS man as he handed it back to his superior. 'Nestle von Kanada,' the man continued.' Herzog nodded as he wrote down the details about the chocolate and its wrapper. He ignored the other food items, including the remaining three hard boiled eggs.

As Anna looked on in disgust the man systematically disseminated her newly-acquired vanity bag. She had heard rumours about Hitler's henchmen, but now was experiencing them at first hand, along with their persuasive tactics. She had always assumed this sort of thing only happened to others, like dissidents, spies and corrupt foreigners but not to a serving U-Boot officer's wife.

'Frau Bauer,' Herzog addressed her in cordial clipped tones. 'As you have not satisfied me about how you came by these English items and the reason why you are writing and asking sensitive questions that could be transmitted and used by an enemy, I have no option but to detain you. You will be held here in Dortmund for further questioning to assess the validity of your story.'

Dortmund, so that's where I am, mused Anna. You're not so clever after all, Herr SS man.

Herzog glanced down at the document on his desk and turned to the civilian. They conversed in low tones and clearing his throat, turned to face her.

'Frau Bauer, as this case is a matter for the security of the Reich, I as a military man cannot deal with it. I now hand you over to Herr Gruber here, who is an officer of the Gestapo.'

Shock and horror coursed through her as she stifled an involuntary gasp and hand-shielded her face as icy fingers of fear touched the sinews of her soul. The mere mention of Gestapo, Hitler's secret police and executioners was reason enough to make any person involved fear for their lives.

They can't do this to me, she reasoned. I'm an officer's wife. To be handed over to the Gestapo was like being one step from the grave. Her mind was in a whirl and she had to think fast as Herzog had washed his hands of her and was already rising from his desk. She decided to try one last bid for freedom and pointed at the telephone.

'Herr Oberst,' she said, 'if you call the U-Boot base at Lorient, you will find that my husband is stationed there, or at least he was. That would settle the matter once and for all, and the same goes for the priest. Please call the church, or the cathedral, they're bound to know him.' She paused as she saw him deliberate, was he weakening? 'Perhaps you can ask him how he came by the English chocolate, potato bread and those hard boiled eggs,' she said defiantly and with a hint of sarcasm in her voice.

Obersturmbannführer Herzog stared at her with dark, sullen eyes; eyes that had seen too many raids and too little sleep. Rooted for a moment, he glanced sheepishly at the other officers, who stood and regarded the black instrument with an uncomfortable and pained expression. But then, how could Anna have known that all of the telephone lines at Dortmund had been disconnected, by courtesy of the RAF?

Chapter Ten

CHAISE LOUNGE

Franz's submarine U-888 was of a similar type as Kurt's, inasmuch it was an ocean-going, long-range boat. It was for that reason both vessels had been selected for the mission in hand. Onboard, her refit was still ongoing and it would be sometime before all was ready.

The last week of April had seen the fitting of the latest anti-aircraft cannons in their quadruple mountings together with a mast for the radar and radio detection equipment. This latest Naxos device was to thwart the Allied ship-to-ship radar that could locate a U-boat at a range of twelve miles and from an aircraft at twenty-five. It was a copy from a British design found on a sinking destroyer and enabled surface ships to pinpoint the U-boats by way of their short wave transmissions. This way, the tables would be turned as the submarine would be alerted to an enemy's transmissions, both from Radar pulses and their short wave radios.

While his crew sorted stores and ordinance, Franz and his first lieutenant, Jurgen Haas, attended lectures on how to operate the new equipment, especially the latest invention, the acoustic homing torpedo, without accidentally becoming its victim.

He submitted his store's requirement for a long sea voyage, this being a period of six months. Some of U-888's torpedoes were offloaded and the latest LUT homing torpedoes placed onboard. The instruction sheet read that the LUT could be fired from a submerged U-Boot at a depth of one hundred and sixty feet; it was then capable of hitting its target using a designated curving search pattern to home in on the propeller noises of its intended victim.

At one briefing, Franz was given the information he was to rendezvous with a second U-Boot; a third boat, U-198, had already sailed for Far Eastern waters on normal operational duties but could be used as a contingency measure to assist in the transportation of the materials and blue-prints. Although the master plan had not, as yet, been revealed it was an exciting time for him and his crew as they realised their next sailing would be of great significance to Germany's beleaguered war effort.

As their date of departure drew near, his Radio Officer had remarked that it was strange that the army code breakers were picking up a mass of signals directed at the local French resistance. HQ was beginning to receive more coded messages from England than usual. It was pure airwave jamming and gobbledygook as they made absolutely no sense at all to him or the back-room boffins that tried to decipher them. Was Tommy up to something? Or was it just a hoax to keep them all confused, alarmed and guessing?

It was now the last day of April as Franz visited the naval base HQ for briefing. Whilst there he tried his utmost to get news of the whereabouts of Anna and her parents. He was informed for the present there was still a total news blackout regarding the recent air raids on the Reich. This was on direct orders from the leader of the Luftwaffe.

That damned Goering, mused Franz, him and his big mouth. He's the one responsible for the mess in the air. With all his bravado and posturing the Tommies, with fewer aircraft, had defeated him. Now with the Amis lending support, things were looking grim indeed.

It was eight-thirty in the evening when he eventually finished his paperwork, and with a quick scrape with a razor and change left Jurgen in command as he hurried ashore for his evening appointment. Whilst in refit and in the safety of the bunker he had allowed one half of the ship's company a rotating roster of shore leave for the duration. If nothing else, they had earned it and he owed them that as all work and no play made for inefficiency and short tempers, especially in the clammy confines of a submarine.

Clearing the bunker it was good to breathe the fresh night air. Walking a short distance he managed to hitch a lift with a passing truck which dropped him off at the Kerentrech station. He was apprehensive as the news, if any, could be good or bad, but he had to find out – either way. All day he had been thinking about it and his only hope now lay with his newfound friend, Lilli. However, as he walked past the saluting guard and through the entrance, he felt a twinge of guilt as his pulse quickened and his troubled conscience reluctantly admitted that he was actually looking forward to seeing her again.

He passed several doors and stopped at the one with its familiar name plate, TELEFON ABTEILUNG. Placing his hand on the door he could not help but detect the light-hearted feeling as something new fluttered inside his chest, spurred on by the knowledge that he was only moments away from her presence. He fought with himself to dismiss the thought. *I'm here for information* he reassured his conscience, but an inner voice mocked him. *You like her, Franz. Ah ha, be careful, you're a married man.* He dismissed the thought and with renewed justification, opened the door.

It was different this time. The girls gazed at the newcomer, some stared as before while others whispered and smiled their secret smiles. But they knew he was spoken for as news had filtered down to all and sundry. He recognised Yvonne by her desk and saw she was about to leave. She caught his eye whilst still applying lipstick and smiling, mouthed her familiar 'Allo' greeting as piercing dark eyes flashed and invaded his senses.

Franz dropped his gaze as he felt himself grow hot and fortunately spotted Lilli, who was busy at her desk, again with her headset clamped firmly in place. He made his way towards her and placed his officer's cap onto her console. Lilli jumped with surprise and turning beamed happily whilst talking into a microphone at her chest. With a welcoming smile and a raised finger of caution she indicated for him to wait.

Nonchalantly this time, Franz glanced around, fished for his cigarette case from his breast pocket and lit up. He felt relaxed now after the initial baptism of friendly fire and looked-on as Lilli withdrew the last jack, along with her headset.

'Guten Abend,' said Franz with a smile as she nodded and reached for a message pad.

'Hallo, Franz. How are you?' she replied with a happy to see you expression. 'I'm afraid the news is not too good. Here, please read this.'

He took the message pad and in anticipation, inhaled deeply on his cigarette.

<u>Polizei Amt Köln</u>   <u>30 April 1944</u>

Fam. Wagner. Home Guard/Wardens have confirmed +Herr und Frau Wagner found deceased in block cellar + All persons in block accounted for + Frau Anna und Kind Eduart Bauer not found in this block + No other children found in this block + End.

He read the teleprinted message several times to let it gravitate and register in his confused mind. On the one hand it was good news, yet on the other Anna had lost her parents. But then where on earth was she? She was not with his parents in Dresden as he'd been able to use the naval HQ telephone and speak to them, being the bombing there had so far been superficial.

'So now we know Franz,' she said softly and interrupting his train of thought. He shook his head as Lilli gently touched his hand and pitiful pools of blue met his tortured gaze.

'I'm sorry about your parents-in-law,' she continued, 'but it's still good news about your wife and your son. They're alive; otherwise the welfare would have informed me. I also called the police in Aachen and they have no record of your family's name as casualties. We must now look on the bright side, ja?' Perplexed, he nodded in agreement as he crumpled the message and stuffed it into his jacket pocket.

'Thanks anyway, Lilli,' he said despondingly as he picked up his cap.

'Aufwiedersehen,' she said with a wan smile and a catch in her voice. Franz turned to leave but as an afterthought, spun round.

'What time are you off duty?' he asked with an inquisitive smile.

'Just finished,' Lilli beamed and indicated with a nod. 'Look, here comes Heidi.' Franz turned as a stunning brunette with permanent waves and a sunflower smile came up from behind. 'Heidi, this is Franz, my, my...' Lilli hesitated, lost for words, 'my ship's captain.' He swallowed hard and once again had that toe clenching moment as the tall, doe-eyed fräulein with an hourglass chassis weighed up the situation and offered her hand.

'Ein Kapitän,' she said with mock surprise and adjusted her shoulder bag. 'Pleased to meet you, Franz, I hope you two will have a pleasant evening.' He nodded with a ghost of a smile as with an approving gaze and a lazy wink, released him.

'So, it's off to the Kaffee Haus, is it?' Heidi purred, as she glanced over Franz's shoulder to share a knowing look with Lilli.

'Just a nightcap,' Franz managed to say, more to Lilli as an invitation than in answer to her friend's premature assumptions. Lilli beamed her thanks at Franz, while answering her friend with a casual nod, being well-accustomed to her man-eating antics. Gathering her things and to a chorus of 'Gute Nacht', she let Franz lead the way to the exit and reclaim his sanity.

***

Back inside the friendly atmosphere of the Café, Franz, with a glass of Cognac in his hand had come to terms with the situation, all thanks to Lilli and her comforting presence, together with her efforts in trying to trace his family. He observed her across the table, happily watching the antics of the sailors on the dance floor.

'Lilli,' he said in a low voice as he leant across the table. She turned her head and met his questioning gaze and was pleased to see he wanted to talk. 'I've been thinking, I just want to say thank you for all your efforts and for helping me.'

She shook her head and reached out for his hand, to touch it in reassurance. He felt her warmth and tenderness as she folded her hand over his, to hold him in their first meaningful touch.

'Franz, I'm doing it because I want to. You don't have to thank me, as you know I have already done the same for others.' She touched his hand as compassionate fingers stroked his senses, her words sounded distant, as a tinge of desire stirred within. With effort he stifled the thought and nodded in understanding as he glanced up to meet her tender gaze. She said nothing, but he discerned a trace of longing in her eyes as she squeezed and held his hand. However, much can be said without a word spoken as their eyes met in warm communion, and like an opening flower at sunrise a numbed realisation dawned that something had blossomed between them. Franz in himself felt good, relaxed, a passing fancy for a pretty girl and still gazing across the table the corners of his mouth lifted and creased into an encompassing smile. She sighed inwardly and felt relieved as she saw the change in him and his mood. She had, at last, brought this man out of the slough of his own despond, to face the world and its challenges once more.

He began to laugh and appeared transformed. He laughed at the absurdity of it all as the Germans now occupied France. He laughed at the picture of the Austrian corporal and erstwhile artist hanging on the wall. He laughed at himself for being here with her, at her choice, when she could have a dozen young men and laughed even more at her bemused features. He laughed at their situation, as here they were, holding hands across the table like two adolescents, each one waiting for the other to break their first intimate touch. But then laughter is contagious and soon Lilli, hand shielding her face, laughed with him as others close by joined in for no apparent reason, other than to forget everything and to be happy that they were still alive.

Slowly their laughter subsided to warm smiles and tear-brimming mirth-filled eyes as they sheepishly gazed round the room to token nods of acknowledgement and raised glasses of 'Prosit'. For her part, Lilli was happy to see the change in him, as his features were less lined and he had suddenly come out of his shell but with female intuition she also felt this was their moment of bonding.

'Sorry about that,' he excused himself. 'I just saw the funny side of it for once. I just want you to know that I shall be forever grateful and in your debt for giving me your time and the things you've done for me.' She held his gaze and with an uplifted heart sipped her wine for inspiration.

'Franz, you don't have to thank me for anything.' Slowly shaking her head she continued, 'And thank you for taking me out this evening.' He was about to say more but was once again distracted by those coral sea eyes, deeper blue than any ocean and her honey curls falling back onto bare shoulders. He felt the warm sap of desire rise in his body as a jealous voice, in the shadows of his mind whispered her name. Of course, Anna was pretty but it had been a long time since he had been with her and now he was to sail again, perhaps never to return.

Once more, the whole issue of Lilli's presence came to taunt him. What if he did enjoy being with her? It was a question that haunted and challenged the married members of his crew, some even here now, chatting with the French girls and nurses. It was constantly debated across mess tables. Now, the very same spectre had finally arrived at his door. What if that would be how it ended, both for him and his crew? Anna would find someone else, he would expect her to but for him and the lads sitting round the other tables, only eternity was waiting and that's a long, long time without the gentle touch of a woman's hand.

Lilli saw he was wrestling with his thoughts again and raised her glass to him. She realised that she had to let him have his say, but had become intrigued now with this man of deep thinking and contagious laughter.

'For the past two days you've given me hope,' he said, 'and thereby peace of mind. For a person in my position, as captain of a U-Boot it is of the utmost importance, both for myself, my submarine and the men I command. Please understand, for as you already know, I am a married man. I have to search my conscience, even now to be sitting here with you. As for my wife and son, I feel somewhat relieved. It's you, Lilli, who's given me hope and the conviction that they are still alive.'

He paused and levelled his gaze as their eyes met in mutual communion – his, penitent and revealing, while Lilli's, soft, azure and understanding. 'You know Lilli,' he continued, 'there's now this thing between us and I think we both know it,' and shook his head

94

to emphasise their plight, toying with his glass as he waited for her response.

Lilli, stabbed by the sudden revelation, dropped her gaze and fingered her drink as she knew her eyes would betray her. She switched to gazing at the candle's dancing flame, an understanding light that touched her heart and could not be extinguished.

She lifted her eyes to meet his in self-reproach and mutual confession. He nodded in acceptance, as undertones of emotion flowed between them, and his eyes, like hers, reflected the quandary of two tangled souls with just one thought in mind. Lilli shook her head in awareness of their dilemma as in her heart the stirrings of love for this man were compounded by painful remorse.

For his part, he felt only relief as finally, this thing that had lodged itself between them was now exposed. He wanted to say more, but with emotional restraint he shook his head and returned to his glass for the only solace he knew.

On seeing his turmoil, she again reached for his hand.

'Franz,' she said quietly. 'Whatever is on your mind, and whatever it is that you want to say to me, I think it can wait?'

Lost for words, he studied his glass as if to find an answer within its golden depths and with an uneven smile, met her emotional gaze. His eyes were calm now, like a brooding ocean in winter as he deliberated his emotional dilemma and self-consciously checked his watch.

'I have to get back, Lilli,' he said. 'It's a busy day for me tomorrow.' She nodded in understanding.

'That's fine with me,' she replied. 'And thank you again for taking me out this evening, I enjoyed it.'

'My pleasure, it's the least I could do.' Finishing his drink he stood and assisted with her coat.

'Bon nuit, Jacques,' they both chimed as they waved to the barman and stepped out into the night. Franz glanced at the sky and made a mental note about the weather as the wind had eased and only a few scattered clouds remained to occult the moon. Apart from that, the blackout was complete. To Franz however the sky spelt danger, a bomber's moon which would occasionally bathe the Brittany landscape in swathes of its pallid light.

Neither spoke as Franz, with Lilli's arm crooked in his elbow, walked back to the compound and savoured the moment of their platonic friendship. They were just glad to have each other's company and if words and feelings were left unspoken, then they both accepted it. Several military vehicles were moving through the rubble-piled streets, their pencil beams of restricted light stabbing the darkness, while sailors in high spirits, staggered noisily down narrow streets towards the fishing harbour and back to their boats and ships.

With the gravel crunching underfoot, Lilli held his arm as they negotiated the incline that led into her compound. It was at this moment that all hell broke loose as the undulating wail of the air-raid sirens howled their dire message and shattering the tranquillity of the night.

Immediately Franz's instinct of survival kicked in as he was once again the commander back on his bridge. They were exposed, caught on open ground and needed shelter, fast. He rationalised the attack would come from seaward in order to avoid detection and anti-aircraft fire. Since the U-bunkers were about one and a half miles distant, the aircraft would attack there and over-fly his position on a straight run, as the town was in a line with them.

They could easily run and make it to the air raid shelter by the dormitory but were thwarted; it was already too late as an aircraft screamed overhead. Franz hit the ground running, pulling Lilli down as the tarmac of the parade ground disintegrated in a searing ball of flame, just paces ahead. *Wrong*, his tortured brain screamed. *It's not just the bunkers they're after, and that shelter, we'll never make it!*

Lilli pulled him up and screamed 'Franz, this way, schnell!'

There it was — a small building tucked away to the side of the parade ground. Grabbing her arm, he pulled her along as they ran for their lives. Cannon shells churned up the remaining tarmac as they gained the building and he pulled her through the door.

It was hot inside and by the illumination of a solitary light he saw the concrete steps that led to a basement. Rapidly he descended, pulling Lilli along with him. As more bombs fell, the brick building shook to its foundations, bringing with it a rain of dust and a mass of soot-stained cobwebs. Reaching the floor of the basement they stood breathless, gazing at each other and collecting their thoughts. He began to laugh and Lilli joined him and both, now grinning like dating Cheshire cats she threw her arms round him, hugging him at the joy and relief of having survived. Moments later came an explosion as the building shook and a blanket of dust rained down from the ceiling and its joists. The stair light flickered, dimmed and the building was plunged into darkness. Slowly, as their eyes adjusted, they became aware of the red glow emanating from the boiler's grate. From its light Franz observed that round the corner of the stairs stood several chairs and an old settee. Taking her hand he guided Lilli across and realised it was actually a chaise lounge from a by-gone age.

'It's hot down here,' said Lilli removing her coat and spread it over the seat. 'All that running, I'm boiling.'

'Ha, ha, that's very original,' said Franz and they chuckled at the unintended pun.

'Well, it might be funny,' she replied, 'but it's very warm down here and I'm not used to running like that. What's more, I lost a shoe coming down those stairs.'

He sat beside her and listened intently to establish the direction of the raid. Several detonations followed in rapid succession as the old boiler house shook in sympathy. Lilli was trembling and sat holding her hands between her knees as she stared vacantly into the open firebox. 'Franz, I'm frightened, this is not a good shelter.'

'It's all right, Lilli,' he assured her. 'That's only our Flak batteries,' and feeling her distress put his arm round her and drew her close. He felt her fear and tension subside as she responded, sliding both arms round him and snuggled up to his neck, to gently kiss him there. Her silent tears meandered and seeped slowly to his chest as he turned towards her and found her soft willing lips brush gently with his. Their kiss was tender and of kindness, of release from anxiety and pent-up emotions, but quickly became pressing and passionate and desperately wanting each other.

The unsaid before was now the act as her fingers removed his tie and unbuttoned his shirt. Her perfume, mingled with tears invaded his senses as he felt her nails trail across his body and pull to release his shirt. Her moist cheeks touched his chest and she felt his muscles tense and his pulse quicken as her searching lips found and nuzzled him there.

Franz felt the agony of his desire as a knot formed deep in his loins. His turmoil was complete and expunged as she pulled him down onto her and to the embrace of her willing body. There, by the glow of the firelight and encompassed by the fur of her coat, their bodies lay entangled. As more bombs fell and the Flack batteries pounded their venom to the skies, two bodies lay surrendered in each other's arms and abandoned to all else except the impassioned fulfilment of each other's wildest dreams.

***

It was the sound of the siren that broke the spell. As the clarion call of the all-clear sounded, even in the confines of the boiler room

Franz could hear its singular and plaintive wail. Apart from the ruddy glow from the grate the room was otherwise in darkness, only the sheen of her hair lying spread across his chest reflecting the glowing embers. The prophetic wail slowly died to be replaced by a supreme silence from the world above, together with the sound of water as it surged through the boiler's rusting pipes. Lilli was asleep and lying in his arms as he gently shook her shoulder.

'Lilli, wake up,' he said in a loud whisper, not wishing to startle her. 'Wake up, Lilli we have to go.'

'Franz,' she murmured. 'Is it over?'

'Jawohl, it's over, they've gone.' He eased himself up and watched the fire in the grate as dying embers dropped into the ashcan below. Sleepily she opened her eyes and observed him in the firelight. He looked younger now, less stressed as if a great weight had been removed from his mind. Lilli cherished the moment and would have loved to have remained there with him in the cosy atmosphere of the darkened room, perhaps forever, but knew deep within herself this was not to be. Reluctantly she stood and adjusted her dress and leaning towards him, stooped and kissed him gently on the cheek.

'Franz, I'm sorry for what happened, please forgive me.' He glanced up and saw the outlines of her face, radiant, lit-up like Easter's Angel in the fire's amber glow. Her hair was now the colour of a golden sunset as she began to comb and coax it into place. Once again her beauty touched his soul as he conjured up a picture of the Lorelei legend and its bewitching maidens, combing their hair as mesmerised sailors crashed to their doom on those treacherous Rhineland rocks.

'Nein, Lilli… Nein,' he stammered. 'Bitte, there is no fault, it's the war. We're just its victims and what's more, we're lucky to be alive.' He felt a heel and hypocrite for saying those very words that he'd so often heard from others, but now in the bowers of circumstance, they applied to him.

He stood and brushed himself down as the bulb suddenly burst back into incandescent life. Lilli found her lost shoe and came to him and adjusted his tie and smoothed and patted his shirt, allowing herself a mischievous smile as she met his sheepish gaze. Checking his watch, he needed to get back to his boat and see about the raid. He picked up her coat, draped it over her shoulders and saucily patted her bottom. 'Come along, Lilli. Mach's schnell, I have to get back.'

'Ja Franz, ein moment, I cannot go back to the girls looking like this. They'll know something more than an air raid has happened.' With her hands Lilli smoothed and brushed the fur and tossing her head let her wave of curls fall over her shoulders. Franz sighed with impatience as Lilli produced a mirror and began to apply lipstick and with an inviting smile, pouted her lips and whispered mischievously. 'Ready.'

However, his cap was now missing and seeing him searching she burst out laughing as she saw his crestfallen face once he found it, firmly wedged behind the seat, and his efforts in trying to bend some shape back into its distorted contours. With a satisfied grunt he replaced it, took her hand and led the way back to the waiting world above.

***

There was only a small crater where the rocket had exploded, together with strafing marks that followed a line to the dormitory. Apart from that the buildings had escaped serious damage. The bomb that had shaken the boiler house had left its mark in the road and had luckily missed its intended target, as it left a ten-foot crater and flattened the nearby trees. Several vehicles were burning but that was about all the damage he could see. Franz was anxious to return to his bunker as he feared the worst for his boat and crew. With haste they walked to Lilli's dormitory and said their hurried farewells. Checking his watch it would be 4:30 by the time he reached the bunkers.

'I'd better get back and see what the damage is,' he said. 'Let's meet in the café at nine tonight, unless you hear different... about the bunkers, I mean.' She nodded in understanding and squeezed his hand and as an afterthought, kissed him fleetingly on the cheek.

'That's a thank you for looking after me,' she said with a smile. 'I'll try and catch up with some beauty sleep. See you later Franz, and please do take care, Au revoir.'

She opened the door to reveal the dim glow of the blue night light and the heavy blackout curtain beyond. With the sound of her receding heels on the parquet floor, he turned to see the first faint streaks in the eastern sky.

Chapter Eleven

SUPERCARGO

As the lorry descended the hill and rounded the last bend, Franz saw with relief the silhouette of the bunkers, still standing and unscathed.

Passing through the main gate, he noted that some vehicles were still smouldering and new craters had appeared. The bunkers however, stood like the ancient Pyramids of Egypt, solid and unshakeable.

'They're still standing,' he said as the driver slowed to a halt by the western entrance.

Franz jumped out and tipped the driver several cigarettes. The youngster called out his thanks, 'Danke, Herr Kapitän, Heil Hitler!' gunned the engine and sped off, leaving Franz to cross the bombed wasteland that led to the blast screen and side entrance. He touched its concrete wall as he entered and repeated the mantra.

'You'll need bigger bricks than that, Tommy.'

Inside, the arc lamps dazzled him until his eyes adjusted to the artificial light. His boat was still moored alongside Kurt's, their combined refits still in progress and undisturbed by the raid. He stepped off the quay and negotiated the gangway, shielding his eyes from the blinding arcs of the welders as they fitted the fifteen-metre snorkel tube, along with its spaghetti of hydraulic pipes and valves.

Climbing through the open deck hatch, he was greeted by the aroma of coffee and Jurgen, with an expression of fazed relief.

'Franz, good to see you back, we were getting concerned. Another hour and I would have had to report you as missing. What happened, you been in a fight?' His First Lieutenant grinned and pointed at his uniform. 'Did the Tommies roll you in a ditch?'

Franz glanced down at himself and gingerly picked and brushed at the remaining flecks of distemper and cobweb.

'Ja, something like that, it was a close-run thing,' he answered with a smirk. 'They nearly caught me with my pants down,' and chuckled to himself at the unintended pun, as Johann arrived with mugs of coffee and freshly-baked rolls.

'We had it bad here, but the bunkers survived,' added Jurgen. 'Doenitz and those workers from the Todt department certainly did their homework when they designed this lot. I reckon Tommy will be back again for another crack, the sooner we get out of here the better.'

Franz nodded in agreement as he sipped his coffee, but his thoughts were back at the boiler house. He thought of Lilli, his guardian angel perhaps now with a few ruffled feathers by the event that between them should never have happened. Jurgen, still puzzled as to his state and absence, decided any explanation could wait and was just glad to have his commander back.

'Are you going to the HQ bunker today?' he asked.

'Nothing planned,' replied Franz. 'Sleep is the priority for me. I'm off to my bunk. Call me if it's urgent.'

'Jawohl,' replied Jurgen. 'I hear that our neighbours will be ready to sail shortly. They're not allowed to display their ID number – any reason?' Franz had heard it too. Both U-boats were not to show any hull identification numbers, not until they were clear of Europe, then they would be used and painted on by the crew.

'Ja, it's all ultra-secret,' Franz replied. 'The less said the better, as the Gestapo have picked up a French master spy, right here under our noses. Der Schweinehund is responsible for some of our recent losses. Chap called Stosskopf, sounds German to me.' He said with concern whilst still trying to straighten out his über-bent cap. 'Anyway, see you later, but call me at fifteen hundred.' Jurgen nodded as Franz disappeared into his cabin and drew the door curtain behind him.

At three in the afternoon, Franz was awakened by the sound of the cook as he placed a tray of coffee and a thick slice of poppy seed strudel onto his desk.

'Danke, Johann, Gott im Himmel, did I sleep through all that racket?' The jolly-faced cook nodded and grinned as the scraping of metal against metal and hammering from topside carried throughout the boat.

'You must have been tired, Herr Kaleu'nt,' he replied. 'That hammering is the new breathing tube being tested. It's the French engineers, they're trying to make it fit,' he added with a chuckle. 'I have your cleaned uniform here, Herr Kaleu'nt, as we have guests onboard.'

'Guests? What sort of guests?' he queried with a frown, as he swung his feet to the deck.

'Civilians, Herr Kaleu'nt. The First Lieutenant is talking to them in the control room.'

'Very well, Johann. Tell him I'll be there in a few minutes. I need a quick wash and a scrape with a razor.' The youngster nodded as Franz made his way to the allocated space that served for the officer's ablutions.

Cleaned up, he made his way to the control room. Two civilians, whom he judged to be in their late forties stood talking to the FO. Franz introduced himself as they shook hands.

'Karl Bach,' said one of the men with a friendly nod, 'and my colleague, Hermann Steiner. We're scientists from the Berlin Academy, Herr Kapitän.'

Franz knitted his brows. On seeing his bemused expression they handed him their papers, together with a communiqué marked for his attention and rapidly excused themselves to attend a meeting ashore. Jurgen watched them with amusement as they struggled up the conning tower ladder. Franz noted that the seal was that of the Lorient Marine Head Quarters.

'Looks ominous, perhaps our sailing orders,' said Jurgen pulling a face as Franz gingerly opened it and peered inside. On seeing the High Admiral's stamp and signature he decided to take it and read its contents in the privacy of his cabin. Minutes later, he called for a muster of the crew.

'Meine Kameraden, I've called you together to inform you as much as I am able about our next mission. I have received a message from Admiral Doenitz that we are to sail with scientists and their equipment. The former are here as you have already met them, while their equipment is still in transit.' Speculative murmurs rippled through the assembly as a young gunner piped up.

'Achtung, achtung, stand by forward tubes, prepare to load stink bomb torpedoes.' This was greeted by a spontaneous outburst of laughter from the ranks but put paid to 'lower deck' rumours and eased the overall tension. Franz shot him an icy glance but thought him amusing just the same.

'Until we have loaded our stores we will remain here at Lorient,' he continued. 'We will train ourselves with the use of the new Flak, the radar detector and the Schnorchel. All those personnel not required will have shore leave as usual.' This last statement was greeted with relief and applause. 'Then remember, when you are ashore treat all the ladies like you would your own sisters...' Murmurs and chuckles arose from the younger members. 'And try to come back sober.'

This time the chuckles and laughter from the ratings were spontaneous. He nodded at Jurgen, who dismissed them. They were happy to be kept informed but he felt a heel for keeping the news about the escalating air raids and the razing of their homeland from them.

'One thing I forgot to mention,' said Jurgen as he followed Franz through the bulkhead door and back to his quarters. 'Those scientists, they brought on board a small wooden box.' He indicated the size with his hands. 'It was heavy, and when I say heavy, I mean heavy.'

'So, where is it, or better still, what's inside it?' Jurgen indicated with his thumb towards the forward mess.

'It's in their quarters. I had to place it under their bunk as they said they were coming with us and said it was not to be opened by anyone as it's dangerous to the skin. By the way this is for your attention, it's just come in.' He handed him a large grey envelope, complete with the seal of the Berlin Ministry of War. Franz thanked him as the First Officer excused himself and left him with his mail.

Franz sat on his bunk, finished the remainder of his lukewarm coffee and opened the confidential envelope. It was the usual restricted list of U-Boot losses, this one for the month of March 1944, and noted with alarm that fifteen boats had been lost. For several of the boats it gave reasons for their demise as witnessed by other U-boats but for the majority, there was just the word 'Totalverlust' and its area of operations.

He was not surprised as many of the boats lacked experienced crews, even his own consisted mainly of youngsters and only a handful of old salts from the early days. Jurgen and he were the oldest onboard, their combined ages being just fifty-seven years. He, at thirty-one being the oldest. The youngsters regarded him as their hero and would follow him to the ends of the earth if needs be. They trusted his seamanship, his skill at choosing action rather than confronting it head on, and so held him in their highest esteem. For them it was he that would lead them into battle and sink the ships of America and England. Some were barely nineteen and came indoctrinated from the Hitler Youth brigades, totally brainwashed and proudly sporting their swastika tattoos. He felt sorry for them as they had been cheated and robbed of their youth, both by their brain-washed parents and by the educational system of the National Socialist state.

Now, it was up to the likes of him to re-educate them in the ways of the real world where bigotry and arrogance could spell their doom. As their captain he had taken over from the classroom, the teacher and their parents because out there in the vast reaches of the Atlantic he would teach them to respect their enemy rather than despise him, but then the enemy was not always human, as the sea could be a greater adversary than any belligerent empire. Fail to respect the ocean and its discipline and the result could be as fatal as a depth charge. Lessons of seamanship had to be learnt quickly, as the Atlantic in winter was an experience and experience is a hard school. Teamwork, sharp eyes and quick wits prevailed on a submarine, perhaps more than on any other seagoing vessel and he would teach them that as a priority.

The youngsters talked freely of victory for the Reich and he wanted that too, that's why he was here but the Master Race and its shallow ideals he never cared for. The problem was some of these youngsters lived and breathed it. He fought for his country, to win and stop this war and for no other reason. It was his duty, he was a German and he fought for the justice of the German nation, as his father before him who had fallen at Ypres in 1916. However he reasoned, he had died for the right of empire and nothing else, alongside the Englender cousins, duped into the same ideal as two Victorian cousins fought for red scraps of territory on a map. But this war was different, an ideal which now lay exposed to the detriment of the German nation. He and the other officers realised that at the rate they were losing the U-Boats they could never win this war. They could only prolong it and only as long as the U-Boats came off the slipways and courageous men came forward to man them.

Then there were the U-Boat commanders themselves. They too were getting younger as the war continued. There were now commanders aged just twenty-one, what experience did such a young man have? He had pointed out to the youngsters that they had a duty first to themselves, in close relation to their boat. They must fight to stay alive, as dead heroes are not much use to anyone. They must use their heads; stay calm and not panic as depth charges rained down. In so doing they would be able to fight their ship, to slip away and with an element of luck, return to base.

As if in a dream, he still held the document and glanced once more at the losses and the names of the commanders, some he knew but many were new names that had gone to a watery grave. His mind wandered to the officers' mess ashore where the wall was becoming festooned with black-framed photos of the lost commanders and on each visit the names and photos were increasing.

He shook himself out of his melancholy and hearing his FO pass by called out to him. 'You can join me for coffee Jurgen, ask Johann to bring it in here.'

Jurgen thrust aside the curtain and joined him. Franz was about to open the remaining document when voices and a faint knock came from behind the curtain.

'Come in,' called Franz as the curtain parted and two anxious faces peered in from beyond. 'Please come in,' he motioned to the two men. 'We're a little cramped but you can sit down here on the bench seat.'

'Danke, Herr Kapitän, we're sorry to put you out like this,' said Karl, as he and his colleague sat themselves down.

'Your name, Karl Bach,' said Jurgen to the older man. 'I've heard that name before somewhere. You're from the Ministry of Research, ja?'

'Right first time, Herr Lieutnant,' said Karl with a modest smile. 'Actually, it's the government research establishment.' He pointed to the envelope that Franz had still not opened. 'Please read the documents as they are our travel documents.' He gave a chuckle at his little pun as Johann appeared with extra coffee, cups and cake.

'Please help yourselves,' said Franz as he proceeded to open the envelope. So much for sailing orders, he mused as he glanced at the letter heading.

KAISER WILLHELM INSTITUT
BERLIN

Kapitän Franz Bauer
U-888
Lorient   Berlin 26 April 1944

Herr Kapitän,

Kindly be informed that Herr KARL BACH and Herr HERMANN STEINER will be joining your vessel as supernumeraries. They will be hand carrying samples and will advise you accordingly.

Herr KARL BACH and Herr HERMANN STEINER are to be classed as civil servants and are to be entered into your vessel's log as such persons of state.

105

They are to be given every consideration and courtesy, together with any other persons joining from this establishment.

Hochactungsvoll,
K. Diebner
Heil Hitler

Franz studied the letter and thought it strange that it should come via the War Ministry rather than straight from the Berlin Institute. Then the signatory Diebner, he'd heard of that name somewhere too. Something to do with conflicting elements and matter. So these were the back room boys and more to come. But for what purpose and where were they all going? Bad enough having to fight his boat with greenhorn youngsters and now he was going to have absent-minded professors staggering about as well.

As Karl, Hermann and Jurgen were talking about the boat's routine he made a mental note about Diebner before reading the second document, which turned out to be a loading manifest. This came from the Admiralty, as it also dealt with the vessel's stability. Not much to go on he mused, except some hefty-sized crates and their weight listings.

Four crates of engine parts and spares. Each crate was three metres in length and one metre wide. Five thousand kilograms in all. That's about the weight of six torpedoes he reckoned as he mentally calculated his boat's stability. Then there was another crate of paperwork, documents and blueprints, amounting to some one hundred kilo.

'Quite a bit of excess baggage here, gentlemen,' said Franz tapping the document with a knuckle.

'Ja, true,' volunteered Karl sheepishly. 'We're sorry about this. They told us about the lack of space on your ship – ach nein, sorry, boat. We had no idea it would be this confined.' He shot a furtive glance at the captain and smiling nervously nodded to his friend. 'We will of course assist you in loading, Herr Kapitän.' Feeling like an intruder, (which he was) he nervously shuffled his feet and added with a pained expression. 'Of course, if you agree and will allow us the pleasure, Herr Kapitän.'

Franz shrugged, realising he had made them both feel uncomfortable but he still needed some answers and decided to try a different tack.

'Any idea where I'm supposed to be taking you and your bits and pieces?' he asked casually as he handed the document to Jurgen. The two scientists cast furtive glances at each other, Hermann nearly choking on his cake as Karl's Adam's apple worked overtime. 'We cannot really say, Herr Kapitän,' said Hermann. 'Perhaps somewhere where we will not be disturbed.' He ran his fingers through his thinning hair and glanced pathetically at Karl, who was clearly uncomfortable with this type of questioning. Hermann glanced back at Franz and with the ghost of a smile added, 'by the bombing, I mean.'

Franz answered with a nod and a sceptical gaze as he sized up the man.

'Ein guter Kaffee, Herr Kapitän,' Karl volunteered, raising his cup with exaggerated appreciation.

'Jawohl, very good coffee,' repeated Hermann. 'Only our Reichsfuehrer Himmler has coffee like this,' he said as he joined his colleague in the welcome distraction of the lifting cup, salutation ceremony.

Franz gazed from one to the other with a calculating frown. This cup-lifting business must be a scientific quirk he reasoned as alarm bells began to sound in the back of his mind. Why, he asked himself should a scientist be having tea parties with the leader of the SS and Gestapo, the Reichsfuehrer and second in command to Hitler?

'What, you have coffee with Himmler?' queried Franz. Karl shifted uneasily in his seat and glanced across to Hermann who came to his rescue.

'What he means is we had a flying visit from Herr Himmler. He has an interest in science as everyone knows, as does our Führer.' Franz eyed them both suspiciously and had a feeling they knew more than they were willing to let on. Let them finish their coffee, he mused, and we'll see what HQ has to say. Checking his watch and with an inward sigh of relief he reckoned that he would not be needed there today. Johann appeared and cleared the table as Karl and Hermann thanked the cook. Hermann glanced at his watch, 'Six-forty,' he said, nodding at his colleague. 'Sorry we have to go, Herr Kapitän,' and shook hands with them before excusing themselves.

'Strange pair,' said Franz, as the FO was about to leave. 'Just check over the stability and draught for me, before we sink ourselves in dock.' Jurgen nodded with a grin as he made his exit, closing the curtain behind him.

At last, Franz was alone. For now, the exigencies of war could wait as he sat on his bunk to relax. He took stock of the mounting paperwork piled on his desk, as his gaze drifted to the silver-framed snapshot of Anna with his son. It had been taken last May, nearly one year ago, so he would be a big boy now. The last time he'd seen them was seven months ago and that was only briefly, during seventy-two hours' leave while they turned his boat round, then back to the Atlantic.

Franz stretched himself on his bunk as events of the night before seeped into his mind. The sudden attack and their run for the shelter. Lucky for them the boiler house was there. And Lilli, her soft, passionate kiss and young demanding body. It was just a memory now and nothing to treasure, just a happening like a sports day at school he reasoned, only no trophies for this one.

Once more he gazed at the picture and recalled Anna laughing at him, as he had at first forgotten to remove the lens cover. He missed her smile, her touch and company and felt so terribly alone without her. But then last night, why did it have to happen like that? It was just supposed to be a social evening and bang, the raid, both running for their lives and finding solace in each other's arms.

Guilt and regret welled up inside him as he was, after all a dedicated family man and loved his wife. There were all those girls in other ports but it had never happened before. I was stupid and a victim of circumstances. Ja, that was it, he decided as he lit a cigarette and studied the crazed patterns of cork on the lined deck-head above. It was circumstances but then what would Anna say if she found out? How would she react if she were told of the circumstances? Wasn't he supposed to be looking all over Germany for her, like a dutiful husband?

He reached under his bunk and pulled out a bottle of Cognac, together with a glass. Pouring out a generous measure he settled back on his bunk to stare vacantly at the deck-head and wrestle with his thoughts.

He turned to look at his son, Eddi, mein kind, I hardly know you, he mused. Would he recognise me if he saw me now? The war, it's not my war, I never wanted to fight the Englander. They're people like us Germans, Saxons only now they're English. What's more, I can speak their language, learnt it at school and at the yacht club in Ipswich and Cowes. I've got many friends there. The Tommies, they've got their empire – it's vast and they're trying to strangle us with it, why? We have our new Reich but the only trouble is we march in and occupy other countries. But then didn't the Tommies do the same, only it was further back in time – then every country was doing it. Trouble is we Germans got there too late. If only we could wind the clock back, all those Hitler rallies and those torch-light parades. Gott im Himmel, it had all been a stage show. He mesmerised us with his torch-light parades and arm-waving rhetoric.

He gazed at his empty glass and reached for a refill and another cigarette. He thought about his chances of getting out alive, to survive the war? If it all ended today that would be fine as just recently there had been an upsurge in loss of boats. 'Totalverlust' and a photo framed in black of its late commander. Is that what's waiting for me?

Then there was this next mission. This could be curtains for me; I've got a bad feeling about it. Once more his glass was drained and allowed himself another generous measure and glancing at his desk, dismissed his waiting pile of paperwork. And those two scientists, his supercargo. He'd heard all about Hitler's secret weapons to destroy England. Was this just Goebel's propaganda and the nation's wishful thinking? Then where am I bound for next, a stores run – perhaps to that lost city of Atlantis…?

***

The scenery changed as the faces of his recent victims suddenly swam before him. Their oil-blackened features, with hollow, blood-shot eyes that stared accusingly down the lens of his cyclopean eye. Choking as they tried to swim and crawl for their lives through the solidifying treacle-like mass. In the background their stricken ship, a tanker blazed from end to end and bows down – as it spewed out its six thousand ton cargo of thick, black crude…

He awoke with a start and soaked with perspiration cursed the recurring nightmare.

'Can't remember nodding off like that,' he muttered and found the empty glass by his side. He got off his bunk, removed his uniform jacket and poured the remains of the bottle into the glass before settling down on his bunk once more. Mental stress together with late nights and the contents of a polished bottle of spirit now took their toll as he lay and gazed at her picture. Franz closed his eyes, 'Anna,' he whispered, 'I'm sorry I let you down.'

Chapter Twelve

ONLY QUESTIONS

Wearily, Anna sat herself down on the plain bed and holding Eddi's hand, helped him onto her lap. As she held him in her arms, he snuggled against her and was soon fast asleep.

Casting her eye round the cellar she took stock of her surroundings. It was a large basement with stored chairs, broken tables and at one end there was a recess with well-stocked, wall-to-wall wine racks. A solitary bulb with a white lampshade burnt to give immediate light overhead, leaving the walls in perpetual half shadow.

She cast her mind back to the last twenty-four hours, her living nightmare. How, at the hands of Gruber and his Gestapo colleagues, she had been bundled into a guard's van and shunted across war-torn Germany to end up here, in this mouldering Munich cellar. They had told her they would be checking out her story, then slammed and locked the door.

As the time passed, she guessed she had been here about three hours and felt certain that common sense would prevail and would soon be released. But then, that man Gruber, he bothered her as he seemed to be taking an unhealthy interest in all she had done. And now she was in München, some three hundred miles from Dortmund and even further from home. Perhaps it was for the better, she thought. If they released her in the next hour or so, she could travel on to be with Franz's parents in Dresden. It's a long way she reasoned, but there's been no bombing and I could be there in a few hours. I would be safe there with them, and Eddi would be able to see his other grandparents.

Cradling Eddi, she was lost without her belongings, as her bag was still with the Gestapo. As for food, she'd been allowed a bowl of weak potato soup, shared with her son, along with two slices of stale bread. This was after Obersturmbannführer Herzog's SS men had questioned her. It was like re-living a second-rate American movie – the intense light and always the same questions. First it was Gruber, then the two SS henchmen with their death's head insignia and Herzog, their senior officer. She kept giving them the same

110

answers to their repetitive questions, all about the paper and the chocolate, the sweets and the English wrapper.

Why had she offered the sailors chocolate and sought military information? Who were her parents and where was she born? They would not believe that her parents were 'conveniently dead' as they put it. The best they kept until last.

'Where is your husband…?'

Sarcastically, she had laughed at such an inept question. Then she had asked them politely, if they found him, would they please let her know. They struck her head with a rolled-up newspaper for that remark. She had screamed at them that she would have them all arrested, then it was their turn to laugh, with scorn and mocking derision in their haughty arrogance and dry humour. She had told them it was an encroachment of her rights as a German citizen to be treated like this. They told her bluntly that, as a spy she had no rights and would be shot.

They had demanded how she could speak English, she had explained her husband was a keen yachtsman and owned a sailing boat. She told them that they occasionally sailed across the North Sea to some east coast ports and met up with British yachting friends.

They demanded the names of the ports and she mentioned Great Yarmouth, Lowestoft and Ipswich but could not recall any harbour master's names, which annoyed them. Had she seen any military installations? She told them that at the time, she was only a young girl, not even married and never cared about things like that.

She went on to say Franz also spoke English, so were they going to arrest him too? Again, a sharp blow from the rolled-up copy of the *Völkischer Beobachter* and in anger she had screamed at them that he also spoke Dutch and that was why he was such a good captain. They left her after that and kept her sitting by herself in the chair for several hours. After a while, they returned Eddi to her and she discovered they had questioned him as well. Just a little boy, but then that was their way.

They had given him sweets and in his best way, he was able to tell her that they kept asking what his mother did at night. Did he have lots of uncles coming to visit him? Did he like butter and eggs? Did his mother make him lots of cakes? They're just pigs, Schweinehunde, thought Anna as she cuddled her son.

Aimlessly she stared round the cellar and still could not believe that she, a U-Boot commander's wife, was now here and a prisoner of the Gestapo. It was a nightmare but then nightmares have endings, whereas this one was for real.

Her thoughts turned to Franz. Perhaps they would contact the U-Boot bases? It seemed incredible that she could not get word to him. Again, she ran it through her mind that if he went to Aachen, to their house and found it damaged, he would not know where she was. She felt foolish now as perhaps she should have left a note. Then, what if he'd been killed, lost at sea? She might even be a widow and the dreaded telegram had been sent to her house.

'Mein Gott,' she whispered as doubt and fear began to creep into her soul. 'I cannot go to Dresden, I must go back home to be there for him.'

Haunted by the demons of her own making, she sat there, frightened and alone. So much had happened to her during the past few days, and now her fate was left in the hands of Himmler's secret state police.

Anna sat mulling things over as the glaring overhead light brought back memories of her interrogation. She thought of those sadistic morons, how, unknowingly, her husband is assisting in keeping them in power as they strutted around in riding boots, black uniforms and their intimidating death's head insignias.

With fear for her safety and anger welling up, she slipped off her shoes, put her sleeping boy down and taking off her coat, placed it over her child. Cold now, as with a mother's self-sacrifice she curled up next to him and fell into an uneasy sleep on the musty horsehair mattress.

Chapter Thirteen

ORDERS TO SAIL

He awoke with a start as a noise disturbed him. In the dimmed light of his cabin Franz peered at the bulkhead clock, 0600. It was daytime and he'd slept soundly for ten solid hours, an unimaginable luxury for him. The main lights in his cabin had been turned off, as now only the blue night-light glowed with its tranquillising luminescence. It must have been the cook, he mused.

As he collected his thoughts he glanced down at the deck. The empty bottle and glass had been removed but their legacy remained as he swallowed hard, his throat as dry as Sahara sand. With the elixir of coffee on his mind he was suddenly jerked back to past events and froze as he recalled Lilli and their date. He imagined her sitting in the café and patiently waiting for him after their arranged rendezvous. He cursed himself for drinking in his bunk, it was a recipe for disaster as, coupled with lack of sleep and mental stress he was now paying the price.

He turned on his bunk light only to reveal the haunting picture of Anna and his boy. With a Mona Lisa smile she seemed to question and gaze down at him but it was Lilli and her yielding body that invaded his thoughts and stabbed his guilty conscience. It was to be a meeting and not a date he told himself but his troubled mind admonished him as he tried to dismiss recent events and a needful desire that crept like a thief in the night into his loins.

Raised voices and scraping noises from outside his cabin distracted him. Stores he assumed, as a knock and a voice beyond the bulkhead brought him back to reality and the friendly countenance of Jurgen appeared from round the curtain.

'Guten morgen. Sorry to disturb you but our stores have arrived and the two boffins are here to check the loading. The crates are all marked V. MOTOR and labelled as coming from Nordhausen, together with the stencilled letters DORIS.'

Franz frowned with curiosity as wide awake now he swung his feet to the deck.

'Nordhausen,' he replied. 'Where the hell's that and what's at Nordhausen besides a fräulein named Doris?'

'Engines, by their markings, I would guess,' said Jurgen as he drew back the curtain. 'But can't say I've ever heard of the place.'

'Right,' said Franz without conviction, as he managed to winch himself upright. 'I'll be out in a minute,' he added with a yawn and a stretch. 'Get Johann to bring me some coffee, and schnell before I dehydrate.'

Jurgen chuckled at his friend's self-inflicted injuries as he called to a passing rating to inform the cook.

'One more thing,' he added with a mischievous grin. 'There are two more visitors waiting for you in the control room.' So saying, he leant back to double check. 'Ja, they're still there.' Intrigued, Franz put on his shoes and gingerly peered round the bulkhead.

'Am I seeing this right?' he said in a whisper, 'they're Oriental?'

'Right first time,' replied Jurgen. 'How's your Japanese, Herr Kapitän?'

'A little rusty,' said Franz with a grin. 'Damn it, I should have known. Give me five minutes to get myself sorted then wheel them in. We can all guess why they're here and exactly where we might be heading, am I right?' Jurgen nodded in agreement.

'Ja, alles klar,' he said with a grin and left to attend to their guests.

Minutes later Jurgen led the way with a tray of coffee as the new arrivals followed in his wake. One man was in the uniform of an officer of the Imperial Japanese Navy, a captain with three pips on his epaulettes, together with the customary four silver rings on his sleeves. The other man was a civilian, sporting a herringbone-patterned brown suit. With customary bows they introduced themselves in broken German as Captain Watanabe of the Imperial Japanese Navy and his colleague, Herr Kaizumi, a scientist.

'Sie sprechen Deutsch,' Franz complemented them for their efforts.

'Hai,' answered the civilian with a toothy grin. 'Ich nur klein,' then to the Germans' utter amazement, he added, 'you speekee Eenglish?'

He was a stocky man, with cropped grey hair. It was hard to tell his age, but Franz reckoned he might be in his early fifties. Captain Watanabe chimed in with a smile and a stiff bow.

'Please, we can speekee all in Eenglish?'

Franz gazed at them both, and weighed up the situation.

'Yes,' he replied, as the irony of what was about to transpire was not lost on him, or his FO. It was after all, an extraordinary situation as here they were; onboard a German submarine in the middle of a war, and everyone was conversing in the language of their enemy.

'I have this,' said Watanabe, as he handed Franz an envelope similar to the one that Karl Bach had produced.

'Gentlemen, please be seated,' Franz indicated to his bunk settee, as the two men bowed graciously and sat themselves down. He opened the envelope and noted it was more or less identical to the other, even down to its signatory, Karl Diebner. Another document related to the Japanese officer and gave his details and was signed by Reichsfuehrer, Heinrich Himmler.

Himmler again, thought Franz. He's got his fingers in this pie as well. What on earth has he to do with the navy? He was disturbed by a signalman who handed him a telex. With a frown Franz read the teleprinted message and quickly got to his feet.

'Have to go up to auxiliary HQ right away – keep an eye on things, Herr Lieutnant, until I get back.' He excused himself with a nod, Jurgen, sensing something urgent had cropped up requested the Japanese to follow him to their quarters.

Franz took a shower, found his cleanest dirty shirt, shifted into his number one uniform and forty minutes later was negotiating his gangway.

***

It had just past eight o'clock when to his surprise Franz met up with Kurt. They found themselves in the lounge of the Auxiliary Naval HQ building which had moved from the Boulevard Suchet after the main building had been gutted in the February 1943 raid. Apart from being summoned at such short notice and not having any idea as to why, they discussed the matters of the previous night and compared notes about the raid. Kurt said he and Yvonne had used the hotel's cellar, along with others, while Franz mentioned his narrow escape using the boiler house as a make-do shelter.

'One thing that did strike me as rather odd,' said Kurt, as he lit up two cigarettes and passed one to Franz. 'Normally the Tommies just bomb a specific target area, keeping their larger bricks for the bunkers. But this time they used Mosquito bombers to bomb, strafe and rocket this place and communications, along with us, the main target.' To emphasise his point, he indicated to a large pile of masonry and several neat rocket holes above their heads, where the sky was now in evidence.

'Hmm, guess you might have a point,' said Franz. 'It's normally just the bunkers. They don't touch the town anymore as most of the locals have been bombed-out and fled. Any further bombing on the town upsets those that remain and word has it that De Gaulle has asked them to stop any more raids. Perhaps we should all stay in town – bunk down with Jacques in his café, eh?'

'Did you see any of it?' said Kurt. 'I was already in the hotel when it happened.'

'See it! 'I was in it. It was definitely a Mosquito, as you said. I can tell those scheisters from a mile away. Those growling Merlins have a distinctive sound. One of them started firing cannon shells at us as we ran for this old boiler house. He hit some trucks with rockets but missed the communications building and the dormitory. I guess he'd already dropped his load before that, probably incendiaries to light the place up for the bombers.'

Franz paused in reflection, as he visualised the boiler's glow and the lingering memory of Lilli's perfume and body pressed against him. 'We managed to stay there until it was over,' he added, recalling their moment of needful release. Kurt merely nodded as he too had his tale to tell. However he did not for one moment suspect that Franz, the family man, had had 'une affaire de passion', by courtesy of the Royal Air Force.

'More or less the same with me,' he replied. 'We just managed to get into the hotel and dived for the cellar as we heard the sirens. Luckily for us, Yvonne said she was tired and we went straight back to my hotel. She must have had a premonition, as she'd found a bottle of wine stashed in the cellar and we celebrated the raid in our normal style.' He gave an amused chuckle. 'It could have lasted longer as we were only halfway through… the bottle, I mean.'

'So, changing the subject,' continued Kurt. 'What's with the telegrams? You must have had one?' Franz nodded and tapped his breast pocket.

'Ja, I have mine. Also that cargo I was telling you about has arrived along with two Japanese guys. My guess is that we're here for our sailing orders and it's the Tokyo or bust run for us.'

'Well, that's interesting,' said Kurt. 'Looks like the cat's out of the bag. I don't have any passengers, only crates of engines, radar equipment and blueprints. So with your Japanese super-cargo pointing the way, it must be Japan we're heading for – all makes sense now eh?'

Franz nodded. 'The only other thing I can think of is by the time we get there it will be no picnic as it will be the typhoon season, a case of from the Atlantic frying pan into the Pacific fire. You ever been in one of those? The ground swell goes right down to forty odd metres, really throws the boat about.'

Kurt pondered the question and shook his head. 'Nein, can't say I have but it sounds interesting,' he replied with a grin.

An orderly appeared and requested them to follow him along the great hall.

'Don't forget to ask them for an extra bag of rice and some chopsticks,' quipped Kurt in a loud whisper as they were hurriedly ushered into a large room through a pair of ornate, floor-to-ceiling double doors.

'This way, please,' said the orderly and led the way round a large rectangular conference table where high-ranking officers from the Wehrmacht were already seated, along with several civilians.

To Franz's utmost surprise the Japanese gentlemen from his boat were also present, along with several others from that country. Remaining seated they politely bowed in unison as Kurt and Franz entered. Unfamiliar with such protocol the two captains stood to attention with their caps tucked under their left arms. Together they clicked their heels then turning towards the Japanese contingency returned their bow, albeit rather stiffly. It seemed to be accepted and honour all round was satisfied.

Franz and Kurt took their places and glanced round the table. They recognised the familiar face of Fregattenkapitän Kals, their naval base commander, along with his aides, whilst others they had only seen on newsreels and in newspapers. Field Marshal Rommel, whom they knew had been in France co-ordinating the western defences, was prominent along with General von Fahrmbacher of the Lorient Garrison and Vice Admiral Matthiae of the Kriegsmarine.

Next to Rommel sat Hoffmann, Hitler's overweight and personal photographer along with Admiral Canaris, head of German intelligence. At the head of the table sat a weasel-faced man with round, black-rimmed spectacles and wearing the black uniform of a general of the Waffen SS. He was flanked by two burly blond giants from the ranks of his own corps, who stood rigidly behind him, keeping a wary eye on the august company.

As soon as the latecomers were seated, the thin man rose. Clearing his throat and glancing systematically around at his captivated audience, he started his address.

'Guten tag, meine Herren,' he began. 'Mein namen ist Himmler, Heinrich Himmler.'

Kurt kicked Franz under the table, as here they were, face to face with the butcher of Europe, the second power in the land and as Reichsfuehrer the head of the notorious Gestapo. Franz glanced at Kurt and gave a non-committal shrug as they tried to reason why Himmler was here in such a remote part of France, along with the Japanese and a smattering of the Nazi elite.

'Gentlemen, you might ask yourselves why I am here,' continued Himmler. 'I am here at the express wishes of the Führer. I have also come to welcome and honour our Japanese friends and allies in our combined struggle against the English and the Americans.' He paused and glanced round the table as the Germans sat, stony-faced, while the Japanese contingent bowed slightly in his direction with inscrutable smiles.

'Because of the Americans now in the war against us, we, the German people are united with our Eastern ally in a common and a united cause.' Himmler paused again for effect as several Germans nodded in agreement. 'It is because of the betrayal by the Jews, whom we Germans accommodated, gave them a home and educated their children to become doctors and scientists that we are here today. These very same Jews, who I will remind you were born in the Fatherland and grew fat on its milk and daily bread, have betrayed us by stealing our secrets and taking them to America. These Jews used our laboratories and were educated at our universities and studied alongside our scientists, only to stab us in the back, this like the noble Brutus before and to betray us like he did Caesar. They are spies, a sub-species of humanity who would steal even their mother's milk as they have robbed the Fatherland of its technology today.'

The German officers nodded in agreement as the Japanese, along with their interpreters, sat with detached expressions and waited politely for him to continue.

'I have here a document.' Himmler picked up a sheet of paper and held it high for all to see. 'A document from the Führer, to allow the latest German technology to be shared with our Japanese ally. Not only our present technology but also that of our latest research in weapons and their delivery. Amongst these weapons there is one, one weapon so unique, it will astound the world. But more so the English and the Americans, on whose heads it will fall.'

'So gentlemen,' he continued, 'that is the outline of our meeting today. But before I hand you over to our next guest and speaker, I would like to take this opportunity and introduce to you our two distinguished U-Boot captains. Please welcome Kapitänleutnant

118

Franz Bauer and Kapitänleutnant Kurt Oblitz. These two commanders will have the honour of carrying our materials and scientists to their intended destinations.' He gestured towards the two officers to be upstanding.

Taken by surprise, the two commanders blanched visibly. Scuffing their chairs, Franz and Kurt stood awkwardly and bowed to the assembly. They, in turn, put their hands together for a rapturous round of applause.

Himmler cleared his throat. 'These two captains will sail their U-Booten to the Far East and with this new technology, we, Germany and Japan, will attack our enemies from both sides of the world, a united attack which is bound to succeed.'

As Franz and Kurt regained their seats murmurs of benign agreement drifted round the room.

'I now bring you to the main topic and the conclusion of this meeting, as I have something of very great importance to disclose to you all. I have with me here a distinguished Doctor, Herr Klaus of the Kaiser Wilhelm Institut in Berlin. He will kindly take the chair and explain to you, in layman's terms, what we in the Fatherland have striven to develop and in the very near future, use against our enemies.'

He held out his hand in a formal gesture. 'Danke, meine Herren. That is all. I give you Doctor Klaus.'

Amidst rapturous applause from some, and strained applause from others, he took his seat.

Doctor Klaus rose nervously to his feet. He was a man of average height, with lean features and silver-rimmed glasses that matched the colour of his thinning long hair. He shuffled his papers self-consciously, adjusted his glasses to sit halfway down an aquiline nose and peered over their rim for silence – like a hanging judge who was about to pass sentence. With a furtive glance towards Himmler, he began his address.

'Danke, Herr Reichsführer,' he began, with a nod in Himmler's direction. 'Gentlemen, what I have to say this morning may come as a great surprise to some of you. Herr Himmler has already pointed out that we have lost some of our best...' Klaus suddenly froze and shook his head as he met Himmler's intimidating gaze. Dr Klaus cleared his throat as he continued. 'As I was saying, we have for reasons of security dismissed some of the foreign workers that we were involved with in our scientific projects.' He paused, satisfied with his timely correction. 'German scientists have weathered this setback as valuable time has been lost, however we have now developed an aircraft that is capable of delivering a payload, an explosive device – a flying bomb, if you like – at over twice the speed of sound.' Murmurs of incredibility and astonishment arose, as others who had witnessed its launch nodded with satisfaction.

'He's crazy,' whispered Kurt. 'Twice the speed of sound, where did Himmler find him?' Franz kicked his ankle, feeling like a schoolboy about to be found out by the teacher. Only, this teacher was the head of the SS and Hitler's secret police.

'It is so, gentlemen,' the scientist continued. 'I can confirm that we have made and launched this weapon. This aircraft is, in fact, a rocket driven by a special fuel. We can deliver a payload of one thousand kilo at a velocity in excess one thousand six hundred kilometres per hour.'

'Sounds too good to be true,' said Franz. 'I wonder when they're going to start using it and pay them back for Cologne? It could never be soon enough for me.'

Dr Klaus held up his hand. 'Gentlemen, please, I have not finished. Kindly let me explain.' He waited for silence. 'We scientists have already successfully flown a much smaller version of this rocket and, within days we shall launch it against England…' He paused, as again, murmurs of appreciation filled the room. 'However, this is not the reason why I have come here today. 'I am at liberty to inform you,' he continued, 'that Herr Himmler has been involved with us scientists and engineers at Penemunde since 1943 and has witnessed our final successful firing of these new weapons.'

As for Franz, the penny suddenly dropped as the signature on his document came into focus. So, Himmler was involved but Holy Virgin, why him? He's Hitler's deputy, not a scientist.

'Gentlemen,' continued Dr Klaus; 'What I now have to tell you will directly concern our two U-Boot officers here with us today.' He indicated with his hand as Franz and Kurt saw a sea of faces turn in their direction. 'We have the flying bombs and the method of delivery. Now we need a destructive device, a bomb of mega proportions. I can now tell you that we, the German scientists…' He paused and began muttering to himself as he had clearly lost his way on the script. 'Ja, here we are,' he said with satisfaction as he peered over the rim of his spectacles. 'We scientists have been able to construct the model of a device that will release the power and the raw energy of the sun upon this earth.' Murmurs of surprise and delight filled the room as the Japanese sat with inscrutable faces and made their own comments as they followed the translated script.

'Gentlemen, let me explain. We are here today because the Führer believes by sharing this technology and the raw materials with our ally Japan; we can save precious time for its construction.' He nodded at an elderly Japanese civilian seated across from him. The Japanese scientist bowed politely, his grey and neatly-cropped hair at variance with that of his German colleague. 'Doctor Joshikura here is working in Japan with Doctor Hedeki Yukawa on a similar project. Therefore, as allies and friends of Japan and with the aid of our Unterseebooten, we will send a consignment of an element called uranium.'

Again he paused, checked his papers and sipped from his glass as all eyes were now riveted on him.

'Together with this uranium, we will send enriched water and graphite in its purest state. These items will be needed for the construction of our new weapon, our so-called Uranium Bombe.' He glanced round the table as his audience sat transfixed by his speech and revelation. Himmler sat impassive as the two SS henchmen continued to stare vacantly ahead.

'Gentlemen, I will now explain, in lay-man's terms, what Germany has developed in order to end this war. We scientists have reluctantly been drawn into this bomb-making affair with the alarming news that the Americans, with the assistance of our traitorous scientists, as well as those others from Austria, are already well-advanced in making a similar bomb. I can assure you all, that I have information from reliable sources that the Americans are using an old gymnasium in Chicago, at Stagg Field University, for this very same project.'

He stopped as more voices and murmuring arose and army generals shuffled with unease, the latter not having been informed until now.

As for the Japanese contingent, they were silent no longer and conversed in loud terms and animated gestures amongst themselves, as this was the weapon for them. It would save Japan. Their Emperor would defeat the round-eyes from the West and they would become lords of the Eastern globe.

'Gentlemen,' Dr Klaus continued, holding up his hand for silence. 'Some of you might have heard of Doctor Einstein, one of our scientists who, in 1921, was awarded the Nobel Prize for physics. He is another that has gone to assist the Americans, but I digress. He is the scientist that volunteered the scientific equation; $E=Mc^2$ well, gentlemen, today it has become the formula for this most powerful explosive device known to man. All that Einstein meant to say was that the mass, M in the equation, could be converted into energy. I have now been informed that Doctor Einstein has been given further information, this by the traitors from Germany and Austria. The picture is not rosy; there are many working against us in the race to create Atomic Fission. Fission gentlemen, is a means of splitting atoms and thus causing a chain reaction.' He paused to run his fingers through his hair and sifted through his papers as a sea of blank faces found themselves at the dawn of the atomic age.

'So, it looks like the Tokyo run for us,' said Franz quietly, nodding his head in resignation.

'I can't believe what I've just heard,' said Kurt with a frown. 'So those rumours about the special weapons were true, after all. What's more they'll be relying on us to get through the British blockade. No wonder we're getting those extra cannons, rubber paint and that Schnorchel fitted as priority. Germany's future depends on us. It's all beginning to add up, eh?'

Franz nodded as he gazed at the old scientist and felt grateful to him for suddenly and un-expectantly giving him hope and a purpose to carry on the fight.

'Ja, looks like the cat's definitely out of the bag now,' he replied, 'and we'll be sailing shortly. I wonder how many others know about any of this?'

'Gentlemen,' the scientist called them to order. 'Before I leave you, I think it only fair that I should perhaps explain, in more detail, what it is we are trying to achieve and your part in the equation.' He stopped to finger combed his hair as stifled chuckles rippled around the room, as the professor's hair now stood at all angles, however he still commanded their respect as he continued, oblivious to his appearance.

'It is because of the harassment by the Allied bombing of our cities, factories and establishments that we scientists, under the leadership of Doctor Heisenberg, have managed to diversify our efforts. We now have many small units working at various sites, many below ground, in tunnels and bunkers. We have mastered the equation;

'$E=Mc^2$ where E is the energy, M is the mass and c the speed of light squared which, as some of you might know, is three hundred million metres per second – or, if you prefer the Englischer version, one hundred and eighty-six thousand miles per second.' A chuckle arose at his non-intended wit as Himmler frowned in response.

Shuffling his papers he went on. 'We have, in our underground laboratories, dealt with the sub-atomic particles simply by bombing atoms of uranium with neutrons. This was intended to achieve atomic fusion. The whole game lies within the rules and structure of the sub-atomic world. Doctor Heisenberg once volunteered his theories about this sub-atomic world, where he speculated that it was impossible to know the exact amount of energy locked-up in a given space at any moment in time. It is an uncertainty, but we are now to justify this uncertainty. What we need to do now is to control the result. Once we have achieved this, we can then harness the product of this fusion, namely a substance called plutonium. Then, but only then, can we build and trigger our Uranium Bombe. Meine Herren, danke, that is all.'

The applause was instant and deafening. Even the inscrutable Japanese officers and scientists nodded and applauded him. Doctor Klaus made a bashful bow, sat and stood to bow once more. He acknowledged them with a wave of his hand and glanced nervously at Himmler, who seemed pleased with his address and offered a condescending smile as he rose, and the room was brought to order.

'Meine Herren,' began Himmler, 'you have heard Doctor Klaus explain to you matters in which I personally have been involved in for the past year. I can assure you, as I saw doubt on some faces…' He paused and glanced with displeasure at Kurt and Franz and swiftly carried on. 'Jawohl, I can assure you all that these machines have flown and are now, even as I speak, in mass production. Because of the Allies bombing the experimental site at Penemunde, this site has been abandoned and moved to an underground factory at Nordhausen. We have code named this secret factory as DORIS and it is our intention, once we have built a sufficient quantity of these weapons, to launch them and strike at England.' Nods of suppressed glee and approval rippled round the table as he continued.

'We will strike and seek our revenge, as they have bombed our cities into ruins. We will do the same to them, only…' He paused and wagged a bony finger. 'We will not only leave them in ruins, but we will leave them in ashes – hot, uranium ashes.' Methodically, he pounded the palm of his hand with a fist. 'Ja, gentlemen, ashes, we will leave them in ashes, grey atomic ashes.'

As loud murmurs arose, he stilled them with his hand. 'It is our priority now to get this bomb into production, as just one bomb will have the power of forty thousand tons of high explosives.' Another murmur, this time from the generals, as never before had such explosive power entered into their calculations, their minds reeled as they relished the thought of Germany wielding such power and might.

'Gentlemen,' continued Himmler, 'you can well imagine the potential of this sizable weapon. We must therefore win the race to build it, otherwise we will be overtaken and lose this war, make no mistake.' It was a revelation that nobody thought they would hear from such a high ranking official as Himmler. 'In order to speed up this programme, our Führer, Herr Hitler, has agreed to share Germany's technology with that of Japan. Together our two great nations will assemble the final stages of our Uranium Bombe and solve this atomic jigsaw once and for all. We have plans to build an even bigger rocket,' continued Himmler. 'A rocket that will be capable of carrying this bomb and using Japan's large aircraft launching submarines. We will be able to launch it in the North Atlantic from four hundred kilometres distant and strike at Washington and New York.' Again, in emphasis, Himmler pounded his fist. 'We will bomb their cities like they have bombed us. Let those Americans feel the effect of burning and falling buildings, of the choking dust and women and children made homeless, destitute and crying with hunger and cold. That, gentlemen, will be all.'

He bowed towards the Japanese, as elated and spontaneous applause erupted, together with a standing ovation. Himmler revelled in the applause and managed a congenial smile as white-gloved orderlies brought in silver trays loaded with lead crystal glasses and bottles of Champagne.

'Look at your Japanese passengers,' said Kurt. 'First time I've seen any of them smile. Guess that's what they came for and we're going to play the underwater taxi for their ride home.'

'Ja,' replied Franz. 'They're in the same boat as us, if you'll excuse the pun. They've lost about all of their aircraft carriers and air power is what counts nowadays.'

'So it's up to us to deliver the goods to Madame Butterfly,' said Kurt, raising his glass. 'I'm all for it. Get a nice sunshine cruise from the grey funnel line and the Emperor builds us a bomb to give the Tommies some of their own medicine.'

'Herr Kapitän,' came a voice. It was a courier from Naval HQ who handed them both sealed envelopes. On inspection they found instructions stating only torpedoes already in their tubes were to be carried. The only spare torpedoes were a number of the LUTs, which were destined for offloading in Japan, and were not to be fired under any circumstances. Cargo would take the place of the empty torpedo racks. Sea routing would be given one hour before departure.

'Looks like our holidays are over,' said Kurt with a grin. 'Better pack your bags, Kapitän Bauer.'

They were about to join the main group in the dining room for lunch, when Himmler with his two SS guards and Bormann, his aide-de-camp, came striding across towards them and held out his hand. Franz and Kurt stood rigidly to attention, and then shook the proffered hand.

'You two commanders have the best U-Booten this far south,' Himmler began. 'Also, you both have good records of success. The Führer and I depend on you to get through with these weapons, so you must make every effort but take no risks.' They met his discerning gaze and nodded in acknowledgement.

'You must avoid all contact with the enemy and his merchant ships and you will be receiving your final orders from me via the Naval HQ here. Good luck and Heil Hitler.' He half raised an arm in the Nazi salute but changing his mind, turned on his heel and strode out of the room. They stood; amazed that Himmler should have shaken their hand, even if they never got a word in edgeways.

'So much for a cosy chat with our deputy leader,' said Kurt, 'he took off like one of his rockets, eh?'

'Didn't even give us a chance to say Heil Hitler, but did you notice his hands?' continued Franz in a loud whisper, 'a bit effeminate, I thought.' Kurt raised an eyebrow as there were rumours but thought better than to voice an opinion and pointed in the direction of the set tables.

'Come on, let's eat before they put us before a firing squad, I can smell those schnitzels from here.'

'Good idea,' said Franz, 'before he changes his mind and comes back to offer us honorary membership of the Gestapo.' Chuckling at their wit they followed the others into the chandelier-festooned dining hall of the General Headquarters building.

With lunch tucked under their belts the two captains made their way back to the main bunker complex to pick up any further documents, together with their respective boats' private mail. Franz noted with disappointment that there were several letters for his crew but nothing from Anna.

Before they left the HQ building they were informed news had leaked out about their mission as they had been given a 'Sonder' rating, which meant that their boats had priority over all the other U-Boats.

'For all his size, Himmler certainly has clout,' said Kurt but on seeing his friend's concern about the mail, he decided to assist in the only way he could. 'Tell you what; let's celebrate our day with a couple of glasses. I've a feeling we'll be away quite soon. Besides, my boat's like a transit camp at the moment.'

'Touché,' said Franz as he checked his watch. 'Four-fifty. It's a bit early, but then it's not every day one has a tête-à-tête with our Herr Himmler, not to mention hearing that Uranium Armageddon is just round the corner.'

'You do realise,' replied Kurt, 'if this gets out, our boats will be number one target on the Tommy hit list.'

'Can't see that it will make much difference,' said Franz sceptically. 'I'm on their hit list every time I poke my nose out of harbour.' Kurt gave an amused snort. It was the same with all of the U-Boats, ever since the Allies had achieved command of the skies.

'Ja, guess you're right,' he replied. 'Anyway, let's not get morbid and daub the devil on the wall. At least we'll get a good table in the café, eh?'

Chapter Fourteen

CELLAR ORDEAL

Anna awoke with a start at the sound of heavy footsteps from beyond the door. With alarm she heard the lock turn as the cellar door burst open and three uniformed men, followed by Gruber marched into the room. One was an officer of the SS with his black uniform and death's head insignia whom she recognised as one of her interrogators, while the other two were soldiers in field grey. The SS Gruppenführer nodded and the Feldwebbel gave the order for the corporal to bring Anna's bag. The soldier disappeared out into the passageway and returned moments later carrying the canvas bag.

'Corporal,' said the SS man, 'kindly give Frau Bauer her bag. She is a U-Boot captain's wife and is to be given every courtesy.' With an icy stare he met her confused gaze. 'Aufwiedersehen, Frau Bauer,' he snarled and turning on his heel strode arrogantly from the room, closely followed by Gruber who, grim-faced, waved a warning finger in her direction.

The sergeant stood facing her and craned his neck over his shoulder as he listened for their footsteps to recede. Satisfied he dropped the military mask to smile warmly across at Anna and taking the bag from the corporal stepped forward to place it at the foot of the bed.

'I believe this is yours, Frau Bauer?' It was the first kind face she had seen since her arrest but she had now become wary of anyone in uniform. Hiding her fear and suspicion she answered with a nod as Eddi clung to her, still traumatised by recent events.

'Anna, please call me Anna,' she replied hesitantly and reached for the bag as the corporal came forward and placed it on the bed beside her. 'Danke,' said Anna with relief at getting her possessions back. She noted by their actions the two soldiers were only too keen to assist but suspected it could well be a ruse. Another one of the Gestapo's games of carrot and stick, she reminded herself, and would be on her guard. 'Bitte can you tell me the time, as my watch has stopped?' In a flash the corporal peeled back his sleeve.

'Zeit? Ja, of course,' he replied, peering at his watch.

Anna instantly recognised it as a British aviator's watch as she had seen them being worn by the yachtsmen at the Ipswich yacht club. It brought back a flood of memories, as Franz had taken her across the North Sea from Kiel and there she had met up with the yachting crowd, several of whom were Fleet Air Arm pilots on their weekend leave from Lee-on-Solent.

She recalled the good times that were had in their company and remembered them checking their watches for closing time at the bar. It was a sort of British game, as they had to get their glasses filled before the man behind the bar rang a bell then called out 'Time gentlemen, please!' The club soon closed after that.

'Two-thirty,' the stocky soldier replied, bringing her back to the present with a jolt. Systematically he checked it again and held it to his ear. 'Ja, two-thirty.' She nodded her thanks as she adjusted her watch and was about to ask the next pertinent question, when the sergeant, reading her thoughts, cut in.

'That's in the morning, Frau Anna,' he volunteered, seeing she had lost all track of time.

'Ja,' said the corporal, 'another new day and it's nearly the end of April and not a potato in the ground.' The remark fell on deaf ears as he muttered to himself and made his way across to inspect the wine racks.

'So, I'm free to go?' Anna queried, addressing the tall Feldwebel. The sergeant had taken one of the scattered chairs and was about to make himself comfortable. Still holding the chair, he pondered the question and hesitated to answer. What this woman needed was a good few days' rest, he mused, and not be running about the bomb-scarred country trying to dodge air raids, the SS and Gestapo.

She met his questioning gaze and reasoned he was not that old. With tired blue eyes divided by an aquiline nose and cheek bones that sported a scar portraying a student who just needed a shave and a good night's sleep. From under his helmet a thatch of straw-coloured hair protruded, completing the image of a true son of the Fatherland.

He sat and relaxed his six-foot frame and casually removed his helmet to reveal his longer than regulation curls. His blond hair reflected the light and would have gladdened the heart of many a lonely fräulein, Anna mused, as they regarded each other.

He sat there still weighing up his answer and proceeded to scratch his head whilst still holding the helmet, which bobbed in sympathy with the efforts of his cranial massage. Satisfied, he placed the helmet on the flagstoned floor. She noted his actions were quite

128

meticulous, as he faced the helmet towards her and it lay sentinel, like Pharaoh's dog by his jackbooted feet.

As if in answer to her question several dull detonations shook the cellar, causing a chunk of ceiling plaster to fall and narrowly miss the corporal at the racks. He was heard to mutter something inaudible as the bulb flickered on its dangling flex. After a while and as no further detonations were heard the sergeant answered her question.

'Ja, Frau Anna, of course you are free to go but I think it is better that you and your boy wait until the bombers have gone.' He emphasised the point by indicating with his head and glancing at the ceiling, with its numerous cracks and chunks of missing plaster. She followed his gaze as several rapid detonations shook the building and loosened flakes of distemper which fell and settled in thin, white patches on her bed like the first snows of winter.

'That's ours,' the sergeant volunteered with grim satisfaction. 'That's our Flak and nothing to worry about, Frau Anna.' Casually he reached into his tunic and extracted a battered chromed cigarette case which he deftly flicked open with one hand and offered across to Anna.

'Nein, danke,' she said, shaking her head. 'I don't smoke.' He shrugged his broad shoulders and extracted one for himself, tamping one end on the case before lighting up and slipping both case and lighter back into their respective pockets. He exhaled the smoke as he watched Anna tidying her hair with the aid of a tiny mirror.

'It still looks a mess,' she added as she tucked the mirror away in her purse. He just sat and grinned as he knew better than to comment on the delicate subject of women and their coiffure. Leaving his seat Anna felt threatened as he came towards her but her suspicions of uniformed men wavered as he held out his hand in greeting.

'Mein namen ist Helmut,' he said. 'Feldwebbel Helmut Vogl and over there is Obergefreiter Wilhelm Brunner – Willi, to all and sundry.' He indicated with a thumb in the corporal's direction. On hearing the mention of his name, Willi dusted off the chalky white flakes from his shoulders and came across to introduce himself.

'I'm Willi,' he said. 'Just call me Willi. It's better that way.' He drew up a bentwood carver which had seen better days, being well-riddled with woodworm. As he dropped himself into the chair, Anna winced, as the infested wood complained under the burden of his mass. Satisfied and comfortable, he settled for a cigarette from Helmut.

Anna guessed he was in his late thirties as his once dark hair was greying at the temples. He was not as tall as Helmut but heavier in build, while his jovial, rounded features were at odds with his uniform and coal-scuttle helmet. He looked uncomfortable wearing it as his demeanour was that of a land worker, or so it seemed. Willi lit his cigarette and removed his helmet, but held onto it as he scratched his head with his other hand.

'I normally keep it on,' he said with a grin as he glanced suspiciously at the ceiling. 'Anyway, it's all the rage and fashion at the moment, right Helmut?' As if to prove his point, multiple dull detonations once again shook the cellar as the light flickered in response.

Anna, observing them both and trusting that the ritual head-scratching was nothing catching, observed as Willi replaced his helmet as more flakes rained down. Nervously Anna glanced up to see the exposed laths that still held the ceiling in place as she protectively stroked her sleeping child's head. It was a distraction, a kind of therapy, as she gently picked the flakes from his hair and face.

'Now this is the real raid,' said Helmut with a painful expression. 'Before it was only the pathfinders and diversionary bombers. We're in for a pasting again.' He checked his watch. 'Should last about forty-five minutes, then we can all go home,' and smiled reassuringly at Anna. 'They're not after us,' he added. 'It's the railroad and goods yards, as we're shifting some of our industry south, into Austria.' She nodded her understanding but it was fear that now lurked in her eyes as she recalled the flames and her parents, trapped in their cellar.

'Ja, we can all go home in forty-five minutes,' said Willy with a sardonic smile. 'That's if they've left us a home to go to. Two weeks ago it was the Amerikaner, a daylight raid and flying too high for our Flak to bring them down. Carpet bombing – they hit everything except the target. After the raid, the rail yards were still intact but they'd hit my farm and injured my wife and children.' He rose from his chair as his face turned into a mask of anger. 'Ja, they are so high up...' and stopped in mid-sentence and pointed with a wagging finger at the ceiling. 'So high that we cannot reach them and they cannot see what the hell they're supposed to be aiming at. We're at their mercy and so are my cows. Some have died of shock and those that are left can't be milked.'

Anna shook her head in sympathy and understanding as Willi strode back to the wine racks, turning and with a warning finger shot them an incensed look. 'I'll catch one of them one day, a dose of bullet pudding up his arsch will teach him a lesson before his feet touch the ground.'

'He lives near Dachau,' explained Helmut. 'That's just a few kilometres north of here with lots of open countryside. There's a large prison camp there and the bombers try to keep clear of it, but twice now they've hit his farm and the cows either die from shrapnel wounds or of fright. He gives their meat away and won't eat it himself while the Wehrmacht usually requisitions the rest.' Anna nodded as she glanced across at the farmer, so out of character in his uniform and did not want to hear any more of how her country was systematically being torn apart.

'What about yourself, Helmut?' she asked. 'Are you from around here?'

'Nein, I'm from Stuttgart,' he replied. 'That's another hundred kilometres from here. Being an industrial city, it's always being bombed, especially as the Allies discovered the new Tiger panzers are being made there.'

'You have a family, I mean, are you married?' Immediately, she realised she had overstepped the mark, as he winced at the thought.

'Family, yes, but I'm not married. Just my mother and father, whose business was destroyed last year. My father had a foundry there and perhaps when all this is over I'll go back and help him to rebuild it. Luckily it was an incendiary bomb; it burnt the place down but all of the heavy machinery is still intact. It can be made to work again.' Helmut paused, pulled out his cigarette case and lit up. 'We made marine propellers, perhaps even the ones for your husband's U-Boot.' His smile faded as he realised he might have said the wrong thing. Anna let it ride, as a ghost of a smile played on her lips and she wondered where her husband might be. She stifled the thought and felt she had to carry on with the conversation as something more sinister about her arrest was bothering her.

'Perhaps you should have joined the Kriegsmarine as an engineer.' Helmut gave it some thought, drew hard on his cigarette and stubbed it out on the sole of his boot.

'Well it was strange,' he replied, 'I finished my university at Heidelberg in thirty-nine, just before the war started.' Subconsciously he ran his finger along the duelling scar on his cheek, his credentials among the upper crust of university life. 'Working at the foundry I could drive heavy machinery and upon my call-up in October of thirty-nine the Wehrmacht needed drivers for their panzers. So at the age of twenty-two, I found myself driving tanks. One year later and because I could ride a horse, I was chosen to ride in the victory parade down the Champs Elysées. It was my hair and height that made me the propaganda machine's favourite soldier. They used me for newsreels and victory parades, and you know what? As yet I've never fired a shot in anger.'

'I wouldn't shout too loud,' said Willi, who had finished studying the wine labels and now carried a choice bottle of Riesling-Spätlese to their table. 'If we get the Ostfront you'll be knee-deep in shell cases before you can say Horst Wessel.' Helmut cast him a sour glance but chuckled at the corporal's dry sense of humour.

'Well that's been my war so far,' he replied. 'Except since about eight months ago when the heavy air raids started and I've not been filming since.'

'Ha,' snorted Willi, 'that's because we've no cinemas left to show them.' Anna stifled a laugh, hand-shielding her face and realised it was the first time in weeks that mirth had passed her lips. She listened to their idle banter and saw the truth and irony of it all. Helmut was about to say more, but was interrupted by Willi, who was making distressed hand signals whilst holding the bottle of 1927 vintage.

'We'll drink this before you bore Frau Anna to tears with your tales of yesterday's hero,' he said jovially. 'Only trouble is, we haven't a corkscrew. I'll go up to the kitchens to see if I can find one, ja!'

'Nein, Willi,' said Helmut, 'you had better stay as it's safer down here. Pass me that bottle and see if you can find our mugs.' Willi handed him the bottle as Helmut, using his bayonet, deftly scribed a circumferential line in the glass below the cork. Holding the blade and with a sharp tap on the neck, sliced it away. Anna sat watching and admired the young man's ingenuity. He probably learnt that at university, after the fencing, she mused.

'Quite a neat trick,' she remarked as Willi returned with two battered aluminium mugs and filled them with the golden liquid.

'That's no trick, that's education,' volunteered Helmut with a grin.

'Danke, to both of you, and Gesundheit,' said Anna, feeling guilty as Willi waited for Helmut to finish.

Once again the cellar shook from distant detonations but the light miraculously remained lit. Willi adjusted his helmet as they listened to the reassuring thump-thump-thump of the Flak batteries replying in kind to their airborne tormentors. Reminded once more of his farm and clearly agitated, he left his chair and made his way back to the wine racks.

'You know that schweinehund Austrian corporal would have been better off painting out my cowshed,' he said in disgust. 'Today another raid and most of my cattle gone as the army took them for the glory of the Reich and their Gulaschkannone up there in the street.' Helmut gave a knowing sigh, indicating to Anna that he had heard it all before as Willi returned with a second bottle of the '27 vintage and leaving it for opening later as he continued with his tirade against the Nazis.

'Ja, that Scheiss Gulaschkannone, that's something else. They set up this field kitchen right here in the middle of the street to feed the bombed-out inhabitants and the gall of it was, they used my livestock for the event...' Flushed with emotion he pointed at the ceiling and with a wagging finger continued his condemnation of the Führer. 'Right here in the square it was where he spoke in thirty-eight with his Lebensraum and Scheiss Master Race rhetoric and now right here in the square they ate my prize cows, only this time without the flag-waving, drums and torch light parades.'

Anna's heart went out to the portly farmer and felt sorry for the man. She was reminded of how her husband and his fellow captains were paraded with flags and flowers as they returned from their destruction of British shipping, and with their numerous Iron Cross decorations.

'I'm sorry to hear about your farm Willi,' she said. 'But I can tell you that my husband has told me on several occasions that we are working on a Wunderwaffe to win this war. Perhaps it will be our turn soon.'

'Wunderwaffe?' Willi spat the word. 'What special weapon is that, the only Wunderwaffe here is our shovels.' He glanced at Helmut who was casually lighting up his third cigarette and had obviously heard all that before as well. However, Anna had now become Willi's new captivated audience.

'Tomorrow,' he continued, 'if we survive tonight that is, I shall be back on the burial squad, as there must be at least three hundred Amerikaner bombers up there. Soon they will have dropped their candy-bars and be finished, München will be finished and very soon, Adolf Hitler and his thousand-year Reich along with it.' He was nearly finished himself, Anna thought, as she saw how upset and flushed he was. He nodded his head in consternation and in emphasis to the reality of it all, as Helmut handed him a re-fill and cigarette. Regaining his composure he cast them a detached look as he sat to finish his wine and lit up – Anna could not help but notice, with an USAF logo, Zippo lighter.

Anna half finished her wine and handed the mug to Helmut and attended to her son. She decided she would leave as soon as the raid was over and now head for Frankfurt, where Franz's brother, Albert lived. He was a soldier but had not heard from him for over a year. That would be about 300 kilometres to the northwest, about the same distance as Dresden but it made sense as it would be on her route back home. She had told the Gestapo that she was going to Dresden. Should they change their minds and come looking for her, which to her chagrin, they might, at least she would be well away from them. Even if her brother-in-law was not home, then Lotte his wife might have some news about Franz and his whereabouts.

As the hours crept by Anna kept her vigil lying awake by her sleeping child. The two soldiers spoke in low tones so as not to disturb them whilst from the outside world only the occasional sound of Flak batteries was heard. It told its own story as Anna decided to wait until first light.

Lying there she relaxed as best she could and thought about her recent ordeal and her brutal interrogation by the Gestapo. She decided to risk asking the sergeant some personal questions, as she needed to know if the Gestapo could find out the one thing that would be her undoing. Her thoughts turned to food but the wine made her feel woozy. Listening to the background murmur of their voices, drowsy eyelids closed as Anna drifted into a much needed sleep, embroidered with dim dreams.

Chapter Fifteen

THE LAST WALTZ

It was less than busy inside the café, as the majority of the tables were empty and their accompanying bentwood chairs stood neatly propped against them. Franz and Kurt made themselves comfortable by a window as men from other ships glanced briefly in their direction; others from the U-Boot flotilla raised their glasses in camaraderie and respectful salute. Across the room in a corner sat some soldiers who were busy chatting with several off-duty nurses. At the bar happily seated were the usual handful of local girls who in turn, laughed and giggled as they conversed noisily and one, known to Kurt blew a ring of cigarette smoke towards them, the only two officers present.

Minutes passed and without any signs of service one of the girls nodded in their direction and slipped behind the bar to call for attention in her local dialect. Soon the beaded curtain parted and Jacques made a flustered appearance. The barman was without his customary beret and seemed put out and surprised at seeing the two officers at such an early hour of the afternoon. Unsettled he picked up a tray and hurried across the room.

'Bonjour Commandant,' he wheezed at Kurt, as his barrel chest heaved with the effort. 'You are early today, gentlemen, non?'

Beads of perspiration glistened on his forehead as he produced a blue handkerchief and methodically began mopping his saddle-bag jowls and sweat-laden brow.

'I'm getting too old, Messieurs, those barrels they are heavy, non?' He wheezed as he stuffed the cloth back into his apron pouch and summoning a cheesy grin took their order. 'Same as usual, une bouteille de vin rouge avec deux ballons de Cognac?'

'Oui Jacques, merci,' replied Kurt with a nod. 'And you should not be lifting those barrels. Let the navy do it for you.' He indicated to the sailors at a table near the bar.

'Oui, Monsieur, merci,' Jacques replied, with a thankful nod and a look of benign resignation. 'Next time, I will ask, certainement.'

135

Lifting his apron he wiped the table with a single swipe of his brawny arm before disconcertedly shuffling away with their order.

'What's all this ballon business?' enquired Franz with a frown.

'It's Breton for one of those large bulbous glasses, Yvonne told me about it, but look...' Kurt indicated with an angular nod to where the barman was leaving a trail of sticky grey footprints, impregnated with straw. 'Scheisse, by the looks of it, chicken scheisse,' he added with disgust.

'I thought I could smell something;' said Franz, with a cautious sniff, 'and not the latest creation from Paris either,' as he disdainfully peered at the floor and the trail of prints that led back to the bar. 'Must have a few hens out the back or in another cellar? At least they're safe down there, as I know some of our lads have been known to raid the local hen houses for their breakfast.'

Kurt nodded with a wry grin, as he recalled his men had recently returned with a cap full of eggs after a run ashore.

'I know exactly what you mean,' he agreed with a chuckle. 'I told my crew to lay off poaching eggs and they immediately saw the funny side of it. I lost the argument there and then, especially when the cook piped up about their poached eggs being ready.

Kurt stubbed out his cigarette with a grin as he shifted his attention to Jacques who was returning with their order. They were happy to see his Gallic composure restored as the customary Gauloise drooped precariously from his lower lip. Kurt and Franz cast discreet glances at his boots as the foul smell still lingered but his footwear was clean and his Breton cap was once more set at its familiar jaunty angle.

The big man off-loaded the tray and with a cheery grin made his way back behind the bar, muttering as he went but not before sweeping and kicking the offending material ahead of him with the side of his boot.

'Schwein,' muttered Kurt, as he glanced down and flicked his shoe at a remaining lump; sending it skittering into concealment under the next table.

'Reminds me of mines,' said Franz with a chuckle as he filled their glasses. 'Just like mines, with the spikes of straw sticking out. It's just lying there under that table and waiting for its next victim.' They burst out laughing, to the bemused glances of the others and sat with their drinks, reminiscing on old college and academy days before the war.

However, as always the conversation turned and in guarded tones discussed the war and their new tactics now that the wolf pack system on convoys had been abandoned. After a while and with great discretion they opened the subject of the day's events. They speculated on the hazards of their mission and date of departure and were not too enamoured with what lay ahead, which for most mariners would have been the voyage of a lifetime.

With the late afternoon turning to evening their second bottle of 'rouge' was half empty by the time the café began to fill and the accordion player began to warm up by playing wheezing chords from local folk songs.

The music stopped abruptly as whistling and the banging of glasses on tables attracted their attention. Kurt and Franz glanced towards the door and its blackout curtain that had already closed in their wake, as in walked a giggling bunch of girls, Yvonne and Lilli amongst them. Chairs scraped to make room as more whistles and eager young voices pleaded and beckoned them for their company.

Kurt collected two chairs as Yvonne and Lilli made their way across to their table with smiles of appreciation for their welcoming audience. Removing their coats they hung them on the back of the chairs as unabashed, Yvonne stooped to kiss Kurt on both cheeks, while Lilli with a rosy glow, offered her hand to Franz.

Their touch was electric as pools of blue met his questioning gaze and her elusive smile would have shamed the Mona Lisa as she meaningfully shook her head. With an inward sigh of relief he understood after which Lilli mouthed the word 'news' and the two girls made themselves comfortable round the table. Without prompting Jacques, like a trap door spider, shot out from the bar and appeared with a bottle of 'blanc' and two glasses.

'Bonjour,' he said in greeting and instantly burst into his Breton dialect to converse with Yvonne. With abundant animation he spoke in rapid bursts as Yvonne hardly got a word in edgeways but kept nodding her head. Finally she reached into her handbag and handed him a slip of paper, together with a bundle of Francs.

'Merci mademoiselle,' he said with a nod and a satisfied growl as he grasped the wad of notes with calculating beady eyes. Placing the note on his tray he stuffed the money into his kangaroo pouch and smiled congenially as he poured the wine for the ladies, before ambling back to his bar.

With Yvonne pre-occupied with her handbag, Lilli sipped her wine. Peering over the rim of her glass, she noted how unusually smart Franz and Kurt were turned out, smart even for submariners!

'You are both looking handsome tonight. Must be your Sunday best,' said Lilli with a flippant smile playing on her lips. Kurt chuckled at the compliment as Franz nodded in appreciation but could only gaze at his drink and search for the words of contrition that might suit the occasion.

'Sorry about last night Lilli, did you wait for me?' he said with a sheepish glance in her direction.

'Well yes, Herr Kapitän. You could say that,' she replied with a hint of sarcasm in her voice. 'It's not every day a girl gets stood up in this town,' she added with mock indignation as he cast her apologetic glance. 'I knew where you were as some of your crew entertained me and paid for my drink,' she added with a friendly nod towards them sitting near the bar. His mind raced as he agonised about himself in his cabin and the empty bottle and Anna's picture. What could he say in mitigation? The cook had cleaned up and would have said something to the others onboard. That sort of news travels fast on any boat and God only knew what his mischievous crew had told her.

'Well, I…' he stammered as Lilli relented and her lips parted in a forgiving smile.

'I hope you finished all that paper work,' she said, 'they told me you were trying to catch up. Burning the midnight oil, ja?' He tried to keep a straight face by not showing too much relief now that he knew from which direction the wind was blowing. So the lads had come to his rescue after all. He glanced across to the bar, I owe them one, he mused as he picked up his drink and held her expectant gaze.

'Ach ja, das paperwork, alles gut, finished. So, here we are again, a free evening once more. We should drink to that.' He waved his arm to catch Jacques's attention as he felt he needed a double Cognac after that mental mauling. As the barman acknowledged, the outstanding matter of the night before reared up in his conscience as his moment of weakness in the boiler house played large on his mind. 'Lilli, about the other night…'

'Franz, nein,' she said quietly, as she took his hand and pulled it to rest on her lap. 'I know Franz. Please not now, not here. It's neither the time nor the place. Besides, I'm a big girl now.' Nonplussed by her remark he put it down to female intuition as she seemed to know what he was about to say. But then he was glad that she had stopped him and what's more, she had already indicated that she had not breathed a word, especially to her chatterbox friend Yvonne.

Lilli felt his tension and knew what it was that he wanted to say as she too felt the same but then, she was not the guilty party and something like that would always keep for another day. There was, she felt a symbiosis that now existed between them and it had, as yet, only just started to bloom.

Still holding his hand she sensed he felt the same as they needed and enjoyed each other's company and, as far as she was concerned she did not want their blossoming relationship to wither on the vine. Not yet, anyway – not at this time, as her loneliness and sense of despair at the war and all the bad things that were happening had been assuaged by this man's companionship and the fulfilment of their recent tryst.

'You have some news for me?' The sudden sound of his voice startled her as her train of thought derailed.

'Ja, Franz,' she said, meeting his questioning gaze. 'Perhaps it's good news as I've been in touch with Köln and their lines of communication are now re-established. In fact the welfare contacted me. I have it here.'

With a final squeeze she released his hand and swivelling round reached into her coat pocket to hand him a slip of paper. 'They informed me that there is a priest who has now given them a list of names, and your wife's parents as parishioners were on that list. They sent me a second list of homeless people for that particular area around the cathedral.' Lilli pointed at the paper with a pink fingernail as she had underlined in pencil the name of Anna Wagner und Kind. 'They told me that this is a list of people that sheltered in his church on the night of the raid. It's mostly his parishioners but he realised later that he recognised her as from time to time she had attended Mass there with her parents. Anna Wagner is how he knew her when she was much younger – which is of course the family name of her deceased parents.'

She tapped the paper with her finger to emphasise the point. 'You see, Franz,' she continued, 'I instructed them to search for your name as Bauer, and your wife as Anna, and of course they could not link anybody in that parish as such. It's taken a little while to unravel but now it's all thanks to that observant priest.'

Franz shook his head in understanding and disbelief, as he read the teleprinted message. She had succeeded where he and others had miserably failed.

'And of course,' she went on, 'since they mentioned a child as well, it has to be your wife Anna and son, ja?'

Like Saul, on that fabled road to Damascus she witnessed the miraculous transformation in him as he read and re-read the note as the final pieces of the jigsaw fell into place. Gone were the anxiety and the uncertainty to be replaced with the knowledge that his wife was out there somewhere and she and the boy had had a narrow escape in an air raid so close to her parents' home. He realised they could have been killed. But most of all, thanks to Lilli his guiding angel, he had been given the hope of seeing them once more.

She met his appreciative gaze but for him it stayed longer than he intended as her full lips brought back memories of their moment of passion only hours before.

Try as he might, he could not exorcise this phantom, more so now, as he owed her an even greater debt of gratitude. He felt the urge to take her into his arms and kiss her in abandonment for everything, and even more. Words did not come easy for him as their relationship had taken a new twist as they were now lovers, regardless of the fact that Anna was somewhere back home and waiting in the wings.

'Lilli, how can I ever thank you, even if only part of this turns out to be correct?' he said. 'You have been an absolute angel to me and have once again given me hope. It's such a long shot that priest recognising her, when she only went there on odd occasions after we married. I know when she was growing up she attended catechism classes and all that, but that was a long time ago. Those priests must be drawing their pensions by now. Perhaps there were others who recognised her as her parents were well known in the community? I've been to the church a few times, when we visited,' he added. 'It's close to the cathedral and her mother usually prepares the flowers...' He left it at that, as that would no longer be the case.

He folded the message and stared vacantly across the floor to where some couples were dancing. Lilli saw his anguish and gently took his hand in hers.

'Franz, listen to me,' she said in a whisper. He turned towards her and she glimpsed a dewdrop glint of moisture in his gaze. 'It's over for them. They have had their lives and have left Anna as a witness to their love. You have to accept that and look to the future.' She squeezed his hand and sensed that he needed someone like her, to share the problem and give the solace that only a woman can give. Unselfishly she would help him, but deep down inside herself she knew she needed him too as it was still uppermost in her mind he had transformed her that night, from a bewildered maid into the realms of womanhood and the memory of that sensuous moment would stay with her for ever.

'Lilli, you're right, thank you once again for helping me. I'm sorry for messing up your evening with my problems again; it seems to be coming a habit.'

She smiled reassuringly as their eyes met and to her surprise he suddenly leant towards her and kissed her un-expectant cheek. Lilli swallowed hard as she felt her cheeks flush with embarrassment but a feeling of desire began to creep ever outwards from her breast. Franz felt pleased with himself to have thanked her in that way but he was only a man and never realised that Lilli, now a woman wanted more than just a peck.

'It's nice being able to help, we're a team, Ja?' she said, raising her glass to him. She wanted to say so much more but was afraid if she did, she might lose him. The irony was not lost on her that it was actually the business of his wife that was keeping them together and for the moment it would keep. With female intuition she knew that his wife was out there somewhere and she would lose him one day, however there was a war, people died and here in France she lived for the present. She was here with him and that for the moment was all that mattered.

'Some team,' he said with a chuckle. Feigning modesty she brushed the innuendo aside as the glow and passion from that night still lingered.

'So, you've been visiting?' She trailed the question.

'Ja, it was the Admiral today. You know how it is,' he said with the hint of a smile. She nodded, as she knew better than to talk freely in places like this but felt relieved that he had once more become his jovial and happy self. She indicated across the table to where her friend was chatting and laughing with Kurt.

'She always talks about him at the exchange, says she's in love. Couldn't tear herself away fast enough this evening – something about a special rendezvous. Seems to me she has one of those every night.'

'Sounds like a touch of the green-eyed monster to me,' replied Franz with a wink as she threw up her eyes in mock disgust.

'Ach, see if I care,' she said, trying to hide her true feelings. 'Them two, a rendezvous, they're just oiling the wheels for later. It's a bottle of Champagne, Napoleon's four-poster bed and a game of periscopes as she calls it.' I've touched a nerve, mused Franz as Lilli, now sipping her wine envied her friend's easy approach to life as she too imagined herself and Franz having a tête-à-tête in a sumptuous four-poster feather bed.

141

'It's alright, I know all about it,' he said, disturbing her train of thought. 'They might as well set up house and home there as even HQ have his room number. Rumour has it that they now deliver his sailing orders via a bell-hop and room service.'

Lilli smiled at his sense of humour and not unlike lovers they laughed at each other's jokes and were well at ease with their conversation.

'Hey, you two. What's going on?' called Kurt from across the table. 'Must be the wine. I think we'd better have the same as you're having.'

'I've had some better news,' said Franz. Yvonne, glancing at her friend had an intuition that something more than happy families was happening right there on her doorstep.

As the two men beamed at each other and chinked their glasses the two girls gave each other those knowing looks that only women can give and decipher. They shrugged their shoulders and smiled their secret smiles.

With the bottles dead and glasses empty, Kurt checked his watch. 'Eleven-thirty. I didn't realise it was that late. Sorry ladies, we have to go as we have an early start.' He rose from the table as Franz glanced at his watch and confirmed the late hour. He signalled with a nod at Lilli, who pushed her chair back and picked up her coat.

'Ah, non! It's early yet,' Yvonne exclaimed. Suddenly she had come alive as she rushed to her feet, leaving her chair to clatter to the floor behind her. She threw her arms round Kurt and fervently kissed him on both cheeks. Lilli and Franz looked on bemused, as Yvonne signalled to Jacques for more Cognac and pulled on Kurt's arm to sit him down again.

'I really have to go, mon petit chou, we have a lot of things to do and must get back to our boats.' Gently, he prised her hand away and as an afterthought added, 'there is a war on, you know.'

'Pouff!' came her fiery reply. 'La guerre, it can wait. Look at Franz and Lilli,' and indicated with a pout of her cherry red lips. 'They are so happy tonight, non?'

Her charcoal eyes glistened with intent and shone like diamonds as she took the glasses from Jacques and with an extra pout, handed Kurt his drink.

Others on nearby tables had noted the disturbance but Yvonne was not done yet. As Kurt downed his Cognac she took his arm and led him out to the empty dance floor. Like an unspoken request Andre came to life and struck up a Viennese waltz as Yvonne held sway on the floor. Kurt glanced across at Franz and with a submissive shrug resigned himself to her mood and to the lilting cadence of the waltz.

'She's a graceful dancer,' remarked Lilli with a side-glance at her man and offered her hand. 'Come Franz, shall we join them?' Franz froze and squirmed in his shoes. He hesitated as his conscience pricked him as he wondered what Anna would say. However Lilli's outstretched arm, engaging smile and loose summer dress melted his resolve, besides – he was happy for once. Self-consciously he checked his watch as Lilli stepped forward in triumph and took his hand.

'I have to get back, early start,' he stammered as she gently but firmly led him in the direction of the dance floor.

'Just this one dance with me, Franz,' Lilli pleaded in mock desperation. 'We'll have this dance and then you can take me back, I promise, ja?' He shrugged and nodded in submission. One dance couldn't hurt either way he mused, as he allowed himself to be led past the tables, occupied by some of his crew.

Reaching the dance floor, he took her in his arms as a boisterous and well-humoured chorus of catcalls, whistles and the soft chink of coins on glasses ensued from his crew. Franz nodded his acknowledgement and smiled somewhat contritely as, together they warmed to the lilting tempo of Strauss and his Danube waltz.

Seconds later, the chandelier lights flickered and suddenly the saloon was plunged into darkness as an air raid siren began its undulating wail. Muffled sounds of distant explosions drowned the dying wheeze of the accordion, as detonations shook the building.

Chapter Sixteen

STEPPE ENCOUNTER

Major Yuri Konstantin sat in the saddle and gazed across the wide expanse of the rolling steppe. The land was flat and featureless, except for the occasional hillock and wooded areas, with many abandoned isbas, gutted and derelict. In the distance, great woodlands flourished and rivers flowed but here, on the open steppe, the water was stagnant now the snows of winter had melted.

The harsh winter of 1943–44 had given way to an early spring and the weather had settled to clear skies and sunshine. Now, it was late April and the air was still. The scrub and birch trees had regained some of their foliage, but not a young leaf stirred as Mother Nature held her breath.

As the sun rose higher the mosquitoes swarmed, the air becoming thick with their brown bodies and the humming of a myriad wings. They rose in clouds from the marshland and settled on man and beast alike. It was the horses that suffered the most. In a feeding frenzy, mosquitoes clung like grapes from their eyes, nostrils and ears until, heavy and gorged, their swollen bodies dropped in ruby clusters to the steppe below. Patiently but calculating every second, Yuri and his men stood ranged and waited for the signal and the assault to begin.

As the sun continued to beat down, a shimmering haze developed across the flat terrain as distant trees floated and danced like spectres at play. For Yuri it added to the difficulty in making out the enemy lines one mile distant.

The Wehrmacht in its retreat had dug in once more and waited for the Soviet's next move which, under the directions of the 'farm boy diplomat', Major General Khrushchev commanded the three-mile length of the Soviet thrust. Khrushchev was under orders from Stalin to keep up the pressure on pockets of the retreating enemy as it would create vibrant headlines back in Moscow, at the same time allowing the Red Army to beat the Allies to the draw by the taking of Berlin.

Yuri swatted angrily as hordes of black flies diverted his attention as they buzzed and bit incessantly, the sound of their wings filling the air in a cosmic hum, the eternal music of the awakening steppe. Still his soldiers waited with their horses, infantry men and tanks, together with four hundred pieces of artillery that stood ranged, facing south at this juncture in the Soviet front line.

It was near the city of Voronezh and the river Don that the main thrust of the Red Army now found itself and intent on purging the Crimea Delta of the invading Hun. For Yuri, it had been a war of attrition since the time his house had been taken and his family shot and buried in a mass grave of lime and earth. He had followed in the wake of the retreating Wehrmacht, as he fought battles of escalating brutality against the field-grey menace for every inch of his homeland.

It was the German army which was now on the defensive and experiencing heavy losses of aircraft, mechanised armour and men. Having surrendered a quarter of a million men at Stalingrad, the Wehrmacht was now in full retreat and their onetime superiority in armour and weapons was now matched and countered by the Soviets. American and British aid via the ports of Murmansk and Archangel had bolstered the Soviet war machine and the local production of arms, tanks and munitions was once again achieved.

But there is a price for everything, as the toll in Russian lives was immense and the retreating Germans, together with their Cossack allies, destroyed the dwellings of peasants and farmers alike. It was a repeat of their earlier victories but set in reverse as, before the event of Stalingrad the advancing army had systematically torched houses and butchered their inhabitants with scant regard for the rules of war.

Treated like cattle, the Soviets were regarded as sub-humans by the misguided ideology of the invader and herded into prison camps and left to starve in appalling and inhumane conditions. Thousands of surrendering soldiers were given no quarter and shot to accompany the butchered peasantry in mass graves dug by their own hands.

Three years from the onset of Barbarossa and across the same Russian wasteland the two opposing armies were still locked in mortal combat. However the Wehrmacht's flood-tide of victory had long since passed as its ebb now exposed the quicksands of defeat.

With the sun at its zenith, it was still only the insect world that moved. Sand fleas now joined the feast and exercised vigorously to bite their human hosts, as the two armies faced each other and waited.

As expected, the order came from the Soviets as a red flag was raised along the Russian lines and three hundred T34s gunned their engines amidst a roaring crescendo and black clouds of lazy drifting exhausts. They now stood poised in battle formation, their engines thrumming and lending an undertone to all that was nature.

With the artillery behind and a rear-guard of a further one hundred tanks, four thousand infantrymen were ready to follow in their wake. A further two thousand were dug in along the three miles of zigzagged trenches and waited, with rifles and anti-tank guns at the ready for any counter attack. At the centre and on the flanks, Yuri had stationed several batteries of M-13 Katyusha rockets, the fearful *Stalin Organs* of the Russian Front.

For their part the Germans were well dug in. However, from their slit trenches they already knew they were, once again, outnumbered but had no alternative than to sit and wait for the inevitable assault. During the cover of night they had prepared a warm welcome for the *Ivans*, now so visibly on parade and were confident that they could hold their part of the front and rebuff the forthcoming attack. Heavy German machine gun nests were hidden by the many hillocks and clumps of high grass and flanking them in their slit trenches were the remnants of a company of the elite 2 Para. of the Witzig group which had command of the anti-tank Panzerfausts and lighter machine guns. On both flanks and in the centre was the armour, one hundred and fifty of the trusty Mk IV Panzers, along with fifty state-of-the-art Tigers with their armour-piercing projectiles and manned by highly-trained and fanatical Waffen SS crews. The artillery was left short, as it could muster only ninety 88mm guns, but this was a fault of Hitler's bunker strategy and misguided overzealous feedback.

It was the steady drone of aircraft that heralded the advent of attack. As the Russian Yak fighters passed overhead, Major Yuri gave the signal for his artillery to commence firing. Red signal flares rose into the sky, hung for brief seconds and slowly fell to earth as the barrage began. For thirty minutes the big guns were in action together with volley upon volley of rockets, their eerie wail blending with the sigh of descending artillery shells as they flew in a barrage of lethal metal towards the German lines.

The surrounding earth trembled as explosions mushroomed in and around the German trenches, killing and maiming as a hail of shrapnel scythed down any living thing that stood in its path. Again,

146

it was the horses that suffered the most, having no trenches to protect them. They stood in lines behind the tanks and died horribly, their piteous screams affecting their riders who, minutes before had cared for them. After the barrage came silence, a lull followed by the sounds of whistles and the waving of signal flags as the Red Army began to move. Yuri despatched fifty of his T34s into the salient together with platoons of infantrymen clinging like leeches to sides and turrets as they careered towards the German trenches. To his chagrin he looked-on as more aircraft appeared and flew over him and the German positions and carried on flying in a southerly direction only to disappear and fade into the distance. It had been expected for them to attack the German rear and the Panzers that lay beyond the tree line but something had gone horribly wrong. Without him knowing, the Soviet plan had been changed.

Exposed, his tanks were now at their most vulnerable, along with their human cargo that steadfastly clung to their sides. At two hundred yards from the Wehrmacht's trenches they began to machine gun all that lay in their path and commenced firing blind their 76mm rounds into the trees some six hundred yards distant.

Suddenly with a bright flash and a roar the earth erupted beneath them as a line of anti-tank mines hurled half their number skywards to land, broken and in flames. Heavy calibre machine guns now opened up to decimate the infantrymen still clinging to the remaining tanks and the solid shot of the armour-piercing projectiles of the Panzerfausts, blasted the remainder.

It was all over in minutes as fifty Soviet tanks lay blazing, with wounded men screaming their last, while German snipers targeted any soldier that moved. For Yuri it had been a calculated risk but without the promised air support he was at a disadvantage. However at the expense of five hundred men and some tanks he now knew the German front line positions and those of the anti-tank guns and expended mines. Perhaps his tanks had not been sacrificed in vain after all as they had torn a gap by triggering and breaching the anti-tank barrier.

Without hesitation, Yuri gave the signal as a second wave of one hundred and fifty tanks lurched forward in an open wedge at flank speed. From behind their lines, his artillery ranged in on the trenches and the Pak positions as a ninety-gun barrage of German 88mm shells screamed in reply. Although outgunned, the German rate of fire was far superior and, coupled with their heavier shells, the majority of the Russian artillery and some ammunition dumps were soon put out of action.

Minutes passed as the Russian fire faltered and the Germans gained the upper hand of the duel. In the trenches the German infantry kept their heads down and held their fire as the T34s closed the range, and at one hundred and twenty yards the Germans retaliated. Down went the camouflage as the remaining Pak commenced firing their 37mm solid shot projectiles piercing the Soviet T34s below their heavily armoured turrets and glacis plates. It halted them in their tracks as heavy calibre machine guns sputtered into life to cut down the infantrymen with their shouts of 'Urrah, Urrah!' running and advancing from behind.

Confused by the anti-tank guns, the T34s broke formation as one hundred Mk IV Panzers broke cover and joined the battle to engage the Soviet armour at three hundred yards. Once again outnumbered several Panzers were hit and went up in flames, however the German superior radio communications soon had the Soviet tanks confused and attacking blindly through the Panzers' smoke screens.

Under normal circumstances the short-barrelled 75mm guns of the Mk IVs would hardly be able to pierce a T34's turret; however, turning to regain their lines the Soviets exposed their vulnerable sides as tank after tank was destroyed. Some of the crews tried to escape the carnage, leaping and screaming in agony from their turrets with their battledress on fire but were mown down by the machine guns of the concealed gunners. Hundreds of the Soviet infantrymen threw their arms up in surrender, shouting 'Kammerad! Kammerad!' only to be cut down in a hail of unremitting fire from both tanks and en-trenched infantry.

Clearly Major Yuri had miscalculated the tenacity of the 2nd Parachute group and was now paying the price along with his lost aircraft cover. His one hundred and fifty tanks lay with the others, gutted and burning together with the loss of another eight hundred of his infantry. He had no option but to use what remained of his artillery to soften up the trenches and re-grouping Panzers, even as several hundred of his infantrymen lay wounded on the field.

As the artillery duel began once more, Yuri's attention was drawn to movement on the German flanks as two lines of camouflaged Panzers emerged from the trees and headed at speed towards his exposed flanks.

Once again the element of surprise was with the Germans as these Panzers were the thirty miles per hour, sixty-ton Tigers. They closed the range to three hundred yards and began to fire 88mm shells at the remaining T34s. The surrounding infantrymen scattered as their shielding armour was decimated, the tanks becoming white-hot burning shells as the eight-hundred rounds per minute Spandaus continued the carnage, cutting the artillery crews to ribbons.

The unchallenged executions continued until minutes later the returning aircraft lent a hand by strafing the German lines and artillery with cannon fire. Fortunately for the Germans the aircraft were low on fuel and ammunition and had to break off the engagement as soon as it began, but it had been enough.

The Germans had lost sixty-one dead and thirty severely wounded, leaving them unfit for battle and a burden for those that remained. Eighteen Mk IVs were rendered inoperative, either burning or stopped, and five pieces of artillery had been hit.

Yuri gazed through binoculars as the remnants of his attacking forces were able to escape back towards the second line of the Soviet defences, allowing the beleaguered Germans to re-group and to lick their wounds.

It had cost Yuri some two thousand lives, two hundred and thirty of his tanks and over half of his artillery, together with stores, munitions and many wounded.

Mother Russia was paying a high price for her freedom.

Chapter Seventeen

ROOTS

At three-forty in the morning, the faint sound of the all-clear siren permeated down from the world above as Helmut, on hearing its steady note nodded in grim satisfaction. He lit up and poured himself a cup of ersatz and saw that Willi was still asleep, being he would be on duty at six. Anna, too, was still resting and lay with her arm cradling her slumbering child.

An uneventful hour later, Helmut shook the corporal awake. Willi gave a good-natured grumble about the early hour, helped himself to the remains of the mashed ersatz and grimaced as he drained his mug. Deftly slinging his Mauser over his shoulder he quietly left the room. With his departure Helmut, in need of rest nimbly hot-bunked it, taking the corporal's place on the palliasse.

It was the sound of silence that disturbed her. Anna sat up with a start as she realised she had been asleep, but calmed herself as Eddi was still beside her and seeing the sleeping bulk of the sergeant, relaxed and checked her watch. 7:30 it indicated as she collected her thoughts. She urgently needed to wash and freshen up. Quietly she slipped off the bed and lit the paraffin stove to re-warm the pan of ersatz and planned her next move.

First and foremost she had to get away from this Gestapo lock-up and the threat of Gruber, with his HQ close by. She would see if any trains were running and in which direction as she now had options, but if possible she would head for home.

With breakfast on her mind she selected a slice of potato bread from her bag, poured herself a mug of the mashed wheat before making herself comfortable in Helmut's chair. She sat watching her sleeping child as she ate her Spartan meal and pondered the circumstances of her stupefying arrest at the hands of the SS.

'Guten morgen,' said a deep voice. 'Did you sleep well?' He startled her as she sat engrossed in her thoughts and turned to see Helmut putting on his jackboots.

'Ach Helmut, you made me jump. I thought you were asleep. I hope I did not disturb you?'

150

'Nein, I'm a light sleeper, anyway it's gone eight. It's time for me to check on what's left of the city. I'll make us some breakfast as Willi has brought some eggs and home-made bread.' He lit a cigarette and helped himself to the dregs in the pan before adding more of the same. Eddi by this time was awake and called out that he was hungry.

Helmut busied himself with boiling several eggs as Anna brushed her boy's hair and told him to be good and wait. Within minutes the sergeant had placed the eggs into his mess tin allowing Anna to nourish her hungry child.

'By the way Helmut, I would like to thank you both for your hospitality. But may I ask you a question, if you please?'

'That's alright, it's been a pleasure and we are glad to help, but what's on your mind?'

'Well that SS officer at Dortmund – he sent me here, along with Gruber from the Gestapo. Is that correct?'

'As far as I know, ja, that is correct, except that the Gestapo do the sending. He and Gruber had reason to believe that you are a spy for the British, even though you have a German husband. In any war, strange alliances are formed, hence the interrogation here at HQ.'

'Mmm,' Anna replied as she sipped her drink and weighed up her next question. 'So, that's all? You haven't heard anymore, or anything else?' She glanced over the rim of her mug for his reaction, having framed the question as casually as she could.

'On the face of it no,' he replied but had an inkling that Anna was about to say more – casually he lit another cigarette and waited.

'So they dragged me halfway across Germany, just because I showed concern about my husband and that stupid business with the English printed wrapper. Is that how they always operate?'

Helmut studied her face as he weighed up her question. He saw a mature woman, perhaps in her late twenties. Her lips were well-formed but plain, without any make-up, and her chestnut hair still retained some curls but needed attention. Even without make-up she was a pretty woman, of medium height with a full figure to match. She really did appeal to him.

'That's how they do it; it's their style of intimidation. You were lucky as you are the wife of a serving officer but they have no scruples. They could have kept you locked up and thrown away the key and no one would have known. That's how Germany is run today.' He beckoned towards her mug. 'Here Anna, have some more schwartzblut, it's just brewed. I'm sorry we have no sugar.'

She looked up at him with a frown as 'schwartzblut' was army slang for the ersatz. She'd heard it before, however some of the soldiers used a more derogatory term for the questionable liquid.

'It's fine and it will help to keep me slim, ja?' They both chuckled at the standing joke as most of Germany had been slim for the past few years.

Helmut continued as he stirred condensed milk into his drink. 'It was the SS officer at Dortmund that must have realised the absurdity of it all. He checked out your story and the Gestapo had no option but to release you. He sent an officer down the line who went to the church and found the priest, but by this time you were already on your way here. Gestapo HQ being a few blocks from here. They are a law unto themselves those boys, and you were lucky. They don't often release people as they did with you.'

Anna felt relieved to hear that as she thought they might dig further. But that seemed to be the end of the matter and she would soon be away from them.

'So, I have the SS Obersturm to thank, I'm afraid I was rather rude to him at the time, however it was Gruber that got to me. He's the devil himself.'

'That officer obviously played it by the book and has probably seen the light as to what these crazy Nazis have done to Germany. But then you're crazy too if you don't mind me saying.'

'I'm crazy?' Anna's brown eyes flashed with indignation.

'Well, I didn't mean to offend you,' went on Helmut, 'but you should never have asked such sensitive questions, especially in times like these. Then to write messages on scraps of paper; English chocolate paper at that, well that's a definite, nein, nein fräulein. They just had to pull you in.'

'Well, you must understand,' Anna replied, a confused smile playing on her lips. 'I was concerned about my husband. That's not a crime in my book and what's more, perhaps I was not thinking straight as I had just lost my parents in an air raid. But then I might also have been suffering from concussion after that landmine explosion.' Her ear still felt sore and it angered her. 'Oh, I'm fed up with it all, dear God, stop all this insanity and give us peace.'

Tears welled in her eyes to roll gently past her cheeks as Eddi seeing his mother's distress ran to her side. Helmut realising his folly, clenched his toes in his boots. He felt a heel for putting her under further stress. Moments later however, he was surprised as Anna leant towards him and touched his arm.

'I'm sorry, Helmut, 'I didn't mean to snap at you, as I know you meant well. You're right and I should have known better and thank you for all you have done for us.' Hugging Eddi, she kissed his hair as the sergeant pulled up a chair and sat across the table from her. 'I trust one day I can repay you,' she added, still toying with the boy's hair.

He met her candid gaze and saw the anguish in her eyes and nodded solemnly in understanding. He felt she needed someone to help her. Perhaps she felt as lonely as he did and she needed a man's companionship? But then, how could he be the one?

'Frau Anna,' he addressed her in earnest. 'I have something else to tell you, as I think you should know.' Their eyes met – hers wide and anxious, his, awkward and a sympathetic blue.

'That Gestapo man Gruber, he had got hold of something else. I heard him mention something about Poland and Krakow and your name…'

He paused as she had already closed her eyes and was shaking her head in disbelief. He decided that whatever it might be she needed time to absorb what he had just said and left his chair to light another cigarette. Anna gazed up at him, a gnawing fire in her heart and mind as from somewhere above, the legendary sword of Damocles hung by its solitary hair.

A noise on the stairs startled them both as the cellar door sprang open and corporal Willi, in typical barn-door style, entered the room.

Helmut was glad of the distraction. As for Anna, her mind reeled and floated in a sea of turmoil. With the mention of Poland, she felt the bottom had just dropped out of her life.

'It's really bad up there,' said Willi. 'High explosives and incendiaries. Several thousand must have died and half of the city is in ruins.' He gasped as he stopped for breath and waved his arm in a hefty sweep. 'Alles kaput.' He took a few paces and placed a small bag of coffee beans on the table, together with a tin of condensed milk. 'I got these from a bombed house. Its occupants won't need them anymore, not where they've gone.' He crossed himself at the thought and poured himself the last of the ersatz. 'We're assisting the Heimwehr in collecting the bodies and supplying them with transportation.'

He glanced at Helmut, who nodded for him to finish his unofficial report. 'It's the transportation,' he went on. 'We're reduced to horse-drawn wagons and hand carts as the petrol dump is finished, still burning. Alles kaput.' Angrily and without ceremony, he opened the tin with his bayonet and stirred a spoonful of the milky substance into his mug. Satisfied, he passed the remainder to Anna. 'For the boy, just mix it with warm water.'

She thanked him as he finished his drink with several noisy gulps, whilst Anna prepared the questionable milk for Eddi. Together they finished their breakfast and, from what Helmut had told her she just wanted to be gone from this place. Anna placed Eddi's empty mug on the table and stood to face them both.

'Well, gentlemen, I think it's time for me to be going. I shall only get in your way if I stay. Danke for all your kind hospitality.' She held out her hand and said her farewells and picking up her belongings placed them into her bag and let her son lead the way to the stairs.

'Auf Wiedersehen, perhaps one day when this is over, we'll meet again up there in the Hoffbräuhaus, if it's still standing.' They could only nod as the suddenness of her departure had caught them both by surprise, especially Helmut, as he liked her company. On reaching the door, Anna turned and with a questioning voice, echoed a woman's perpetual plea. 'Please, gentlemen, where's the bathroom?'

'Ja, Anna,' Helmut volunteered with a grin. 'It's further along from the Klosett you used, it's marked Waschraum. Only, I don't think there's any water. Go up the cellar steps and you will see a door on your left, it leads into the kitchens. There's a laundry and also a tub in there.' She nodded and smiled her thanks at his understanding of her situation.

'Once you come back out of that door,' he went on, 'turn left and go further along the passageway. That will lead you into the beer hall and out into the street.' He paused and with a parting smile added, 'so Anna, it's Auf Wiedersehen. Good luck with everything and be careful up there.'

She thanked him and was about to go but turned, came towards him and Willi and gave them both a peck on the cheek. It left them speechless and with Eddi in the lead they made their way up the dark and musty staircase.

'Looks like we've got the place to ourselves again,' said Willi as he began to clear the table. 'We'll have a glass of wine, make some real coffee and back to assist the home guard.'

'Sounds reasonable to me,' said Helmut. 'I'll come with you and see for myself, as I have to report back to the guardroom.'

Using the butt of his bayonet, he crushed the beans as Willi poured out two mugs of wine. Helmut extracted two cigarettes, lit them and handed one to his friend. With the coffee beans brewing, he thought about her and admonished himself for letting her slip away without a meaningful word of farewell, as he really had taken a shine to her but then, what was a man to do under the circumstances? Perhaps it was just an infatuation, the damsel in distress syndrome, he reflected?

With a shrug he dismissed the encounter as they sat down to their wine, smoked their cigarettes and debated the war and their own chances of survival?

Chapter Eighteen

QUESTIONS

Chairs and tables were scattered as the café's occupants rushed for the safety of its cellar. Franz pulled Lilli by the hand as he followed the chain of local girls, whose plaintive cries of 'Mon Dieu! Mon Dieu!' along with their click-clacking heels, was an aid to his blind navigation. Once on the stairs, he found the tubular handrail which, to his relief, speeded up everyone's descent as the Flak batteries opened up, along with the thunderous roar of low-flying aircraft. Further sounds of detonations now lent an air of urgency as matches were struck and lighters flickered, with the last of the barflies gaining the safety of the cellar. The yellow light of a candle flared briefly, but more were soon lit. Jacques stood on the last step of his cellar handing out advice and candles as thirty-five of his guests made themselves as comfortable as an air raid would allow. They took their places noisily, choosing packing crates, barrels and chairs and found several straw mattresses, musty and well-used from previous raids.

Franz found a large crate covered with a horse blanket and called for Kurt and Yvonne to join him. He leant back against the stone wall as Lilli beckoned and made room for her friend.

'Seems only light stuff tonight,' said Franz as he placed his candle into a recess of the wall.

'Sounds like fighter bombers to me,' agreed Kurt. 'Rockets and small bombs so far and our Flak. Maybe the big stuff will come soon enough. That being the case, we should be safe up this end of the town.' He pulled out his cigarette case and lit three smokes and handed them round. Lilli hitched her arm with Franz and contentedly leant her head on his shoulder.

'Perhaps they're after the barracks and your nice parade ground,' Kurt added with a chuckle. 'You know how it is with those Tommies. They've got this phobia and just can't stand us marching across Europe and goose-stepping at our Sunday parades.'

A few sailors within earshot joined in and laughed, which helped to ease the tension as everyone settled for the routine of yet another raid and a night in a cellar.

For Lilli it was different as she felt his warmth and heartbeat against her cheek and was reminded of the raid and events from that other night but in more congenial surroundings. It aroused in her a warm sensuous feeling, new but not alien, as it spread its warm tentacles in search of fulfilment. Inside herself she wanted him to embrace and kiss like that once more and to feel his hair and body against her. In that way she wanted him, just one more time and alone. She tried to reject it, to concentrate on the outside world, her work, explosions and the sudden death they brought but her aspect on all those things had changed, as she was not alone any more or afraid – like before. But the sensation returned and refused to be denied as it crept slowly, like a serpent, and ever downwards. She contained the feeling within herself as she put her feet up and snuggled against him and draped an arm across his waist, happily closing her eyes as the two men conversed in lowered tones.

She now felt contentment, even in an air-raid and a divine happiness which in all of her twenty-four years she had never experienced before. For her it was the happiness which one only read about in books but now was aware it existed. But the feeling was soon marred as the thought of Anna entered and clouded her mind. Perhaps they could share him, she mused. But what would she do if the situation were reversed? Yet, had she not already helped his wife by lifting his spirits, calming his tortured mind? Lilli lay there with dreamy eyes watching the flickering lights of the lambent flames and made herself a silent promise. She would only borrow him as long as it lasted, look after him and return him. Yes, that's it, she decided. Like borrowing a fountain pen, use it carefully and return it – perhaps with a little less ink. She settled for that and gave him an affectionate hug and he responded by placing a protective arm round her shoulders and running his fingers through her hair.

Detonations were now less frequent and only felt as ground vibrations rather than heard, except the timpani accompaniment of the Flak batteries whose response was still evident. By now many had dozed off while those that stayed the distance conversed in low tones. Girls giggled occasionally as they sat talking with the sailors who as air raid veterans had brought their drinks with them.

Lilli cast her mind back to them and their cheers and wolf whistles for their captain. They would now take her as his fräulein she reasoned, perhaps even his mistress. She turned the word over in her mind. No, I cannot be a mistress, aren't they supposed to be close by, near the unwitting wife? No, she reasoned, I'm his guardian angel and I will look after him for her. The cellar shook with the sound and force of an explosion. Franz shifted uneasily but Lilli did not mind as she was safe with him. It's true, she mused, in time one gets used to anything, even bombs and being a mistress.

'Sounds like a light raid,' said Kurt. 'No heavy stuff so far. It's been two hours now so it can't be the bunkers.'

'Guess you're right,' replied Franz. 'One of those Tall Boys is enough to shake the whole town.' His voice startled Lilli as it boomed in her ear and gave him a dreamy squeeze, snuggling once more against his chest. 'Could be a diversionary raid,' he continued. 'The Allies are up to something, as some of our Schnellbooten have reported a mass of activity along their south coast. They sank three of those Amerikaner landing craft and clobbered a few more, said they saw a long line of lorries along the coast. Then there's all this radio traffic to the Maquis from the BBC. It's all gobbledegook to our decoders, but the French resistance seems to act on it as they've been busy blowing up our railway lines and vehicle convoys. By the way,' he said gazing round the cellar. 'Where's your mademoiselle?'

'Over there, I think,' said Kurt. 'Ja, there she is with Jacques,' and indicated to the back of the cellar. 'Said she would get us a bottle of his special vintage, you know these air raids don't seem to bother her. Not like your sleeping beauty here,' he said as he glanced down at Lilli. 'She's used to the bombs, even stays in her house during some of the raids. Says they're not after her and it's all my fault – the war, the bombs and anything else that happens around here.'

They chuckled at that as it was true, as once the U-Booten arrived the bombers came too. They watched in amusement as Yvonne and the old barman were engrossed in animated conversation, now and again glancing in their direction until Jacques nodded in resignation and produced a bottle from a rack close by. They looked on in anticipation as Yvonne, with her bottle and provocative swaying hips weaved her way like a rugby forward past several reclining bodies and over to where they were sitting.

'Ah, c'est bon, you have a nice seat here, non?' she said with a winning smile and stooped to brush Kurt's cheek with a kiss. 'Here, this is from Jacques. It's one of his special vintages for two of his special customers.' And beamed passionately as she handed it to him.

'Merci mon petit chou,' he replied with a grin. 'Is this for now or later?'

'Certainement later, mon chéri,' she replied with a teasing pout. 'And of course there are no glasses down here – but listen, I think the guns have stopped. I think we can go now, non?' Even as she spoke the all-clear sounded with a steady and welcoming wail.

Slowly the cellar's occupants stirred as most of the youngsters were asleep, albeit with a helping hand from the bounteous god Bacchus. Excited voices, mostly from the local girls rippled through the candle-lit cellar as Jacques led the way back up the steps to his bar. Franz shook Lilli awake as her head was still lying on his arm.

'Come along, Lilli, it's over and I have to get back.' Dreamily she opened her eyes and greeted him with a contented smile.

'Ja, Herr Kapitän you must go back to your boat,' she replied with an accentuated Prussian accent. She lifted her head only to let it fall back as she pressed herself to him once more. 'Thank you for taking care of me,' she whispered. 'I had such a nice snooze,' and kissed his neck before prising herself into a standing position.

Lilli beamed down at him as she brushed the creases from his jacket and handed it to him. 'Here you are, Herr Kapitän. Good as new.' Franz stood as he took it back from her and they held each other's gaze in warm communion.

'Danke Lilli,' was all he could say as he felt his tortured heart beat fast against his chest. Self-consciously he dropped his gaze and gave the jacket a final shake and brush.

Lilli fixed her hair and leaning towards him whispered, 'Ready.'

Franz inhaled her perfume and with that one word was immediately drawn to another time and place. As he glanced back at her he saw her respond as her pink lips parted so invitingly in the candles' lambent flame. The memory of his lips on hers aroused his senses, as a burning desire crept into his loins. Suddenly the cellar became a cramped place and he needed to get away, to an open space as once more guilt needled his conscience.

Annoyed with himself, he took one of the candles and with a directive nod allowed the girls to make their way towards the stairs. As they followed and bringing up the rear Kurt tapped Franz on the shoulder and nodded in the direction of one of the crates they had used as a seat. The horse blanket had slipped to reveal, in bold stencilled letters the words WD-USA DEHYDRATED EGGS. Two candles were still burning in alcoves and as they peered around they saw several more of the same crates. Another close by was marked WD-USA TINNED BUTTER along with WD-SPAM.

'So that's his little game, smuggling supplies,' said Franz with a hint of suspicion in his voice.

'Smuggling be damned,' snarled Kurt. 'How the hell did he get hold of that lot? The last time I saw something like that was on a British freighter before I helped myself to a few tins and sinking the rust bucket.' Kurt took a second look around. 'Better inform the military police. What do you think?'

'Ach, nein, it's only a few crates, let him have them. They were probably washed up from that same old freighter of yours,' he added with a chuckle as he started up the stairs, indicating with his head for Kurt to forget it and follow him.

Back in the café an oil lamp was already lit. Only the hardy stalwarts remained waiting to be served as the local girls along with the music had disappeared. Yvonne and Lilli were saying their goodbyes as having decided it was reasonably safe to walk back, especially as Yvonne had invited Lilli to stay with her.

Yvonne rendered Kurt a volley of kisses, whilst Lilli gave her man a peck on the cheek. However, taking his hand and brushing his ear with her lips, whispered softly, 'Je t'aime.'

He stood speechless for the seconds it took his befuddled brain to come to terms with the reality of the situation as Lilli released his hand and with a saucy smile, turned and followed Yvonne to the door. Franz could only gaze after her and knew, deep down he felt the same, however for him it was a feeling he dare not mention.

The two commanders allowed themselves a nightcap and left the café, with Jacques waving a cursory 'Bonne nuit' in their direction. Once outside they saw the dying flames of buildings and workers clearing the streets of rubble. Further along a large building was burning and fire engines were still engaged in quenching the flames.

'Looks like the place we visited this afternoon,' said Franz. 'The Ministerium, isn't it?'

'Ja, I think it is,' replied Kurt. 'Must have been a rocket attack, as there's not much structural damage. Strange for them to waste their rockets on that place. They must have missed, as there's a fuel dump not too far behind it.'

They walked on, past houses that had also suffered hits, their occupants now standing in the road, homeless. Women and children stood and sobbed, their tears reflecting the flames and the ruddy dying glow of their homes as both friend and foe worked to assist in dousing the flames and consoling their erstwhile occupants.

'Not much we can do,' added Kurt disconsolately as he gazed and followed the flying embers, checking the limpid sky for friendly clouds. 'Reckon they'll be back for the fuel dump once they realise their mistake.'

'Ja, you could be right,' said Franz and glancing behind him added, 'we're in luck. Here comes our lift.' They stood in the road and flagged down an army transport heading down towards the docks and asked the driver about the raid. They were glad to hear the bunkers were not harmed and were even more surprised that neither were the docks.

***

Days went by as the two U-boats waited for the remainder of their stores. June was now upon them but it was a grey and dismal day as dark clouds threatened and the barometer was falling to herald the inclement weather to come.

Inside the Admin. Bunker the two captains held a joint meeting of their respective crews. As senior officer, Franz addressed the men:

'Gentlemen, I have been informed by Herr Himmler due to certain difficulties the expected supplies will now arrive in five days from now. I have been assured by General Feldmarschall Rommel in order to expedite matters the army will supply a special convoy escort for reasons that we already are well aware of, namely the Marquis – or, better said, the local bandits. Some of these have now been rounded up but those that escaped are being supplied by air from England. We are in possession of their plan "Vert" and "Rouge" that deals with immediate sabotage. Be alert and report anything suspicious and always stay in numbers when going into the town. Our guests in the meantime will not be staying onboard but will stay here in this bunker so we can enjoy the extra space until such time as we are ready to sail. Shore leave is granted to all off-watch personnel for both boats. Are there any questions?'

'Herr Kaleu'nt,' one of his mechanics piped up. 'Is there a chance of us calling in at Singapore?' A loud murmur arose as the man voiced the sentiments of others.

'As you know,' replied Franz, 'I cannot divulge any of this and ask all of you to keep tight-lipped when ashore. Our very existence depends on it. However you would all have guessed that with our guests and their origin we will be heading for the Far East.' Welcome murmurs arose from the respective crews. 'Anyway Shultze, why Singapore? What's so special besides the Raffles bar?' Jovial laughter and belly laughs turned to respectful silence as Franz raised an authoritative hand and nodded at the youngster to continue

'Herr Kaleu'nt, it's my wife, she's a local girl. I got married there in '43. We have a baby girl.' Immediately a hearty cheer went up as Jurgen called for silence.

'Congratulations Schultze,' said Franz with a grin. 'I will speak with Admiral Dönitz and see if we can divert to see the baby.' Again more cheers as Jurgen called them to attention and dismissed them. The men were marched back to their bunker as the officers and NCOs followed.

'This business with the stores,' said Kurt as they gained their bunker and walked to the end of the quay to watch another boat returning from its patrol. 'I heard that some of the supplies for us are being waylaid by the resistance. They shot up a goods train a few days ago, killed most of the soldiers and took their weapons. Machinery and torpedoes they blew up and left a crater sixty feet deep.

'Ja, I heard about it, Lilli mentioned it. Said the French girls working with her were getting edgy. They don't want to work with the Bosche anymore, is how she put it. It's the Maquis; they're beginning to flex their muscles as the Tommies are dropping more and more equipment to them.'

'Ja richtig,' agreed Kurt as Yvonne had warned him about her fellow countrymen plotting revenge. He lit up and handed one to Franz. 'Just look at this boat coming in, the crew I mean. They look washed-up, two years ago they would have been cheering with pennants flying and the boat dressed-overall with bunting but now not even a single kill to their credit. Look at them, they're lucky to be wearing their pants.' Together they acknowledged the commander with a cursory wave as he manoeuvred his boat into the adjacent pen.

'I tell you one thing,' continued Kurt. 'The sooner we get out of here the better. We deliver this fantastic bomb and rocket material and see what happens. I know we cannot go on like this much longer and I reckon that Dönitz knows it too.' He turned with a yawn. 'I'm off to my bunk to catch up on my beauty sleep. Say we meet up at seven tonight? Better make it on my boat, as that schwarzblut of yours gives me the cramps.'

'Jawohl, I'll see you at seven if nothing else crops up.' Tired from the previous night's ordeal, Franz made his way back to his submarine where dockyard workers were still hard at work modifying the boat.

It was mid-day as Jurgen, in the control room called out, 'Someone here to see you, Franz. I'm afraid it's rather urgent.'

'Jawohl, I'll be right there,' said Franz – busy with his new suit of charts and routing. 'Anyone we know?'

'Can't say, but he could be Gestapo.'

'*Gestapo!* What in the name of hell fire are they doing here? Tell them to wait.' He thought about Himmler and their recent meeting and linked it with that.

Minutes later, he was on deck where a tall and athletic-looking man in his early forties stood waiting. He wore a brown leather overcoat with a wide-brimmed hat to match. Franz judged him to be some sort of pugilist as his heavy build, pummelled ears and flattened nose seemed to fit that category. Up on the quay stood two armed men in black uniforms with machine pistols and steel helmets portraying the chevron insignia of the Waffen SS.

Franz's mind reeled as he assessed the situation. These guys mean business, he mused, as here were Hitler's henchmen at their best, or worst, whichever way one looked at it.

'Kapitän Franz Bauer?' The man addressed him and held out a hand the size of a dinner plate. Franz accepted the proffered greeting but his mind was racing as to why this pockmarked stooge of the SS had come to visit. 'Dolch, Rudolf Dolch, Herr Kapitän,' the man volunteered and as an afterthought added, 'Gestapo.' So, Jurgen had hit it on the nail, thought Franz as their eyes met. He noted the man's dilated pupils and the cloying smell of absinthe on his breath. Notwithstanding the man's viperous gaze remained locked on him as the two guards gazed down from the quay.

'Bitte, Herr Dolch, my cabin is at your disposal.' Franz indicated to the open hatch. 'I trust that none of my crew have been up to any mischief in town?' The Gestapo man eyed him suspiciously and allowed himself a wry smile, revealing a set of tobacco-stained teeth as he indicated to the soldiers at the gangway.

'Bitte, Herr Kapitän, they are your escort. I have orders to bring you to Gestapo headquarters immediately. Shall we go?' He said, indicating towards the gangway. Franz was struck dumb as here he was being arrested on his own boat. Alarm bells rang in his fuddled mind. It was he the Gestapo wanted, not any miscreant from his crew. But why?

'I cannot leave my command just like that, Herr Dolch, is there something that I should know?' With an exasperated intake of breath Dolch weighed up his opponent as patience was not his forte. Seeing his agitation Franz decided to use the official approach, as that would be the best way to deal with the police, secret or any other type. 'Herr Dolch, have you any papers or warrant, as both I and my vessel are under sailing orders.' Once again Dolch took a deep breath.

'Herr Kapitän, I don't know the answer to your question, I have my orders to escort you to Gestapo headquarters, immediately. Now, can we go before there is any unpleasantness?' Once more, he indicated towards the gangway with the sweep of a giant hand and glanced from Franz to the two chiselled-faced guards who stood eyeing events and took one marching step forward.

Franz weighed up the situation and realised he was caught between a rock and a hard place. He glanced up to his conning tower where Jurgen and other officers stood waiting on events. Admitting defeat he shrugged and nodded at Jurgen, as he had no choice but to see what they wanted. He would play it their way, as this was the rule in Hitler's jungle. Nobody messed with the Gestapo as even an admiral would not be exempt.

Jurgen arrived to find out what was happening, although he had already guessed after seeing the SS guards.

'Any idea what all this might be about, Herr Leutnant?' Franz demanded with a wink at his Number One.

Jurgen, pan-faced, answered dryly. 'Nein, Herr Kaleu'nt, I cannot recount any of our men having been involved with any misdemeanours ashore. A little too much wine, perhaps, or fraternising with the mademoiselles. But then, that in itself is not a crime – not in my book, anyway.'

Dolch's hands balled into fists as the two men glared at each other. Franz quickly stepped in between them. Jurgen knew that Dolch had no authority over him, as Dolch was only the messenger. It was Franz they were after and Franz they would get. Franz was grateful for the loyalty of his First Officer and his complete disregard of Dolch's status, but this was as far as he would let it go.

'Ja gut, Herr Leutnant, that's all I wanted to know. I shall be leaving the boat with Herr Dolch here, so will ask you to take charge until I return.' Jurgen nodded as Franz turned to face Dolch. 'I will just secure my cabin Herr Dolch, kindly wait here.'

Without waiting for Dolch's reply, Franz left him in the pleasant company of his FO. He returned minutes later to see them both still glaring at each other, like prize fighters waiting for an imaginary bell. Jurgen's temper was only held in check by the presence of the guards and their Schmeisser machine pistols slung from the shoulder.

'So, Herr Dolch,' said Franz, 'let's go,' and indicated for the man to lead the way up the gangway.

'Nein,' said Dolch, 'I will follow you Herr Kapitän.' Once off the boat the guards clicked their heels and saluted Franz as he stepped onto the quay and smartly fell in behind him as they made their way out of the bunker.

***

The Mercedes curved smoothly into the gravelled driveway of the Gestapo building. Red Nazi banners flew from its portal, with their black swastika emblems portraying what might lurk within as uniformed SS men stood guard with snub-nosed Schmeissers slung from their shoulders.

As the car slowed, Dolch leapt from its running board and opened the door at the same time shouting orders at the guards. Franz sat bemused until stung into action by the gruff stentorian bawls of his escort.

'Raus, Herr Kapitän, Mach schnell, raus!' The escort followed as Franz, with Dolch leading, was led into the building and down a marble corridor, echoing hollow – to the jackbooted strides of his guards. They swept into a dimly-lit room, where two Gestapo officers were seated behind a large oak desk lit by a solitary green-shaded table lamp.

'Kapitän Franz Bauer, Herr Oberst,' said Dolch as he methodically stood to attention.

With deliberate scepticism, the two men eyed their visitor as Franz politely removed his cap and stood at ease, returning their hostile gaze.

'Please be seated,' a voice rang out from the desk. Dolch immediately sprang into action and moved a plush Louis XVI chair from the bay window to a position in front of the desk. Franz nodded in appreciation and sat down to face the two men, placing his cap onto his lap as he waited for all to be revealed. He was offered a cigarette and a light by none other than Dolch, who had positioned himself several paces between Franz and the door. He took the proffered cigarette and noted the ashtray on the desk already contained several stubs, these being of varying length. Obviously, I'm not the first customer he mused as with a determined set jaw he waited for all to be revealed.

A side door opened and a tall, thirty-something Gestapo officer appeared, together with an older Oberstleutnant of the SS who carried a bundle of files. They cast a discriminative eye at the room's occupants and quickly seated themselves at one end of the desk.

A pregnant silence filled the room as the Oberstleutnant shuffled his papers and commenced the proceedings by clearing his throat and casting a steely eye at Franz. Not to be intimidated, Franz returned the calculating stare and nonchalantly leant forward to stub out his half-finished cigarette. Respectfully and in true naval fashion he folded his arms, sat back and waited.

'Kapitän Bauer,' the SS officer addressed him in a clipped Prussian tone. 'My name is Müller and I am here, together with my officers, to ask you a few questions. Have you any idea why we have brought you here?' Müller stared menacingly as he let his words penetrate and removed his cap to reveal a full head of grey, closely-cropped hair. It was cropped with military precision, neat and flat at the top to a height of one centimetre which accentuated his bullish features and square Pomeranian head.

'Nein, Herr Oberst. Perhaps you would be so kind as to enlighten me?' Franz replied, holding the man's gaze. However the man's cap distracted him as it lay on the desk with its silver death's head emblem facing in his direction, to taunt him with its vacuous grin.

'Then I will help you,' said Müller, as he glanced at the documents before him. 'You have a fräulein here, ja?'

Franz swallowed hard as all eyes were riveted on him. He detected their glee, knowing they had driven the first nail into his coffin. His mind was racing with thoughts of Lilli and any connection she might have with the likes of Müller and the Gestapo. Had she reported him? Was she an agent? He sat motionless and weighed up the question. It was such an innocent question, a Ja, or Nein answer, but he felt exposed and vulnerable before the close scrutiny of such interrogators as these.

It was the Gestapo man on his right that broke the silence.

'Herr Kapitän,' he said quietly, but with a threatening tone. 'We are waiting. Kindly answer the question.'

Franz kept his nerve and addressed Müller. 'But of course, I know several ladies from the town. Is that a reason to arrest me?' He relaxed as he thought about the stupidity of bringing him here to answer such petty questions. He met their individual hawk-eyed stares with difficulty as, cunningly, the lampshade was set at a refined angle for the light to just dazzle and interfere with his line of sight. It made it difficult to see them properly. 'Gentlemen,' he continued, 'we could all save each other a lot of time if you came to the point as I have to return to my boat. You cannot hold me like this as my vessel is under sailing orders.'

In a flash the second Gestapo man on his right sprang to his feet and with a bony fist banged on the desk, causing the ashtray to bounce and fly off the desk and land at Franz's feet.

'*Herr Kapitän*,' he bawled, '*we will ask the questions here and you will answer them.*' He leant forward, supporting his bulky frame on outstretched arms and balled fists. Franz met his demented gaze as the policeman jutted his jaw and was disturbed to see the man's veins stick out from his neck, all red and purple, like rain-fed worms.

'Answer the question, Kapitän Bauer,' chimed a soft Austrian voice on his left. 'We are waiting and like you, we too are busy.' Franz noted that it was the voice of the tall Gestapo man that had entered with Müller. The carrion comes from all over the Reich, he mused.

His menacing outburst having had no effect, the man on his right sat as Franz pulled out his cigarette case and lit up. He realised that he had to stay cool, calm and collected as the whole thing was a farce but they were after something and Lilli had been mentioned, but as yet, not by name. He would play it like a depth charge attack – play for time, dodge and weave and run silent, but get distance between himself and the hunter. Needing an ashtray he picked it off the floor and placed it back on the desk and addressed Müller.

'I cannot see how this can help but I do know a fräulein by the name of Lilli. I'm afraid I don't know her family name, I never asked.' He gazed at Müller and the others in turn but they sat motionless, disdain written large upon their questioning features. Müller glanced at the document and continued without raising his head.

'Kapitän Bauer, did you at any time inform your young lady, this Lilli person, about your movements or the movements of others, or even about your next mission? Did you say anything at all like that to her?'

Again silence filled the room, as four pairs of questioning eyes and suspicious minds were directed at him and, once again, waited for an answer. Franz clenched his toes as the light and the questions irritated him and tried to think of his next answer. It dawned on him matters would get serious if he did not convince them, here and now, that theirs was purely a platonic friendship, so to speak. They would have to guess the rest or draw their own conclusions, as nobody knew their secret – unless she had told one of her friends. However, this, for the moment was not in question.

'Herr Oberst, as you are already aware of my friendship with fräulein Lilli, all that I can add is that I did have a drink in her company, on several occasions. During one of those occasions I was involved in an air raid, where I escorted her to her compound by the parade ground.' He stubbed out his cigarette as he gave his next answer some thought. 'With regard to my mission I have never divulged this to anyone, not even to my crew. That goes for any mission, past or present. However, it's already an open secret that we would be going to the east, as you yourself are undoubtedly aware that I have two Japanese guests on my boat.' He glanced at them now as individuals, one by one and faced Müller again. 'I have never spoken to anyone about my movements, Herr Oberst, and that is probably why I am still alive today.' Franz felt good with that answer, until the man to his right cut in.

'She has a friend, ja?' came the probing Austrian voice. Franz was once more thrown back onto the defensive ropes, as clearly these professionals were not gulled by his answer.

'Ja, but of course, she has many friends.' His thoughts immediately turned to Kurt and Yvonne – did these people know about his friend and was it perhaps them they were after? Oberstgruppenführer Müller of the SS division Gruppe Deutschland drummed his fingers on the desk with impatience as this was dragging on too much for his liking. This navy smart arsch was playing a cat and mouse game with him and they all knew it.

'Kapitän Bauer,' said Müller in a firm yet friendly tone. 'We are aware that you would like to get back to your boat. If you have nothing to hide just answer our questions, because it is important and will affect the security of the Reich. If you choose not to co-operate with us we would have no other option than to interro… to question you further but at another place. Now is that clear?' He paused to let his words register and was satisfied as he witnessed Franz's unease. 'We know about your friends, all of them, so please stop this nonsense. I will ask you for the last time to answer our questions. Names, if you please, Herr Kapitän?'

Müller sat back and shuffled his papers in agitation and met his gaze. Franz cleared his throat; he needed time to think as he brushed ash from his uniform. Shrugging in submission he decided to let them know what he knew as it was nothing that could compromise the security of the Reich.

'Herr Oberst,' he spoke quietly to the effect that it made them all lean forward, to catch his every word. The ploy seemed to work, he was playing their game and it would give him an edge, a minor battle won, he mused and continued, 'I realise that you are doing your duty here in the same way that I carry out mine at sea.' He paused. They listened intently, but he could see that cunning and suspicion was written large on their features, their inherent trademark. His placid tone had also taken some of the sting from the interrogation as he continued, 'As you are aware from my naval records I am a married man with a son. Because fräulein Lilli works at the exchange, I requested her to try and get word to my family. Because she carried out this compassionate favour,' he continued, 'for that is what it was, I invited her for a drink at our local café, along with her friends and other officers. That, Herr Oberst, is all I can tell you.' Franz eyed each one in turn, then pulled out his cigarette case and waited for their response.

'So, Herr Kapitän,' he replied in dulcet tones, 'that is better. We seem to be getting somewhere. Now the names of all of your friends at the café, ja?' Crunch time again, mused Franz. The old goat is hanging onto my shirt tails. However, he reasoned, they must know all of the names already. Once again, he shrugged it off, realising that these people were not going to be denied their pound of flesh.

'Well, I suppose Lilli's closest friend would be Yvonne. She works with her at the exchange.' He felt a heel, and thought that all was needed now was for them to offer him the thirty pieces of silver. Once more a shuffling of feet and several grunts of satisfaction from his interrogators. 'She's French and a good friend of us Germans.' But even with that statement he felt the betrayal was complete.

'This French fräulein,' said the Austrian, tapping his notepad with a bony finger. 'She is very popular, ja?' He glanced at him over the top of the lamp as Franz noted the weasel glint of his triumph. 'So, she has many friends. Perhaps we could have their names?' He sat back and watched as Franz stubbed out his half-finished cigarette.

'Well, I believe you already know Kapitän Kurt Oblitz, just as you seem to know about the girls. We're old shipmates from the pre-war days, so we meet up here on our boats and make up a foursome at the café.'

'Ja, we know about Kapitän Oblitz,' said the Gestapo man on his right. 'He has many French friends. We need their names, the French girls too.'

So that was it! he mused. Why didn't they say? Of course it had to be Kurt they were after, probably for fraternising a little too amorously with the locals. And the bar girls, they would know them too. With the proverbial cat out of the bag, he could let them have their names.

'Of course Yvonne has friends. She's French and she lives here,' replied Franz with a sweep of his hand 'As for Oblitz, I cannot say. We meet socially at the café and we just talk about old times. Perhaps you should ask him yourself,' Franz replied with a hint of sarcasm and returning Müller's bullying stare.

'Perhaps we will, Herr Kapitän. Perhaps we will,' said Müller in a slow and menacing tone.

'Herr Obergruppenführer,' said Franz in exasperation. 'I have listened and answered your questions. To the best of my knowledge the ladies are only acquaintances who, but for the war, I would never have met. If you want names, well there's Mimi, Lulu, Yvette and Jacqueline to name but a few. Then Andre the old accordion player, Jacques the barman, and Monsieur FiFi the queer cook, so what else can I tell you?' They sat in stony silence as he squinted against the light. Sensing victory he took the initiative. 'Then if you have no further questions I would like to be released and return to my boat. I have a war to fight and perhaps win it for us all.' He fished in his uniform jacket pocket for his cigarettes and lit up and blew the smoke defiantly at the Gestapo men to his right.

Müller once again re-shuffled his papers and glanced at this troublesome sailor who had said a lot but told him nothing, or rather that which he already knew. Glancing once again at the file he rose from the desk and turning his back on Franz made his way towards a hand-painted portrait of Hitler. He stopped in front of the picture in its gilt frame and with hands clasped firmly behind his back, began tapping his boot in annoyance on the polished parquet floor.

Müller, still gazing at the picture admitted defeat as, without turning and in his clipped Prussian manner, spat out the words for Franz's release. 'That will be all, Herr Kapitän. Guten tag, Heil Hitler.'

Seething with anger at the man's impertinence, Franz leapt to his feet and made for the door. Dolch, ever alert and showing due courtesy, was already holding it open.

Chapter Nineteen

COMMIT TO THE DEEP

I-59 moved mainly by night. Having left mainland Japan in her wake the ocean giant passed through the East China Sea leaving the chain of the Ryukyu Islands to port.

Itachi made his way towards the relative safety of the Formosa Strait. During daylight hours he would set *I-59* on the seabed, safe from the eagle eyes of prowling American patrols. In deeper water however, he had no choice than to keep his boat moving, but then only at slow speed in order to save his batteries and to maintain control of depth and steerage.

He had one advantage inasmuch that he had sailed these waters since the outbreak of the Sino-Japanese war and knew the location of the many uncharted reefs and sandbanks which had claimed ships and the lives of their crews throughout the ages. Shipwrecks from this latest conflict now littered the tropical islands and shoals of the Eastern seas and shallows of the North Pacific Ocean. They lay abandoned, beached and derelict, resting their rusting frames on the white coral sand.

For Itachi however these very same hulks served him well as nine days later he approached the Pescadore Islands to the west of Formosa. In an easy and well-practised manoeuvre he nosed his submarine alongside the stern of an old freighter that had been gutted by fire and touched ground in the shallows of the uninhabited island. As he lay in the wreck's shadow it allowed him to take stock and use his radio to communicate with Tokyo and to scan the sea and skies for hostile ships and aircraft.

With the three hundred foot bulk of the wreck as a decoy it would be impossible for any Radar to target him, even the latest American short-pulsed sets would not be able to decipher the fat 'blip' that painted itself on their screens. It was from this vantage point that Itachi evaded the searching fingers of the electronic beams as his engineers carried out their maintenance.

The off-watch crew went fishing with bamboo spears while others swam leisurely around their boat. As his lookouts scanned the sky, Itachi walked his deck and longed for the moment when he too would have the innovative German weapons and anti-Radar devices.

He was interrupted from his thoughts as lookouts shouted a warning and pointed towards the eastern sky. He raised his glasses and observed as the specks of aircraft flew towards the north. He looked-on with dismay and anger as the American planes winged their way in the direction of his homeland and that of its southernmost islands. Their fighter escorts went unchallenged as he knew only too well his country lacked the experienced pilots to fight the planes that remained serviceable but even that paled into insignificance, since the remaining aircraft carriers were not in fighting condition to launch them. Takayuki, on hearing the commotion came on deck as Itachi pointing, handed him the glasses.

'Looks like American fighter bombers to me,' said Itachi with conviction.

'Avengers, I guess,' replied Takayuki. 'Better keep our heads down.' He peered through the lenses at the rapidly disappearing aircraft and handed them back with a contemptuous snort. 'Looks like they're after coastal shipping,' he added. 'Our supplies come down past Formosa.'

'Hai,' agreed Itachi. 'I'm sure the pilots saw us down here – the wrecks, I mean. They're like a landmark. Wonder what they'd have done if they'd known about us?'

'Looks like your idea is a good one,' said Takayuki as they watched the men returning with several sticks of skewered fish. 'What bothers me is where those aircraft came from. They must be off a carrier?'

'Well for the moment I don't wish to find out,' said Itachi as he watched the last of the fishermen return.

The two men remained on deck and marvelled as they observed the full glory of the setting sun. The heavenly body became a shimmering fireball as the rotating Earth rose to meet it, reflecting its crimson fire in the torpid waters of that eastern sea as behind them it lent an embellishing touch to the old freighter's rusting plates.

They watched in silence, spellbound at nature's grand finale, the end of her day as the glowing fireball kissed the western horizon and in firmamental glory slowly sank from view. With the rapid onset of the tropical night it was the signal for their time to leave their opportune sanctuary with its rusting hulks and fringe of leaning palms.

Regaining his bridge Itachi gave orders to clutch in the motors just as the boat's signalman came on the tower and handed him a message. He scanned its contents and with a satisfied grunt handed the paper to Takayuki. The lieutenant read the message as Itachi told him to make an announcement to the crew. Eagerly Takayuki flipped the switch of the intercom as an electrostatic hum coursed throughout the boat.

'Attention all ship's company; this is the First Officer speaking. Our German allies have launched their first salvoes of new weapons on the British Empire. As of yesterday, the 13th of June the first V-1 rocket bombs targeted London.' From the depths of the submarine, a rousing cheer was to be heard as excited voices enquired for more news.

'Sounds like our round-eyed friends are keeping to their word,' said Takayuki as he glanced with satisfaction at the teleprinted text and handing it back to the signalman.

'Hai, in that case we had better be there to meet them,' said Itachi and gave orders for slow speed astern.

With electric motors humming in unison, the metallic leviathan gave a shudder as *I-59* began to move. With the added buoyancy from her venting tanks the submarine lifted clear of the clutching sand to return, once again, to her natural element. Now with the mantle of night to conceal them Itachi turned his boat and nosed his way out of the shallows and set himself on a southerly course in the direction of the Luzon Strait and the northern Philippines. *I-59* cruised at twelve knots under a light blanket of cloud as five men and the OOW kept watch through wide-lensed night glasses.

For Itachi, the cloud cover was a blessing as it would be difficult to spot him from the air. With instructions to the duty officer for him to be called should anything be sighted he left the bridge for the sanctuary of his cabin. Sailing submerged by day and surfaced at night, good progress was made and the days passed uneventfully but the friendly clouds had thinned as distant cumulous mountains were a reminder of the monsoon that was soon to come. Days later Itachi stood with the lookouts on his bridge as his boat entered the Straits of Luzon. He would be safe here he reasoned, as the northern islands were still in Japanese hands, but was wary of prowling American submarines and reconnaissance aircraft.

On 19 June there came a change to his sailing orders as the commander-in-chief of the Japanese combined fleet; Admiral Soemutoyoda had transmitted new orders. *I-59* had been expected to rendezvous with the two U-boats to the west of the Malacca

Strait but this was before American B24s and 29s had the island of Singapore in their bombsights.

With the Japanese warlords withholding the news of the advancing British and American forces, Itachi and his officers were misinformed and now blind to the reality of events. Events that were rapidly tipping the balance against Japan's war machine. With his new orders Itachi scanned the skies and it seemed to him he would see more and more of the Americans and not a Zero in sight.

By late afternoon *I-59*, still heading south had made good progress and was now twelve hundred miles from her Kure base. Itachi gauged the weather as the clouds had thinned, revealing the late afternoon sun. Turning to Takayuki he indicated at the sky.

'We'll dive the boat, I don't like the look of those drifting cotton wool blankets.'

'Hai, I will give the order.'

The lookouts left the bridge as over the address system, Takayuki gave the command to dive the boat and left the bridge for his diving station. Seconds later the sudden roar of engines made Itachi freeze as in an instant he realised he had been caught, still surfaced by hostile aircraft. Two twin-boomed aircraft screamed at him from converging directions. With cannons blazing and firing rockets they levelled out over the water. One rocket found its mark and exploded close to the deck gun, instantly shredding it into an item of scrap metal as the unfortunate gunners were still on deck and about to leave for their dive stations.

Not to be thwarted, the anti-aircraft gunners scrambled to return to their gun and opened up with twin 25mm cannons. The attacking aircraft jinked their way clear and banking in a wide circle once more made for the surfaced boat. Itachi ordered full speed and turned his boat to meet them as they re-grouped off his starboard bow. Now and for first time Itachi experienced the formidable fire power of the Lightning P38 fighter bomber. He was about to crash dive the boat but knew in those vital seconds, as his hull floundered on the surface, he would be at their mercy.

Long seconds passed as time was lost in assessing the damage but luck was on his side as both aircraft had taken a wide turn and were not as organised in their second approach as before. It would be an equal match, he reasoned, as surprise was no longer an item and his second gun-crew now at their station opened up with quadruple cannons.

'*Steer 275!*' screamed Itachi into the bridge communications. Moments later, with the boat turning rapidly towards the west the rapid firing cannons spat smoke and flame as their explosive shells and tracer streaked at the incoming aircraft.

With grim satisfaction Itachi watched as the leading P38 suddenly blossomed orange and a wing, like a wind-blown leaf in autumn, tore away. From the corner of his vision he saw a parachute, it seemed to partially open as at the same instant the second aircraft pressed home its attack. Only two rockets were fired but once again, *I-59* was hit. A part of the stern outer casing was torn open and oil was soon spreading over a large area of the surrounding sea.

In anger and desperation Itachi gripped the conning tower rail letting his binoculars drop and hang loosely from his neck. His knuckles showed white, as still gripping the rail he cursed the planes and the downed pilot now floating only half a cable's length from his bow. He looked-on angrily as the remaining aircraft circled him from a distance and seconds later headed away in an easterly direction towards the Pacific.

He ordered slow speed and damage reports but noted with misgiving that the boat was scribing a large circle. Reports of a jammed rudder were now being made as the damage control party was already checking the damage on deck. Several seamen dealt with the fallen gunners as they placed three bodies into hammocks and weighted them down with shells from their gun. In final salute they lowered them down the casing and committed them to the deep. Itachi looked on grimly and checked his watch.

'Four thirty-five,' he murmured and gauged the elevation of the sun as the damage control team began to cut away the tortured metal. Takayuki was summoned to the bridge, along with Mori, the engineering officer.

'Konnichiwa,' said Mori with a slight and courteous bow. 'We have to check the rudder,' and nodded to emphasise the point. 'The dive planes are functional but the rudder is jammed at twelve degrees to port.'

Mori stood motionless as sweat glistened on his forehead and streaks of black oil had made their indelible mark on his once white overalls. He stood a head size lower than his captain but his bearing indicated that of a martial artist. Itachi nodded and once more checked his watch.

'It's a long time before dark. Can we dive, Mori?'

'Hai, captain,' replied Mori, nodding quickly to emphasise the point. 'We have a leak on the port after tank but I have already transferred most of the fuel. We can flood that tank and if necessary, de-ballast it later.'

'Yoroshii, we dive.' Itachi nodded to his FO, who immediately activated the diving alarm as the damage control team scrambled off the deck and to their diving stations. 'We dive, even if we have to go in ever decreasing circles.'

Takayuki grinned at the pun as the water rose rapidly and closed over the hull. Itachi allowed himself a last glance towards the eastern horizon before the pressure-resistant hatch closed with a dull thud just inches above him. *I-59* levelled out at sixty feet and with only the port motor running to offset the turning motion of the jammed rudder Itachi kept his boat at depth. However, he was still unable to steer except in a large circle and occasionally used the starboard motor in reverse to steady the boat.

Minutes later came the report that all internal checks for leaks had proved satisfactory which meant the submarine was only superficially damaged after all. With the hull's integrity checks completed, Itachi raised his secondary periscope which was able to be elevated at a greater angle and scan the sky for aircraft. Satisfied other aircraft had not been summoned he swept the ocean in azimuth for tell-tale signs of funnel smoke but fortunately, the sea was empty.

He lowered the scope, and moved across to raise his main periscope for a more detailed scan of the ocean. Through its wide lens he once more scanned the surface but still saw no evidence of any surface craft. Several pieces of wreckage from the downed aircraft were sighted but with daylight rapidly fading he could not find any trace of the downed pilot.

As soon as darkness fell Itachi ordered *I-59* to surface. Tanks were blown as the submarine emerged and wallowed in the swell like a wounded whale. With the sea still cascading from the tower the hatch was flung open and lookouts scrambled with night glasses to their stations. Rapidly they scanned the sea for any signs of movement and listening intently for the noise of aircraft as the AA gun crews followed and took up their stations. Except for the lapping of the waves and the throb of the diesel exhausts, there was no other sound. They were alone on a hostile sea with major repairs to effect and only the mantel of the night to shield them.

With several shouts and frantic indications from the main deck the AA gunners fired several rounds as Itachi rushed to his bridge. His officer of the watch pointed and with his eyes adjusting to the night, he saw it too. There he was, the American airman waving a hand as the gunners again fired in his direction. Itachi leapt onto the gun sponson, shouting *'Iie, Iie!* and grabbing a gunner struck him a blow to the head as the OOW called for his captain to stop.

'Iie, Same! Same!' yelled the officer as Itachi, somewhat confused suddenly grasped the situation as he saw the tell-tale phosphorescent trail along with the triangular fin now circling the unfortunate airman. The sound of running boots on the casing drew his attention as his four remaining deck gunners rushed to the pilot's assistance. Forming a human chain down the steep and slippery side of the hull they pulled the man clear of the water and laid him on deck.

Silence followed as one man ran to the bridge. Still drenched from the rescue he bowed to his captain and with wide peasant eyes, explained the man had lost a lower limb. It was only his Mae West that had kept him afloat as the shark had taken away his leg. The gunner went on to say the man was still alive as there was a pulse to be felt at his neck. Itachi called for the doctor to examine the airman but in the meantime gave orders for the submarine to be ballasted down by the head.

Twenty minutes later the stern section of *I-59* was several feet clear of the water and the damaged rudder clearly visible. Oxyacetylene 'gas axes' were rigged to burn away the twisted metal from the outer casing and rudder. Welders were set to work to fabricate and replace a damaged section of the rudder assembly and by midnight the work had been completed. There now remained the matter of the American airman who, after having been treated with bandages and morphine, was sinking fast. Gripping the doctor's arm he whispered 'Thanks Tojo,' before he breathed his last. Itachi gave orders for his dog tags to be removed along with his life jacket. A shell from the deck gun was to be strapped to the remaining leg and his body returned to the sea.

With the aid of a line the remains of the airman were lowered down the submarine's side. Once released, the corpse sank rapidly to join the unfortunate deck gunners in the cradle of the deep.

Hours later, with repairs effected and trim regained, *I-59* gathered speed and proceeded surfaced on her southerly course towards the west coast of the Philippines and its northern island of Luzon.

Chapter Twenty

TRAPPED

Anna and Eddi reached the top of the stairs and found themselves in the unlit passageway of the beer hall's service department. Doors led off to various rooms but even in the dim light that filtered through from a distant window, Anna made out the door that Helmut had mentioned. She entered and found herself in a lobby where another three doors were clearly marked with enamelled signs in Gothic script. Immediately in front was a door marked Küche, while to her left the sign read Klosett. The door on her right was ajar and here she saw the laundry facilities of the establishment.

'Eddi, be a good boy and wait for me here,' said Anna as she placed her bag down beside him and utilised the facilities behind the door marked Klosett. On emerging it was his turn and with nature relieved they went through the open door marked Waschraum.

'Now, my little boy, it's bath time,' she cooed. He shrank back with a grizzled face on seeing the wash-tub and what his mother had in mind. 'First we'll have a nice wash and afterwards we can go for a walk in the sunshine, ja, mein kind?'

He nodded in benign agreement but was not too sure that he meant it. Anna closed the door and seeing its lock was broken used a nearby chair to prop under the handle, wedging and jamming it closed. Just like in the movies she mused and stepped back to admire her handiwork; reasoning it would suffice as the place was, after all empty except for her two soldier friends down the stairs.

Glancing round she saw she had the barest of essentials as everything was a throwback from a by-gone age and suffered from disuse.

On one wall two taps protruded and close by stood a wooden wash trough with sloping sides. It was mounted on two trestles and inside lay a tarnished scrubbing board accompanied by a wooden bung. The floor consisted of terracotta tiles leading to a central drain while in another corner stood a kiln-type fireplace, its smoke-stained bricks supporting a cast iron cauldron. It stood there dominating the room with its rusty door wide open as if waiting for its next feed of coal. Two more pine chairs stood close by and made up the remaining furniture. Anna clicked her tongue at the lack of facilities but she needed to freshen up and at this moment in time could not be choosy.

'Now Eddi, let's see what we can get out of these taps. Perhaps they will work for us, ja?' She spoke more to herself than to her child as he clung to his mother's skirt and nodded with side glances at the black, gaping maw that beckoned in the corner. He recounted Grimm's tale about a wicked witch and her oven and knew that this sort of thing could devour little boys like him.

The old brass tap was stiff as Anna, now using both hands managed to turn on the nearest one. Rusty water exuded and after a while eased to a trickle and soon stopped altogether. Not to be thwarted she moved to the second tap. This one was easier to turn but to her chagrin produced the same rusty water, however it kept running and slowly the discoloured flow eased to form a steady stream of clear water.

'Rain water Eddi, we're lucky today,' she said as the precious liquid flowed to the drain. 'Quickly Eddi, help Mutti pull the bath, we mustn't waste it.'

With much scraping and pulling she managed to drag the trough and trestles the short distance to the taps and adjusted the supports once her 'bath' was in position. With everything back in place and the tap still running clear she inserted the bung and soon had enough water for them both.

Under strong protest she undressed her son and lifted him up and over into the trough. Eddi let out a gasp as the water swirled around him. Shivering he drew a deep breath as Anna reached for the cut, half bar of soap.

'Kalt Mutti, kalt!' he cried as his little feet marked double time and splashed her.

'Look Eddi, here's your special red soap. You like this.' Not giving him a chance to reply she soaped him down and with a rapid rinse – it was over. 'There, what a brave little boy,' she added as she whisked him out and towelled him down. 'It's all over and you feel better now, ja?' He nodded half-heartedly as he shivered but still had a cheeky smile for her as she reached for his clothes. Dressed once more he said he did feel better as his cheeks were glowing and he smelled pleasantly of carbolic, courtesy of a priest and a misappropriated parcel from the British Red Cross.

'Now Eddi, it's Mutti's turn,' and adding discreetly, 'you can hold the towel for me and look in my bag for a sweet.'

As Eddi occupied himself, she undressed and using one of the chairs stepped up and into the makeshift bath. The boy was right she realised, it was quite chilly as she splashed water over herself and rapidly soaped herself down. Not many in Germany today can have the luxury of soap like this she mused, dear God where will it all end?

Anna rinsed off and felt invigorated from her bath and the vibrant tang of the soap. 'The towel please Eddi, pass me the towel!' He'd hung it over the chair by the door as he stood waiting by the bag and enjoying his sweet. It was at that moment she heard the footsteps in the passageway. They sounded slow and deliberate and to add to her angst, stopped outside the washroom door.

'Eddi! Schnell! Pass me the towel!' she said in a loud whisper and frantically gesticulating towards where he had left it. At his own speed he went to collect it and reached out for it but froze as the door handle began to turn. The door remained closed as the wedged chair held, however as force was applied it began to yield. The door was now ajar but only by a few inches and was once more jammed by the chair as a leg caught in the groove of a broken tile. Anna gazed, transfixed and was horrified as a long bony hand snaked round the door. Spidery fingers groped for the chair, located it and forced it away from the handle. The door swung open as Anna, exposed and vulnerable met the cold hypnotic stare of Rolf Gruber.

He stood facing her and half closed the door behind him as Anna, horrified at the intrusion instinctively sat back down and placed a shielding arm across her exposed breasts. With grey calculating eyes he savoured the moment as he gazed wantonly at her nakedness and his vulpine features transformed into a lecherous and leering mask. Anna sat rooted in fear and humiliation as once again she felt helpless, trapped and vulnerable by the Gestapo agent.

'Guten tag, Frau Bauer,' he greeted her in a mocking tone. 'We meet again, ja?' He held her gaze as he bent and placed a hand on Eddi's shoulder and gently but firmly propelled him out of the room. 'We meet again and such pleasant circumstances, ja?'

He took a step backwards as he closed the door behind him and not taking his eyes off her he slid the chair back with a foot and propped it under the handle. Anna's mind was racing; she had to extradite herself from this nightmare, but how? Like a wild animal caught in a trap her eyes remained riveted on Gruber's as she waited for his next move. His lower lip quivered and drooled saliva as he stepped towards her and methodically began to remove his black leather coat. She thought of screaming, calling out for Helmut but he would not hear from this distance and it would only frighten Eddi, who must be just beyond the door.

The coat landed on her chair as he took another step and methodically began to unbutton his jacket. As the space between them narrowed, Anna's mind raced to recall recent events. The Gestapo had released her so he must be here by his own volition. She had heard stories about the cranks, sadists and social misfits that had joined their ranks and Gruber was a prime candidate and fitted the picture, full square.

Blind rage welled within her at his affront and disregard of any vestiges of human decency.

'Get out of here, you swine!' she hissed. 'You have no right or authority to be here. I shall report you.' Gruber smiled mockingly as he reached into his breast pocket and with a leering grin pulled out a Luger pistol and casually levelled it at her face only an arm's length away. Anna shrank back in horror and disbelief as she had imagined many things but nothing like this. Gruber, his greying temples belying his age sprang forward and still brandishing the gun deftly kicked out and dislodged the protruding bung. Water drained and spurted, soaking his highly polished shoes as he cursed under his breath and indicated with the pistol.

'*Raus, Jude! Get out, you Jewish whore!*' With one word, with that one particular word, her whole world caved and crumbled. She sat motionless in the now empty wash-trough, her eyes staring blankly in his direction but not seeing or focused as the reality of her situation pervaded her soul. So here it was, Gruber of all people had found her secret, her Achilles heel.

'Raus Jude!' he hissed. 'Get out, you Jewish swine, your bath time is over,' and waving the Luger indicated direction towards the chair.

Anna, mortified at the revelation and still covering her modesty as best she could stared transfixed down the barrel of the gun. He stood and savoured the moment as with a perverted grin he relished the sight of her nakedness. It was a moment in time for her, as time stood still – her mind was racing and she looked on with apprehension and eyes wide with fright as his knuckles whitened on the levelled gun. She sat frozen with listening fear as his jaw muscles tightened and waited agonising seconds for the inevitable bullet and oblivion that lay beyond. He stepped closer and his eyes narrowed to slits of hatred as he again motioned with the gun towards the chair. However, having lowered the gun it dawned on her he was not going to shoot her there and then and must have something more basic in mind. Seconds passed between them as Anna glared at him but kept her wits about her. The despair of being branded a Jew in Hitler's Germany now released a pent-up dam of frustration, humiliation and anger. First in line was her tormentor Gruber and his affront on her dignity. Followed by her treatment at the hands of the SS and the whole Nazi system and for all the others they had abused, humiliated and murdered. She knew she had to act fast and weighed up her chances. Gun or no gun he was a man and as the nakedness of woman is the work of God, she would use His works to good effect.

'*You are the swine!*' she screamed. '*You and your scheiss, Nazi filth!*'

With satisfaction she saw his surprise as it unnerved him and he took half a pace back. '*Schweinehund!*' she screamed and hurled the soap.

Startled by her actions and the sight of her quivering breasts his concentration wavered. It was enough – Anna seized the moment and gripping the sides of the trough launched herself bodily in his direction.

Unfortunately for her there is a universal law which states that for every action there is an equal and opposite reaction, as now the trough shot away from under her and the trestles went flying. Anna lost her balance and landed awkwardly on the wet floor, however her momentum carried her forward as she hurtled towards him.

Gruber, taken off-guard, attempted to sidestep but was too late as her naked body slammed into him. Still clutching his gun he toppled backwards as together they fell heavily to the floor.

Anna, bare and humiliated, turned into a five-foot-five bundle of fighting fury as she landed with Gruber under her. Straddling his body she clawed at his face and eyes and clutching his head repeatedly struck it against the unyielding wash-room floor.

'*Schweinehund!*' she screamed repeatedly as she carried on pounding his head and digging her thumb-nails into unseeing eyes and bleeding sockets.

At first a stinging pain seared his cheeks as her raking nails left bleeding furrows in their wake and was rapidly losing consciousness as a myriad of blazing lights stabbed his battered brain. Sightless and with one hand he struggled to save his eyes as Anna carried out her venomous assault. But it can be said that the instinct of survival is most prevalent before the final blow is struck as Gruber, with a strenuous heave of his body managed to free his trapped arm. Anna, caught off balance toppled sideways and screamed in terror as the Gestapo agent, still holding the gun pulled the trigger at point blank range.

Chapter Twenty-One

CHILD'S PLAY

The door had closed and he was alone in the gloomy passageway. He stood facing it with its wrinkled brown paint and could hear the raised voice of his mother and the deeper tone of the man's. Eddi was not frightened as he'd seen the man before and accepted it as, just of late, he and his mother had travelled many miles and met many strangers.

With nothing else to interest him he decided to wander off and walk back along the passageway to where the window allowed a beam of sunlight to play on the wall. He searched around for something to play with but finding nothing dug into his pocket for his toy bus. He began to play with it, driving it up and down the sunlit wall, but buses need a conductor and he too, could play that role.

Once more he dug into his pocket and brought out his whistle. He tried blowing it and it made a sound, finding it still worked it fired his imagination.

I'll be a train instead, he mused and placed the bus back into his pocket. Stamping his feet as hard as he could he started running back down the corridor towards the cellar steps and blowing his whistle as loud as his little lungs would allow.

***

They were still discussing the war when they heard the shrilling alarm and the heavy, stomping footfalls. Helmut flicked his cigarette into orbit and grabbing his pistol leapt into action. He cleared the cellar door and negotiated the stairs, two at a time. Willi spilt his wine and forgot his rifle as he followed the sergeant at his own pace.

Frightened on hearing the drumming and resounding echoes of their boots, Eddi stopped his game just as Helmut raced round the corner. He saw the boy standing there wide-eyed and about to burst into tears as he dropped the whistle beside him.

'False alarm!' yelled Helmut with relief as Willi came lumbering and panting on the scene. Eddi gazed at them sheepishly as he recognised their friendly faces and Willi, with a wagging finger bent down to pick up the offending whistle and hand him back his toy.

'Where's your mutti, Eddi? Has she left you all alone?' Willi asked and patted his head now that his pulse rate had settled. Eddi took back his toy and pointed with it along the passageway. The silence was suddenly shattered by a woman's distant scream and the muffled report of a gun.

Once again Helmut sprang into action as he knew instinctively that that scream could only be Anna's. He doubled along the passageway and with his pistol levelled for action launched himself with a jackbooted kick against the wash-room door. It yielded in an instant as with a tortured sound of splintering wood the propped chair skidded across the tiles and crashed into the far wall.

As the strapping sergeant lunged into the room he checked himself in shock and disbelief at the bizarre scene that met his gaze as this was not what the soldier had expected. It took several seconds for his confused brain to grasp and assess the situation and to absorb the goings on.

He barely recognised Gruber with his mauled and bleeding face as the Gestapo agent righted himself to a sitting position and straddling Anna's body. She lay prone and motionless with blood oozing from under her matted hair. Helmut stood transfixed as there was nothing in the army handbook about a situation like this. Here was an assault on a naked officer's wife and by none other than a Gestapo agent who was a law unto himself. He hesitated as Gruber half turned his head at the intrusion and gun in hand glared menacingly from bleeding sockets in his direction.

'*Gott im Himmel, Gruber!*' Helmut yelled. 'You've killed her, get off her!'

Helmut was still pointing the pistol at him but lowered it, knowing he had no jurisdiction over this man, even in a gross situation like this. Gruber leered contemptuously at him and still breathing heavily from his ordeal raised the Luger threateningly at the sergeant. Instinctively it triggered a response and throwing caution to the wind Helmut took a pace towards him and levelled his pistol at Gruber's head.

'*Get off her, you swine, or I'll shoot!*' he screamed.

Gruber hesitated in the Mexican stand-off, however seconds later Willi stormed into the room. At a glance the corporal appraised the situation and with a deft movement of his arm and a resounding

184

crunch of glass on bone, brought the bottle of Rheinland Spätleese squarely down on Gruber's head.

***

By now it was early afternoon and Gruber had been dead for several hours. It was his body that now occupied the wash-trough as he lay with a crushed skull and sightless, staring eyes. Helmut and Willi were busy cleaning up the mess once they had righted the trestles and placed the trough in its place.

'Rather ironic,' said Helmut as he squeegeed the last of the blood towards the drain. 'I mean Gruber and her. They never made it in real life and now their blood is together, intermingled you might say.' Willi stopped to ponder the question and nodded with a wry smile.

'Ja, ja, guess you've got a point. Like one of those Magyar gypsy weddings,' and indicated a cutting motion with his finger. 'The happy couple they prick themselves with a knife and mix their blood, right!' They chuckled at their morbid wit and the paradox of it all as they carried on wiping down the wine and blood-spattered surroundings. 'Bit of a waste,' he added with a chuckle. 'That was the last bottle of the '27 vintage.'

With Willi on duty in and around München's Marienplatz it was easy for him to leave the building without arousing suspicion and to dispose of the evidence of their justifiable act and cleansing operation. He threw the blood-stained shards of the bottle onto a nearby bomb site and Gruber's coat and gun onto a passing horse-drawn wagon piled high with civilian corpses.

Helmut recovered the spent 9mm bullet which had lodged itself in the wall and its ancient horse hair plaster and enlarged the tell-tale hole to expose the brickwork beneath. To complete the disguise he dislodged several more chunks, which he left where they fell. Finally with all evidence of the incident removed, he secured the broken door with a wedge and joined Willi and his unit in assisting the Home Guard at clearing the streets.

Chapter Twenty-Two

THEY'VE LANDED

Seething with anger Franz returned to his ship using the same stately transportation that fetched him only hours before. A telegram awaited him from HQ at Boulevard Suchet to say that there would be some further delay in the despatch of the stores. No reason was given. He did a quick inspection-round of the boat to satisfy himself that all was ready for sea, while the off-watch 'Liberty Men' were sprucing themselves up for their night of action ashore. They asked about sailing and he told them that they could remain ashore if they so wished. A hearty cheer arose as he gave the Duty Officer his night orders and his own whereabouts in case of need.

'Back to the Kaffee Haus,' said the officer with a conscious grin.

'Jawohl Klaus, back to headquarters,' he replied and trying to make it sound as rueful as he could. 'Perhaps I will get more information there than I get from Berlin.' They laughed at that as it was another of the boat's standing jokes. 'I'm just going next door to see what orders they might have,' and with a wink continued, 'then I might just consider the café.'

'Jawohl, Herr Kaleu'nt,' replied the Duty Officer. 'I just hope the bombers give us a miss tonight.' Franz nodded in agreement, picked up his cap and made his way on deck and crossed over to see Kurt. He found him sitting in his cabin, a cigarette in one hand and a glass in the other.

'Hallo Franz, how's it going?' said Kurt as he pointed to a folding chair and handed him a glass. Franz sat and helped himself to a measure of Cognac and noted that his friend was also in his number one uniform.

'How am I, you might well ask?' said Franz. 'Pretty choked up with the whole damn bunch.' Kurt could see he was angry and already had more than a hunch as to the reason why. 'Those SS Schweinehunde and their Gestapo poodles gave me the third degree this afternoon. Didn't they ever? They grilled me and asked about all my friends and the people that I associate with around here. You've got to believe it, those boys know all my business.'

He paused as he helped himself from a tin of Players and lighting up, continued. 'They were keen to know about you and your French fräulein. I gave them all of the names, even the bar girls and hit the roof with them.' Kurt nodded in sympathy as he gazed across at his aggrieved friend.

'Mmm... How interesting,' he remarked. 'As you can see I'm not dressed up just to go to the ball. I've been there too, same thing as yourself, only...' He paused and continued with a smirk. 'They wanted a little bit more detail from me, intimate detail, you know what I mean? What I did in my spare time type of thing. I told them to go to hell. That Müller fellow he laughed at me and told me that it didn't matter as he knew anyway. Then that Schweinehund König, our welfare officer for the base, he's been spying on us all this time. Told them that if they didn't arrest me there and then I would walk out and I did. I just walked out in disgust.'

They sat in silence for a few moments, each with their own thoughts and ideas about why it had happened. Kurt picked up a telegram and handed it to Franz.

'I see you have the same fan mail as me,' he said as he glanced at its content. 'So you're leaving on the sixth. That's Tuesday – tomorrow, in fact. I'm to follow one day later.' The telegram gave details of the sailing plan and a grid reference rendezvous point for both boats, twenty-four hours apart. Franz handed it back as Kurt put the document marked 'Ultra Geheim' into his safe and hid the key under a crate of Cognac.

'I don't know about you,' said Kurt, 'but I'm going up the road for a quick beverage with my crew and say adieu to my fräulein. Care to join me?' Franz nodded as he stubbed out his cigarette, glad they were going for a last run ashore.

It was early evening as the two men arrived at the café after hitching a ride from the army. However they did not take too much notice of the two soldiers on guard, who clicked their heels in salute as they entered. It was odd they commented, that the usually brightly-lit room was in semi-darkness as only the centre chandelier was lit and one of the local bar stool virgins was no longer sitting in front but now serving behind the bar. Two more of her colleagues were serving the tables, to the delight of the crews as they wiggled around.

They found a good seat as the café was reasonably empty. Only the hardened drinkers along with the local bar flies and Andre with his accordion were to be seen. The latter sat, as usual at one end of the bar with his customary Gauloise dangling from his lower lip and an enchanted glass that was never empty at his elbow.

'Something's wrong here,' said Kurt. 'Jacque's not around and the whores are serving the bar.' Franz had thought the same as they entered and nodded as he lit up two cigarettes and handed one to his friend.

'Seems like there's been a funeral round here,' said Kurt. 'I've seen more life in a morgue.' He gave a humorous snort as he drummed his fingers, trying to weigh up the situation while at the same time trying to catch the eye of one of the serving girls.

'Seems like the locals know something that we don't,' he said as Lulu sashayed across for his order. 'Sometimes they get a tip-off and get their heads down before the event.'

Franz nodded as that sort of thing was common knowledge and even the Germans used it as an early warning system. He watched as the girl came across in her low-cut dress to take their order. She said nothing but simply stared at a point on the table as she took his order and returned to the bar.

Kurt knew the girl as one of Yvonne's friends and was normally quite friendly towards him. He leant back in his chair and asked one of the sailors from the harbour if he knew what was going on. The man's reply nearly knocked him off his seat.

'They've shot him, Herr Kapitän,' Kurt stared at the man in total bewilderment.

'Shot who?' said Franz, with concern.

'Jacques, the barman,' replied the sailor. 'He's dead and the rest of his family are all locked up. Also, there's something about him and a radio transmitter and his pigeons being used as couriers.'

'What! Jacques with a radio transmitter, are you sure?' replied Kurt with a frown. 'Do you know who did it?'

'Gestapo, Herr Kapitän,' and indicated with his head to a far corner of the room where two men were seated.

Kurt nodded his thanks but could not make out the men as Lulu returned with their drinks and noticed her eyes were red from spent tears. As he tried to converse with her she cut him short.

'Merci, Monsieur Commandante;' at the same time casting her eyes and indicating with a glance at the two men sitting in the shadows before returning to the bar, but this time without her enticing wiggle. Intrigued he glanced in the general direction and with alarm tapped Franz's foot.

'Don't look now but our two friends are over in the corner.' Franz picked up his drink and casually glanced in their direction. His jaw muscles tightened as in the gloom he made-out the pockmarked face of Dolch.

In low tones they put the day's events together and were certain that Jacques had something to do with their interrogations. They let it ride as they had already fathomed out the string of events and reason for their grilling.

As they discussed Kurt's imminent departure, men from their own crews arrived and brought some life and atmosphere back to the bar as they requested Andre to play the zeitgeist tune, 'Du Schwarzer Zigeuner'. As life returned and glasses chinked Kurt was eager to speak with Lulu and tried to catch her attention.

She skirted them but serving the next table smiled as she said in passing, 'Oui monsieur, un moment, s'il vous plaît.'

Franz noted her trim figure and chestnut hair and was reminded of Anna, only her skirt was never that short. She returned minutes later with two Cognacs and with a defiant pout made out the bill and placed it under Kurt's glass. He paid her without looking at the paper and patted her pert bottom as she put on a special show for him with a well-practised wiggle back to the bar.

'You know her, then?' said Franz with a grin as his friend seemed familiar with most of the girls.

'Jawohl, she's a friend of Yvonne's but works a little late sometimes,' replied Kurt with a chuckle and picked up the bill. Ignoring the price he read the scribbled note and his blood turned cold. Under the order of '4 x Cognacs' was a hastily scrawled note. *Yvonne arrestation.*

So they've taken her in too, he mused as he forced a laugh and handed it across to Franz.

'Your turn to pay the next round,' he said as Franz caught his drift and took the bill.

Franz glanced at it. 'Ja,' he said slowly, 'I think it's my turn, fancy another?' He saw the concern in his friend's eyes as he played the part and put money on the table. Yvonne was in trouble, he mused, and there was nothing either of them could do. Lulu came across with two more drinks but said nothing. Her eyes told their own story as brimming tears glistened on pink Breton cheeks.

They sat talking about events when the blackout curtain parted and Franz immediately leapt to his feet as Lilli entered along with two other girls from the exchange. He collected three chairs as Kurt rose to greet the newcomers and caught Lulu's eye.

Lilli came and sat with Franz and immediately began to relate in lowered tones about recent events as Kurt ordered more drinks.

Franz noticed her swollen eyes and trembling hands as she told him about Yvonne, how they had come for her and at gun-point and dragged her by the hair out of the building. Dew drop tears glistened as she finished, adding that she had heard that her friend would be shot.

Franz offered her his handkerchief and told her that that was not possible. They would have to release her. Composing herself she took hold of his arm.

'Haven't you heard the other news?' she whispered. 'The Englanders are dropping parachutists; only they're dummies, made to look like soldiers and stuffed with straw.'

Franz shook his head and knitted his brows, bemused as he tried to fathom out why on earth they should want to do that.

'That's not all, Franz,' Lilli went on. 'Our phone lines have all been cut and we cannot get through to our HQ at Caen, or anywhere else here in France. We can only communicate by radio and that is being jammed. There have been heavy bombing raids all over France, especially Calais. Lots of messages too from the BBC to the Maquis. I think something big is going to happen, we are not safe here.'

As she spoke, the other girls from the exchange were telling the men the same stories. Soon, the whole café was openly talking about it and conjecture was already overtaking events. It had become common knowledge the Allies were up to something big, as each man in turn would add more to the story. The two Gestapo men could only listen as they were powerless to stop this flood-tide of information and open debate.

'We sailed out with our Schnellbooten as there was supposed to be a naval raid on Cherbourg,' said a sailor. 'But then we were recalled as it was a false alarm, the Tommies were only dropping tin foil and trying to blank our radar.'

'All very confusing,' said another. 'I have been on constant alert for the past three days but after that straw dummy business we were all stood down.'

'Better get another round in before the dummies get here, Fritz,' said a voice from the back as the café exploded with laughter.

Suddenly the air raid sirens started and the lights flickered momentarily as the place was plunged into darkness. Soon came the familiar drone of heavy bombers and the café began to shake as the detonations from Flak batteries and bombs shattered the tranquillity of the night. But things were different now as helpful Jacques was no longer there with his guiding light and the raid was intense as hundreds of detonations were heard. More by instinct than vision everyone made it down into the cellar as candles sputtered into life and the nightly vigil began. Even in the candlelight Franz saw immediately that all of the boxes had disappeared and nudged Kurt.

'I see that all those American boxes have gone.'

'Ja, I did notice,' Kurt replied, 'and I think I know who has them.' He indicated with a nod in the direction of the Gestapo men. Everyone now spoke in loud whispers so as not to miss the pattern and the fall of bombs.

For his part, Franz welcomed the raid as he could speak to Lilli about recent events and any news she might have about Anna. Next to them the torpedo-boatmen were still debating their tin foil strips and coded messages that were absolute gobbledegook, and some soldiers were relating the many different leaflets that had rained down earlier that evening, again in code and garbled French.

The local girls were huddled in a corner by the wine racks and spoke in cowed whispers. Andre pulled up a palliasse for them and they sat themselves down to await the unfolding events.

'Sorry Franz, I have no news about Anna,' said Lilli. 'I've tried, but it's now even more difficult to get through as the bombing raids are worse than ever. Soon there will be nothing left for us to go home to.'

'Thank you Lilli, perhaps no news is good news, after all.' Detonations came closer and began to shake the cellar. 'That's a whole bomb load gone,' he said. 'We should be safe. Guess he was off target!'

Lilli's two friends were crying silently behind her while Kurt had gone to their aid and was doing his best to calm them. Lilli, frightened as ever, moved closer to Franz and put her arms round his neck.

'Hold me please,' she whispered. 'I can't take any more of this, something terrible is going to happen, I know it.' She clung to him as he felt her warm tears on his neck and her perfume reminded him of that other night and raid. He gave her a reassuring squeeze but from what he had heard this evening he was not too sure himself now. Things seem to be coming to a head around here, he reasoned, and what's more Lilli's alluring perfume was once again invading his senses.

'They came for her this afternoon,' said Lilli after a while. 'I'll tell you that first, then something else.'

He still held her close for no other reason than there was a raid and it seemed the right thing to do. He felt her trembling body against him and her fear as she rested her head on his shoulder. But then, what else could he do? After a while Lilli had calmed herself enough to relate the events of the day.

'It was early this morning when they came to see me,' she began. 'They asked me lots of questions about you and our relationship and about Kurt and Yvonne, even about her and myself. I didn't tell them anything that was not common knowledge. I said that we were all just good friends. I also reminded them that as a Kriegsmarine officer they must give me more respect. They dismissed it and said I could be arrested.'

'What about us?' said Franz, 'you didn't...'

'Ach nein, nothing like that,' and she gave him a reassuring hug. 'I only told them about trying to locate Anna for you. Then they asked about Jacques and how he was involved with Yvonne. Of course I knew nothing about that. I said he was a barman and that Yvonne was my friend. Then they asked me about pigeons. Did I ever get involved with the pigeons? Of course I had to laugh. They had to be joking!'

'Pigeons,' said Franz. 'We all knew he kept pigeons but then so do a lot of people.'

'Well, I didn't know it at the time,' she replied, 'but I got the story from one of the other girls whose boyfriend happens to be one of our soldiers. Listen to this. It seemed that one of our coastal batteries was getting a bit bored one afternoon and they went down to the beach for some target practice. One of them shot a pigeon; he picked it up and found it to be a courier as it had a message canister tied to its leg. They took it to the military police and the Gestapo got hold of it. They in turn traced it to Jacque's loft and café. They came down here and found some food boxes, which had been dropped by air. Those must have been the ones we sat on the other night, ja?' Franz nodded and squeezed her arm for her to continue.

'Well they went through his back yard and found a radio transmitter. He had concealed it in one of his chicken coops.'

'Gott im Himmel,' said Franz as he released her. 'It all adds up, we came here the other day and his feet were covered in muck. We had come in early and must have surprised him. Even Yvonne was acting strange. Remember when she gave us that bottle of wine down here? Said it was a present from Jacques. The old rascal was trying to put us off the scent. Excuse the pun, ha!' he said with a chuckle and continued, 'I think Kurt had better know about this before the Gestapo have another go at him.'

'Ja, of course, but one moment Franz, there is just one more thing you have to know.' She took both of his hands in hers and gazed at his face in the lambent candle light and wished they could be somewhere else, all by themselves as she felt their own little world was closing in on itself and would soon be gone forever.

'Please continue, Lilli, I would like to get to the bottom of this as it affects us all. We could get tarred with the same brush. Being a U-Boot captain would be nothing to them. They would lock all of us up, or worse, ja?'

'Well it was Jacques,' she continued. 'He was a spy, I know. But he was a brave man too as he saved Yvonne that afternoon. They accused him of being a spy for the Englanders. But rather than being questioned by the Gestapo he had a gun hidden away in one of the coops. Knowing the game was up, he pulled it out and they shot him. He wanted it that way.'

'Who told you that?'

'Yvonne did,' she whispered. 'She trusted me. Said that Jacques never shot anything in his life and the gun wasn't even loaded. With him dead they left to round up the usual suspects. After that they came for me but that was later on and Yvonne had already returned to the exchange. After telling me about the shooting they came for her. It was awful Franz, that poor girl.'

Her tear-filled eyes gazed into his as he felt something more than just a passing attraction for this woman. As she leant towards him her shoulders began to heave in heart-rending sobs. He drew her into him and gently ran his hand along her shoulders. She raised her head and he kissed her tears. It's the war, he said to himself as he held her in his arms. We're all its victims; however he was at a loss as to what to do with this poor girl who was taking over his mind, body and soul.

'Danke for looking after me,' she whispered, using his handkerchief to dab her face and kissed his cheek. He felt her face still hot from spent tears and her tender lips searching for his. It was all he could do to contain himself and she felt it too. Lilli wanted him to love her just one more time, as another stick of bombs shook the cellar and Jacque's bottles rattled in sympathy in the racks.

'We have to tell Kurt as soon as we can,' he said. 'He has to know.' She nodded in agreement, her head against his but with female intuition felt the spell was already broken.

'Franz, another thing,' she said, dabbing her eyes. 'It's very important.'

'What is it, you can tell me?' He spoke like an anxious parent to a child as Kurt heard him and joined them to see what was going on. She gazed at them both.

'I picked up a few things on the radio link,' she said with a hushed voice. 'When we managed to un-jam the frequency, it's about the Allies. I think they have started the invasion, Sie kommen.'

Franz glanced at Kurt and nodded. 'You know something, from what I've heard tonight and this long raid…' He pointed to the ceiling with a thumb. 'I think she's right.'

By two o'clock that morning the raiders had gone and the all-clear sounded as everyone trooped back upstairs. Inside the café it was calm but the windows were out and the blackout curtains billowed like sheets in the wind. The sound of flames crackling and licking hungrily through several buildings nearby was their only source of illumination. Wild angry shouts, both French and German only added to the confusion as the two commanders walked the girls back and managed to flag down a truck heading for the dock and their U-bunker.

***

Tuesday, 6 June dawned as a blustery day, but a moderating westerly had taken the place of the bombers. The U-bunkers had survived yet another onslaught however; the fishing port was left in a twisted mass of devastation.

Kurt reported to the controller and was informed he had to wait for his sailing orders until such time that the sweepers had cleared the mined channel. He was concerned that there was definitely a flap on as some of the smaller submarines, along with several of the S-Boat squadrons, both here and further along the coast, were given orders to sail. Kurt checked their destination on the grid map and noted it coincided around the area of Cherbourg, the Isle of Wight and once again, Lyme Bay.

'What's all this?' he queried. 'What's going on in the Channel?'

'We have another one of those alerts,' came the reply from one of the MTB commanders. 'The Luftwaffe have reported several destroyers along with battleships steaming slowly this way and from the Isle of Wight area. Same as last time when we saw a few of their landing craft. We'll surprise them again, ja? Catch them with their pants down.'

Kurt mulled it over and did not like what he heard, especially after what Franz had told him and what Lilli had said about an invasion. Her words '*Sie kommen*' were still ringing in his ears. He returned the torpedo boat officer's comment with a wan smile and wished him luck. Sounds like he's going to need it, he mused. Especially if the British are sending battleships. What was puzzling him was the dummies, why drop straw dummies and risk aircraft for nothing, he wondered? The Tommies were not stupid? But then it had to be nonsense as the weather was against them. It had been nothing but gales for the last few days, surely Eisenhower wouldn't invade under such conditions?

'This is for you, Herr Kapitän,' said a pimply-faced clerk. 'Came in just before the raid.' Kurt took the brown envelope, which was marked SONDER-GEHEIM / Kapitän KURT OBLITZ and wax-sealed with the Kriegsmarine seal and Swastika emblem. Quickly he tore it open.

ULTRA GEHEIM

Berlin Montag 5 Juni

2330 Uhr

An... Kapitän K. Oblitz U-835

1. U-835 to sail 1200 hrs 6/6/1944.
2. Proceed and clear Lorient. Submerge until clear of the coast + surface at cruising speed towards Gran Canaria... Grid ref... To be advised via R/T.
3. Wait for arrival of U-888 + proceed at cruising speed towards Singapore Island via Cape and Indian Ocean. Grid ref... To be advised via R/T.
4. Rendezvous with Japanese U-Boot *I-51* or *I-59* (to be advised) and transfer stores as detailed in previous orders.
5. Under no circumstances are you to attack targets unless confrontation is unavoidable.

I wish you a successful voyage,

Karl Dönitz

Hochadmiral der Kriegsmarine.

Heil Hitler

Kurt studied the document and mulled it over in his mind. So here it was at last. He was to sail with the blessing of the Admiral himself. Should get my Iron Cross decorated for this one, he mused as he

195

carefully placed the secret document into his breast pocket and made his way back to his boat.

Once onboard he informed his first officer to make the boat ready for sea and smoking only to be allowed on the weather deck.

Back in his cabin, he put his feet up and rested on his bunk as the cook brought him coffee and croissants, freshly made. He noted with satisfaction as the boat became alive once more as pumps and motors began to run and watertight doors were closed and clipped. Ignoring the sounds, even as the lights were dimmed, he thought about Yvonne and realised how much he missed her now she was gone. She had been fun to be with and they both knew the risks she had taken, especially from her own people, for fraternising with the enemy.

He felt a pang of guilt for having to abandon her but another thought had begun to loom large on his conscientious horizon. Perhaps the Gestapo had a point: he should be out there giving his mind to the war effort rather than chasing after French girls. Well it was all done now he reflected; too late for remorse. He would sail and do his duty when the time came but then, didn't he always?

He sipped his coffee and added a livener of Cognac but had to forgo his customary cigarette. His mind drifted back to her. Why had she been with Jacques, especially at that time in the afternoon when she should have been on shift with Lilli and the others?

Tired he shut his eyes, as thoughts about Lilli's hunch and the threat of an Allied invasion played on his mind. He conjured up a picture of the Isle of Wight with its white cliffs and the Needles. Then the comments of the MTB men in the café once again sounded warning bells in his mind and a caveat once at sea. He tossed and turned in his bunk as Lilli's words of bombs on Calais and Caen and prowling shadows of battleships began to haunt his dreams.

He awoke with a start, sweating from a troubled sleep. There it was again – someone was knocking and calling his name.

'Kurt, it's Franz!' He blinked as he rubbed the sleep from his eyes.

'Ja, come in!' he called as the vanity curtain parted and in walked his friend with a beaming smile and two cups of coffee.

'Here, Herr Kapitän, room service.'

Kurt raised himself on one elbow, yawned and checked his watch.

'Seven-thirty,' he said. 'What's happening?'

'Everything, change of plan,' replied Franz. 'You are to leave shortly. Lilli was right. The scheisse has hit the proverbial fan: they're here. Our coastal defences have all been shelled by battleships and since midnight real parachutists have been landing outside Brest and Caen.'

'What! They must be fools. The weather's against them,' said Kurt as he struggled from his bunk. He took a few sips of the scalding liquid and fought with his shoes as he had left the laces tied.

'Some of our U-Booten engaged a battleship but without success,' said Franz with concern. 'There's just a mass of Allied ships and we can't strike back. We're outnumbered, at least twenty to one.'

'Where's all this coming from?' asked Kurt. 'I thought you went back to your boat? Didn't you sleep?' He finished the remnants of the previous evening's Cognac, tipping the last precious drops into his cup. 'Ha, that feels better; I can face the Englander now. Priorities, eh, Franz?' Franz shook his head and grinned at his friend's light-heartedness and wondered what sort of constitution he might have.

'Listen Kurt, you will be sailing soon,' and reached into his pocket and handed him an envelope. 'These are your amended sailing orders. I was handed them as I came past the office.'

'So you've been out on the tiles, eh?' said Kurt, clicking his tongue.

'Ja, in a way, if you like. Only I had to see Lilli. She told me last night that it was important that I see her. She starts at six and we had breakfast together and she told me the rest of the story about Jacques. Listen to this, as it affects us all.'

'Jacques? He's dead. Have the Maquis resurrected him, or something?' said Kurt with a chuckle. Franz cast him a sobering glance and shook his head.

'Nein, worse than that, my friend. It was Yvonne who was the brains behind it all. She was the real culprit. Apparently she had been passing back information she gleaned from the exchange and also from the likes of us.' Kurt knit his brows as in a flash he was suddenly wide awake. 'Well it was Yvonne who was behind the other night's raid,' continued Franz. 'Remember the one on the HQ building? She had gotten wind that Rommel was coming and staying here and an important meeting was taking place the next day. She didn't know that Himmler was going to be there as well. Had the whole thing clicked, then our top brass and the Japanese would have been eliminated in one fell swoop.'

'That's no great loss as far as Himmler and his cronies are concerned,' said Kurt. 'And, as for the Japanese, well it would have saved us all a trip.' His face wore a sour expression as the thought of sleeping with a spy, a honey trap, the betrayal rankled and stuck in his craw.

'Well anyway, getting back to Yvonne, it seems by the time her and Jacques managed to get the information to the Allies it was too late to bag Rommel. There must have been some confusion with the timing of the messages, as the place was attacked twice if you recall. Maybe it was us disturbing him that afternoon when we got there earlier than usual?'

Kurt shook his head in consternation as he recalled the event. He knew at the time that the barman had been acting strange. He of all people should have twigged.

'So she knew all the time,' he said solemnly. 'Now it's beginning to make sense. You remember that night in the café? I wanted to leave but she dragged me out onto the dance floor and all of a sudden along comes your friendly Mosquito to wreck our HQ and as luck would have it we shot down a couple more.' He shook his head in disbelief. She was so pretty and we had good times together he mused and now all this scheisse. 'But can you imagine she could have said nothing. She could have let me go my own way and be caught out in the open with a dozen rockets up mein arsch. What can you say to that?'

'Not a lot,' replied Franz. 'She knew through Jacques and his radio the bombers were on their way as he sent the damned message.'

'Ja, it makes sense now,' said Kurt. 'The cunning swine! But you've got to hand it to her, she saved our lives that night.'

'Ja, my friend. She obviously had a soft spot for you. But then of course there was Lilli, her friend and myself. We would have been out there too.'

'And the pigeons…?'

'Well this is what she told me about that episode,' said Franz, as Kurt called out for more coffee. 'As we know the Maquis have a network all round France to gather information, ja?' Kurt nodded. 'Well, this time, Tommie's birds are dropped by parachute on a dark night. It happens all the time – agents, transmitters, saboteurs and those crates. You name it and down it comes and we cannot do anything about it except when we catch them red-handed. Well Jacques receives them in a basket and attaches a detailed drawing of what and where to bomb, as all the VIPs are holed up there for the night. He releases the birds to make their merry way back to England. Whoosh off they go, and it's Trafalgar Square here we come. Simple, ja? Now I don't know how his own birds get to England and arrive back here, if any were sent out in the first place; but the Tommies have ways and means of collecting them. They take his birds back to Churchill's loft and once released with new codes and messages; they all come back here to roost, all under our very noses. Fait accompli, as they say around here, ja?'

Kurt nodded solemnly. Then allowed himself a wry smile as he visualised the pigeons in orbit round Nelson's column and fat old Churchill holding his cigar and bottle of Scotch trying to coax them down.

'Well it all sounds simple, too easy,' replied Kurt, 'but what about her being present when Jacques was shot? Why was she there in the first place, when she should have been on shift? She would have been missed and reported.'

'Lilli mentioned that, as Yvonne had told her the whole story before they came for her, she knew it would only be a matter of time and managed to slip away in the confusion as Jacques was shot. She had to tell her you see, my dear chap, as she felt she had to warn you. It was her way of saying she loved you and perhaps you could somehow avoid being on this mission. She felt guilty, like Judas she said as she confessed to Lilly. Guilty as hell as she had also told Jacques to send the information about our boats and our Japanese guests…'

'What!' croaked Kurt as he spilt his coffee. 'You can't be serious! How the hell did she come by that?' Silence descended in the cabin as Franz shrugged and glanced across at his friend.

'Hey, just a minute,' retorted Kurt in a mask of surprise and disbelief. 'You don't think that it came from me, do you?'

'Nein, I don't. But our friends at Gestapo HQ might have a different opinion. Anyway, getting back to Yvonne, she only got that information at the last moment and then went AWOL. She rushed to see Jacques but he had no more birds left. He chanced his arm and used his transmitter but they homed in on his transmissions along with his empty pigeon loft and message capsules. They both took a chance – a gamble if you like – and as we now know, they lost. You see, she never knew from her source when we were leaving.'

Kurt sat on his bunk with his head in his hands as Franz checked his watch.

'Eight-forty, time's marching on. I'd better get going and leave you in peace. You'll be away within the hour.'

Kurt finished his half spilled coffee and led the way back up on deck.

'You know,' said Kurt as they stood by the gangway and lit up. 'I've never had this feeling before when sailing but this time it's different, too many loose ends and I have to sail halfway round the world while the Tommies are camping on our doorstep.' He paused for thought and drew on his cigarette. 'And what about my girl, who's going to speak up for her?'

Franz glanced at his friend who for once, showed stress and concern. He realised Yvonne had made more than an impression on him, even now after she had betrayed them all.

'Listen Kurt, your best bet is to get the hell out of here as soon as the boom is raised. Once the Gestapo get her to spill the beans they will be after you like a rat up a drain pipe. Fraternising works both ways, you know.'

'I know, I know,' said Kurt, sounding irritated. 'It wasn't platonic but I swear she never asked me anything. We just had a good time together and now, in her hour of need I'm running out on her.'

'Nein, you're not running out on anyone, she made her choice. For all you know she could have been using you as a blind, a ticket to get her in and sit amongst us. I think from the sounds of it she got emotionally involved with you, clouded her judgement so to speak. She got herself caught with her knickers down, if you please. Now it's your turn. Don't let it cloud your judgement as you'll need all your wits about you to even get out of Biscay, let alone carry out your mission. If not both then one of us has to get through. If we succeed we can still win this scheiss krieg.'

'Ja, of course, I know you're right,' replied Kurt, realising his friend made sense. 'Thanks for that. She played both ends against the middle, but you know how it is. Like you and your wife, I still can't get Yvonne out of my mind.' Franz nodded as he knew only too well of late what it was to get emotionally involved.

'Look Kurt, if it makes it any easier for you, I'll see what I can do. I'll try to see her if they let me.' Or if she's still alive, he reminded himself.

'Danke, I'd appreciate that,' he replied and flicked his dog end into the oily water. 'Tell them that she never asked anything from me, and that's the truth.'

'Ja gut, and what shall I tell her?' Franz said with a hint of a smile behind his eyes. Kurt stared hard at his friend, as if poleaxed by the question that had come like a bolt out of the blue and chuckled heartily as he realised he'd been neatly caught out by his friend.

'Tell her Bonne Chance, nothing else. So it's Auf Wiedersehen, my friend, I'll be starting main engines. Good luck to us both, ja?' They shook hands and clasped each other's shoulders. 'Hope to see you down by the Azores and we'll rendezvous as before. Our own code, ja?' Franz gave a sombre nod, as it was another reason why they had survived so long in the war. 'And thanks again for letting me know about Yvonne. I thought we had something special between us. You know, maybe after the war...'

'C'est la guerre, mon ami,' said Franz with a Gallic shrug. 'Bon voyage and remember – it's your first round in the Bamboo Bar in Tokyo.' With hearty chuckles they shook hands but saw in each other's eyes the lurking spectre of uncertainty and looming defeat.

Chapter Twenty-Three

TRAUMA

Once again, Anna was back in the cellar. Helmut and Willi had carried her down and had dressed her wound as Eddi stayed close to his mother and played with a wooden train, a present from Helmut. He was told not to make any noise and to let his mother sleep.

It was the savoury aroma of food that roused her. Anna felt a stab of pain as she tried to open her eyes. With effort she raised herself onto an elbow and gingerly felt the side of her head where it hurt and tried to collect her thoughts as she explored the bandage which encased her ear and temple. Recollections of past events seeped into her mind as her eyes began to focus on familiar surroundings but a throbbing pain and the light affected her sight. Tired, she lay back and recalled events in the wash-room, her bath and that man Gruber with his gun. That gun she reflected and its ear-shattering report as her right ear was affected with a high-pitched ringing noise. However this paled into insignificance as Gruber's leering face swam into view and the word Jude came back to haunt her. Confused from her ordeal, even how she got back in the cellar she now feared for her life as realisation dawned that Gruber would be back and remove them both to a Jewish work camp. Both... Gott im Himmel, where's Eddie? What's happened to him?

Frantically she tried to raise herself up but the effort made matters worse as a stabbing pain affected the side of her head and the light her vision. Exhausted she fell back onto her pillow and through cracked and feverish lips, tried calling his name.

'Eddi, Eddi, are you there?' she whispered, 'Come to me, please.' There was silence at first followed by the sound of metal on metal and again the smell of food. Painfully she turned her head as she heard the noise again.

'Na ja, wie geht's?' came the familiar voice in its local dialect. She focused on the voice as Willi's jovial features swam into view.

'Willi, where is my boy?'

'Your boy's right here, Anna,' he replied waving his fork. 'Don't worry, I'm looking after him, you just rest – here, I'll help you to sit up if you like?' He came to her and moved her pillow of blankets as Anna struggled to sit up against the brass headrails.

With a happy laugh and holding out his new toy Eddi ran to her side. Lovingly Anna reached out and drew him close and kissed his forehead. He gazed at her bandage and tried to touch it, but Anna drew away.

Contented weariness now overcame her as she settled her head back on the pillow but rest did not come easy as she tried once more to piece together events. However it was always Gruber that dominated her thoughts as she tried to recall his intrusion and taunts but the throbbing pain and the constant ringing in her ears unsettled her mind.

The aroma of food made her realise she was hungry and tried to fathom out how long she had been here like this. Was it hours, or days? What day was it? Then Gruber again, he would notify his cronies at the Gestapo and once he informs them, they would come down here and arrest her, only this time – for being a Jew. She gave up with her dim thoughts and once more raised herself up as she heard Willi busy with his meal.

Turning towards him she saw his mess tin loaded with sauerkraut, dumplings and the local sausages and was happy to see him as he jovially waved his fork in her direction and gestured that she should join him.

'I've given the boy something to eat, Frau Anna, don't worry about him but you should have something too.' Without waiting for a reply Willi forked some of the steaming cabbage from a large pan into a canteen and took it across to her.

She managed a lopsided smile; 'Danke Willi, only it's my head and back, I cannot move too much.' With effort she adjusted her posture and winced as her whole body felt tender and bruised.

'It will be alright later, Frau Anna, you were lucky the bullet only grazed the side of your head. With rest and care it will soon heal,' he said as he handed her the segmented metal dish. 'This is your breakfast and dinner,' he added with a grin, 'courtesy of my house and not the army. Please eat; it will make you feel better.'

Anna tried to come to terms with the word bullet. She was alarmed at the thought she had been shot. It explained the pain and the dressing but then a woman like her should never have been in a position to be shot. How could all this have happened to me? She asked herself, as Gruber's leering face once again swam into view.

'Danke Willi, it smells good.' He nodded his appreciation as Anna feeling the warm metal on her body suddenly realised what she was wearing. She was in a long-sleeved embroidered nightdress, scented with lavender and never seen before. Mortified she recalled her naked body in the wash-room and now this. Of course, they've dressed me...

She cast a furtive glance at Willi who sat nonchalantly munching his meal and deeply engrossed with his wine. She felt helpless and shamed by the fact that this stranger had to look after her in every sense of the word. Ja, and Helmut, him as well. He must have had a hand in all this as they would have had to dry and dress me... Well amongst other things it must have made their day, she reasoned and knew Franz would have thought it amusing.

Franz, she felt guilty for not thinking of him before but it was Gruber that was uppermost in her mind, he would be back to haul her in as a Jew. Better ask Willi what was going to happen to her now. Perhaps he was guarding her for the Gestapo? She decided to ask him about that once he had finished his meal and with an aching jaw she ate part of the meal and beckoned for Eddi to join her.

'Here Eddi, you can help Mutti eat her dinner.' The boy came across as Anna spoon-fed him. He soon demolished the remainder and quickly slipped off the bed to carry on with his game. 'Danke Willi, it was very tasty and I think I was hungry too.'

'Ja, it's all from my farm, tastes gut, ja?'

Finishing his meal and not waiting for an answer he emitted a resonating belch, wiped his lips with the back of a podgy hand, and repeatedly kissed his teeth in an act of dental refinement.

'Willi, what time is it?' asked Anna, concealing her abhorrence at such farmhouse manners.

'Time?' he queried and checked his watch, peering at its dial with child-like satisfaction. 'I make it eight-thirty.' He glanced up at her and seeing a puzzled frown added, 'that's eight-thirty in the evening. You've been asleep for most of the day, Frau Anna.' She frowned at that and shook her head but that hurt. Beckoning Eddi to come to her she covered him with one of the blankets.

'Bedtime Eddi, it's already late but first a little prayer for us here and your daddy on his boat.' She clasped his hands together with her own and together began to say the special prayer. 'Vater unser...'

Heavy footsteps sounded from beyond the cellar door as the Lord's Prayer faded from her lips and Anna glanced anxiously across at Willi. He shook his head and waved his hand in dismissal as the heavy footfalls grew louder. With old hinges creaking in protest the door swung open and Helmut strode into the room.

'Guten abend,' he greeted them and nodded with a courteous smile in her direction. 'I see you are better now. Did you sleep well?' He beamed the question and grinned with amusement in her direction. She met his gaze and felt the blood rise to her cheeks. He's more jovial and familiar now, she mused as she self-consciously adjusted her nightdress without any form of support.

'Danke, I am feeling better now,' she said quietly but feeling ill at ease in his presence. 'Only my head is still hurting.' And managed a wan smile and fussed with Eddi's blanket as she envisioned her naked body on the wash-room floor.

It was then she saw it and realisation dawned the reason for their levity as there, right next to her and on the bed-post hung her pink brassiere and panties, a present from Franz whilst passing through Paris but which now was displayed like a barrack-room trophy, for all to see. With a composed expression Helmut averted his gaze as Anna painfully reached out to recover this intimate part of her wardrobe.

'Well that's good now,' he replied, stifling a smile as Anna tucked the embarrassing items from general view. 'I'm glad you're feeling better.' He turned to meet Willi's questioning gaze. 'It's done, finished,' he said in a commanding tone. They eyed each other as Helmut nodded and Willi understood.

Dismissing her dented pride and feeling her composure returning, Anna addressed them both as she tucked Eddi into his blanket.

'Can you please tell me what's going to happen to me now, I mean is Gruber coming back to arrest me?'

Helmut glanced at her and nodded, walking across to the door he closed it with a flick of his boot. Methodically he felt around in his tunic pocket and drew out his cigarette case, lit two cigarettes and passed one to Willi. 'Frau Anna,' he said, choosing his words. 'Let me inform you that your persecutor Gruber is no more.' He met her wide-eyed gaze as she tried to come to terms with the revelation. 'Unfortunately, he met with an accident and was killed in the air raid.'

'Air raid?' replied Anna with a frown. 'While I was asleep?'

'Ja, it was a bomb and the building collapsed,' Helmut replied. 'For your own safety and ours you will kindly not mention it again. Is that understood?' His eyes narrowed as he waited for her response. Confused she glanced from one to the other and with a discerning nod accepted her tormentor had somehow met his end.

For her it was enough and felt a sense of relief and like Pilgrim upon seeing the Cross, a great burden had been lifted. However another thought struck her, Gruber might be dead but what about his associates at Gestapo HQ? They must know all about me, she reasoned and leaving was once again uppermost in her mind.

'What happened with the air raid?' said Anna. 'I mean, is there much damage and what about the railway station? Is it still standing?' Eagerly she searched their faces for an answer.

'Can't say at this moment in time,' Helmut answered with a shrug. 'I've been up there with the Heimwehr, burial party and that sort of thing. I had to call in at the police headquarters, or what's left of it.' He took a final drag on his cigarette and casually stubbed it out on the heel of his boot. 'The Heimwehr estimate some thirty thousand buildings destroyed and several thousand dead and injured. It's sheer carnage up there. The police and the Heimwehr can't cope. At this rate there'll be an epidemic.'

'Ha, the Heimwehr,' Willi sarcastically interjected. 'Old codgers with buckets and spades more like it.' His cheeks grew flushed with indignation as he pointed at his forehead and drew circles with his finger. 'They're all crazy up there and the likes of me have to pick up the pieces. I'm a farmer and that scraggy, scheiss chicken-breeder Himmler should have stayed one too. As Reichsführer he's right up Hitler's backside. You know, they'll have to nail planks to his feet before he gets himself lost up there. Look at the state we're all in and soon we'll have those Russkies to deal with. Lieber Jesus! We're all done for, thanks to him and his cronies.' Indignantly he rose from his chair and angrily made his way across to study the bounteous wine racks once more.

Helmut, amused by his colleague's outburst smiled with a shrug, as it was not too well-publicised the Reichsführer; the second in command of Germany, had at one time been an unsuccessful chicken farmer.

'What about the trains, Helmut?' Anna anxiously repeated her question. 'I've to get away from here.'

'You can forget about that, Anna, as most of the city has been affected. In many places there are just bodies and rubble. Not much will be moving in any direction from here, not for a long while.' He saw despair etched on her bandaged features but could not help as transportation was not his forte within the army. Casually he lit another cigarette and blew a smoke-ring towards the light.

'I went past the Gestapo headquarters,' he continued, it's still standing but the doors and windows are out and a lot of their confetti is blowing up and down the street.' With a wry smile he called across to Willi. 'Did you hear that? Good news, ja? I think those boys will be leaving us alone for the time being.'

Willi made his way back to his chair and sat to examine the selected bottle and nodded with indifference.

'Corporal Stern here will have his hands full when he goes on duty,' continued Helmut. 'Better leave that for later, eh?' Willi pulled a face at his sergeant as he raised himself with an audible sigh. 'First aid and burial party, mass graves and funeral pyres for our good citizens. Better get yourself ready to go on watch, my friend, before they send a search party and I'll have to be the one to charge you as absent from place of duty, eh, Willi?' Helmut indicated with a jerk of his thumb as Willi reluctantly took up his rifle and with a clatter of his steel helmet and canteen made for the door.

'I'm sorry Helmut,' said Anna. 'I do apologise. I had no idea the bombing was that bad.'

'Nothing you can do or say, Anna,' he replied. 'The Allies can now bomb us at will and we can't stop them. However, there's one more thing.' He fumbled in his tunic pocket as he made his way across to the bed and produced a bent and dog-eared envelope. 'This, I believe, now belongs to you.' With an outstretched arm he handed her a letter-sized brown envelope.

Her mind raced as alarm bells in her already confused mind began to sound once more. Dear Lord, she thought, is there no end to this? It was an official-looking envelope and once more felt threatened. 'For me?' she said anxiously. 'I don't have any letters, Helmut.'

With hesitation she took it from him, her eyes wide and questioning as she met his benign gaze. Anna saw its flap was already open; in fact it had never been sealed. She noticed there was neither a name nor an address, just a matchbox-sized stain at one corner. Her mind froze as she realised it was blood.

She peered up at Helmut for an answer as he must obviously have seen its contents. In the poor cellar light was it fear that he saw hovering there, or defiance, like that of a wild animal, cornered and steeled to fight? But then it was his grim expression coupled with a sobering nod that now bade her to examine its contents.

Twenty-Four

GAUNTLET RUN

At 0400 hours on 6 June they came. After the early morning bombardments of the coastal defences there was a lull in the south as the Americans and British established their presence on the beaches. The Kriegsmarine was unable to have any effect on proceedings, having lost several of the U-boats to the Allied defence screens and the Luftwaffe was noted by its absence.

So, it was at 1000 hours on D-Day morning that Frigattenkapitän Kurt Oblitz manoeuvred his submarine out of the U-bunker and followed the Blavet estuary and out into the broad Atlantic. As Kurt's boat cleared the Gavres headland he noted surprisingly, the weather had moderated to force four on the Beaufort scale but the westerly swell was still six feet as the U-boat followed in the wake of the boom defence vessel, through the swept channel and out into the Bay.

Kurt was on the bridge with the OOW and two lookouts as they scanned the distant horizon and the surrounding sky for any signs of hostile ships, periscopes or aircraft.

The low cloud base was a blessing as aircraft could be easily spotted but the heavy swell made the boat roll and pitch with a slamming motion as the sea, on the starboard bow, broke against her in a welter of spray and foam. It soaked men to the skin and made their lives a misery as they peered through the spray and continuously wiped their lenses. They used towels wrapped around their necks to arrest the water that seeped with icy fingers past their oilskin hoods, trickling down and ending in their sodden boots.

Kurt scanned the northern horizon with his Zeiss lenses and watched with a certain sense of melancholy as the land on his port quarter slowly fell away. Some three miles out his escort's Aldis began to stutter, to signal 'good hunting' as the minesweeper veered to starboard and turned back into the swept channel. Kurt, still peering through his glasses, weighed up the situation and guessed with all that was happening in Normandy they would not bother him this day of all days as he was happily headed in the opposite direction. An ill wind for some, he mused but it's turned out right for us.

He was a veteran of many actions and a born survivor as now he sensed the presence of the enemy if nothing else. With one hundred and fifty feet showing beneath his keel, he ordered his men below and gave the command to dive the boat. With bows already submerged he was the last man down as the tower hatch slammed shut only inches above his head and the waters of the Atlantic closed over the boat.

With dive tanks flooding U-835, devoid of her recognition number, levelled off at one hundred and twenty feet as Kurt ordered a reduction in speed to dead slow and sufficient revolutions to maintain steerage and depth. In the silence of the deep they heard – through the hydrophones the faint but distinctive pitch of high-speed propellers, coupled with a whine of electric propulsion.

'Just as I thought,' said Kurt turning to his number one. 'It's a submarine and not one of ours. I knew they would have a reception committee parked on our doorstep. It was the lack of aircraft that made me suspicious. Normally there's a patrol but if they've got one of their own boats down they would not want to compromise themselves. They've learnt their lesson on that one as a while back they clobbered one of their own.'

He took the phones from the operator and listened as the man tuned for maximum sound and direction; satisfied Kurt set a new course of west by south, at 40 revolutions.

'Keep at dead slow until we lose him,' he ordered. 'Then alter to the west until midnight at the same speed. Any problems, call me. I'm going to catch up on my beauty sleep. Oh, by the way, Fritz – don't hit anything,' he added with a grin. The pimply youth stared wide-eyed at his captain, not knowing whether this was a joke or an order. With true Hitler Youth spirit he gripped the controls with extra zeal as he kept his eye on the gyro compass.

'Jawohl, Herr Kapitän,' he replied stoically as his mates sniggered at their diving controls. 'Steering two-five-five, Herr Kapitän!'

As the submarine nosed its way out into the Bay the crew settled down to their silent running routine; twin E-motors hummed in unison as the boat successfully distanced itself from the prowling intruder and land.

Kurt lay on his bunk as the monotonous tone of the motors washed over him. They hummed hypnotically, like noontide bees swarming in the summer heat. He closed his eyes to rest awhile before surfacing for the long night ahead. He had ample time now to contemplate events as he lay there, trying hard to relax but the haunting demons came early to taunt him and to stoke the fires of his despond.

So much had happened to him during the past twenty-four hours and now the Allies had landed in France, it was the beginning of the end he mused, unless Hitler could pull a magic rabbit from his battered Tyrolian hat. He, along with fellow officers realised the U-boats could do nothing to stop them. They had long since lost the battle of the Atlantic and now were being picked off on their own doorstep, both here in France and in home waters.

His thoughts turned to Yvonne. Why had she done it? Did she really do it? Without seeing her he could not believe she had done this thing. He had trusted her and loved her company and they had been the best of lovers; how could the woman do this to him? What would be her fate in the clutches of the Gestapo? If she really was an agent of the resistance at best they would put her against a wall and shoot her, no further questions asked; otherwise it would be humiliating torture and deportation to one of the work camps.

But no, this was his girl and had known her well over a year. He had taken her under his wing, cared for her with victuals from this very boat, coffee and cigarettes, even gave her money for dresses. Now it was over, just a memory of dispirited love and dastardly betrayal. Perhaps after all a women's love is brief, or was it because he was German and she just had to do it? A patriotic French woman, a modern Joan of Arc? Better she would have shot him, there and then in that hotel love-nest of theirs…

It was the knock that brought him back to reality and a call from the cook, who entered the cabin holding a steaming mug of coffee.

'Elf Uhr dreizig, Herr Kapitän,' he sang out in his Alpine lilt.

Kurt checked his watch. He had slept a full nine hours and felt better for it. It was still half an hour before midnight and surfacing but he had already decided to bring it forward by twenty minutes. Never surface on the hour, he had taught himself. Others might have the same idea or be waiting, already surfaced. Also the watches changed and they would be less alert on the handover.

He made his way to the control room, checked with the hydrophone operator they had shaken off their previous companion and ordered the boat to periscope depth. He carried out a three-sixty degrees sweep and, satisfied, ordered the boat to surface. As the duty-watch manned the tower a rapid sweep with night glasses proved they were alone on an empty ocean. The crew erected the mast with its radar detector as Kurt ordered half speed on diesels and shaped his course in a westerly direction to clear the jutting coast of neutral Spain.

Chapter Twenty-Five

COWARDS

After seeing his friend depart, Franz made his way along the quay and into the bunker office which had a direct link to the bomb-damaged but still functioning HQ building in town. There were two teleprinted messages for him stating his stores were still in transit. Someone had hastily written in pencil 'due to events in Normandy'. He had listened in to radio reports and the news seemed disastrous as British and American tanks were already ashore and had breached Rommel's defences. Little wonder, he mused, as the Allies had air superiority and could strafe and bomb at will.

He was informed that the fast motor boat flotilla had sailed and were at Cherbourg for refuelling and were to head towards the Allied landings to try and attack battleships and tank landing craft. Speedboats against battleships and aircraft, it did not sound good, he mused but now there was something more alarming and closer to home as the Flak gunners who, between raids hung around drinking coffee, informed him that several of their men had been murdered by the Marquis. These bandits had suddenly become bold by sniping at soldiers in broad daylight.

They advised him that it might not be such a good idea to wander into town without an armed escort now the locals were once more getting bigger than their Breton clogs. Franz chuckled to himself at their mode of expression and made a mental note about the locals. Making his way back along the quay he made out the uniforms of two SS soldiers and winced as he saw Dolch accompanied by a young Gestapo officer.

'Ach nein, not again,' he muttered as the fresh-faced youngster detached himself and strutted to meet him. Franz was taken aback as the young man's arm shot up in a Nazi salute like a creation from Geppetto's workshop.

'Heil Hitler, Herr Kaleu'nt.' Bemused, Franz glanced at the zealous youngster as he observed this latest product of the Hitler Youth who had yet to invest in a razor. Franz nodded and waited for him to continue as the man unnerved by the captain's gaze glanced back at Dolch.

'Can I help you?' said Franz without batting an eyelid but had a shrewd idea why they were here.

'Herr Kaleun't, wo ist Das Boot, U-835?'

Franz knitted his brow and methodically gazed round the pen. 'I cannot see it here, Herr Leutnant, can you?' The youngster turned in exasperation to Dolch, who was already striding to the rescue, followed by his SS guards.

'We meet again, Herr Kapitän. Where is the other boat and Kapitän Oblitz?'

Franz fixed him with a steely gaze and with a disarming smile, confronted his erstwhile tormentor.

'You should know better than that, Herr Dolch. Never ask about a vessel's movements in wartime. I could have you shot for that.' The Lieutnant took a sharp intake of breath and shifted his weight to the other foot as he nervously licked his lips. Dolch's eyes narrowed and his jaw muscles worked overtime as he spat out the words through clenched teeth.

'We are looking for Kapitän Oblitz and are not playing games, Herr Kapitän. Now, tell us where he is.'

'I'm afraid you are too late, Herr Dolch. Kapitän Oblitz sailed from here some time ago. It would seem you have missed the boat.'

Franz had never enjoyed himself more and stifled a smile as he watched the colour rise in the man's face. For his part, the young Lieutenant looked on, wide-eyed with apprehension, as Dolch glared threateningly at Franz. Muttering an oath, he turned on his heel and went back along the quay and out of the bunker. Franz watched him and his stooges leave and made his way back onboard to the delight of several of his crew, having witnessed the proceedings with animated glee.

Back with his men he put them in the picture of events ashore, both with the Normandy landings that morning and also with the business in the café. He advised them to go ashore in groups and to stay together. Any men with local girlfriends should also stay in groups, as none of them could be trusted. That went down like a lead balloon with those concerned, amongst a chorus of loud jeers and friendly guffaws from the boat's 'bar fly' contingent.

At seven o'clock that evening, Franz went ashore and was dropped off by the cratered parade ground. He walked into the dormitory building and asked a passing colleague of Lilli's to let her know of his presence. She came down after a few minutes with her handbag and coat and was happy to see him but her eyes, joyless and dimmed told their own story.

'I thought I would not see you again,' she said with an engaging smile. 'Thank you so much for coming to see me,' and affectionately pecked his cheek. Franz led the way past the sentry and back out into the open. They passed the boiler house in silence, each cherishing their thoughts about their little love nest, as Lilli, savouring the moment, crooked her arm in his.

Once inside the café they realised it was no longer the same. The cosy atmosphere, along with Jacques, had gone and like the barman, never to return. Some of the girls were still there and spoke in whispers. Gone too were their giggles and shrieks of happy laughter as the Germans sat glumly round their tables, conversing and speculating in lowered tones. It was easy to find a table as Franz and Lilli sat and Lulu came across to take their order. He asked for his usual Cognac and as a surprise ordered a bottle of Chateau Pontet Canet for them both.

'Only the best,' he said as Lulu beamed at them and wiggled off with the order.

'Times are changing,' said Lilli as she gazed around the room. Gone was the snug, smoke-filled atmosphere, the chink of glasses and the welcoming sparkle of the chandeliers. Several soot-stained oil lamps burnt in their stead and a solitary light bulb glowed from behind the bar.

By the windows the blackout curtains hung forlornly to one side as the windows had been sealed and boarded-up since the last raid. At the sad sight of her surroundings Lilli shivered involuntarily. 'Feels like someone's just walked over my grave,' she said rubbing her arms through her summer dress. Franz nodded, as without its charismatic host, music and chandeliers the place had gone to the dogs.

Lulu returned with the Champagne and popping the cork, to the delight of those at other tables, poured their drink. Like lovers they chinked glasses, 'Prost Gesundheit' they chimed, however their smiles were distant with branched thoughts of the parting that was soon to come. Lilli stared vacantly at the bearded bubbles winking invitingly at the brim. Any other time it would have been a joyous occasion but now it was the sorrow of parting, perhaps never to see her lover again.

Seeing her melancholy Franz recharged their glasses. 'So, what's the latest news – about Yvonne, I mean?'

'She's gone,' replied Lilli, shaking her head. 'They've got her and are holding her to ransom. Unless several of the locals who are part of the Maquis surrender they will shoot her. If they surrender, the Gestapo have promised they will only be sent to the local prison, as prisoners of war.'

'Fat chance of that,' said Franz, shaking his head. 'They'll put them against a wall and "bang".'

'Not really Franz, haven't you noticed? There's no music. It's Andre. He's given himself up.' Tears welled in her eyes as Franz reached for his handkerchief and pressed it into her hand.

'That's ridiculous, what, old Andre a terrorist? I can't believe it.'

'Nein, he told them to take him and to let her go. Now both of them are under interrogation and the last I heard they've been sent to a place called Auschwitz-Birkenau. Is that in Deutschland?'

'Never heard of it,' he replied with a frown and shook his head in disbelief and told her about Dolch and how Kurt had slipped away. 'Had they come sooner, they would have arrested him. He'd have been guilty by association.' Lilli nodded and dabbed her eyes and fumbled in her bag.

'Here, take this,' she whispered and passed him a note under the table. Franz glanced around the café, but no one seemed interested in them. Casually he opened the crumpled note and discreetly shielded it with a beer mat.

'Kurt Mon Cher, please forgive me, I will always love you and will pray for your safety when I get to heaven. Love, kisses and sweet memories...
Yvonne'

'Gott im Himmel, how did you get hold of this?'

'It was wedged into one of the jack sockets on my desk. She knew what was coming. Ach, that poor girl.'

He said nothing as he thought about his friend out somewhere on a windswept ocean, whilst here he was betrayed in his own bed.

He decided to change the subject. Lilli was too upset and he needed to know for himself what news she might have. 'What's going on with the landings? Where are Rommel's panzers? The artillery? Have you heard?'

'Rommel?' She shook her head in disgust. 'He was at home, Franz. He took the weekend off. There was nobody in high command to resist the initial landings. It's hard to believe, but it's true.' He shook his head in disbelief as she reached for his hand. 'Franz, we've lost the war, haven't we?' She met his level gaze and

215

saw only anger in his eyes. He nodded at the question now on everyone's lips and thought about his own chances of survival.

'We lost the war the day we marched on Moscow,' he said bluntly. 'Now with the Allies on our doorstep we can only hope Hitler surrenders while there are still bricks left standing.'

'What about your mission? I heard something about that?'

He leant towards her and spoke in earnest. 'If we get through there is a chance the Japanese can pull it off. It's our only chance and I'm going to make sure I deliver the goods to Madame Butterfly.' It was the first time he had told her about his movements. But with Yvonne's spying activities it was now an open secret.

So it was all true, she mused as she squeezed his hand. He met her concerned gaze and it was good to feel a woman's touch. Her loving gesture reassured him as she was the only person who kept him sane. Now, as they gazed at each other they saw in each other's eyes the sadness and sweet sorrow of the parting that was to come.

'I would like to thank you for your kindness as tonight will be our last night together like this.' Lilli with brimming pools of blue shook her head and placing her half-finished drink to one side released his hand.

'Please Franz,' she said quietly, 'take me back. I cannot bear to sit here one minute longer. I don't want to come here ever again.'

'Jawohl, let's go.' He finished his drink, left money on the table and assisting her with her coat waved goodnight to those sitting at the bar. He led the way past the blackout curtain and out into the silent mantle of the night.

They walked back, arm in arm and in silence with only their footfalls sounding on the cobbles, content to be in each other's company but both dreading the moment of parting to come. Passing the boiler house she squeezed his arm as they met each other's gaze and she kissed his cheek. He gave her a token smile, kissed her hand and felt a heel for not summoning the courage to tell her how he really felt.

They passed the sentry and walked inside the building. Lilli turned and put her arms round his neck and began to cry, quietly at first as with a heavy heart, he held her tightly to himself. Awash with tears she clung to him.

'Franz, I don't want you to go, please don't leave me. I love you, Franz. I'm sorry but I love you, I love you.'

His heart went out to her as he felt like saying the same but like a knife Anna came between them. He was in a tight spot of his own making and felt himself drowning in a flood of his lover's tears.

'Lilli, I'll come back,' he whispered as she kissed him again with her departing tears. 'I'll come back to you, I promise if I cannot—' A flash and the sound of shots and another flash, then darkness…

It was the sound that drew his attention, a loud crackling sound. Franz opened his eyes and realised he was lying in the open and the noise was coming from a burning building. He collected his thoughts as he lay there and to fathom out what had happened. His head hurt and a blanket had been draped over him but his back was cold. Again he tried to recollect what had happened as realisation dawned that he was hurt. Cautiously he moved first one leg, then the other, and the same with his hands.

I'm still in one piece, he mused and his thoughts turned to Lilli. Ja, where was she? He remembered he was holding her and came the flash, the sound of a shot… *Where's Lilli!* His distressed mind screamed.

Ignoring the hurt he threw off the blanket. A uniformed nurse came to his side and told him to lie down but seeing his determination to stand she assisted him onto his feet.

'What happened?' he asked as he felt the lump on his head and the tacky, congealing blood. He winced as she fussed and adjusted the cumbersome field dressing.

'Cowards the lot of them,' said the middle-aged woman angrily. 'They knew there were only girls here, Schweinehunde Franzosen but we caught them and they're all dead.' She pointed to where a pile of bodies lay and the blood which had oozed into a large congealing pool. It reminded him of a deer shoot in the Black Forest. He had piled the carcases up on that occasion, only this time they were human.

'Scheiss Franzosen,' he muttered as he checked his watch. It read nine-fifty but had stopped.

'What time is it, please?' he asked the bustling woman as she picked up the blanket and draped it round his shoulders.

'Ten-forty, Herr Kapitän. You will have to go to the hospital. I will get you some transport.'

'Nein, I have to find the girl I was with. Her name is Lilli.'

He peered round and in the amber glow of the flames he saw another three bodies lying on the ground. The nurse tried to stop him but he swept her aside and she was left clutching the blanket. He saw the boots of the sentry and a Frenchman who lay uncovered, his beret shielding his face. Then to one side he made out the bare feet and the light-coloured hair of a woman with the rest of her body covered. He feared the worst as slowly he lifted the blanket and his heart sank – it was Lilli. Kneeling down beside her he took her hand in his. Some warmth in her lifeless fingers still remained as he kissed them and held them to his cheek.

'I'm sorry Lilli. So sorry my love, please forgive me,' he whispered as he tried in vain to choke back the brimming tears that were mute witness to an unrequited love.

Chapter Twenty-Six

BISCAY

Franz had returned to his boat having had a grenade splinter removed and a head wound dressed after the insertion of numerous stitches. The following afternoon he attended the brief ceremony as Lilli, along with others was laid to rest. He had learnt that she'd died instantly, having shielded him and taken the full force of a grenade that fateful night. He stood there in the van of circumstances, bareheaded by the yawning tomb. He felt numbed by her death, even blaming himself for what had happened. He waited for the priest to finish and bent to place a single red rose onto the coffin, a flowery token to bind her to the earth as it was lowered to join three of her colleagues and the unfortunate sentry. He placed the flower as a token of gratitude for her efforts in trying to trace his family but also as a fitting farewell to a friend and surreptitious lover.

He remained there, rooted by her side for many poignant minutes in a sense of companionship, not wanting her to be alone in her final moments beneath open skies. He became lost in his own thoughts as feelings of guilt returned to haunt him. Once more he reproached himself for her death, as the burial squad commenced their solemn task and the first earthy sods drummed down in resounding requiem. He no longer felt guilty about their relationship, as here before him was the reality of war and what humans, whatever their creed or country, could exact on each other. The war brought out the best and the worst in all of mankind. Who could cast the first stone, given their circumstances where life that night had hung in the balance and their subsequent loving liaison, nature's remedy in times of stress, with love's healing surrender.

He would always remember the unselfish person Lilli had been, along with her uplifting camaraderie and the love she had so freely given. She had saved him from himself he reasoned as before their meeting, he'd suffered a sailor's stress of loneliness, together with swingeing bouts of melancholy and despair as he waited for news from home. Since their affair he had come to the conclusion in the fog of war, one's sense of values and perspective change and to survive, both mentally and physically, one had to adapt.

As he stood in final farewell and the alien soil of France rained down to bury her, Franz swallowed hard as a wave of emotion welled up to engulf him. Silently, he swore to her that he would fight on until the bitter end and to final victory, or die like her and her companions in the attempt. Eyes brimming with tears he stooped and clutching a handful of soil cast it in lonely grief at the rising mound.

'Adieu, Lilli,' he whispered and gingerly replaced his cap. Turning and with leaden feet, walked solemnly away.

***

On 8 June, news filtered through Allied bridgeheads had been established in Normandy and the Wehrmacht could not stem the tide of the British and American assault on the beaches. The Luftwaffe had by this time lost several bases, along with the remaining aircraft. It was now a race against time for the Kriegsmarine to get out of France.

At 2200 that night, Franz loaded the remaining parts of a V2 rocket engine and as the pen's gates opened, U-888 with her number replaced by a lucky Sylvester mushroom symbol slipped her moorings to proceed on her vital mission. He headed his boat down river and through the narrow south-western channel, cleared the shallows and rocky islets as he sailed in line astern with a minesweeper and two other U-boats acting as Flak ships to maximise U-888's chances of reaching the open sea and the safety of the deep.

Minutes before midnight, Franz acknowledged the sweeper's Morsed light that he was clear of the minefield. With guiding lights extinguished, the sweeper turned back to base as Franz took the way off his boat and lay listening on hydrophones for any underwater activities. Inside the submarine the crew settled down to their routine as the watch above listened out for the tell-tale drone of aero engines. Way to the north and inland the look-outs discerned numerous flashes that would occasionally light up the night sky. The Normandy beaches were some three hundred miles distant but various flights of bombers were attacking all over France that night.

Forty-five minutes later, and with no underwater or air-borne sounds present, Franz was satisfied and gave the order to proceed at ten knots, surfaced towards the Canaria Isles and a course of west by south. This would lead him to the safety of deeper water before heading on a westerly course into the Bay and his rendezvous with Kurt and U-835.

As the boat gathered speed, no other sound was heard other than the throb of her diesels and the rush of water as the sea broke over her bows and deck. Time and again U-888 dipped her nose under as she continuously plunged into the long, Atlantic swell. The moderate seas climbed her deck and ran along its length until crashing in a welter of foam and spray against the structure of the tower.

With the Naxos rigged, the radio watch listened out for radar transmissions, this in a special sound room, located below. In the tower the deck-watch kept their night glasses trained on the limited horizon but knew with every turn of the screws the chance encounter with aircraft diminished. Soon, with the fathometer reading three hundred and fifty feet under his keel, Franz gave orders to increase speed to twelve knots and leaving nothing to chance left the Flak cannons manned for any eventuality. Four lookouts remained and equipped with their powerful Zeiss glasses were stationed on the conning tower with instructions to watch out for the tell-tale white streaks of any fast-moving ships that might indicate Allied submarine hunters.

Satisfied, he went below to 'relax' in the pitching and rolling boat and plan his best course for avoiding ships and aircraft, especially near Gibraltar. He steadied himself against the chart table as he plotted his course. Johann brought him a mug of coffee when suddenly the Naxus alarm gave warning of a radar transmission. Seconds later came the OOW's excited shout of 'Flieger! Flieger! Kapitän to the bridge!'

The mug crashed to the deck as Franz, with reflex action made it up the ladder in record time and was immediately confronted by a blinding airborne light. Permission to fire was given as the gunners, shooting over open gun-sights replied in kind as tracer shells streamed down on them from behind that dazzling curtain. Cannon shells traced a line in the water and missing the bridge as Franz ordered flank speed and helm hard to port.

The light suddenly died as the aircraft roared clear and two canisters splashed with great fountains to one side where seconds before the boat had been. The gunners, their sight restored kept firing as the four-engined aircraft melted into the night and two hull-shattering explosions hit the surfaced submarine with sledgehammer blows. Twin columns of tortured water climbed majestically into the night sky as Franz corrected his turn and steadied the boat.

'Dive!' screamed Franz to his engineering officer waiting below. 'Schnell, engine room, make clear to dive!'

Agonizing seconds passed as the diesels died, dive tanks now open to the sea flooded and the bows already down as the E motors took the strain. Men scrambled and shot down the tower to land in a heap as the engine room secured the remaining valves. Franz took one final look at the banking plane, easily spotted with its line of engine exhausts belching purple and blue. He remained poised and calculating as his bows sank deeper, keeping a wary eye on the bomber as it levelled out to begin its second approach; however, this time without the aid of the light. With seconds to spare he slammed down and dogged the hatch as the swirling waters surged over the tower. The E-motors howled in protest as Franz ordered full power and spun the boat by ninety degrees. U-888 heeled to obey her rudder as she continued to claw for the safety of the deep.

At two hundred feet, he levelled the boat as two detonations once more shook the hull, but these were mercifully too distant and shallow to have any real effect. Franz had reasoned the aircraft would circle and follow in the direction he was heading before the attack and dive. It was airman logic, a basic reasoning but he was not done yet. He gave the command for slow speed and altered course by forty-five degrees towards the north-west. As the E-motors settled into their regular low-pitched hum he brought the boat up to forty feet in order to clear the rapidly shallowing seabed and the many wrecks in the area. He trimmed the boat to proceed at slow speed on her amended course.

As order returned, the crew congratulated themselves on a lucky escape and for the vital few seconds of warning their scientists had been able to provide. Franz explained to them about the newly-developed Leigh Light the British were using to surprise surfaced submarines at night.

'It was the Naxos, it saved us,' said Wolfgang, the bo'sun and lookout. 'Picked up his radar, after that we heard him as he was approaching from the east and down wind, the crafty devil.'

'That new light contraption of theirs is deadly,' chirped Walther, the gunner. 'But at least it gives us something to aim at. Put out that Tommie's lights didn't we?' he said with a chuckle.

'Alles gut,' said Franz in agreement as the cook brought him a fresh mug of coffee. 'It's a good job we had our gunners ready and that Naxos device. All you need in this game is an edge, right?'

Jurgen nodded and murmured agreement as the twin motors hummed their tune of battery-powered propulsion. Course was again corrected as Franz made his way out into deeper and safer waters of the Bay.

Eleven days later, U-888 was cruising surfaced on a southerly course with the Canary Islands to starboard when the look-outs spotted the small but distinctive black speck in the distance. In brilliant sunshine U-888 flashed her identification signal as back came a Morsed acknowledgement and friendly reply. It had been an ordeal but as Franz gazed across the tranquil blue water, he gave an inward sigh of relief. They had run the gauntlet of Biscay and survived.

As twilight fell, the two U-boats moved towards the islands and one rubber dinghy was launched from each boat. They landed close to the light house and the town of Maspalomas where the islanders were friendly and none too fussed whose money they took, especially as they were paid in gold sovereigns.

Well after midnight, after enjoying the local hospitality and loaded with fresh produce they returned to their respective boats drifting in the calm water as they waited for a third U-boat to join them. The following day was spent waiting and drifting. With the onset of the night, Wolfgang won the prize of a bar of chocolate for spotting the approaching U-boat at a distance of four miles. No mean feat in the gathering dusk.

U-863 arrived with its commander, Von Esch and exchanged official despatches together with a new routing plan for the two boats as the aircraft carrier HMS *Victorious* would soon be operating in the Indian Ocean. He went on to explain there was a change of plan as he had orders to proceed to the east and there receive further orders but using the western route, down the coast of Brazil, round Cape Horn and into the Pacific. He explained he was carrying Radar equipment and two U-Boot specialists who were experimenting with hydrogen peroxide as a power source, together with a consignment of mercury.

The latest news for Franz and Kurt was Dutch submarines were now operating around the Cape Town area and British submarines were operational in and around the Malacca Strait. They wished each other luck and proceeded surfaced towards their distant goals – perhaps, God willing, to endure and meet again on the other side of the World.

Chapter Twenty-Seven

A MATTER OF BIRTH

Anna stared at the envelope and pondered the stain. Was it her blood or Gruber's but reasoned she had not lost any letters? Nervously she pulled out a document and several photographs. Not pictures but photocopies of legal documents. Here, in bold type and stamped with an eagle and swastika at its margin was a document file heading with her name, ANNA MARIA WOLF and in capital black ink lettering the name GOLDBERG had been added.

Once again she feared for her life and that of her child as here it was, in black and white – a photographic copy of her identity and evidence to reveal her blood-line and roots. It had to be that Gestapo lowlife Gruber, she reasoned as she recalled how he'd called her a Jewish whore and nobody else had mentioned her roots.

Like in a dream she held the incriminating records as recent events drifted like evening shadows through her mind. Her arrest and the train journey here to Munich. Her naked body and fight with Gruber. She closed her eyes as she recalled the gun and the gaping hole where the bullet would emerge and end her life. His leering face and incisive scream, '*Jude*'. It still sounded, like death's trumpet in her ears.

With a sigh she shook her head; it was a sigh of utter weariness, of despair and resignation as she re-examined her birth certificate. She avoided Helmut's gaze as a sense of guilt, of not belonging overcame her. All her life she had been brought up as Deutsch, an ordinary German girl and it was only during the last few years of the Nazis which had so conditioned her and the rest of the country that to be Jewish was to be a non-person. She had always believed with her married name of Bauer and being the wife of a naval officer she would be safe, her true origins concealed by the passage of time and matrimony. However it was not to be.

She thought of the past, how the Fatherland of her parents and her childhood had changed dramatically once the Brown Shirts began to march. How fate had dealt her an unkind hand as the cards were now face-up on the proverbial table, its wood carved from the tree of bigotry and hate.

Self-consciously she toyed with the documents as here she was, with two soldiers and herself branded a Jew and topping the Gestapo most wanted list. She had no desire to read any of the other copies as, at a glance, some were familiar – especially the copies of her birth and baptism certificates.

However another document caught her eye, as it had Gruber's signature and a Berlin Archive letter heading. It was all too much as once again those cold fingers of fear began to claw at her soul and with a heavy heart she forced herself to examine the document. The bloodstain, it had to be that swine Gruber's, she reasoned as it was on the envelope and now also on her certificate of birth. That swine is still with me, she told herself, even in death he's following me, stamping his filth everywhere.

GEBURTSBESCHEINIGUNG

Vor und Zuname	Anna Maria WOLF (Goldberg)
Geburtstag	9 Juni 1917 um 8 Uhr 50
Geburtsort	AACHEN
Religion	Römisch Katolisch
Vor und Zuname, sowie Stand des Vaters	----------------------------------
Vor und Zuname der Mutter	Maria Lisa WOLF

Yes, that's me, and thought about her parents killed in the air raid. Her birth certificate had been kept by her mother and stepfather at the flat; so this copy was now all that remained except for the original, either in Aachen or the Berlin archives. The irony of it all did not escape her as it had returned to her by the hands of Gruber.

Again she thought about her parents and the story her mother had related when she became a teenager. Her mother had married after the war, and her father was actually her stepfather, her real father having been killed in the war. She had cried when her mother had explained she was grateful for being married to him as he had always been good to her.

He, her stepfather had been her real father's best friend. Her mother went on to say he had married her out of a sense of high moral duty, having promised his dying friend on the battlefield he would look after his pregnant girlfriend and ended up with her as his wife. He kept his word and Jurgen Wagner married her after the war and gave her his name. There had never been any problem with that, as her mother's maiden name of Wolf hid her roots. Only Franz knew, and that sort of thing had never bothered him, especially as many German Jews had given their lives in the Great War. That would have been the end of the matter, had it not been for the incident on the train and Gruber's grubby digging in the Aachen registrar's archives and its local church. To the Nazis, she was a Jew and the likes of her and her son must be sent to a camp for the final solution.

She scanned through the documents but had seen enough. Her wound had begun to throb and her headache had returned with a vengeance. She glanced across the room to where the sergeant stood smoking and held out the documents.

'Helmut, please you can read them as they will explain why I am still here. Perhaps it will explain other things and you will understand matters between Gruber and myself.'

He responded slowly, as he had already examined the papers and copies, as well as the remaining contents of Gruber's pockets. Therefore with some pretence at modesty he acted out the scene so as not to embarrass her and did not accept them immediately. It felt reminiscent of a school play, only now the actors were for real.

He lit another cigarette and made his way across the room and took the papers from her, feeling uneasy at having to deal with such private and personal matters. However, he noted that Anna had missed to read an important piece of paper.

'I will have a quick look Anna, if that's what you want,' he replied. 'Better lie down and rest your head. I'll make some coffee and don't worry; I'll stay here with you until Willi returns.'

She smiled her thanks as he sat and shuffled the documents into their chronological order with Gruber's Gestapo headed note paper as the fourth and final document.

He picked up the first photocopy of a baptism certificate, the standard of the Catholic Church. There was a picture of a baby lying in a cradle, complete with an embroidered border and date; a second copy had the seal of St Josef's Kirche Register, Aachen. He recognised it to be some sort of testimony, written in faded ink and with a scholastic Teutonic longhand. The large magenta seal of the Gestapo graced its bottom left corner, its eagle and swastika emblem now dominating the once plain document.

Helmut nodded to himself as he admired the priest's long and
elegant hand, as well as that of the young soldier's gallant and sworn
deathbed testimony. He glanced across at Anna who was lying and
observing him with red-rimmed eyes. He carried on reading,
occasionally nodding to himself as the bare facts of Anna's birth and
turmoil now lay exposed. Another document was her marriage
certificate to a Kriegsmarine Offizier: Leutnant Zur See Franz
Bauer.

'So, they weren't married then? Your real father I mean?' Anna
closed her eyes and managed a resigned nod from her pillow. 'It was
the war,' he continued, 'and I understand there were thousands like
him. They tried to legitimise their offspring but the church and state
wouldn't hear of it. It doesn't matter now, does it?'

He read the final document and casually stuffed it into his pocket
and shaking his head, more out of pity for her and her trying
circumstances, stood and handed back the rest of the papers. Anna
felt a flood of relief as tears of gratitude and self-pity welled up and
meandered past pale cheeks to join and embellish the stain.

Seeing her distress he came to her side and touched her shoulder.
'Kaffee Anna, here drink this.' It was Helmut who now took
command of the situation. Having witnessed her distress and
torment he knew for her and the sake of the child he had to break
the Nazi spell which the organisation had so ruthlessly implanted
into the German psyche.

Through a vale of tears, more in loathing of Hitler's Germany than in self-pity she gazed at him as he held and offered the mug of questionable liquid. He felt awkward as he had touched her through her dressing gown and it reminded him of how little experience he'd had with girls. The sensation was like hot coals as he withdrew his hand from the cotton material and the softness beneath.

Anna wiped her eyes with a handkerchief and composed, sat up and gratefully accepted the drink.

'Danke Helmut, for being so understanding, 'I'm sorry but I must look a real mess.'

Helmut swallowed hard as to him it was to the contrary. The damsel in distress syndrome struck a chord with him as his heart went out to her. He shook his head as, to him she was an enticing woman and was happy to be close to her. He felt ill at ease to witness her anxiety and tears and felt nothing but compassion for this brave woman, who had visibly aged during her short stay as a prisoner of the Gestapo. But he knew he had to get her away from himself too, as a tender feeling of more than kindness was beginning to brush his emotions.

As Anna sipped her ersatz, Helmut lit up and pondered his next move and how to get her away from the hornet's nest that was Nazi Munich. She had become a danger to him and Willi now that Gruber was dead. There would be an inquiry, questions would be asked and he did not want her here when that happened.

He strolled over to the door and stood smoking as he listened out for any unusual noises from above. Satisfied, he glanced across at Anna and looked-on with satisfaction as with the aid of a small mirror she had adjusted her bandage and was now applying lipstick, a sure sign her confidence was returning. She even managed a coy smile in his direction to the effect of raising his heart rate an extra beat. That's typical, he mused. Who's going to see her down here?

However without a second thought, he realised he had already answered his own question.

'So your real father was in the army and was killed before he could get married?'

Her eyes grew distant and misty as she cast her mind back to his picture hanging in its oval oak frame on their dining room wall. He looked resplendent in the Kaiser's uniform of a Lancer on horseback, with a wide moustache, piercing eyes and Pikelhaube helmet. She could still hear her mother's voice as she related stories about his bravery.

'You've read the documents Helmut,' she said in a faltering voice. 'It's nothing to do with my legitimacy. It's the blood in my veins. I'm half Jewish and that's my crime in Germany today.' She waited for his reaction but only saw his facial muscles twitch as he stared embarrassed at his boots and the flagstone floor. Anna finished her drink as a brittle silence began to invade the room. Helmut shuffled his feet uneasily and self-consciously drew out his cigarette case and lit up another cigarette.

'I'm sorry, Anna. You know it doesn't bother me.'

She had felt a gulf spring up between them now that her roots and paternity had been so crudely exposed. To fall out with him was the last thing she wanted as the matter of her Jewish roots was not her doing but an act of Mother Nature.

Perhaps I should have told them, she reasoned, but then how could she? How was I to know what that man Gruber had unearthed? Of course it was not Helmut's fault, she reminded herself. He was a soldier serving his country, just like her husband. The thought had occurred to her he, too, was part of the system. Ja, that's the irony of it, she mused. They're both fighting to uphold this hideous system which is keeping the Nazis and their evil regime in power.

She stared at her empty cup and the remains of the mashed wheat, not knowing what to say. He meanwhile stood smoking and keeping his thoughts to himself, as to harbour a Jew could mean a firing squad for them all.

'That's alright, Helmut,' she said at last. 'It has nothing to do with the likes of you and Willi. I cannot thank you enough. But I have to get away from here, before the Gestapo find me again.'

'I don't think they'll come for you at this moment in time, Anna,' he replied as reassuringly as he could. 'That last raid damaged their building and several of the staff were killed. However there is one more thing…' He paused, took a final drag of his cigarette and methodically crushed it with the toe of his boot.

Nein, what next? screamed an inner voice as she steeled herself by the nature of his tone and looked-on as he drew out several papers from his pocket.

'These belonged to Gruber,' he said, matter-of-factly and met her wide-eyed gaze. 'They gave him the authority for your immediate arrest and deportation to Buchenwald.'

Anna gasped, her mind in free-fall. 'Nein!' she cried in a loud whisper and clasped a trembling hand to shield her face. 'Nein, they cannot do that Helmut, I'm an officer's wife. Mein Gott,

Buchenwald, that's the women's internment camp. They send the zigeuner and undesirable people there and get those injections, Franz told me.'

'Bitte Frau Anna,' said Helmut in a soothing tone. 'Please read these documents as they are the ones Gruber acted upon. He cannot carry out the order now but I feel as it concerns you, you should know.'

He crossed the room and handed her the papers. Anna adjusted her nightdress and took them from him and with trembling hands began to read the orders that would have sealed her fate. Gruber was to have taken her to the nearest SS collection point for transportation by rail to Weimar district and the camp at Buchenwald. The second document related to her son. He was to accompany her and his father, Kapitänleutnant Franz Bauer must not, under any circumstances be informed of this.

She shook her head in disbelief that her own people could do this to her and her family. This was to be the final solution that she had heard about so many times but had felt so secure in the presence of her husband. So now it's me and the answer to Hitler's Judenfrage, she mused as silent rage built up inside her. We Germans must be so stupid to be taken in by the Nazi rhetoric and now we are paying the price. Swine, like Gruber are roaming the country at will, whilst our honest folk are fighting and dying for the Fatherland. It's a joke, but the joke is on us.

'Here Helmut, take these,' she said brusquely and handed back the documents. For his part Helmut felt uneasy, both as a man who knew what had been going on with the Jews and now in uniform he was branded as part of the system. Out there as a soldier, it had been different; he had been one of many. But here with Anna, it was on a personal and humanitarian level. Guilty by association he thought, as he took the papers from her.

'I had better keep these documents; you must understand if they are found on you, it would be difficult to explain how you came by them.'

'You can keep them,' she replied coldly. 'Tomorrow I shall be away from here and these murdering swine. What have we Germans become? Answer me that?'

Once more, silence filled the cellar, only to be broken by the rasping sound of flint on metal as Helmut lit up another cigarette. Anna, still visibly shaken by the threat of her deportation to a work camp, now observed in astonishment as he nonchalantly dangled the cigarette from his lower lip and casually applied the yellow flame to the incriminating pieces of paper.

'They're safe now,' he said with a satisfied grin as he ground the ashes with his boot. 'We'll make a plan of action for you and your boy. But first we'll have to wait for Willi to return. Please don't worry; we'll get you away from here, all in good time, ja!' He gave her a benign nod and a reassuring smile as he sat to finish his cigarette, together with his lukewarm drink.

Anna cast her eye across at the ashes and heard him as if from a distance, perplexed now she had witnessed his making amends for her immediate incarceration and demise. Conscience-stricken, she reproached herself for being angry and needlessly snapping at him. Now, having witnessed his act of kindness and appreciation of her situation, it left her a trifle wrong-footed. There is goodness in my people after all, she reassured herself.

'Danke, Helmut. Danke vielmals that you'll do this for me, I thought you might hand me over to the Gestapo once you found out about my roots.' She paused; not immediately finding words to express her thoughts. 'You know Helmut, you and Willi are taking a great risk for me. If they found out you would both be put against a wall and shot. Nobody helps Jews in Germany today.'

'Ach nein, Anna. They have to catch us first. Willi and I are born survivors we play their game and hide away down here when the going gets tough. As long as they don't send us to the Eastern Front, we'll survive. I'll make some fresh coffee for us, Willi will soon be back off watch but tell me, Anna...' He stopped as he lit the stove, his mind searching for the right words. 'You are half Jewish. How come you have managed to get away without detection for so long? Up until now, that is? Did your husband pull strings?'

'I was never Jewish,' she snapped defensively. Helmut sensed he'd touched a nerve, but in order to help, he needed the facts. 'They brought me up as Wagner,' continued Anna, 'and my mother's name was only used on my birth certificate as they married soon after. Our local doctor knew of course, but then he was Jewish so that was easy and by the time I attended school the wounds of war had healed. My real father's parents, my grandparents they came to see me as oft they could and gave my mother money, they lived in Belgium and traded in diamonds. We were all happy that way. Later I met Franz. He knows my story but it never bothered him. Many of his friends are Jews and one is even serving on his boat.' She paused to check herself as perhaps she should not have mentioned that. She glanced at Helmut as he met her questioning gaze, but he simply shrugged his indifference.

'It's all right, Anna, there are a few Jews in the Wehrmacht. Those with blond hair and blue eyes get away with it. As you know it doesn't bother me. Please finish your story.'

He's right, she mused, that crewman does have fair hair. 'Anyway, I don't even know where my husband is, let alone any of his crew. To him I'm his wife and the mother of his child and I know he loves us both.'

'That's a pretty good story, Anna, but you know we were the same down here. We only watched as the Brown Shirts and thugs arrested and harassed the local Jewish community. They smashed their shops and took great pride in pinning yellow Stars of David on their coats.' He poured out two cups, handing one to her. Anna took it gratefully and felt relieved she had told him her story. She had nothing to hide anymore; her cupboard skeletons had all been exposed and laid to rest.

'That was in the thirties,' he continued and lit up and blew a ring of smoke at the light. 'Ja, we were all so young then and easily led. Hitler gave us work and pride in our country. We were a German nation once again, united under a new flag.' He paused to reflect on the memory.

'Ja, I remember those days too,' said Anna. 'Once more we had money in our pockets. I was courting Franz and we were all so happy. Franz was not a Nazi; he did not like their ideals and the method of their elections. As far as he was concerned my past was not to be mentioned to anyone outside our immediate circle of family and friends, especially as the fledgling Nazis were targeting Jews as scapegoats for all the ills of the past and present. To him I was a true German girl, whose father had died fighting for his country and was proud to mention it.' She paused as Helmut nodded, more in reflection than anything she had said, and sipped his drink.

'Once the Brown Shirts gained power,' she continued, 'most of the Jews with money or businesses just left. They had seen the writing on the wall.' Anna glanced at him at her unintended pun. Helmut acknowledged the irony and chuckled in response. 'After that, two of my friends married Englanders, paid them handsomely for the privilege and with their new identity, left the country for London. But the majority were just rounded up and sent away to the work camps. Then of course there are the likes of me.' She cast her eyes in his direction and gave a benign salute with her cup. He was glad to see she had perked up as Anna, by coming to terms with her situation and the threat of deportation lifted, no longer felt inhibited about herself as she continued her story.

'It was the night of the fires and the orgy of window smashing that settled it for us. You remember the Kristalnacht?' Helmut nodded grimly in reply.

'Ja, who can forget? That was in '38. They came to my father's works and demanded a list of all Jewish workers and went round to their houses and smashed up their homes. Their shops were burnt and all the windows broken. I distinctly remember the music shop as the following day we were told not to play Hoffman any more. All Jewish arts were suddenly banned.'

'It was the same with us,' continued Anna. 'Franz used to say that a nation that buries its culture is denying its history and is on a road to hell in a hand-cart. I was studying in Berlin at that time and it was awful. We…' She paused for a moment. 'They had to wear those yellow Stars of David and the shops were daubed the same. That's when people started to disappear and the rumours of the camps started. But you know it wasn't just the Jews. Gypsies, cripples and deformed children too, just disappeared. Later, in '41, I heard many of the disabled were given injections and so done away with. How could we let this happen? Did Herr Hitler order it? I never saw anything in writing to that effect.'

Footsteps sounded on the cellar stairs. Instinctively Anna froze as Helmut calmly checked his watch and waved in broad dismissal.

'Keine angst, it's only our valiant soldier, Willi.'

Willi entered, smiling profusely. With his rifle in one hand, he clutched a small parcel in the other. Still beaming he strode across to Anna and handed it to her. Anna, who had propped herself against her blankets, sat up and thanked him as she eagerly unwrapped the newsprint.

'Gott im Himmel!' she exclaimed in surprise. 'It's a meal for the Kaiser himself!'

Later that evening both Anna and her son ate heartily for the first time in many days. Willi had brought her a roasted chicken from his farm, together with noodles his wife had prepared. The two soldiers opened wine for themselves and Anna sipped from a glass, again courtesy of Willi. He gave them the latest news from the outside world and in lowered tones discussed with Helmut their plan for the disposal of Gruber's body.

Chapter Twenty-Eight

FLANK ATTACK

The Red Army had now regained Voronezh, Kursk and Minsk as it pushed the Germans back westwards on a wide front towards Warsaw and Hungary. To the east of Lovov, in the Ukraine, a pocket of the First Panzer Army had resisted and dug in as the Soviets concentrated their efforts to regain Lovov.

On 23 July 1944, Major Yuri Konstantin found himself fifty miles to the east of the city and ordered his men to flush out the remaining Germans using tanks and artillery. After the great mechanised battle for Kursk, where both sides had lost over three thousand tanks, Yuri found his unit with only two hundred and thirty tanks and even less artillery. He was by now well-acquainted with his enemy and if nothing else, respected their ability to fight in tight corners. However the Germans had lacked air power ever since the D-Day landings which had forced Hitler to send his eastern-front aircraft to defend the Reich. It now left them vulnerable and it was here that Yuri's detachment received full air support, both in strafing and bombing of the German positions and vital aerial reconnaissance.

Breaking off from the ensuing assault on Lovov, he was ordered to move his tanks and artillery to within a mile of the German pocket and sent out scouts to gain information.

To the south-east lay a woodland that had been skirted by the Red Army days before and left in abeyance (by orders of Stalin) as the hard core pocket of German lines now stretched for three miles before him. Orders had come from Marshal Konev that he was not to take any unnecessary risks. He was to wait for re-enforcements and air support.

By now, the sun was at its zenith and the heat stifling as Yuri sat, glass in hand, swatting flies and talking to a wounded officer. A sudden commotion on his left flank drew his attention. He heard shouts then the unmistakable 'crack, crack' sound of rifle fire. His Smirnoff went flying as he dashed from his tent and witnessed a group of several hundred men, some dismounted, others still on horse-back and riding hard towards his left flank. Seconds later came the whine and moan of his own artillery shells as they passed overhead and landed, with an explosive 'crump', amongst his troops.

There followed a further onslaught as one of his Katyusha batteries was ranged against him, the rockets of the 'Stalin Organ' causing mayhem amongst his men. Stockpiles of ammunition and vital fuel brewed up in a great fireball, killing and maiming as more shells and rockets found their mark. Hundreds of soldiers resting in their tents were killed as they scrambled out to be greeted by a hail of shells, rockets and bullets.

'*Fascisti, fascisti!*' he shouted at a young lieutenant.

'Nye pa-ni-mâht!' The confused officer yelled back and shaking his head vigorously, began shouting orders into a field radio.

'*Fascisti Kosaka!*' screamed Yuri, as realisation dawned his flank was being attacked by a large band of rebels, the majority in field-grey uniforms of Von Pannwitz's command and others in traditional Cossack garb. Through his glasses he could see them, some still mounted and with sabres and pistols attacking his artillery crews, hacking and slashing while others had turned his guns round and were firing down his own lines. He witnessed three of his tanks turning and using machine-gun fire to great effect however, in the confusion the same guns were also mowing down his own men and stampeding his corralled horses.

'*Ivan, get the horses. Davai! Davai!*' he shouted above the din and gesticulating in their direction.

Dropping the headset the lieutenant leapt to his feet to shout orders at his dismounted infantry troops. Signal flags and flares added to the confusion as only a handful of his mounted troops swung into action. Some fifty men were now mounted and rode hell for leather down the line with their familiar cries of 'Urrah! Urrah!' as shells continued to scream over their heads to land and slaughter indiscriminately.

To add further to the mayhem the German artillery now opened up and 88mm shells began to rain down in rapid succession on the exposed lines. Yuri's last remaining and precious armour was caught in the open and quickly dispatched as the tanks brewed up into blazing wrecks.

Amongst all the chaos the Soviet cavalry, having regained their wits, charged heroically at the Cossacks as a cut and thrust duel on horseback ensued. The Russian troops were no match for the skilful Cossacks, who would gyrate from their saddles to hang and shoot from under their mounts' necks, but soon the Red Army's superiority in numbers began to tell. As more Red Cavalry arrived and the infantry men having recovered from their initial surprise, began running and shooting, along with their deep throated cries of 'Urrah, Urrah'!

Having achieved their mission, and with the covering fire from their German allies, those Cossacks that had been firing the guns and rockets remounted. Others, the walking wounded or those without mounts were swept up effortlessly, buzkashi-style by their comrades, to ride double-mounted back to the safety and cover of the woodlands.

As the battlefield cleared the badly wounded Cossacks were left to their fate, namely to be systematically dispatched by Yuri's men who, on Stalin's orders, ('Take no prisoners or wounded,') shot any man, friend or foe which moved.

Chapter Twenty-Nine

KELLER HAUS

'I've arranged for an army truck to take him away,' said Willi as he finished his freshly brewed ersatz. Anna grimaced, as she recalled her recent ordeal and did not want to know any more about the matter in hand.

'Excuse me gentlemen, I think this is not for me. I will rest my head for a while.'

'Ja, but of course,' Helmut replied, pulling up his chair to talk business with his corporal. Willi allowed himself a glass of wine, took several gulps and savouring the moment, emitted a satisfying belch. He eyed the sergeant who by his nonchalant expression made allowances for his Bavarian farmer's etiquette.

'I took the liberty of using your name,' said Willi. 'So when we take the body up to the street you will have to sign the paperwork.'

'*Paperwork?* What bleeding paperwork?' replied Helmut with alarm.

'Ach nein, don't worry,' said Willi, waving a podgy hand in dismissal. 'It's just for the truck, the transportation. It needs a signature, you know how it is.' He grinned at his bemused friend's unease as he studied his empty glass. 'We'll have to deliver him to Dachau, as we've already buried the air raid victims. No questions will be asked there as it's an army transport. They'll just incinerate him along with a few more Jews, gut ja?'

Pleased with his plan he beamed at Helmut as he allowed himself another glass. Helmut froze visibly as he glanced with embarrassment in Anna's direction but was relieved to see she was mercifully asleep. Better explain matters to Willi, he thought and making a mental note as Willi was oblivious about Anna's background. He knew the corporal did not mean what he said as it was just one of those clichés which was now accepted and on every browbeaten German's lips.

'Sounds reasonable to me,' said Helmut accepting the corporal's fait accompli and nodding in agreement, at the same time glad they would get rid of Gruber without any risk to themselves. He lit a cigarette and blew the smoke ring contentedly at the light and joined his friend to finish the bottle.

'How's it looking up there?' asked Helmut after a while. 'I have to go and report at twenty hundred. Hauptman Kessler wants me to guide a convoy of lorries through the town. They're heading for Austria – some important and secret stuff to avoid the bombing around here, I guess.' He glanced at his watch and methodically wound up the timepiece. Willi nodded in agreement, as many such convoys had passed through the city.

'They counted the bodies and took names as best they could,' he replied. 'The police and the Home Guard, that is. I was consigned as first aid party. We had to clear the streets of rubble. You should be able to get through by now.'

Helmut nodded in mute satisfaction as he rose from the table and strapped on his pistol belt.

'They think I'm a doctor you know, little do they realise I'm just a farmer. I can treat livestock, broken limbs and deliver lambs and calves but to treat broken heads and burns, that turns my stomach. Half the time I feel like throwing up and for what, eh?'

Again, Helmut had heard it all before as Willi, clearly upset left his chair and drained his glass. He glanced down at Anna, who with Eddi was asleep as he brushed past her bed before settling himself down on a straw mattress on the floor.

'Give me a shake as soon as you return and we'll get that hund out of here.' He indicated with a nod towards the stairs as he settled his bulk on the yielding palliasse.

'Jawohl, und gute nacht,' said Helmut as he switched off the light and quietly closed the door, the sound of his receding footsteps echoing on the cellar stairs.

He had only slept for a few minutes, or so it seemed as Helmut shook him awake.

'Come on, let's go,' he said in a loud whisper. 'It's twelve-thirty and the truck's waiting.' He shone his torch down at the corporal's feet, its blue light emitting an eerie beam as Willi, still half asleep wrestled with his jackboots.

They made their way up to the level of the washroom and into the kitchens. There inside an empty meat store lay Gruber's body. The cooler lacked its blocks of ice, however his corpse remained limp as they manhandled it along the corridor and out through the beer hall's doors.

Without ceremony they heaved his body into the canvas-covered truck. Helmut handed the young driver the required identity papers which stated that it was the body of a French resistance fighter. He had given the name as Pierre Yves Doumont and supported the evidence with the dog tag still on the corpse. Once at Dachau the driver was to obtain a signature with an official stamp and return the document to him personally at the barrack's guardroom.

With a curt 'Heil Hitler!' for good measure Helmut slammed the door and the truck sped off into the night, taking Gestapo agent Rolf Gruber on his final journey to oblivion.

'That was smart,' said Willi. 'But where did you get that tag from, and those papers?'

'Fate, my friend,' said Helmut nonchalantly. 'He did it himself – Gruber, I mean. I found them in his pockets. It seems he was a busy man, our Herr Gruber.'

They stood for several minutes in silence, each with their thoughts, at the same time listening intently for any indication of aircraft but thankfully they heard nothing. Willi pulled out two cigarettes, handed one to Helmut and with a shielded flame, lit up. Once more they stood listening and gazing at the open sky and the patient brilliance of the moon. With relief they savoured the moment of the tranquil night and glad to be rid of the incriminating corpse.

'It's too late for them now, they won't come tonight,' said Helmut breaking the silence. 'I'll be off now, as I have to report to the barracks but I'll get you excused for the morning muster – just report to me at the guard house at twelve.'

'Ja gut, I'll get my head down and catch some beauty sleep, I'll stay with Anna so you'll know where to find me. We've got to work this out between us – to survive I mean. I just hope our lot will not be sent to any front.'

'I doubt it, we're only a small detachment,' said Helmut. 'Besides, they need us here to keep law and order and clear up the mess.'

Ja Anna, he reminded himself as Willi had mentioned her name. He liked her even more now since assisting her in that washroom incident and having to carry her naked body back down into the cellar, but the memory faded as Willi brought him back to the present.

'I heard the Russkies are heading for Czechoslovakia, Yugoslavia and Rumania to cut off our oil. We're not that far away from there.'

'Ach nein, that's over one thousand kilometres from here, we'll stop their advance once our new tanks get there. Our best bet is to shoot down more of those damned American bombers. They'll lose their stomachs to fight and Roosevelt will make the Englander fight their own battles. We can then give them a second Dünkirchen.'

'Hmm, I don't see it that way, that lousy whisky swiller said the other night that he will only accept our total and unconditional surrender. I heard it myself on my radio – it was on the BBC. They translated his speech into French and German and what about their bombers? The Englander have hundreds of them now.'

'Radio? I thought you handed that in?' said Helmut with surprise, as he lit up two more cigarettes.

'Ja, I did but I kept the crystal set, it works fine. I've stretched a thirty-metre aerial inside my barn and the BBC are transmitting with extra power, so I listen in some nights.' Willi took the cigarette. 'Doesn't work too well in the day-time, something to do with the atmosphere.'

'Better watch out,' said Helmut. 'Don't tell too many people about that or you'll be getting a change of atmosphere.' And indicated with his thumb in the direction of Dachau.

'Na, not me, I'm a farmer and too well-known around here. They don't come searching around the likes of me,' and made a wide yawn. 'I'm off now, see you up here in the Hoffbräuhaus, I'll get a couple of Steins in.'

Helmut managed a chuckle at Willi's satirical wit as he thought of the dry cellars and the empty beer hall.

'By the way, Willi, I have to tell you something. It's about Anna.'

'Anna? Why? What's she done now?' Willi said, with concern, as he paused by the open door.

'Nein, nothing. She's alright. Alles gut,' Helmut answered awkwardly. 'Only, I have to tell you that she is Jewish. That's why Gruber had it in for her. He found out, ja?'

'*Gott im Himmel!* So that's it, eine Judin. If they find out we're harbouring a Jew we'll be in the grosse Scheisse.'

'Ach nein Willi. It's now only the two of us that know. I'll tell you the full story later but just be careful what you say down there, be discreet, ja?'

Willi nodded, stubbed out his cigarette and shaking his head, for once was lost for words.

'We'll be alright Willi,' continued Helmut. 'Don't worry. Just keep schtum about it, ja? So, I'll see you at twelve, at the guardroom, but make it sharp. You're buying the first round.'

He grinned and with a wave made for his combination. One kick and the BMW sprang into life. Helmut roared off and was soon swallowed up by the blackout as Willi returned to the cellar deep in thought as he tried to dismiss the dire consequences in harbouring a Jew, here in Münich of all places.

The lorry returned at four o'clock that morning and Helmut was there at the guardroom to meet it. He examined the signed papers with the stamp of the SS and the Dachau concentration camp and handed them to his superior officer who, after a quick scrutiny and a shrug, handed them back to Helmut.

'In the morning take them to the Gestapo HQ. They're nothing to do with me. We're soldiers not spy catchers and executioners. I want nothing to do with those SS fanatics up the road.'

'Jawohl Herr Hauptman,' said Helmut with relief as he placed the papers and the dog-tag into an envelope and concealed it in the inside pocket of his great coat. However seconds later the officer turned and eyed the sergeant with a questioning gaze.

'By the way, Feldwebel Vogl, how is it that you're involved with the Gestapo?' Helmut froze in his jackboots as he met the officer's unsettling gaze and tried to think of a plausible answer.

'It was the air raid, Herr Hauptman. Their HQ was hit and they had no transport. They saw us clearing the streets and requested for us to move the body for incineration. It was a plain-clothed officer by the name of Gruber – he told us not to ask questions and as I was the senior NCO, I just did as he requested. As you know, Herr Hauptman, it is better not to ask questions, not from those people. You know how they operate – they treat us like underdogs.'

The officer nodded in mute satisfaction but his rancour clearly showed as he angrily spun on his heel and marched out of the guardroom.

After the midday muster Helmut detailed off his squad for their next assignment. They were not given a specific task only to assist as required during bombing raids. Willi's orders were quite convenient as he was to man an aircraft listening post. The device, with multiple dishes was ranged close to his farm together with a Flak battery and radar-guided searchlight. After any air raid, he was to take his men into Munich and there assist the Heimwehr with first aid duties. Helmut supplied him with a truck as Willi and his eight-man squad set off in the direction of Karlsfeld.

Helmut picked up his coat, threw it into the side-car and set off on his combination to the Gestapo headquarters at Wittelsbad Palais. Once there he requested to see Herr Gruber, but was informed that he had not been seen since the afternoon before the raid.

'I have some documents for him,' said Helmut. 'Can I leave them here?'

The orderly, wearing a red swastika armband gave the sergeant a quizzical glance as Helmut produced the official brown envelope with its Dachau Stalag stamp.

'Here, please follow me,' he said in a clipped Prussian accent and motioned for Helmut to follow. They picked their way past large chunks of plaster and masonry as they headed down a wide and dark corridor. The orderly stopped at an open door and indicated inside. 'This is Herr Gruber's office, you may leave a message.'

Danke,' Helmut replied as he took in the scene. Office, or what's left of it, he mused as he brushed past the pompous orderly. 'I'll leave a message where he can contact me, ja?'

'Jawohl,' clipped the man as he indicated to a notepad lying on the floor. 'The wall and window will be fixed shortly,' he added as he followed Helmut's gaze. Helmut was amused by his posturing, as the man was clearly agitated by the intrusion and continued to glare in his direction. He picked up the pad and placed it back on the ornately carved desk and noted there were several scribbles and some Berlin phone numbers but three familiar words focused his attention: 'Anna Bauer – Jude'.

So here it was he mused, Gruber's discovery about Anna was still on his pad and as yet, they'd not missed him. He must have received the information and photocopies then made his way to see if Anna was still at the cellar. Being Gestapo he would know all about the trains and their schedules and took a chance that she would still be there.

Helmut's mind worked overtime as he tried to second guess Gruber's activities. Probably no one else has seen this as a plan of action flashed through his mind. Helmut picked up a pencil and began to write as the orderly stood by the door and observed his every move.

'Ach, Geheim,' said Helmut with a grimace and in mock alarm, methodically scribbling out the words. 'That's restricted, secret, I can't write that,' he muttered loud enough for the man to hear. He stood watching suspiciously now that Helmut had torn the sheet from the pad. With great deliberation Helmut wrote out another message and stuffed the crumpled paper into his tunic pocket. 'That's it,' he said with an authoritative glance at the orderly. 'He can find me there and pick up the documents at the guardroom, as I cannot leave them here like this.' As an afterthought he pinned the pad down with a crystal, swastika-embellished paperweight.

Leaving he chuckled to himself as he saw the bemused look clouding the man's features and realised he had to act fast to dispel any suspicions.

'You had better get that hole and window fixed before the blackout,' he said in an assertive tone. 'My men will be coming round later to check on lights and security.'

'Jawohl Herr Feldwebel,' replied the orderly in a high-pitched and irritated manner. 'It is already in hand. It will be done before dark.' He was vexed that this soldier had so blatantly invaded his sanctum.

They made their way back down the corridor as Helmut strode ahead, his steel-tipped jackboots echoing along the flag-stoned floor, past grim-faced men in black uniforms working to clear away the debris and salvage their mountains of paperwork.

At last he was there, at the entrance with its splintered door hanging at a crazy angle from a solitary hinge. Men with shovels, wheelbarrows and shoring timbers were already in evidence, as was their horse-drawn transport. The orderly in his black uniform with death's head insignia seemed out of place with the rubble at his feet but meticulously, like a guarding ant he made sure Helmut, his charge and intruder vacated the building.

Once in the open Helmut heaved a sigh of relief, the scrap of paper burning like hot coals in his pocket. He leapt on his machine and with one kick the BMW sprang into life. Revving the engine he roared away and allowing himself a backward glance noted with grim satisfaction the orderly still standing there, deeply suspicious and now flanked by two SS guards.

Chapter Thirty

SUMMER OF '44

With the trains still not running, Anna and Eddi remained in the cellar.

Helmut had informed her he did not think the Gestapo would bother her again as Gruber was dead, and the memo he had torn from the note-pad was the only evidence which linked her to him. He still had possession of the dog tag from the unfortunate Frenchman and no one had contacted him with the note he had left on Gruber's desk – not yet, anyway. It seemed once Gruber ceased to exist, all such matters died with him.

As spring turned to summer, their life in the cellar became a routine event. Anna was safe there from the occasional air raid and used the beer halls' defunct facilities for meals and sundries. On odd occasions she ventured with Eddi outside, taking snatches of fresh air and watch fascinated, as the sun reflected on a thousand vapour trails as American and British bombers filled the sky.

For her, night time was the worst. She grieved for news of her husband but Munich was a long way from the sea and the only news she ever received was by way of Willi's humble crystal set. The German news was all about the Wunderwaffen which would soon be in operation and the German Volk should take heart as these weapons will win the war.

Then, the U-Boats were mentioned as stoic fighters and according to *'Germany calling, Germany calling'* radio transmissions with its presenter William Joyce, (nick-named 'Lord Haw-Haw,') these were sinking many ships in the English Channel. However, the German radio could not suppress the news from the Eastern Front as it filtered through from the thousands of wounded as they returned back to their homes. They related stories of bitter fighting, hardship and humble retreat.

Then there was Helmut. He had been kind to her but she could not help thinking he was giving her more attention than was justified. On occasions he took her and Eddi out to see the new Tiger tanks which were being transported to the Russian front. The boy was taking to him as well and now called him and Willi 'Onkel'. She could not blame Helmut as she knew she was still attractive and in the confines of the cellar those sorts of things could develop and rapidly get out of hand.

It was the air raids, these made one realise how thin the thread of life can be. Often he would sit with her and Eddi, to put a comforting arm round her as she cuddled her son and the building shook and masonry fell in chunks. With air raids one needed the closeness and the touch of a fellow human being for comfort and reassurance and was a psychological thing which few people – except those who sent them, realised. Anna knew and was alert to the danger of such friendships, which if left to run their course could soon blossom into full relationships.

It was a wet afternoon in early June when an excited Willi rushed down into the cellar. Anna was busy teaching her son the sounds of the alphabet and paused, alarmed at the noise, as he stomped down the cellar stairs.

'*Anna, it's happened!*' he shouted from the door. 'Sie Kommen!' Confused, she gazed at the excited soldier.

Whose coming Willi? She said with a frown and once again, expecting the worst.

'They've landed,' he said with a sweep of his arm. 'The Americans and the English, they're in France.' He paused for breath, his chubby features flushed with emotion. 'Helmut told me at the camp and it's all over town. We're sending our reserve Panzer troops and aircraft to stop them. Now we shall see who will win the war?'

Anna's world folded like a house of cards. France, Lorient, Brest, my husband he's there somewhere. What will happen to him? Mein Gott, he will be killed for sure.

Willi was beside himself, telling her about troop movements, battleships and parachute drops, but the words washed over her in a maelstrom of fear and meaningless sound.

'Frau Anna, I'm sorry,' said Willi as he saw her distress and tried to quell her fear. 'Look, the way I see it is our navy would have pulled out of France long ago as they must have seen the build-up for the attack. Makes sense, ja?'

He paused, as deep within him he knew she had just cause to be alarmed. Anna stared at him in shock and disbelief as he tried his best to calm her.

'We've heard nothing to say that Franz has been injured or anything else...' His voice trailed off, the words meaningless to her as she tried to come to terms with the news.

'Nein!' cried Anna, and composing herself shook her head. 'Sorry Willi, it's my nerves. I'm at my wits end thinking about him. Nobody knows I'm here, no one. I don't exist. I must make contact with the Kriegsmarine, or his parents in Dresden.'

'But of course, Frau Anna but please, if you make any official enquiry then there is the Gestapo and who knows what can happen? If they find you again then we will all hang.'

A stony silence transcended as she shifted her gaze to three flies in decreasing orbit round the glowing light bulb. He's right, thought Anna, but I must get away from here to somehow make contact with the navy in France or Kiel.

'We'll wait for Helmut to return,' said Willi. 'See what other news he has and what our unit will do now. We can discuss it all better then, ja?' Still trying to calm her he sidled across to the paraffin stove, poured out two mugs of real coffee, added the luxury of sugar and handed one to her.

'Ja, you are right,' she replied. 'I'm sorry for cutting you short. It's the war – it's getting on my nerves and you're right, we'll see what Helmut thinks.' She sat down at the table and instinctively began to straighten out the embroidered cloth, a present from Willi's wife. 'Perhaps with the landings the bombers will not come again,' she added, voicing her thoughts.

'They're still there,' said Willi. 'The BBC said they are now sending one thousand bombers at a time. I can't believe that but then we shot down eighty of them in the last raid up country. Either we're getting good, or the sky's full of them.'

'Well the last bombers just flew over us, didn't they?' said Anna and stirring her coffee. 'They were headed towards Italy and Austria. So what's there to bomb? The opera house? '

'Ha, they're all getting it now,' said Willi with a snort. 'If those gutless, turn-coat Italians didn't scheiss their hosen so easily we could have stood our ground and saved Italy. Mussolini and Hitler are a bright pair. If they hadn't let Rommel run out of fuel in Africa, we would all be in Cairo by now.' Willi paused, clearly agitated by the mention of the Italians.

I've touched a nerve, thought Anna. This is the other side of the man.

'And where was their navy in their scheiss pond?' Willi continued, gesturing with a podgy hand and a face like thunder. 'All that Mussolini guy's posturing and his bragging of Roman legions and an Italian sea. It certainly didn't deter the English Navy – they sent him to the bottom of it.' Anna nodded with a sympathetic smile as she had heard similar comments from others.

'So, how much longer can this war go on? What do you think'?

'Christmas,' said Willi disdainfully. 'I reckon Hitler will be compelled to ask for terms. I've heard it from the officers. They've had enough already but that damned Austrian keeps yodelling about these new weapons. Who knows, maybe he's got something? As for me, it can't be soon enough, one way or the other.'

Shaking his head in disgust he fished for a cigarette from his tunic. Lit up, removed his helmet and sat to finish his coffee. Anna was glad she had managed to change the subject and put him in a better frame of mind and hoping he was right about Christmas. She thought about the landings; Franz might be a prisoner of war now that France was being liberated. Who knows?

They both turned as the familiar sound of boots reverberated on the cellar stairs and Helmut entered carrying a small cardboard box.

'Here, Frau Anna, it's for you and the boy.' Surprised at any such offerings, she took it from him.

'Go on, open it,' said Willi cajolingly with a wink at his friend.

Eddi left his game as he sensed that something important was going on. Quickly he ran to his mother's side as she began to open the box.

'Lieber Himmel!' cried Anna, as she saw the cake with its icing and five tiny candles. 'Look Eddi, it's for you! Tomorrow is your birthday, remember?' He nodded with a happy face, not daring to take his eyes off the treat in store.

'Danke, danke,' was all she could say as not for a long time had tears of joy and happiness caressed her faded cheeks. She hugged her boy and leaving her chair kissed each soldier's cheek. Thanking them for the treat and for bringing back some semblance of sanity into her life.

Chapter Thirty-One

TREK EAST

From the Canaries the two U-boats headed south, keeping five miles distant to give themselves maximum lookout coverage but still in visual distance of each other. Twenty-two uneventful days later, they rounded the Cape of Good Hope, keeping well to the south and the British naval base at the Cape and Simondstown. The immensity of the British Empire was hammered home to them as even in these great waters the lion roared.

Rounding the Cape, they used their snorkels to good effect but the device continually played havoc with their ears and lungs as the long Atlantic swell slammed the air valves shut and starving the diesels, which then sucked the air from inside the submerged hull.

Steamships were sighted as the two submarines were now in the busy shipping lanes on their long trek east, taking them across the Indian Ocean and towards the Malacca Strait.

How times have changed, mused Franz as he observed the fat hulls of the British vessels pass sedately across his bow. How easily he could have dispatched them as they steamed into his sights.

Heading ever eastwards, they passed well clear of the islands of Mauritius and Reunion as, once again, the Royal Navy was in residence. Eighteen days later they found themselves entering the narrow channel of the Malacca Strait. It was time to say Auf Wiedersehen, as the two boats would now proceed independently and ten miles in line astern through the Strait that separated Malaya from the historic Spice Islands of Indonesia. Once through the Strait, it would be onwards to the South China Sea and their rendezvous with destiny.

They ran submerged, again making good use of their snorkels as here, the seas were calm but the threat of Allied sea and air patrols was ever present. At the southern end of the Strait the fortress island of Singapore was still in friendly Japanese hands, with its airfields at Changi and Sembawang able to send out daytime reconnaissance patrols. Yet again these posed a danger as their Japanese allies would shoot first as any submarines of their size and structure would immediately be classed as hostile, being either British or Dutch. Royal Navy ships were in the area, including two aircraft carriers operating in support of Admiral King and Nimitz's American 5th Fleet.

It was from a carrier that a recognisance patrol swept low over the Strait and an Avenger aircraft dipped its wings as it sighted the tell-tale wake of a snorkel tube to the west of Singapore Island. The fleet was informed and a British 'T' class submarine dispatched to lie in wait for the approaching boat. Several hours later a 200-foot column of water and the dull sound of an explosion signalled the end of Frigattenkapitän Kurt Oblitz's mission, together with the loss of V2 rocket parts, blueprints of the Uranium Bombe, Heavy Water and a valuable consignment of mercury.

On 25 August, Frigattenkapitän Franz Bauer passed through the 700-mile length of the Malacca Strait, unaware and ironically sailing over the wreck of U-835 and her crew. He past Singapore Island to port and travelled east, through its Strait and to emerge without incident, into the waters of the South China Sea.

As Franz surfaced his boat a heavy curtain of monsoon rain reduced visibility to almost zero. It was perfect submarine weather with a moderate swell which kept them hidden from ships and aircraft, even those that possessed the fledgling Radar. He stemmed the north-westerly current and ran at fourteen knots surfaced. At 2000 hrs, and well after nightfall he eased back to his cruising speed, having run the gauntlet of the two Straits. The night was black, with only a few stars as Franz made a brief radio transmission on the 600 metre band in order to establish contact with his consort but only the mushy sound of static and a background ethereal hiss was heard.

'Must be bad radio reception in this weather and humidity,' said the radio operator.

Franz acknowledged with a nod and reasoned that Kurt might still be travelling submerged. He gave instructions for the helmsman to steer the boat towards the north-east and the Spratly Islands.

At 0400 hrs, and before the advent of the eastern dawn, Franz called on radio the German naval attaché in Tokyo. The coded reply came through an Abwehr G 312 device that he was to proceed to the harbour of Bulinao, Western Luzon, and to rendezvous with the Japanese submarine *I-59*. Franz acknowledged the Enigma-coded message and submerged as dawn was fast approaching and the island of Singapore would still be visible astern.

Eight days later and having sailed a total of seventeen thousand miles, U-888 was met by a Japanese picket boat and escorted into the coconut-fringed harbour of Bulinao. A welcoming party from *I-59* was there to greet them as Franz nosed his vessel alongside of the Japanese giant. As the officers were entertained in Captain Itachi's spacious cabin, a rapid offloading of their precious cargo commenced.

With the aid of his two Japanese passengers and Itachi's smattering of German they all made themselves understood.

'It is strange Captain, don't you think,' said Franz, 'here we are, both sworn enemies of the British and Americans and yet the only way we can converse and relate with each other is in their language.' The irony was not lost on Itachi as he gauged the German's character and reasoning.

'The Americans are back in the Philippines,' explained Itachi. 'Like yourselves, we are slowly being driven out of our conquests. We cannot fight against the might of America, they have too much technology.' Franz nodded in agreement as he acquainted himself with a glass of warm rice spirit.

'Not only that,' continued Franz, 'but we Germans have the same technology, if not better. However the American factories and houses have never been bombed. With your help we should be able to construct a bomb that will flatten the whole of New York in an instant, and then we shall see how they like it.'

Itachi gave a benign nod. 'I've been briefed,' he replied. 'Our scientists are also working on such a device. I know the principle behind it, but I understand the Americans are also constructing such a bomb.'

'Yes, that's true,' said Franz with a grim nod as he recalled Himmler's rant about Einstein and Fuchs. 'And the winner of the race will triumph in this war. It is a gamble and a race for the end game.'

'Yes, Captain Bauer,' replied Itachi. 'As soon as we are loaded we will depart. Is there any news about your other boat? It was supposed to be meeting one of our submarines further to the north. I ask, as I can only load two of your special LUT torpedoes. We incurred some hull damage during an air attack.'

Franz shook his head. 'No word as yet. Doesn't look too good, I'm afraid. Perhaps we can put the other two to good use on our way home,' he said with a smile. Itachi nodded, and wished he could do the same.

'I'm afraid the waters around here are infested with hostile craft,' said Itachi. 'It's from the air that we have our greatest threat, not to mention all these uncharted shoals and sandbanks we occasionally run into. Singapore is still a good base for us with all those dry docks and facilities but the British are trying like mad to get it back and there are now many American air raids. We could have gone there ourselves but with all the bombing our rendezvous was moved to this more secluded spot.'

'Yes, I understand,' said Franz. 'We have two of our U-Boats trapped there at the moment. Perhaps they will never get out.'

'Well, Captain, we will have to do our best,' said Itachi, eyeing his counterpart. Never, in his wildest dreams, did he ever think that these white, round-eyed people, who somehow gave orders to a crew in the same vein, would one day assist him and his country.

'Hai,' said Franz with a grin as he drained his glass and they all laughed but in a more sober tone added, 'We'll load our return cargo and take our sailing orders from Tokyo. Perhaps we will spend a few days here for rest and maintenance before we head back home.'

'Please be our guests, I will ensure you have a pleasant stay.' Itachi spoke rapidly to his aide. He beckoned the hovering steward to serve another round of Saki together with a tray of Filipino rice and coconut cakes.

That evening, *I-59* slipped her moorings and proceeded with her cargo and the scientists for the open sea. Gaining deep water the submarine turned to starboard as Itachi set his course in a northerly direction and the beleaguered islands of Japan.

U-888 remained for another week to effect repairs and load a cargo of copper and wolfram. With General McArthur's 'private war' and army knocking at the gates of Manila, the Japanese in this remote location were left to their own devices, to wither on the vine as McArthur weeded out Manila.

Bulinao and its fishing harbour remained quiet, a backwater of the war as Manila lay one hundred miles to the south. However, the occasional American reconnaissance aircraft did from time to time keep check on known Japanese positions, but the wily troops under jungle camouflage withheld their fire.

To Franz and his crew the Filipino were friendly but only up to a point as they could not grasp the true situation. To them any white person went by the name of Joe and was by default, an American. They had suffered terribly under the Japanese yoke, with brutality and starvation their daily diet but now the wheel had turned, as the oppressors were compelled to seek local produce and favours in order to survive. With Franz speaking English it was easy for him and his crew to make friends and during their short stay were well-entertained, especially once the U-Bootmen handed out English cigarettes and American-labelled coffee.

They all enjoyed the hospitality of the small bamboo-decked bar close to the market place which served Cerveca and the local brew of Tuba, their own brand of coconut rum. Some of the men struck up relationships with the pretty girls but that was perhaps a less amorous affair than a sailor's want and the girl's need to be commercial.

On 9 September and well after a breath-taking sunset, U-888 slipped her moorings and proceeded through the narrow channel marked only by bamboo poles and coconut palms at its entrance. Franz set his course to the west, then south-west, for the long trek back to the Fatherland. He was in a melancholy mood having heard that Kurt's boat, by now well overdue, had not kept its designated rendezvous.

Once again dark clouds hung low and threatening, which suited him but the seas were rough. He proceeded at eight knots surfaced, as in this weather only a ship's Radar might pick him up but even then he would be indistinguishable on the screen's noise and clutter.

Ten hours later Franz submerged, having left the Philippines some eighty miles in his wake. He dived the boat, continuing warily at snorkel and periscope depth as he headed for home. Surfaced by night they passed the many shoals en-route, travelling onward and past the Spratley Islands, back towards the island of Singapore and the daunting Allied gauntlet of the Malacca Strait.

On 18 September, Franz found himself in shoal waters off the numerous islands which surround the entrance to the Singapore Strait. In the strong current he was swept along, only to take the ground and ride up onto an uncharted shoal. Franz cursed his luck and with engines running at full astern the boat could not be moved. The diesels soon faltered as sand was being sucked into the cooling water intakes and clogging the filters. At snorkel depth there was insufficient ballast remaining to blow the tanks and have any effect.

Although without a great tidal range in this part of the world, it was enough to expose part of the conning tower at low water and to attract the attention of the local fishermen. Fortunately for Franz he had grounded at about low water and while he waited for the tide, cargo was shifted aft in order to lighten the bows. With his bows clear, Franz waited for the flood but keeping his AA gunners closed-up with the men knee-deep in water. He peered anxiously through his glasses towards the south, where several dots could be seen in the sky which could only mean aircraft, carriers and their escorts.

By late afternoon Franz stood on his bridge chain smoking and drinking enough coffee to launch a battleship, as the incoming tide crept at a snail's pace up the side of the tower. With several tons of cargo shifted aft and an extra five feet of water under his keel, Franz took a last sweeping glance at the sea and sky before closing the hatch and giving the order to re-float the boat.

Engaging maximum electric propulsion astern and with his men aft jumping up and down in unison, they felt a judder then a sudden lurch as the boat shifted and with a hearty cheer, twenty men collapsed in a pile on top of each other. Free at last from its shoal encounter, U-888's bows reared high and surfaced like a wounded whale as the controller opened the forward ballast tanks to the sea.

'We're in luck today,' said Jurgen checking his chart, Franz glanced in his direction and acknowledged with a nod. The boat settled on an even keel and grounded gently on the ocean floor. Franz and his engineers took stock of their situation and without any signs of damage they decided to reverse their course and to stay submerged at ninety feet until well after dark. It was then that they heard the fast high-pitched whine of propellers, followed by the unmistakeable slow and distant ping of an Asdic device as it probed the depths with an acoustic finger.

'Looks like we've been rumbled,' said Franz with concern. 'There's not supposed to be any Allied surface ships so close to the island, what's going on? We'll lie here close to this sandbar as it will give us protection. Pass the word, Jurgen. No noise whatsoever.' The man nodded and disappeared aft to the engine room. Several depth charges were heard, but at a distance. 'Good thing here is there are quite a few wrecks about,' said Franz as he sat with his controllers.

'As long as they don't intend making a new one, Herr Kaleu'nt,' quipped Johann, returning with two mugs of coffee. Franz side-glanced the cook and acknowledged with a sombre nod as the man had voiced his own thoughts.

Hours ticked by and with no more sounds from above, Franz brought U-888 to periscope depth and made a 360-degree sweep of the sea. To his chagrin the ships were still there, together with several score of local fishing boats which were all around him, eerily illuminating the scene with their oil lamps flickering from glass jars. It was reminiscent of a water gala, only the oil lamps now silhouetted several hulls of Allied warships close by. He had no option but to vent tanks and settle back on the seabed and remain there, for to manoeuvre in these restricted waters with warships in

253

proximity would be his undoing. However, he reasoned that his saving grace was the warships could not pass easily through the armada of small boats, or use explosives without due care and attention, or so he thought.

In the early hours of the following day and as the air in the submarine thickened, the sound of propellers was heard once again along with the Asdic pulses as they probed and searched the depths. Several explosions were heard more than felt, but this time they were closer. As the minutes turned to hours and the air turned foul, soda lime cartridges were utilised, breathing sets were broken out to assist in breathing and curtail the build-up of the life-threatening carbon dioxide gas.

After twenty-three hours submerged since their last breath of fresh air, their situation was becoming critical. Even with bursts of oxygen from the storage banks the air had become almost un-breathable as above them, the swish, swishing sounds of propellers was ever present.

All the men, except Franz and the hydrophone operator were in their bunks, sweating profusely and trying to control their breathing which came in laboured gasps. Franz gambled with the idea of surfacing as he still had his torpedo tubes loaded but then it would be an uneven fight, now four hours after dawn, he would become a sitting target. It was one of the senior torpedo men who came gasping to the control room.

'Yes, what is it, Prinz?' said Franz as he eyed the man and his deteriorating condition.

'Herr Kaleu'nt,' he rasped, 'we have been thinking,' and stopped for breath. 'We have two of those LUT torpedoes left, the ones we didn't offload. They are those special acoustic ones, ja?' Franz nodded. 'Well, Herr Kapitän, can't we fire them off from here and see what happens?'

Franz gazed at the man as he tried to mull the idea over in his oxygen-starved brain. It was difficult to think and reason as the vice-like pressure on his temples made his head spin with every shallow breath he took. He observed the man's grey complexion, his glazed eyes and sweat-soaked apparel, which told its own tale and that of himself and the rest of his crew. Another hour, a maximum two, and they would never surface again he reasoned and checked his watch. To fire a torpedo would be admissible, as he had completed his mission. Now, to stay alive and to fight his boat would be his duty.

'Ja, Prinz, I think we'll give it a try,' he said, his chest heaving with effort. 'Pass the word quietly. Un-ship the "eel" in number 2 tube and re-load with the LUT. Make everything ready and short range setting.'

'Jawohl, Herr Kaleu'nt,' wheezed the man and quietly went back to his station in the bow. Being the senior torpedo-man Prinz made ready the LUT's sophisticated mechanism. Running-distance, set to minimum, 'curve-track' and the modified acoustic firing mechanism deployed, running depth 12 feet. Finally the battery made 'live', and the weapon loaded into the vacated tube.

'Jurgen, pass the word to the engine room,' croaked Franz. 'Get ready on the E-motors. We'll start the motors, as to fire blind we might hit the sandbar and damage the boat. I'll point the bows in the general direction of the propeller sounds and give the order to fire the eel. By the way, get hold of the gunners, make ready the scuttling charges.'

Jurgen, wide-eyed at the mention of the charges nodded at the plan, lines of strain etched in furrows across his sweating brow. Soaked with perspiration he went aft to inform the engineers and the gunners, still resting in their bunks.

For Franz the action would be transitory, a chosen moment in war which for him and his men would be their triumph or nemesis. It was their only chance he reasoned, as he tried to second-guess the enemy above. The ships knew he was there and would keep him down until he perished on the seabed, or came up for the life-saving air only to face a deadly hail of naval gunnery. It was after all, a game of cat and mouse and he – the mouse – would have a not-so-timid first bite. As U-888's E-motors and pumps engaged, so the propeller activities from above rose to a crescendo.

The hunt was on; with laboured breathing Franz gave orders to flood the number 2 tube. With the pressure equalised torpedo-man Prinz opened the bow-cap as Franz manoeuvred the boat in the general direction of the approaching propeller noises. He gave orders for an 18 degrees bows up inclination and fired his special tin-fish. Ballasting down to compensate for the loss of weight they waited with bated breathing and checking seconds against their watches as the LUT sped on its way. Agonising seconds ticked by as with the E-motors on dead slow, Franz was able to maintain trim and steerage. With their last reserves of energy and the torpedo well on its way he turned the boat 180 degrees and distanced himself at 40 revolutions from the hunters above.

In the control room the chronometer ticked away; their life seconds numbering as the foul air became unbearable, making men weak to the point of collapse. Jurgen, with stop-watch in hand counted, as endless seconds slowly passed...

***

After its six hundred yards run the LUT's mechanism switched to its acoustic searching mode, at the same time its 40 second straight run changed, as its 'course curving' mode deployed. Jurgen, still counting the seconds slowly shook his head as with labouring lungs, Prinz in the forward torpedo room squeezed his thumbs and waited anxiously as the countdown continued. A hundred yards into its second searching curve, and with 88 seconds elapsed running time the magnetic / acoustic pistol engaged and fired its 650 pound high explosive charge.

If not causing the vessel immediately to sink, it caught the Allied ships by surprise. The homing torpedo had done its deadly work by blowing off the stern of a warship which soon settled low in the water, while a destroyer went in hot pursuit of the offender. The remaining destroyer assisted the stricken ship, as the local fishermen watched the spectacle from ringside seats.

'Gustav bring her up to periscope depth,' Franz rasped to his engineering officer and allowed himself a quick glimpse of the surface through his attack periscope and watched with relief as an American destroyer headed towards Singapore and its Strait. He grunted with satisfaction as he housed the scope and at having witnessed a cruiser-sized warship, ablaze and settling by the stern.

Perhaps they thought it would be his obvious course, but the noise and detonations onboard the stricken vessel now masked his engines. Slowing his boat to maintain depth and steerage, he gave orders for the Snorkel Tube to be made ready.

On opening its valve, the pressure build-up vented with a roar as the foul air escaped to atmosphere. Merciful life-sustaining air was sucked in, flooding the boat with its life-redeeming qualities as Franz started his diesels and at four knots put distance between himself and the muffled explosions of the sinking ship. He changed his plan as he shaped a new course, away from the shoals as he headed south by east, along the east coast of Sumatra. He would slip in between the larger islands which were still occupied by friendly forces and some four hundred miles later, slip through the Sunda Passage for the long and hazardous trek home.

Chapter Thirty-Two

OBEY THE RUDDER OR THE REEF

I-59 made good progress by night but was again restricted in speed by having to submerge during daylight hours. Once surfaced Itachi contacted his base on HF radio; however, unknown to him and naval HQ in Tokyo, the Americans had long since broken the Japanese super-enciphered codes, including additives and knew, within some two-square miles of ocean, his submarine's position. It was only a matter of time and opportunity during this period of inclement weather before they would act. Without knowing its vital mission it was enough for the Americans that the submarine was there, it posed a threat and therefore had to be eliminated.

Unfortunately for Itachi the enormous build-up of operation 'Forager' was well underway, involving hundreds of ships and aircraft of the US 5th fleet for the eventual liberation of the Marianas Islands. Itachi's radio signals were picked up by Admiral Nimitz's command ship and investigative action taken.

Four destroyers and a cruiser were dispatched to search for *I-59* as for the present, sending up aircraft from carriers was curtailed due to the weather. Steaming at reduced speed the five ships made their way towards the north-west and three days later picked up a target. It was only a small blip on their Radar screens but a positive pulse to be investigated as both British and Dutch warships were also in operation in those seas.

On a westerly bearing and some 230 miles NNW of Batan Island they closed the range. At four-thousand yards the first star shell salvoes screamed through the night to straddle the surfaced submarine. Caught unawares and now illuminated, Itachi crash-dived his boat as shells from destroyers spouted menacing geysers and shrapnel damaged the hull.

They came running in at high speed, slowing to comb the depths with Asdic, as minutes later patterns of depth charges rained down like autumn leaves on the hapless crew of *I-59*. An intense pressure wall of water caught the submarine in its vice-like grip as numerous 600 lbs charges of amatol exploded and slammed against her hull.

The steel leviathan heaved and plunged like a child's toy caught in a millrace as it tried valiantly to escape the explosive hammer-blows of its pursuers.

Inside the boat Itachi held on grimly to his periscope controls as *I-59* clawed for the safety of the deep. Water began to hiss and flood the boat as a result of the shelling combined with the ever increasing pressure, as the deep began to act on the hull. With E-motors howling in protest the planes-men fought to steady the plunging vessel but the quest for sanctuary in the depths began to turn into a nightmare as the stricken submarine spiralled ever downwards.

In the control room all eyes were riveted on the gauges as the manometer needle crept towards the hull's designed maximum depth. Wide-eyed, they could only watch as the controllers fought to steady the boat and agonising seconds ticked by as the vessel, now at 330 feet had reached its limits, but the needle carried on, ever downwards. Itachi wiped the perspiration from his forehead and frantically ordered all ballast tanks blown as the needle indicated 380 feet and remained steady. However water was still cascading into the boat from damaged seals and valves and metallic groans were heard along the length of the tortured hull.

On the surface, depth charging continued as the destroyers still picked up the sound of *I-59's* motors and pumps but the detonations were more heard than felt as the settings by now were too shallow. With ballast tanks empty, the plunging vessel steadied momentarily but again the depth began to increase as the crew worked frantically to shut off valves and replace sheared bolts on flanges and seals. Monitoring the increasing depth, Itachi met Takayuki's gaze and resignedly shook his head. The FO nodded solemnly as the gauge indicated 408 feet and still falling.

It was fortunate for Itachi that he was close to Formosa as with a sickening lurch, *I-59* hit the abyssal ooze. Lights and fittings shattered and red emergency lamps glowed dimly as the fathometer needle settled to point steadily at an indicated depth of 438 feet.

'*Stop motors!*' Itachi screamed, 'leave all pumps running.' Now, well beyond the boat's operating limits and with the vessel still making water, the crew frantically carried on with repairs. Using wooden dowels and canvas tourniquets on pipes and fittings, they staunched the flow. The forward torpedo room was vacated and its watertight door shut as, gradually, order came from chaos and the main lighting was restored. Now at last, without the giveaway noise of his motors, a dripping silence descended as they waited in hope, listening intently and thankfully hearing the sounds of receding propellers. Long minutes ticked by as the engineers worked frantically and soon the main bilge pump was back in commission. But now another problem began to rear its ugly head as the stealthy killer of submariners crept into their midst. It was every submariner's nightmare as an acrid smell of chlorine began to fill the boat. The deadly yellow gas was emitted from fractured batteries and sulphuric acid storage flasks. As the acid leaked, it combined with sea water in the battery room.

Itachi had no choice but to surface his boat, however the hull still had negative buoyancy as the depth gauge remained at 438 feet.

It was Mori who came to the control room and with a slight bow approached the two officers. Speech was difficult with the gas affecting eyes, throats and lungs. Itachi nodded at his engineering officer. 'Permission to blow the port after fuel tank, Captain, and also discharge bunker fuel from the main tank?' Itachi gazed at the man and recalled the damaged fuel tank which was still flooded.

'Will it empty, Mori, sufficiently I mean?'

'Hai,' came his laboured reply. 'It was only leaking slowly; I can empty it along with some bunkers. Enough to give us buoyancy and we can use our motors once clear of the sea bed. We can afford to discharge one ton of bunkers, it will help.'

'Hai, Mori, do your best as the batteries cannot last much longer.' The engineer disappeared and seconds later pressurised air was forced into the damaged tank. Time stood still as men in the control room had eyes only for the gauge and its long, slender needle which remained stubbornly at depth. It was the engineers who shouted in unison as the stern shifted and agonising seconds later the control room needle began to move, slowly at first but the depth was decreasing.

Itachi ordered re-breathing sets to be distributed as the choking gas took hold. After what seemed an eternity, but was only minutes, *I-59* surfaced, bows down. Itachi opened the hatch and regained his bridge, to his relief the visibility was reduced to zero as the rain god was smiling. Takayuki got everyone on deck as the rain came down in sheets and everyone was in a happy mood, laughing and slapping each other's backs in celebration and joy of deliverance from a watery grave. Standing at the base of the tower the two German scientists stood apart and conversed in low tones. From their crestfallen appearance and ashen faces, Itachi guessed they were not happy with events. There again, neither was he.

As the rain continued the boat was vented as hatches were opened and the effects of the shell damaged area examined. They found the empty hangar had a five-inch hole on both sides where a shell had passed through without exploding. Fortunately this was not part of the main pressure hull, but a pressure hull within itself and could be left flooded, as was the case.

It was only the great capacity of the sub's reserve buoyancy and its air-tanks that had enabled them to overcome this extra weight. The outer casing had suffered and the deck was torn, along with some valves and pipes and, once again the already weakened steering gear had jammed. They tried to free it as best they could but still the rudder remained with a tendency of settling to port.

'We'll have to use the engines to assist in steering the boat,' Itachi informed his FO.

'Hai, it should work, at least until we can get closer to home for an assisted tow,' said Takayuki with a hoarse whisper.

Choice was not an option as Itachi gave orders to proceed and to distance himself from their present location as long as the poor visibility remained. However, hours later he found himself grounding on one of the eastern Formosa Islands and their many shoals. This time luck was against him as, on Lan Lu island (some ninety miles east of the southern tip of Formosa), no wrecked shipping lay close while only fishermen's huts on bamboo stilts were in evidence.

Again – and unfortunately for him, he radioed Tokyo to request assistance, this time in daylight. Inevitably the transmission was picked up by the US Navy and rapidly decoded. Two hours later and still hard aground, several aircraft were spotted by the boat's lookouts. Itachi gave orders to abandon the submarine and went to his cabin leaving four gunners to man the AA guns. As the crew waded ashore the closed-up gunners opened up on the incoming Hellcat fighters.

Rockets, bombs and cannon fire struck the stranded hull. One aircraft was hit and, trailing a fiery cloud, nose-dived into the sea. The pilot had bailed out and a parachute blossomed but *I-59* was already transformed into a blazing wreck. The carrier-based aircraft circled over their downed colleague and with a waggle of wings disappeared in an easterly direction and were soon lost from sight. Three of the valiant gunners had succumbed to the onslaught and as *I-59* settled by the stern, Itachi was seen struggling in the water trying to save the last man. Raising her bows in final salute *I-59* slipped back into deeper water as fishing boats came out and picked up the pilot along with the bodies of the gunners, Itachi and the injured man. Hours later and silhouetted against the fire-ball of a tropical sunset, Itachi's pursuers returned in the shape of several US warships. Not seeing the submarine but many men on the beach, a pinnace was launched carrying an armed landing party.

Fishermen led them to the downed pilot and indicated in the dishevelled submariner's direction. Itachi got Takayuki to approach the landing party by carrying a white flag, as a second landing party came to pick up the crew. The aspiring German scientists, with animated relief showing on their faces were treated with kid gloves, destined to be fast-tracked to America. The fallen gunners were buried, above the high-water line by their shipmates as the Americans looked-on. However, they could only watch in horror and disbelief as Itachi, weighed down by the stoicism of his ancestors, suddenly sank to his knees and holding a concealing white cloth to his abdomen, committed the final act of honour to his Bushido ancestors.

Chapter Thirty-Three

ADRIFT

U-888 skirted the Sumatra coastline but kept well to the east as the Japanese were already isolated on this island, with the Dutch once more trying to regain control. After an uneventful five-day run, Franz waited until nightfall before negotiating the strait between Java and Sumatra and heading towards the west was once again back in the Indian Ocean. He remained surfaced in order to maintain a speed of thirteen knots and began to run his westing down. One hour before dawn he reported his position to Tokyo and submerged his boat to run with diesels and snorkel as he made his passage home.

That evening, as Franz surfaced the boat, the setting sun sat like a blazing figurehead on his bows. Many of his off-watch crew came out on deck to witness the glorious spectacle and breathe the salubrious sea air. They were able to celebrate and enjoy the moment, including a cigarette as smoking was restricted below deck and with beer bottles in hand watch as the glowing fireball sank in firmamental glory below the distant horizon.

Happily they debated events and their lucky escape from danger thanks to the homing torpedo. They reasoned and counselled like all sailors that for the next three weeks at least they would be safe as there was only the aspect of open water ahead until they closed the Cape once more. Franz relaxed the watches to two men on the bridge and allowed himself a glass of Cognac as he made out his log and war diary.

Hours later, as a sea mist descended and towards the end of the middle watch the sleeping men below were rudely awakened by the sound of the clanging alarm bell and the dreaded cry of *'Achtung! Achtung! Kriegsschiff! Kapitän to the bridge! Steuermann, hard to starboard!'*

Below, men drugged with sleep tumbled from their bunks as Franz gained the conning tower and took in the situation at a glance. In a single instance, his peace and confidence was shattered as a large ominous mass with a creaming bow wave came bearing down.

It was pointless to man the guns as the vessel was too close and would, within the next few seconds strike his boat.

'*Full speed, helm hard to starboard! Alle raus!*' he screamed to the men below. '*Loosen the rafts, all men on deck. Schnell! Schnell!*'

They stumbled on deck with the submarine already heeling at fourteen knots as it responded to an already altering helm; but it was too late. With a metal-grinding crunch, the titanic bows of the troopship struck the U-boat a glancing blow abaft its tower. In an instant it was over as the blacked-out liner steamed on into the night, quite oblivious of having rammed a U-boat with its concrete-enhanced bow.

Men were in the water, shouting and struggling, as U-888's stern section slowly reared up, its screws still turning and sank in a fiery glow of phosphorescence and the sound of tortured air. The conning tower and forward section remained for a time as it settled lower and lower in the water and minutes later, gracefully, at the speed of a Caribbean sunset the vessel performed her last dive.

Men swimming choked on the oil as it rapidly spread on the surface, but it had an effect of calming the sea. They swam in circles calling frantically to each other as pieces of debris and flotsam came bobbing to the surface. A rubber raft appeared with several men, followed by another as others hailed from the water. Franz swam to a raft and was helped on-board as the others collected round it, clinging in desperation to its grab-lines. Methodically he took a head count and found from a complement of fifty-seven men, seventeen were unaccounted for. One was Ludwig, the young helmsman, whom he knew had valiantly remained at his post, while the others were mainly from the engineering department.

Franz took stock as in the east the sky began to lighten and it started to rain. He surmised that the nearest land, being Sumatra and Java, was now well behind them but the wind and current would drive them in the opposite direction, out into the vast emptiness of the Indian Ocean. They were without food or water except the clothes that each man was wearing and that, to him, spelt a torturous oblivion.

They took it in turns to occupy the rafts, as only ten men at a time could sit cramped on the square space, while the others clung to its side. For the most the sky was cloudy, with the occasional cloudburst shielding them from the effects of the sun. Thirst now became their main enemy as, with every cloudburst, they licked the sweet water from cupped hands. One raft managed to collect three floating bottles, containing vinegar, olive oil and Cognac.

As the day wore on, they debated their fate. Someone mentioned sharks but Franz calmed the men in the water as he lied blatantly by saying they only appeared around the Cape. Taking turns to stay on the inflatables they counted themselves lucky that no one was injured and after a while they all agreed to say the Lord's Prayer and Franz was not alone when he asked God silently for the sight of a British destroyer.

By nightfall men became weaker and those whose turn it was on the rafts assisted by holding their shipmates in the water. However at around sunset they noticed several gulls alighting on the water but some remained higher, standing and pecking at a distant object. With the men in the water pushing and others using their hands as paddles they made their way towards them. To their amazement they found an upturned boat covered with strands of green, slimy weed and festooned with molluscs.

Using the rafts as a platform they managed to right the water-logged boat and found a galvanised bucket lashed to one of its thwarts. Again with the aid of the rafts – one port side, the other opposite – they managed to raise the boat sufficiently for the gunwales to be just clear of the sea. Untying the bucket and with one man bailing furiously the clinker-built boat soon regained its buoyancy to float, with a list on account of the proliferation of orange-grey shells.

Two men boarded and a set of oars was found together with a discoloured white steering oar lashed to the thwarts along with a boat-hook and a barnacle-covered canvas sea anchor. The latter lashed securely at the bows. Murmurs of approval were to be heard as the men praised the unknown seamen which had maintained this ship's lifeboat.

As a precaution against overloading or straining the waterlogged timbers, Franz kept nine men on each raft and lashed their painters to the stern. Others scraped away the barnacles and molluscs which helped to trim the boat. On further examination, two copper tanks were found under the thwarts which miraculously contained fresh water; however, on sampling the liquid, it was found to be tainted and discoloured. Notwithstanding it was retained by decanting one tank into the other by removing a screwed bung and the aid of the bucket. Now they waited with the bucket at the ready for the next squall to come their way.

Franz and some of the men occupied the thirty-foot lifeboat and as the sea life was removed from the stern the faint outlines of a name became visible. Slowly the brass letters ROOSEBOOM came into view.

Life is a fickle thing mused Franz, sitting in the stern, as in less than an hour of staring death in the face they were now surviving as they eagerly picked the shellfish from inside the boat and piled them into the stern for their first meal. Some men still had their lighters and waterlogged cigarettes and matches, these they would dry out for later. They deployed the sea anchor, which acted like an underwater counter-sail, steadying the boat as it drifted, by keeping its bows into wind and sea.

By this time, it was midnight and the weather had eased to a light breeze and a long swell. Franz suggested they should give thanks for their good fortune and those that knew the words (the older members) murmured the Lord's Prayer in thanks for their deliverance. Later that night, even as the rain came down in torrents and the wind chilled them to the bone they still counted their luck as the bucket filled and the precious liquid was poured into the vacated tank.

After surviving a chilled and rain-soaked night, they were thankful once more as the eastern sky lightened and the sun's crimson disc climbed above the horizon. Its warm rays kissed the boat to bring new life into chilled bodies and aching limbs. Men busied themselves with scraping more mussels from the hull as the sun climbed ever higher in the morning sky.

Franz gauged the weather and noticed the sudden lack of clouds but said nothing. His attention was distracted as a young torpedo man shouted with glee as he caught a fish with the boathook that had been greedily feeding off the mussels. Now everyone wanted to go fishing. Using several strands from one of the grab-lines they made up a six-foot line and using their lapel pins as hooks, baited them with molluscs. After losing several bites they had success by allowing the fish to swallow the pin-hook completely and soon had several varieties of fish for a meal.

Although they had the oars, it was decided to drift towards the north-west as the wind was south-easterly which, unfortunately would set them out further into the Indian Ocean. However it was agreed that they would still be drifting, with the current in the general direction of the northern shipping lanes.

As the day wore on the flotilla drifted. Without fuel for a fire they chewed on the raw fish. Japanese style they termed it and if nothing else, it assuaged their hunger and passed away the time. Water was strictly rationed. Franz allowed them two fluid ounces per man per twelve hours. Again, they had been in luck as unscrewing the brass caps on the tanks attached to them were small chains holding a copper graduated dipper, marked off in English fluid ounces. On seeing this it became obvious that the lifeboat with its Dutch name was actually British-built.

By this time too their cigarettes were well dry and were pooled and rationed and lit with the aid of the sun and a spectacle lens. At six-thirty that evening as the sun once more dipped its crimson orb, not a cloud was in sight. Franz's worst fears seemed well founded – being mid-September, the South Eastern Monsoon had all but moved on.

After five days at the mercy of the elements, exhaustion along with hunger and dehydration was beginning to affect them, especially the younger members. From the start, they had made a makeshift awning from jackets and shirts, using the oars as supports, however on the seventh day the first youngster became delirious and died that same night. Franz said the Lord's Prayer as his friends committed his body to the deep. Unfortunately they could not weigh the corpse down and it seemed to follow them, to drift with them as if not wishing to be left all alone on an empty sea. Minutes later they noticed several dark triangular shapes which circled the body and in a spectacular feeding frenzy made short work of their recent shipmate. The ever greedy fish then continued to circle the boat and began to nudge the rafts.

Franz organised a watch rota in order to keep some men awake – if anyone slept too long they would sleep, never more to wake. The rota also had the added advantage that should a ship be sighted the alarm could be raised. Neutral shipping could easily be seen and recognised as these had their lights blazing but unfortunately they were not in any shipping lane. Franz with Jurgen calculated they still had some eight hundred miles to drift before they'd meet up with such shipping. Then there was always the chance that any belligerent submarine could find them, or their Japanese allies might still be operating in these waters.

To pass the time they reminisced about the war and now realised how wrong Germany had been to try and take on the British Empire. The youngsters in his crew could only stare, hollow-eyed and not comprehending as the others condemned Hitler for unleashing this war. The teenagers had at all times adored the Führer and his Hitler Youth, the mountain treks and torchlight parades. Then the Hitler Mädchen, the girls so young and eager. But it was like a passing dream which had become a living nightmare as they lay in the bilge of a stinking lifeboat, adrift in a hostile sea.

Two lads died the next day as dehydration and hunger took its toll. However, they had now cannibalised the oars to support a makeshift sail from the clothing of their dead shipmates. Franz, sitting in the stern, retained command but this was the tenth day and again no clouds were in sight. He reckoned that another few days of this and they would all be beyond help as their fresh water would be gone. Since all of the molluscs had been consumed, used as bait or dried off in the sun there was no more food to be had and harpooning with the boat hook took too much energy for a poor return.

That same night they lost one of the engineers. He'd been caught drinking sea water and became delirious and without anyone's notice he had lowered himself into the water and just swam away. In the dark it was only his cries which alerted them as the prowling sharks closed in for the kill. With four men gone, Franz moved the remainder from the two rafts into the lifeboat which now contained thirty-six souls. He calculated that the boat had dried out sufficiently and could take this extra burden; besides, the sharks had become bolder and were constantly nosing and nudging against the air-filled tubes.

The eleventh day was more of the same torment as the merciless sun beat down from a clear blue sky. They lay listless, hardly speaking as the day wore on and waited for the onset of night, to make kinship with its canopy of stars and the harbingers of the cold, and misery to come.

On the twelfth day, with all of the fresh water gone, they opened up the second tank which held some three gallons of the tainted water. As before it tasted foul and made them vomit so they decided instead to sponge their faces and necks, as the medic (a civilian and non-combatant) informed them that the moisture would be taken up by the organ of the skin. It had a cooling effect and would help them to survive but he also informed them in text-book style that it was just a matter of time before their internal organs failed and the spark of life would be extinguished. That did not bring any cheers.

The next day they saw a steamship, it was hull-down, but the masts and the smoke were there for all to see. Hope returned for several hours as some began to discuss what they would drink first after being rescued, whilst the remainder lay listless and unresponsive, conserving what little energy remained. The ship sailed on, on its south-westerly course and was soon lost from sight.

On the morning of the fourteenth day, two more youngsters failed to respond to the morning call as by this time the watch system had been abandoned. Once again the gory spectacle was observed as the ever-present sharks made short work of their unfortunate shipmates. Towards evening their luck changed in two ways. With the aid of the extra clothing from the deceased they were shielded from the debilitating rays of the scorching sun and as a school of flying fish had miscalculated their flight path, now landed in the boat. They sucked feebly at the flesh, chewing as best they could with loosened teeth until Johann hit on the idea of dipping the fish in olive oil. It seemed a good idea as Franz tried it for himself.

'Well done, the cook,' he said with a croak, as each man received their share of two and a half fish. It cheered and revived them as later they took their sponge-bath, wiping the tainted water over shrivelled skins.

With the re-hydrating ablutions completed, everyone settled back to loll in the comforting shade of the makeshift shelter and once more observed with sunken eyes the sun's lower limb settling on the far horizon. As the tropical twilight faded, a feathered visitor came gliding on the scene. The albatross swooped low over the water, picking up the remnants of their meal and catching the fish that fed off them. The giant bird flew in a graceful arc and banked with its six-foot wingspan skimming the water and came towards them as if to settle on their bow. Johann wanted to strike it with the boat hook but Jurgen, propped against Franz's knees called out for him to leave well alone.

'Don't touch it! Remember the Dutchman,' he croaked. Sullen eyes swivelled in his direction and stared at the First Officer. They stared with indifference, not conversant with the tale of the accursed sailor as the bird by this time had changed direction and headed into the gathering dusk.

'It must be flying towards land,' he added to hide his superstition. 'I'm sure we can make it if we carry on for another day or so.'

With the wandering bird now just a memory they settled down for another night of discomfort and drifting. Franz calculated the set of the current to be north-easterly and, with light airs from the south, the bird might be heading in the same direction as them he reasoned. Only those birds hardly ever touch land.

Three more youngsters died that night and as the red giant once again climbed into the eastern sky they were committed over the side. Jurgen mumbled the Lord's Prayer and thinking that if help did not come soon, he would be joining them. Franz looked on from his position in the stern and leaning for support on the lashed steering oar watched once more as the now familiar sharks went into their frenzied role. In minutes the naked corpses were gone, unceremoniously disposed of by Mother Nature's sextons. Mercifully for those remaining, the boat soon drifted away from the gory scene.

In desperation Franz suggested that every man should now take some olive oil as it might help. The liquid was poured into the dipper and taken by the dipping of the fingers as they only had three-quarter litres remaining. For him it soothed his parched throat and lips and they took it in turns as they passed round the oil-filled dipper.

'You should have left us some olives, Johann,' croaked a torpedo man. If nothing else it raised a chuckle amongst them. Franz reckoned that their fighting spirit was still there as the spark of life, even here was hard to extinguish. If only they could hold out until they got further north and the shipping lanes.

'I estimate we've drifted over two hundred and fifty miles in this post Monsoon counter current,' he said to Jurgen who was intently observing half a dozen triangular fins that were never too far away.

'What about the sail?' he croaked in reply and turning his head with effort.

'The breeze has been mostly south or south-westerly, two knots, so we might have gained another half knot sailing from that,' said Franz as he cast a jaundiced eye at the questionable sail. 'I reckon with the current and the wind we must be drifting at about two knots and must be back over the Equator by now and a good way out in this ocean. I'd say about three hundred and fifty miles west of Sumatra and a long way up that coast as we were already three hundred towards the Cape when that ship hit us.'

Jurgen tried hard to think as thirst parched his throat and tantalising water was all around him but he had observed the stars and knew they were definitely drifting towards the north. The problem was they had no instruments or charts but the angle of the Southern Cross was slowly changing and that was a good indication. He thought about his albatross, it flew away in a north-easterly direction. It was his own gut feeling that that bird was flying towards where the fish were more numerous, to shallow water and land.

'Ja, in that case I make it about four thousand miles to Capetown,' he candidly replied. Franz thought about Jurgen's reply. Was he going mad, four-thousand miles in this thing? 'Remember that Bounty boat; we need Mr Bligh around here, ja?' He gave a gaunt nod and looked-on in deep thought as an empty arm flapped on the sail as if to wave them on. Franz still in the stern was not quite sure what to make of the man or of his statement, factual or not. But then Bligh had sails, a compass, water and a sextant, he mused.

'We saw that ship,' replied Franz. 'It must have been coming from the Malacca Strait, so I reckon we are much closer to those shipping lanes than we think. Pass the word round, by tomorrow we should see shipping. It will help to boost their morale.' Jurgen nodded and spoke to the man next to him, who passed it on.

A murmur of hope arose and died as the thirty-one survivors now accepted anything that was said, the will and energy to reason being beyond them. As the sun set on the fifteenth day Franz once again issued the 'three times finger dipping' ration of olive oil and in rotation the men moved their positions to relieve those lying in the ever flooding bilge.

As another day dawned, Jurgen reported to Franz that all the men had come through the night. It seemed that the teenagers had all succumbed and this was now his hard core of men – if anything, his would-be survivors. As the sun climbed higher they scanned for clouds or a squall but the vaulted sky was open, powder blue and deadly.

However with the morning came a breeze causing ripples on the swell. Now the moving air helped to cool them and to raise their spirits as the sail filled and took the strain. Jurgen checked the water and assessed today would be the last day of their sponge bath as the tank was all but empty. By eleven the heat of the day began to bite as men shifted uneasily, their sores permitting, but now the boat actually left a wake as the breeze continued to act on the sail.

At noon or thereabouts, with the sun directly overhead they had their last dipper-bath, Franz being the last man to use the moistened cloth. He wiped the precious liquid over his leathered skin and settled back at his station by the steering oar. Looking astern, he gauged the boat was making some three knots through the water as he altered the steering oar in line with the southerly breeze, being aware there was also the current to consider.

As the sixteenth day wore on and the western sun was at a low elevation, a man lying in the bows was suddenly heard to croak, 'I can hear a sewing machine. Listen everyone!'

Some men bothered to raise their heads, however they settled back as only the sound of the lapping waves was to be heard as the boat rose and fell on the long swell. Franz raised an eyelid at the man but said nothing.

'It's a sewing machine, so what?' muttered Horst, one of the gunners lying in the bilge.

'You'll be the next one for shark bait,' retorted a pal, who then sat bolt upright as he thought he heard it too. 'Listen!' he croaked with excitement. 'Everybody listen, I can hear it!'

Those that could muster the energy now sat up and in a flash they all saw it; a glint of sunlight reflecting on glass in the northern sky.

Chapter Thirty-Four

BUNKER FESTIVITIES

As the summer days merged into autumn, the evening chill reminded them winter was not too distant. Anna had now been in her cellar house (as she'd termed it) for seven months and as the rains of late autumn turned to the first snow flurries of winter, Willi's prediction of an end to the conflict seemed as remote as ever. To her intense relief, after Gruber's death there had been no further enquiries, from the Gestapo or anyone else. As for those 'gentlemen' in the Munich office all they knew was that she had been released on information received from the SS. Any other follow-up of Gruber's died with him, expurgated in the ovens of the Dachau camp.

News of heavy bombing raids was relayed to her by Willi but there were no further raids on Munich. Further news of the Russian front came to her by way of Willi's relations as five of them joined her in the cellar, refugees from the Sudetenland. They explained to her they were farmers in the part of Czechoslovakia which had been seized and annexed by Hitler in 1938; it was a German-speaking part of the country so language was not a problem.

They related to her the ferocity of the fighting between the German and Soviet armies – how the Soviets had repeatedly smashed their way through the retreating Wehrmacht, taking vast numbers prisoner. Stories of the rape and pillage of their land and how everything that could be moved was sent back to Russia. They told of countless atrocities having witnessed German soldiers begging for mercy and being shot in cold blood or being sent back to Siberia in cattle trucks without food or water. Anna listened horrified to hear of their ordeal as the rumours before were now verified by these simple country folk.

Helga was Willi's older sister, a flaxen-haired, buxom woman of thirty-nine. She was stocky and her weathered features belied her age. Helga was the typical image of a working farmer's wife who always wore a full flowing skirt and a headscarf to match. Karl, her son was twelve and his sister Maria, a year younger. Her husband had been posted as missing after the battle of Kursk that June. Only her in-laws were there with her, who owned the farm that now belonged to Comrade Stalin.

For Anna it was a relief to have others there with her as she could now afford the luxury of going out on her own and to seek information as to what might lie ahead. She reeled at the sight of the devastation in and around the city and of the sorry plight of its inhabitants.

On the night of 26 November the Allied Forces once again bombed Munich. No one can know or understand the misery of being continuously bombed, to find shelter, only to be bombed out once again. It affects the mind, breaks the spirit and the will to carry on but as the city burnt and the cold was intense, Churchill, its inhabitants vowed would never break their resolve.

Christmas came and for once the bombers had kept their distance. Anna and her enlarged family celebrated Christmas Eve for the children whilst further up the street Helmut and Willi's flak battery kept their lonesome vigil.

For the event Willi had procured some candles and a Tannenbaum cut from his farm. Many toys had been salvaged from the stricken houses and handed out as presents to the children.

At eight o'clock that evening there came a loud knock on the cellar door. The children recoiled and froze in all angst as Helga, gently propelling him, ushered her son to open it. There in his field-grey uniform stood Der Weihnachtsmann – complete with red hat and cotton wool whiskers.

'Guten abend, kinder,' croaked Willi. 'If you have been good, I have some presents for you.'

From a sack he produced several red apples, nuts, dates and raisins and handed them to the delighted children. With great pretence he rummaged further and produced toys for them including a wooden boat for Eddie, complete with three black funnels. They sang Stille Nacht, oblivious to the stealthy exit of St Nicholas as he donned his steel helmet.

It was during the early hours of 7 January 1945 that the bombers returned. As the sirens wailed their undulating lament the first bombs of the New Year began to whistle down. A short raid but with three hundred aircraft dropping high-explosive devices the devastation was complete.

In the harsh light of dawn and the welcome sound of the all-clear Anna and Helga took stock of their situation. Although not hit directly, the proximity of fires and infiltrating smoke, together with a slow flooding of their cellar made their new-found home untenable.

'Anna, you know you cannot stay here anymore,' said Helga. 'Look at the water. That wall could collapse at any moment.' She pointed to a large crack in the brickwork and shifting her scrutinising gaze to her brother, called out to him. 'Willi, get away from there before it falls on your head.'

'Just a few more minutes, nearly done,' he replied over his shoulder as he placed several bottles into a leather holdall. With the water already inches deep he made his way back to the steps where the two women now stood waiting and stooped to rescue Eddi's boat from amongst the floating debris. 'Here you are, Eddie,' he said as he handed it back to the anxious boy standing behind the grown-ups. 'It can sail on a better pond than this,' he added with a snort.

'Ja, I can see that it's dangerous,' said Anna with a shrug as the light began to flicker and with a 'ping', plunged the room into darkness. In the stillness of the cellar the steady trickle of water was heard and acrid smoke from burning electric cables added to the chaos.

'Raus!' shouted Willi. 'Get out, all of you!'

Helga's children bounded up the stairs, dragging Eddi with them as Anna and Helga carried their possessions and Willi brought up the rear. At the top of the stairway stood Helga's in-laws, the not so young Hermann and his wife Engeltraud who had been loading the wagon they'd brought with them. Once more it would assist them in their nomadic wanderings across the Reich.

'You said you had an aunt near Essen. Can't you go there?' said Helga once they were clear of the building and out in the open.

'That's right,' replied Anna. 'She lives about thirty miles north of Köln but it's a long way and there's no transportation. I don't even know whether she still has her house as it could be like here,' and gazing at the destruction added, 'she might even have joined the angels.'

'Ach nein,' said Helga. 'Don't think like that,' and with a beckoning wave added, 'you'll have to come with us.'

'Where are you going? There is nothing to support you at Willi's farm and he's got no room there either. Besides he's been kind enough to me already, I cannot burden him any longer.'

'Look Anna, we have already discussed this before, remember? We'll head east and away from these bombs and the cities, away from the Russkies too. We'll go to our friends and distant relations of my husband's in the Drau valley, over there in Austria. They have a nice dairy herd too,' she said with an endearing smile, 'and a brass bell for every cow.'

Anna stifled a laugh as she gazed at this good-natured, salt-of-the-earth woman. She made it sound like the Promised Land itself, mused Anna, with only the burning bush and a staff lacking in those callused hands.

With the Hoffbräuhaus as a backdrop, Anna made her decision. She would accept and go with her newfound family as there was safety in numbers, she reasoned. These people were from the land and understood better than anyone what was happening and how to avoid the Russians at all costs.

One thing did bother her and gnawed away in her mind was that she was for ever travelling further and further away from the sea. How on earth was she ever going to find her husband or even enquire about his whereabouts? But with the cellar flooding and more air raids to come, it was not the time to ask those kinds of questions.

'Anna, you'll come with us,' said Helga. We've decided for you, Hermann and Karl have gone for the horse and will be back soon. Willi has given us some extra blankets and several live rabbits.'

'Rabbits?' queried Anna.

'Ja, rabbits,' replied Helga with a chuckle. 'They're pedigree not your skin and bone hedge hoppers one sees around here, we rear them for the table.' Anna wrinkled her nose but declined to comment for fear of upsetting her. They were distracted as a military convoy passed through. Wistfully she watched them roll by, the soldiers with their wan, ashen-faced expressions taking in the scene of destruction that was all around them. They marched behind tanks and field guns, grim and resolute, lacking both nourishment and sleep. They were followed by the many homeless inhabitants struggling with their scant possessions, walking silently amongst piles of cleared rubble, lost in their own thoughts as they headed towards Passau and the Danube crossing.

Anna and Helga waited patiently in the dry cold of the January dawn as their children sat snuggled on the wagon, well-wrapped against the weather and the journey that lay ahead. An hour later Hermann and Karl returned with the horse and once in its shafts they moved off to Willi's farm.

That night they stayed at the farm. Came daybreak, Willi arrived home with a few hours leave granted to him by Helmut. He gave them a second horse along with two goats and several rabbits. They were about to set off on their two-hundred mile journey when the sound of an agitated motor horn was heard from further down the track.

An army truck bounced and laboured its way along the frozen and rutted track, coming to a screeching halt alongside them. Helmut beaming from ear to ear jumped from the passenger side and made his way to the tailgate.

'Anna, Helga, come over here!' he called and indicated with a wave. The two women hastily climbed down from the wagon to join him. 'Here you are, help yourselves courtesy of the Wehrmacht,' and indicated to a large pile of clothing, shoes and blankets.

'Such wonderful clothes!' cried Helga as the two soldiers in the back handed her a generous armful from a mountainous pile. Anna tried on several pairs of shoes and boots and carried them back to the wagon.

'Kinder clothing too, Wunderbar,' cried Helga excitedly and fetching a sack.

'Here Anna, these are for you,' said Helmut as he returned from the cab holding several coats.

'Ach nein,' she cried and shaking her head in disbelief. 'They are so beautiful, are they mink?'

'But of course!' he replied. 'Only the best for you Anna, they'll keep you nice and warm on the journey.'

'Danke Helmut, but where did you get all these clothes? And the coats? They've hardly been worn. Look Helga, how do I look?' Anna did a graceful pirouette with her new possessions, clutching them and feeling the luxurious fur.

'Wunderbar,' beamed Helga as she systematically crammed more clothing and shoes of all sizes into her sack.

'And one for you, Helga,' said Helmut with a grin and avoiding Anna's questioning gaze as he handed Helga an ankle-length coat, its fur shimmering a vibrant chestnut-brown in the rays of the winter sun.

'Danke, danke Helmut,' she cried in surprise and discarding her worn woollen coat donned the rich fur, bathing in its luxurious warmth and texture.

'Well, ladies, you are all now ready to climb the mountains,' said Helmut with a satisfied smile, however Anna detected a tremor in his usual commanding voice as their eyes met. Instantly she knew from his expression he wanted to say more. Holding her gaze he came towards her, took her hand and raised it to his lips.

'Auf Wiedersehen Anna,' he said in a trembling tone. 'I hope you will have a safe journey.' They gazed at each other as he fondled her

276

hand in both of his. With a laden heart she saw the tear in his eye. Anna took the initiative and kissed his chilled stubbled cheek as she whispered words of thanks and comfort.

'Danke Helmut,' she said, searching his eyes. 'Thank you for all you've done for me. I can never thank you enough as you've twice saved my life. Thank you.' She could hold back no longer as she felt her warm tears creep past cold winter cheeks. 'My family too,' she added with barely a whisper. 'I want you to know and remember that.' Squeezing his hand their eyes met as he tried stoically to mask his feelings. 'Auf Wiedersehen, my soldier friend. I shall never forget you.'

'Anna,' he replied with a nervous whisper, 'if it does not work out...' and paused in mid-sentence, swallowed hard and held her tearful gaze. 'Please get in touch, you know what I mean.' Once more he held her hand in both of his and expressed his clumsy proposal with a cautious smile. Anna sensed his turmoil and felt humbled by this man's candour and care. Reassuringly her lips parted in an understanding smile and like a departing vessel casting off its lines, she slipped from his grasp.

'Jawohl, Helmut, I understand. I'll not forget but we'll wait for the tide to come in, ja?'

'Adieu,' he said with a resigned nod, acknowledging she had tactfully reminded him of someone else. Their eyes met once more in parting until the sound of Helga and her family's goodbyes broke the emotional spell.

'Auf Wiedersehen Anna,' said Willi as she returned to the wagon. Without ceremony he flung his brawny arms round her waist and gave her an emotional hug. 'Have a safe journey Anna. Come back to visit us when it's all is over.'

'Danke Willi, thank you for everything. I shall never forget you and your kindness.' So saying she affectionately kissed his cheek while his wife, standing on the threshold, beamed and looked on approvingly. Anna made her way across to her and said her farewells amid hugs and kisses from her and her two children and re-joined the others already seated on the wagon.

With deft clicks of his tongue the horses took the strain as Herman released the chunky wooden brake. The women waved their goodbyes before fussing and covering the children with Anna's spare fur coat. As the wagon rumbled on Anna glanced once more in Helmut's direction. He was standing by his truck, arms by his side and reminded her of an adolescent child lost in an adult world.

Chapter Thirty-Five

THE NAVY'S HERE

'Schnell, Schnell the lighters!' croaked Jurgen and tried several of them, the lighter flints sparked but the petrol had long since evaporated. 'Matches, get the matches,' he rasped as Franz squinted and tried to observe the moving dot in the sky.

Fumbling fingers scraped the dried phosphorous sticks and it took several attempts before one suddenly ignited. More were added followed by the tail of a cotton shirt, well dried but stiff with salt. The material sputtered, caught alight and died. More matches were lit as Johann produced the bottle of Cognac. With the aid of Napoleon's finest, the material burst into flames and was lowered into the bucket as another shirt was added over the dancing flames.

'Not enough smoke, we need black smoke!' croaked Jurgen as Franz called for Wolfgang to hand him his seaman's dirk. It was quickly passed to the captain and he leant over the stern and punctured one of the floats, cutting a piece of rubber from the deflated tube. Quickly it was passed to the fire team and holding it over the flames the material was soon alight and emitting dense clouds of choking black smoke. Using the boat hook they held the bucket over the side as Franz hacked off more of the raft's tubes.

Excited they began to speculate. Was it British, American or Japanese and would the pilot see them? As vital seconds turned to minutes they watched in anticipation and hope, even to the point of willing and coaxing the pilot to see them.

'Come on, look this way!' some croaked, waving frantically and expending their last ounces of strength.

Franz thought it rather ironic as here they were making smoke signals whilst anywhere else in the Atlantic his U-Boot would have attracted the whole British Home Fleet by now. However it was not to be as the aircraft was soon lost from sight and as they continued feeding the flames and sprinkled on water to make even more smoke they were so preoccupied that no one noticed several grey hulls emerge from below the southern horizon.

Less than two miles distant, the piercing triple shriek of a cruiser's steam whistle heralded the end of their ordeal. As the warship closed with its outlaying destroyer screen, those that could muster the energy stood and waved at their would-be rescuers. Others sat watching and waiting – transfixed as a cutter was smartly lowered from its starboard side. With oars dipping in unison the seamen closed the distance to their boat.

For Franz and his men it now came as a culture shock to see dark-skinned sailors coming to their rescue. How the wheel had turned mused Franz, as others began to weep unashamedly with the emotion of it all and their timely deliverance. The cutter came alongside and without sentiment a young Indian seaman passed across a bottle filled with water as the Killick threw a line to be tied to the lifeboat's bow.

'Cut the rafts adrift!' he called to them, indicating a cutting motion and pointing at the inflatables. Franz understood the man's thick English and did as the Leading Hand requested as by now all was made fast and the old lifeboat taken in tow.

A scrambling net had been lowered and sailors were at the ready halfway down, ready to receive and to assist the survivors on board. Those too weak to accomplish this feat were transferred to the cutter which was raised on its falls to deck level. Willing hands and stretcher parties were there to accommodate them as the remainder were hauled to safety and taken below to the sick bay. The lifeboat was holed and sunk as the Royal Indian Navy cruiser and its screen gathered speed and proceeded towards the north-west to re-join the fleet heading towards the fortress island of Ceylon.

Days later and having recovered physically from their ordeal, Franz and his crew stood fascinated as they entered the harbour of Colombo. They were astounded by the hospitality of the British, Indian and Ceylonese Navy officers and ratings and amazed they were not blindfolded as they remained on deck to see the battleship *King George V* fitting out.

At this time the harbour was home to Force 57, the British Far East Fleet which was building up its strength to strike at Japan. Franz was amazed to see two U-boats tied up alongside a quay with several of his countrymen still onboard. If this is war, he said to himself the British have a weird and wonderful approach to it.

Moments later and with a gentle touch the cruiser brushed against the dockyard's fenders as heaving lines sailed in great arcs over the heads of the waiting linesmen ashore. A gangway went up and Bosun's pipes shrilled as several three and four ringed officers, in immaculate white 'tropicals', were piped onboard.

Franz and those of his men which were able to walk found themselves dressed in RN fatigues and after many farewells and humble thanks he led his men ashore. They were escorted by an eight-man squad of Ceylonese ratings shouldering Enfield ·303s to where a canvas-sided lorry stood waiting. The stretcher cases followed as a second Bedford appeared along with a jeep. Soon they were whisked away to be hospitalised at the nearby RN barracks and a record made of the approximate position of U-888's demise.

After a week's recuperation, Franz was free to roam the hospital. During which time he learnt from the other U-Boot crews the British had long since broken the Enigma code and was probably why they had known of his whereabouts. This being the case he did not hold out much hope for his friend Kurt – or Itachi for that matter. He found the British as friendly but stiff towards him and his men as, understandably, they had a war to fight and finish and POWs only got in their way. It helped that he could speak English and they used him as an interpreter, especially with his crew and their medical requirements.

From the local doctors he gleaned the European war would soon be over. Hitler, they said, was 'in very much retreat, Sahib'. So now the concept and build of the Uranium Bomb was dead and buried – unless Itachi did manage to avoid destruction. He doubted it, as with the codes broken his chances of survival were poor. However Franz had instructed his men not to divulge anything about their mission, their homing torpedo and the Japanese connection as Germany was still at war and one never could tell...

Having recovered from his ordeal the naval authorities put him into a messing block which was kept under guard with other POWs like him. As he settled down in the two-storey building he knew it was only a matter of time before his war would be over. Sitting on his bed he thought about Lilli and their brief 'affaire de coeur'; he missed her and felt sorry about the circumstances of her death. He was to blame he told himself, but that was the war and its effect on the whole of humanity. He reminisced about their boiler room love nest and felt guilty but dismissed it as a singularity. It happened and that was that, just a pleasant memory of their friendship, platonic at first and turning to needful and spontaneous intimacy as the bombs rained down.

'It just happened,' he muttered and gazed out across the veranda but guilt never fades for it is a jealous and artless emotion; even as he turned his thoughts to Anna and his son the thought of Lilli and her nubile body still caused stirrings within. Dismissing the thought he could not wait for the whole shooting match to end and be with his wife once more. Perhaps, he mused, absence does make the heart grow fonder but fancies' silken leash still tugged at his senses and more often than not, such pleasure never is at home.

But his guilt remained as another thought came to mind; would he tell her about Lilli? '*Nein*' an inner voice shrieked as his demons returned to haunt him. It would only bring her unnecessary grief, he reasoned. It would only stir up anger as Anna would not understand. Again the voice began to mock, '*Would you understand if the coin was flipped?*' He clenched his jaw as he already knew the answer and swore an oath – such liaisons would never happen again he promised himself, even if opportunity beckons. However his guilt remained and like all relationships of that ilk, it never fades…

Still battling with his conscience he lit a pusser's Woodbine and gazed out at the tranquil coconut palms and the mirror of a silver sea beyond. On the walls the lizards 'chit-chatted' as they scampered and clung from the ceiling and overhead a fan swished, creating a welcoming flow of air. Lost in thought he stepped past the louvre doors and out onto the veranda to catch the last rays of the setting sun. It was so quiet and peaceful here, he mused, and envied the British and their lifestyle – they had it made he reflected, as he flicked the dog-end to land on the neatly cut grass below.

As dusk settled he looked-on with interest at the sewing lady as she laid out her bamboo mat and set up shop on the corner of the block, an oil lamp, shaded and flickering close by. She was old and wrinkled and had her grandchildren with her but seemed at peace with herself as she took orders for clothing and, stitch by stitch, sewed on uniform badges for the British sailors. He envied the woman and her simple way of life and promised himself that once re-united with his family he would strive to build a better and more caring life for them all.

Chapter Thirty-Six

LIENZ

It had been a hard winter. However, after many ordeals and kind acts of charity from isolated farmsteads they were nearing their journey's end. After crossing the river Inn at Rosenheim, they carried on to Salzburg and began the ninety-mile trek south through the Austrian Tyrol and its snow-capped mountains. Cow sheds and barns had been their only solace and shelter from the elements when in early March of 1945 Helga's group arrived at Lienz, their final destination in the Drau valley.

By then spring was in the air as the winter snows melted and the mountain streams swollen to capacity with melt water, roared down to the river below. Anna was for once at peace with herself as in her innermost thoughts she reasoned she would survive the war. Only that morning she had heard a BBC broadcast at one of the farmhouses which seemed to be stating the facts of what was happening in her country. There were no boasts or hollow cries of victory only the pertinent facts of the allied advance and where most of the fighting was done.

With thoughts of peace and the re-unification of her family uppermost in her mind it gave her strength as she carried on and took it in turns with Helga to walk behind the wagon, as by now they were in the mountains and the horses were flagging.

Late one afternoon, after another day of steady walking and as the sun dipped behind the mountains they arrived at their destination. Dogs barked and geese honked their alarm as the wagon and its weary occupants pulled in at a small farm. Immediately a plump dirndl-clad woman came out to investigate the commotion only to shriek with delight at seeing her kinfolk again.

A young teenager wearing a green farmer's jacket and leather britches joined her, to be informed that these were his uncle, aunt and cousins whom he had heard about and only seen in faded photographs.

'My name's Alfred,' he said, 'but you can call me Peppi,' as he shook their hands in greeting. A tall muscular man now came on the scene, dressed like his son except he wore a Tyrolean hat that sported an ibex's beard and edelweiss clumped together on one side. 'Servus, I'm Heinrich, welcome to my farm,' he said and politely raising his hat. So these jolly people are Helga's relations? Anna mused and was quickly introduced and given a hearty welcome.

Days later and having settled into her new surroundings, life on the farm for Anna was a new experience as being a city girl she found the earthy aromas a challenge for her delicate senses. For Eddi however it was fun all the way as there was always something new round every corner. He played with the other children and quickly learnt which animals could be chased and teased and what others did the chasing, nipping and biting. It was the geese that frightened him the most. In a cacophony of honks they raised the alarm at his every approach; hissing and with outstretched necks they rushed towards him, to nip and beat him with their wings.

Feeling guilty and in order to earn her keep Anna volunteered and assisted as best she could and did most of the light chores round the farm. On occasions she heard the sound of aircraft and witnessed the Americans heading east, towards Klagenfurt, Graz and Vienna. It was times like these that she counted her blessings as she looked-on until they disappeared out of sight over the mountains.

Towards the end of March, the small community received a reminder of the ongoing war when chickens and geese scattered in all directions as the roar of low-flying fighter planes shattered the peaceful scene. It was later established they were in pursuit of a straggling Wehrmacht column that was fighting its way home in a rear guard action. Small groups of Italian partisans were seen from time to time and would shoot first and never ask questions, seeking only vengeance, guns, food and ammunition.

By now Anna had mastered the art of milking and was only too pleased to contribute and help in this way. Even for the likes of her, a city girl, the work as such was not demanding. In fact and to her amazement, she enjoyed it.

It was on a warm spring afternoon as Eddi was running from the antagonised geese that it happened. The geese gave up the chase as they changed direction and stretched their necks to hiss and fly at the newcomer. Anna heard the commotion but thought nothing of it until the sound of gunfire and the whine of ricocheting bullets spread fear and panic in her soul. A child's fearful scream rent the air as Anna leapt from her milking stool.

'*Eddi!*' she screamed but Peppi was already making for the open door when to their amazement a soldier burst through half carrying half dragging her frightened boy. He wore a corporal's stripes and the uniform of the crack Austrian Jaeger division of alpine troops. Releasing Eddi to be with his mother, he did not bother her a second glance as he brushed past and made his way to a window and cautiously peered over its cobwebbed sill.

Satisfied he turned to face them, 'Fuat, die Hund san'scho fuat,' he said, with an impish grin.

Peppi now checked the window as Anna, returning to her milking stool, cuddled and calmed her frightened son. Warily she observed the youngster whose Alpine dialect she could not comprehend. Peppi returned from spying at the window and nodded in agreement as the sound of occasional gunfire faded in the distance.

Anna sat bemused as the two youngsters conversed as if they had known each other all their lives. Peppi dipped an enamelled mug into a churn of the warm milk and handed it to the corporal who eagerly gulped it down. With a lip-smacking grin he wiped the golden stubble with the back of his hand and as an afterthought, grounded his weapon.

'Servus, mei naumen is Werner,' he volunteered as he shook their hands. That bit Anna understood as he introduced himself and carried on talking with Peppi in the dialect of the Alps.

Minutes later the question and answer conversation came to an end as Werner pulled off his rucksack. Squatting, he opened it to reveal a field-grey greatcoat and handed it to the lad. Anna could only gaze in horror at the garment and shook her head.

'Nein Peppi, it's not for you,' she cried. 'Don't accept it. If it was ever found we could all be shot?'

The lad grinned with the impudence of his tender years and shrugged his young shoulders. Accepting the coat he stuffed it into a manger and concealed it with hay. Again they conversed in their dialect with Peppi pointing in the direction of another door.

'Wiederschaun,' he called out as he picked up his telescopic rifle and rucksack before making his way to the back door of the cowshed which led out to the lane beyond.

Once he'd gone, Peppi sat down and explained to Anna what had been said. Although she had a shrewd idea, as the odd word like Russki, Partisanen and Amis were familiar, as was the word München. She guessed the soldier was trying to get away from local Italians to fight or meet the Americans at Munich. This turned out to be the case, as Peppi explained how the advancing Americans had hounded the young corporal's unit out of Italy and the partisans were now taking the bit between their teeth and getting in on the act. With Allied support they were able to seek revenge for the SS atrocities of shooting defenceless civilians and the gratis guns and ammunition were an added bonus to be used in choosing their next government.

'What was that about the Russians, where are they now?'

'He was not sure about them but said they had already taken Vienna and were rapidly moving this way, towards Linz and Graz.'

'That's not possible,' said Anna, wide-eyed and alarmed. 'We heard it only yesterday the Americans were heading this way and the Russians would stop well to the east, in Hungary and north of Vienna like Prague. Gott im Himmel, we will all be sent to Siberia if they come here.' She was once again fearful of her and her son's safety and could not mention to this young country lad her private fear of rape and plunder as had happened in the Sudetenland. Already a plan of escape was forming in her mind as she held her son and watched Peppi striding out in search of his parents. Anna finished with her cows and with Eddi clinging to her skirt got them back to their pasture where the spring grass was already sprouting lush and green.

That night she spoke with Helga and her family about their future plans once the war had ended. Helga sat crying as she had heard on the radio that the Sudetenland was now in the hands of the Russians and would remain with them. They had lost everything and could not go back. She would stay here in Austria and help on the farms as they had no money, only some items of jewellery which they could sell, and would lease their horses for ploughing and such.

Anna mentioned her fear of being trapped here by the Russians; however Heinrich calmed her fears by adding that he had heard the Americans were now approaching München and heading for Austria. It seemed reality had dawned on the Allies that that nice guy at Yalta was after as much of Europe as he could encircle with his tanks.

'Those Russkies will be in Berlin shortly and that will go right up Herr Churchill's nose,' he added as he filled his glass from a bottle which sported no label. 'Nein, Anna,' he continued. 'You will be safer here with us as very soon, there'll be a lot of refugees on the roads. It's better that you stay here until it all blows over, ja?'

Anna thanked the farmer and Steffi his wife for their generosity as the woman attended to Anna's glass.

'Come then,' said Heinrich. 'Let's drink to the end of this war and to our future happiness.' In unison, they all raised their glasses.

'Prost, Gesundheit,' they chimed and downed their drinks with a satisfied gulp, all except Anna who having taken a sip leapt up from her chair to make for the kitchen sink.

'Mein Gott!' she cried as water came to her eyes. 'What on earth is that?'

'Slivovitz Anna,' said Heinrich, as they tried to hide their mirth. 'That's home-made plum brandy from the Sudetenland.'

'Bitte I can drink Schnapps but not this fire water, you can keep it and your Sudetenland,' she said regaining her composure amidst bemused chuckles and returned to the table clutching a life-saving tumbler of Alpine water.

On 22 April the BBC broadcast in three languages to state that the Red Army had commenced its final assault on the German capital. Berlin was fighting for its very existence against an artillery barrage of hundreds of guns. Again it was reiterated that British and American forces had, since March, crossed the Rhine and were also making for Berlin and east, towards Münich and Austria. It then went on to say several thousands of dead and dying bodies had been discovered by the Red Army at a work-camp named Auschwitz in Poland. The information was scanty but it was believed there were many incinerators at this camp where even more people, mainly Jews had perished.

Then came a list of all the German units that had laid down their arms in total surrender. Anna sat glued to the homemade one-valve radio and listened intensely until the accumulator battery ran out of power. Peppi ran to get a replacement as Anna waited impatiently to hear the rest of the breaking news. She desperately wanted to hear everything, especially about the U-Booten. However by the time the lad had returned the bulletin had ended.

On 25 April a large wing of American bombers came from the direction of the Italian Alps to start their descent and bombing run as they headed north in the direction of Linz. After six years of relative peace, the war had at last caught up with the congenial farmers of the Austrian Tyrol. Unbeknown to them they had made history as it was one of the last great bombing raids of the war.

Three days later the BBC announced the Red Army had entered the suburbs of Berlin and were, at that moment shelling Hitler's bunker. It went on to say the Americans were making their way towards Dresden and the British had liberated Holland, along with

286

General Montgomery taking the surrender of a large section of the Wehrmacht's fighting forces in both Saxony and along the Rhine. The broadcast ended with a bulletin stating Soviet forces had captured Prague and Vienna and Americans had entered Munich. This was followed by the usual announcement of all the German surrenders, along with a final statement addressed to all remaining Wehrmacht personnel that any further resistance was futile. All German servicemen, wherever they found themselves, should lay down their arms at stipulated collection points and await further instructions.

They sat in stunned silence in the farmhouse kitchen. It was unbelievable, even to these simple farmers that Hitler's much vaunted Third Reich had collapsed and Hitler was still out there somewhere, hunted and cornered like some wild animal with no means of escape.

Anna was the first to snap out of the numbness that had settled in their midst.

'The Russians are coming,' she said as the radio carried on reporting events from all fronts. 'Wien – that's only five or six hours from here,' she said with alarm. 'Two hundred kilometres. We will all end up in Russland and they will take everything.' Helga nodded and sighed, having witnessed it first-hand.

Heinrich rose from his seat with an air of decision and with several attempts, lit his cherry wood pipe.

'I think we had better make plans in case they do get here,' he said. 'But I have heard the Americans are already at Passau on the Danube and coming this way. Let's not panic ourselves, just take precautions, ja?'

'Hermann, you only have the two horses and your wagon, there's not much we can do there. Peppi, you and I will drive the cows higher up the valley, including the goats and pigs. Cowherds will look after them up there, it's all been arranged. Any valuables, our silver and jewellery, we will bury in the field. We will rig up an iron bar and suspend it on the quince tree and if the Russians do come, it will be rung as a signal to all. The other farms are doing the same, as we discussed such matters only last week in our Wirtzhaus.' He paused for a moment with his pipe. 'I think the women should stay together, here with the children. Hermann, you and Engeltraud speak good Russian and Anna, English. It could save our bacon.'

Under normal circumstances it would have raised a laugh but today it only hammered home the reality of their plight.

As the sun rose ever higher and the days grew warmer, April gave way to May. On 2 May came a special news bulletin from the BBC.

'This is London. It has been announced that the Berlin garrison has fallen and Hitler has been found dead. Unconfirmed reports...'

'It's over!' cried Anna. 'We're free! Hitler is dead.' Tears of relief and emotion welled in her eyes as she clutched Eddi to her bosom.

'Thank God for that,' said Heinrich striding into the kitchen and immediately stuffed his pipe with an extra charge of tobacco. He crossed himself in respect of the fallen, even if he did include the late Adolf Hitler.

'But who is running Austria now?' queried Helga anxiously. 'Is it the Russians, now in Wien?'

'Na,' said Heinrich breaking into the vernacular. 'But I did hear from one of the Heimwehr's old codgers that the Amis are in Innsbruck and that's only two hours away. I think if that's the case, we're safe.' He drew on his pipe. 'And another thing...' He glanced round at his audience with a glint of steel in his grey eyes. 'The retreating SS are shooting some of us as being turncoats and cowards; they're fanatical and have itchy trigger fingers. Lucky for us that last raid on Lintz scored a direct hit on the Gestapo headquarters and an SS building. Some fifty of them were killed.'

He took a final puff at his long-stemmed pipe and tapped out the ash on the back step. 'Their bullyboy tactics are over; however, to play safe we'd better stay close to the farm the next few days. They're even enlisting young teenagers like Peppi to face the Russian tanks armed only with grenades and rifles. There has to be some truth in it as old man Schuster our headmaster told me only this morning and he's always been a stickler for detail.'

'Well, it's nearly over,' said Anna happily hugging her son. 'If that news about the Americans is true we have nothing to fear. They are good people.'

Heinrich nodded in agreement but kept his thoughts to himself about the SS. He would not let them get his son and glanced at his hunting rifle hanging in the corner. Anna was startled as the silence was suddenly broken and gazed at the clock as it chimed and the cuckoo came flying out of his little door. Eddi watched it with delight as she rose from the table.

'Four o'clock, my cows will be waiting, come along Eddi let's go and bring them in.'

With Hitler pronounced dead that same afternoon a deathly hush crept over the valley. Nothing was moving except the eagles that soared high over the valley as the people stayed close to their homes and waited.

It was the children that made the discovery as they were helping to carry the valuables out to the corner of the farm's kitchen garden. As Heinrich and Peppi herded the livestock away from the farm Greta, Peppi's sister, who was only thirteen and had never seen a fur coat before now draped Anna's fur over herself and called the others to see her fashion show.

'I'm off to the ball in Vienna,' she said with a chuckle. 'Do you like my coat?' They all laughed and giggled as she twirled round the room until she trod on its hem and tripped. There were more laughs and giggles at her antics as Greta remained on the floor.

'I think I've hurt myself,' she said quietly and trying to hold back her tears. 'Look, it's my knee.' The other children bent down to help as Greta pointed to the bleeding cut and at something sharp in the bottom lining of the coat.

Karl remarked that it was just a scratch as he bent and examined the tiny bulge in the hem. He was able to work the object free, past the rudimentary stitching and found it to be a brooch. Little fingers loosened more of the thread and lining to reveal an assortment of clear beads, rings, ear rings, and several necklaces which were stitched further along and up the back of the coat.

With squeals of delight, they called for their parents. Steffi was first on the scene to see what all the fuss was about as Helga and Engeltraud followed close behind and stopped in their tracks as they saw the little treasure hoard lying on the pinewood floor.

'Gott im Himmel,' cried Steffi, 'schmuck!'

Anna arrived in the kitchen carrying her buckets of milk as the children ran to meet her and hastily explained what had happened. She left the pails and went to investigate.

'Here, auntie!' cried Greta. 'From your coat, it came from here.' And pointed at the lining.

'Mein Gott!' cried Anna, clasping a shielding hand to her mouth. 'I know nothing about this.'

Helga stooped to pick up the clear stones and held them up to the light.

'These are diamonds, if I'm not mistaken, look at their size and sparkle, Wunderbar.'

'Diamonds?' said Anna with a suspicious frown.

'Look at this,' said Helga and holding out her coat. 'My coat too, I can feel something here in the lining.' Eagerly she opened the makeshift stitching and like a stage magician produced a pearl necklace, followed by rings and a lady's gold watch. 'Mein Gott, from where did that man get these coats!' she cried, gazing wide-eyed at Anna.

Greta found something more revealing in Anna's coat lining. It was a scrap of paper which she handed to her mother. Steffi saw that it had been written with purple ink and an indelible pencil and slowly began to read it out.

'It says Jacob Rosenberg, Kirchheim, München. There's a number here but it's illegible, it tails off and seems to have been written with a hurried hand.' Steffi handed it to Anna, who read it and passed it on to Helga. Their eyes met in shock and horror as they realised the full implications as both women knew Feldwebel Helmut had had dealings with the internment camp at Dachau.

Helga picked up her coat again to check for any other clues. She found a small ribbon with chain-stitched embroidery and a name linked with an accompanying address in Vienna.

'I have the same,' she said sadly. 'It says Rebecca Koch and their address in Wien. Those poor people they are in that camp at Dachau and we now have their belongings.' A guilty silence filled the room as no one spoke, wisely keeping their thoughts and misgivings to themselves, especially Anna who was once again reminded of her roots and how close she had come to ending up at a similar place.

Having overcome their initial shock the women collected the jewellery and placed it into a tin box, to be buried with the other items of the farmer's heirlooms.

When they had a moment to themselves, Helga and Anna decided to leave the coats – not to wear them but to return them and the jewellery to their rightful owners once the opportunity arose. Anna felt that being Jewish she had a moral duty to return these items. Deep down however, she had a nagging doubt as to how Helmut had come by them.

The following day was memorable for the whole valley but none so much as for Anna and the other women as two jeeps with white stars on their bonnets hurtled into the farmyard and screeched to a halt. Out climbed a lanky American lieutenant followed by a GI with his chinstrap hanging loose. The second jeep's occupants remained seated, their jaws moving in unison and guns lying conveniently across their laps.

Anna, Helga and Steffi, electrified by the sight rushed to the doorstep, followed by Hermann. It was their first sight of an American soldier and also their acquaintance with the enemy.

'Hi, ik bin Amerikaner,' said the lieutenant with a cautious smile whilst the soldier carefully swept the windows for signs of sniper activity. 'Spreken Sie English?' continued the lieutenant in his best German.

Helga nudged Anna with her elbow but little did anyone realise Anna felt like rushing to hug and kiss this wonderful, beautiful man. *My ordeal is over, it's over*, was all she could think of as with a happy heart she stepped forward.

'Ja – I mean, yes, I speak English,' said Anna through a veil of joyful tears and wiping her eyes with the back of her hand. 'Sorry, I have to cry, please can I help you?' The lieutenant turned his head and said something to the soldier who nodded, dropped his guard and signalled with a wave to the others.

'We're kinda lost around here, Ma'am,' drawled the lieutenant. 'Can you tell us where this road leads to?'

Anna turned and called to Helga, who disappeared inside and came back almost immediately with a pitcher of milk and several mugs.

'You are near Oberdrauburg, in the Drau valley and close to Lienz,' said Anna.

'Yeah, Lienz, Ma'am,' he drawled. 'We juss' came from there, but Ober what?'

'Oberdrauburg, it's a few miles that way,' said Anna and indicated the direction.

'Oberdrauburg, yeah, that's where we're spose' to git to.' He turned and shouted the name to the others in the jeep. 'Seems we gotta stop somewhere here,' he said more to himself than to Anna as he pulled and checked a map from his pocket. 'By the way, he drawled, 'have you seen any Russkies about, Ma'am?'

'Russians?' said Anna raising her eyebrows, as Helga beckoned for the soldiers to take their milk. 'No, there have not been any.' Anna turned to Helga to translate what was being said. In unison the two women shook their heads and waited eagerly for his next question.

'Well, lady,' continued the lieutenant, 'there soon will be but can we stay here and use your barn for a while?'

Her mind reeled, could she be hearing this right? Was this soldier actually asking her if he could use their farm? Wasn't he the enemy who according to the propaganda minister Goebels, was supposed to take everything? She could hardly come to terms with that before the other occupants from the jeep came up and started to offer them cigarettes and chewing gum. In return they took the milk jug to fill several mugs, which they eagerly gulped down.

From the second jeep Anna heard one man talking into a walkie-talkie field radio and listened intently for the reply. She made out something about Russians and the name of Judenburg, followed by some other military jargon that was beyond her comprehension.

'Well yes, of course you can,' said Anna with a welcoming smile. What else can I say, she mused? They're the victors after all and better them than the Russki.

'Gee, thanks Ma'am,' drawled the lieutenant. 'We're mighty sure obliged.' He half turned and was about to stride away, changed his mind and turning met her questioning gaze. 'Ma'am, you don't have to worry your purty li'l head about those Russkies, they're our friends.'

Anna's pensive frown gave way to a wan smile as she recalled the horror stories she had heard about the Russians and their way with western women. With a cursive nod and a casual salute the lieutenant made his way back to the second jeep and its crackling radio.

For the farming folk their first encounter with the enemy was over and they returned to the house talking excitedly while the children peered from the half open door. The Americans made themselves comfortable in an outhouse to casually listen to their field set, smoke and play with dice as the children looked on in awe and fascination.

Just before nightfall, several canvas-covered lorries thundered past and the two jeeps left the farm to follow in their wake. They headed east, in the direction of the township of Oberdrauburg, Klagenfurt and Vienna.

***

On 4 May, the BBC announced that the American 5th Army advancing from Italy had met up with the 7th American Army at Innsbruck. It also stated British forces were making their way from Italy and Yugoslavia but facing pockets of Nazi fanatics who refused to lay down their arms.

With the threat of the advancing Russians diminished, Heinrich and Peppi went up and returned from the snowline meadows with all of their cattle and to observe as daily the American and British transports sped-on by. On 8 May 1945, Prime Minister Winston Churchill was heard on the radio to say that the war was over. Germany, now under the leadership of Hochadmiral Karl Doenitz had unconditionally surrendered.

Chapter Thirty-Seven

A GORDON FOR ME

They sat in the farmhouse kitchen and, while the smell of steaming sauerkraut and gammon prevailed, Anna made plans to return to her home in Aachen and find out, once and for all, the whereabouts of her husband. The problem was locally there was no information as the phone lines were down. With no trains running and the roads flooded with displaced persons, it was dangerous to travel unless in a group.

Hermann, despite his advancing years agreed to take his wagon and the two horses back to München and to take Anna with him, as from there the trains might be running. He would also be taking smoked farm produce, as the city was desperately short of food and they needed the money that it would bring. This time it would be easier as the wagon would not be overloaded, as Helga and her children would stay at the farm.

Anna packed her belongings and items of food for the journey and for barter for needful things along the way. She agreed with Helga that the matter of the jewellery and coats would be sorted out later as they had the names and addresses. However, she would call at Willi's farm to see if his wife knew anything about the coats, as the two soldiers, if still alive would by now be interned in a local POW camp.

It was now 12 May. The war had been over for four days and the wagon was loaded ready to set off, when into the farmyard roared an American jeep with the same fresh-faced lieutenant from before. He leapt out, closely followed by a British Army officer, while their GI driver sat watching, chewing gum and waited. Anna was still saying her goodbyes as they heard the vehicle and its slamming doors. With a polite knock, the lieutenant called into the house as Anna, quickly fussing with her hair came to greet him.

'Howdy Ma'am. Nice to see you ag'in,' he drawled and gave her a lazy salute. 'May I introduce Captain Hanson of the British Army. My name's Mitchell, by the way, Gary Mitchell, Ma'am.' The British officer of captain rank nodded with a pencil-lipped smile, as Anna stood and was left wondering why they had returned. 'Please Ma'am, may we have a few minutes of your time?' said the lieutenant removing his cap as he spoke.

'Why, yes of course,' Anna replied as she waved and signalled for Herman to wait for her on the wagon. 'Please gentlemen, come inside.' She indicated towards the kitchen table as with a scraping of chairs the children made a hasty exit and Helga stood to greet them.

'Please be seated,' said Anna as Helga offered them coffee, just made.

'Well thank you lady, that would be mighty fine,' drawled the lieutenant as the British officer nodded in agreement and placing his cap on his lap. As Helga busied herself with their drinks Anna waited as the lieutenant cleared his throat. 'I would like to thank you for your hospitality when we came by here the other day, but I think you've already guessed that's not why we've come to visit.' Anna nodded expectantly and waited politely for him to continue. Helga in the meantime handed them their drinks. 'Ma'am,' he said, as Anna stopped him with a raised hand.

'Please lieutenant, you may call me Anna, my name is Anna Bauer, and this is my friend Helga.' It was a good enough explanation, she mused, until she heard what they had to say.

'Well now, Lady Anna, we've come to ask you to help us being you speak such good English.' The captain nodded in agreement, and took a sip of his coffee, only to recoil in horror as his taste buds took the brunt of the attack.

'Arrrgh!' came his strangled cry as he rapidly pulled out his handkerchief. Coughing and spluttering he dabbed at his lips. 'What in blazes is that?' he demanded in an Eton school accent. Anna clasped a hand to her mouth to stifle her mirth, as Helga's jovial features turned crimson.

'That's our weizen kaffee. We roast the wheat here in the oven,' said Anna apologetically side-glancing the distressed captain and pointing at a tray with the roasted grain.

'Well excuse my saying so,' said the captain, 'but it tastes jolly well foul.'

Anna was highly amused by his antics. She had met his like before, only they were the Royal Naval types who usually ended up as the butt of a yachting club joke.

'As I was saying,' drawled the lieutenant, discreetly sliding his mug in the opposite direction. 'We would like you to help us to act as an interpreter.' He paused as he waited for Anna's reaction, but she sat expressionless and met his questioning gaze. 'We'll pay you, of course, Anna,' he added as the army captain agreed with a benign nod. 'Please consider it and we'll wait in the jeep for your answer.'

The two men rose from the table as Captain Hanson carefully moved his unfinished drink across the table towards the much-embarrassed Helga. His move was purposeful, like an advancing bishop on a chessboard as Helga took the cup and peered dumbstruck at the disillusioned man.

'I shouldn't try giving that to the Russians, madam,' he said with a glance in her direction. 'They might shoot you,' and replacing his cap followed the lieutenant back to their jeep.

Anna stifled a smile as she translated the captain's comment, leaving Helga to stare at the tray of innocent looking ersatz which was now the accepted beverage and lot of the nation. Anna called Hermann back and began to discuss the offer. They both agreed that she should take the job as the only money available at present, Hitler's Reichsmark was in short supply. Payment in US dollars or Sterling would enable her to buy food and clothing they told her and she could still come back to the farm as this was now her home. In addition they would look after her son whilst away. Anna thanked them for their kindness but had already decided on another plan as she walked confidently out to the yard to negotiate terms with the victors.

'Gentlemen,' she addressed them in a business-like manner. 'I will accept your offer on two conditions, one being that you will allow me to take my son.' They nodded with listening eyes and were visibly relieved that she had accepted the job. 'The other condition,' she paused, eyeing them both, 'is that you will help me find my husband as I don't know what has happened to him. It was now their turn to think things over as the two officers exchanged glances as the army captain noisily cleared his throat.

'We cannot make promises, you realise that, Mrs Bauer,' he said testily. 'But I see no reason why we cannot assist you in this matter. All we need from you are some details. Which army unit was he with?'

Anna's eyes glowed with triumph as she savoured the moment. 'He's not in the army, sir,' she said proudly. 'He's a U-Boot captain.' Surprise was written on their faces and the proverbial pin could have been heard to drop as they mulled over her request. Here they were negotiating with the wife of a submarine commander whose husband had taken part in bringing Britain to face starvation and to the brink of an unequalled maritime disaster.

Once again, the captain cleared his throat, this time with a loud 'Hrrumph', but remained schtum as the lieutenant pensively rubbed his chin.

'Guess that shouldn't be too difficult, Ma'am,' he drawled. 'You let our intelligence have the details and we'll try our best to find him for you. Yessiree, Ma'am, you've got yourself a deal.' So saying, he held out a long bony hand as Anna, with a happy heart, accepted his handshake while trying her hardest not to scream and let her elation show.

Two days later a British army jeep arrived at the farm and took them into the town of Lienz, close to river. The Drau sparkled in the sunshine with the snow-capped mountains lending an idyllic backdrop as the jeep sped on its way. She saw cows, their udders swollen and ready for milking and was saddened she would not be there for them today. After a while the jeep began to slow, before turning into the horseshoe-shaped driveway of a large, mustard-yellow building.

Two flagpoles flanked the driveway and from their halyards flew the Union Jack and the Stars and Stripes. As the jeep came to a halt, a young British soldier came to greet her and with a smart salute took her suitcase. Anna, holding Eddi's hand followed him into the building and to a room on the first floor.

The squaddie opened the door and invited her to enter. 'This'll be yer room, laidy. If yer be wanting to gae oot, ye'll hae tae inform tha Sarn't. Hae's doon tae hall. If you or tae bairn be wanting oot, jess use tae phone. Ask for Gordon, that's me, laidy. Yer ken?'

'Yes, thank you,' said Anna, trying hard to decipher what he had said in his Scottish brogue but not quite sure what he had actually said. She did notice however that his regimental badge indicated he was from the 8th Battalion of the Argyll and Sutherland Highlanders. Making his exit he gave her a broad grin, revealing his missing front teeth before closing the door behind him. Suddenly they were on their own, as silence reigned supreme. Anna, deep in thought, savoured the moment as she stood by the bay window that overlooked the Drau valley. At last she had her privacy and what's more, the whole of the British army as her guardian angel.

They slept soundly that night, mother and child. At eight-thirty the following morning Anna awoke dreamily from under her eider duvet to greet her first day of true freedom. After a quick ablution she picked up the phone which was immediately answered by a cultured English voice.

'Good morning, Mrs Bauer.'

'Good morning, please, what am I to do?'

'Kindly join us for breakfast,' said the voice. 'I'll send my batman to fetch you. Your boy too.'

'Thank you,' said Anna as the other phone clicked and moments later came a knock on her door. Anna and Eddi followed the man to the lounge and a place to one side, where officers sat at tables laid for breakfast. Eyes were raised in her direction as she entered and was ushered to sit with several officers enjoying their cooked meals. The sausage, bacon and eggs aroma was unmistakably British and reminded her of her time in England with Franz as a guest of the Ipswich Yacht Club.

With introductions and formalities dispensed, Anna ordered the same as the others. She was not an officer's wife for nothing, she mused as the adage of 'When in Rome' came to mind. The meal over, a local kindergarten lady asked Eddi if he would like to play and once Anna had calmed his fear he nodded and followed the dirndl-clad woman. The meal over, the table was cleared and a map of the locality spread out across it.

'Well, Mrs Bauer...' Anna half raised her hand and stopped the colonel who had addressed her.

'Please, call me Anna,' she said. 'I would like that.' The officer nodded and carried on.

'This is a map of the locality. I understand that you are not from these parts, Anna?'

How on earth did he know that? she wondered, before answering with a shake of her head.

'No, that's correct sir,' she replied. 'I'm from Cologne, but I lived in Aachen before my house was bom—'

'That's quite alright,' cut in the colonel as the others shifted uneasily in their chairs. 'What has happened Anna is the Russians have taken rather more of the territory than was agreed at Yalta and now we are trying to get them to move back, as it were?'

'I see,' said Anna, but wondered why they wanted her as she did not speak Russian.

'You might be wondering what all this might have to do with you,' said the colonel. Anna met his gaze and noted his silver hair, which looked becoming on the less than middle-aged man, and answered with a slight nod. 'Well,' he went on, 'the problem is we have been saddled, if you'll excuse the pun with several thousand Cossacks that fought on the German side and they have surrendered to us.' He glanced at the map to where a red circle had been added and the word Peggetz Camp inserted. 'The problem is, Anna, the

Russians want them back as agreed by us and the Americans at Yalta.' Anna nodded but again, could not see where or how she could help.

'We have requested your assistance,' continued the colonel, 'as a lot of the Cossack officers speak German and one such officer is German, so we need somebody, especially a neutral, a civilian, to explain to them our wishes. It's a tricky situation as they don't want to be repatriated and for obvious reasons. But we thought if a woman could speak to them, especially if she was German, they might listen and trust us more than if it came from one of my men.'

The officers nodded in unison as anxious eyes were cast in her direction. Anna saw from their concerned expressions they were willing her to accept; however in some untrodden region of her mind alarm bells were ringing as the caveat, plot and danger entered her thoughts.

'I see, sir,' was all she could think of to say as she gazed at the map and its tiny, innocuous circle of red ink. As silence descended pipes and cigarettes were lit. Anna glanced round the table and back at the colonel. 'And what makes you think they would trust me, sir?' Several officers nodded at the question and cast shrewd glances from her to their commanding officer.

'Well,' he replied, 'we think you being German and especially now we know you are a U-boat officer's wife, we reasoned they would listen to you. Besides, they are Cossacks and have always had an eye for the ladies.' Several chuckles went round the table as Anna felt a flush to her cheeks but holding her own reasoned she would be compromised; both by the Cossacks and by the Allies and she was being used by the British to pull their chestnuts from the fire.

'And what if they refuse to listen to whatever you want me to say?' said Anna in a suspicious tone, being that her femininity was about to be exploited. Uneasily, some sucked at their pipes, whilst others stubbed out their cigarettes and stared apprehensively at the innocent red circle.

'My dear, they have no choice,' said the colonel bluntly and holding her questioning gaze. Anna stared back at the man in disbelief and at the others as by their solemn expressions and sheepish manner she realised the die had already been cast. Notwithstanding, she decided she would accept once she had seen her brief. It would only mean reading from a document, perhaps answering a few questions. Besides, she and her son would be well looked after here and there was the promise of payment. But now she needed them to keep to the most important part of the bargain.

Anna, with a bargaining smile addressed the colonel. 'Perhaps if you could let me have a brief of what I would have to do or say, I would be able to better decide. In the meantime, would it be possible sir, for you to find out the whereabouts of my husband?' She reached for her handbag and withdrew a folded piece of paper and handed it to him.

The colonel raised his bushy eyebrows and examined the handwritten note. It stated her husband's full name, rank and number and Aachen address. He handed it to a lieutenant with a nod and the man immediately excused himself and left the room. Deep inside Anna's joy knew no bounds. Her heart skipped a beat as she reasoned perhaps, within the hour the British intelligence machine would have the answer and she would at long last have the relief of knowing her husband's fate.

'Well, Mrs Bauer – sorry, Anna,' the colonel said with a congenial smile. 'I think we can sort that out for you and trust we can bring you good news. With regard to the Cossacks, our Mr Macmillan here can let you have the details of what all this Cossack business is about, perhaps we can meet up after lunch and you can assess the problem first hand.'

Anna nodded and thanked him, as the others rose and excused themselves. She was left with a tall, middle-aged man with bushy eyebrows and a certain charm of manner.

'Let's see now,' he said as he bent down to reach for his papers. 'Here we are Anna, perhaps you would be kind enough to read through these. As you see, they are in English and this one here is a translation into German. Handing her the papers he was about to leave. 'By the way,' said Macmillan, 'my name is Harold.' Anna acknowledged with the ghost of a smile and was relieved to find hers was only one page of script.

'Thank you, sir. May I take them to my room?'

'Why not, I think that would be in order but as you can see, they are marked restricted and confidential, so I would ask you not to reveal their content to anyone.'

'Of course,' said Anna with a meaningful smile and warming to his polite manner. However, she was puzzled as to why he was wearing civilian clothes, when all around were in uniform?

Back in her room she was able to collect her thoughts. She read the documents, both in English and German and found they were a precise translation. She could handle that but what she really wanted now was the news about her husband.

Anna skipped lunch but after an hour there was a call from the colonel. He politely asked whether she had decided to accept the job of interpreter. Anna said that she would but what about her son? What would happen to him whilst she was away? He explained that he would be able to join the other children under supervision of the army, along with the children of the soldiers' families.

'So that's that. We'll meet you at two-thirty in the foyer,' said the colonel in a brusque tone and hung up.

At two-fifteen Anna took Eddi with her to the entrance hall where the kindergarten lady was already waiting. Corporal Gordon was there too and she could not help but notice his highly-polished boots. As soon as she had said goodbye to her son the corporal escorted her to where a black Hillman staff car was waiting. He opened the door for her and was immediately greeted by the colonel and Mr Macmillan.

'Glad you took the job, Mrs Bauer,' said the colonel. 'Sorry, I should say Anna. We'll take you for a drive round the place; see what we're up against.' He tapped his cane on the window and with a typical Hillman gearbox whine, the saloon set off along the dusty road in the direction of the Peggetz camp.

Within the hour they arrived at a large clearing and encampment. Here, Anna could not believe the sight that met her eyes. She sat dumbfounded. This must be the mother of all camps, she reasoned. Before her were hundreds and hundreds of horses and tents and above all this, a seething mass of pitiful humanity. All around were fearsome-looking men with black beards and curling moustaches. Many were dressed in costumes of a bygone age, their faces gaunt, devoid of expression, their bodies lean from lack of nutrition.

There were thousands of other men, again with handsome moustaches but in the familiar field-grey uniforms of the German army. Women and children were everywhere and old men and grandmothers just sitting and waiting. There was some semblance of order as the tents were ranged in rows along with a several wooden barracks. British soldiers were directing with gestures to where a continuous line of men on horseback and others with horse-drawn wagons, were throwing their rifles and sabres onto an ever growing pile of discarded weaponry.

Anna looked on as the car drove slowly down the lines of canvas until it stopped at a marquee tent flying the Imperial Russian flag. A tanned Asiatic soldier wearing a field-grey tunic and Caucasus britches strode purposefully towards them and opened the car door. He bowed as the colonel, followed by Macmillan and Anna stepped onto the flattened grass. A tall athletic man with an olive complexion and wearing a white Cossack hat appeared and saluted the colonel then shook his and Macmillan's hand.

'This is Frau Bauer,' said the colonel as the elderly Cossack held out his hand to her.

'Frau Bauer, Sie sprechen Deutsch?' the Cossack asked with an admiring glance. Anna met his discerning gaze and nodded as she felt a flush to her cheeks. His silver handlebar moustache, swept in an upward rake was something reminiscent of a Grimm's fairy tale, or the lancers on horseback in the painting on her mother's wall.

'Jawohl, Herr...'

'Sultan Keletsey Girej at your service,' he said with a broad grin, a bow and a loud impish chuckle at her unease.

But Anna was a good judge of character and saw in his dark, piercing eyes a lurking sadness as he glanced furtively around his surrendering command. He still retained his Luger pistol and sabre as his hand drifted down to hold its trusty hilt. He stood majestically, like a Tartar warlord in his long black coat, with heavy silver-embroidered emblems, but now could only await the victor's bidding.

'Anna,' said the colonel. 'Kindly let him know who you are. A U-Boot officer's wife and that you will be our interpreter. Also we will not keep him as we have to move on, but hopefully will have news shortly about some sort of compromise we can reach with the Soviets.'

Anna nodded and faced this lord of the Steppe, repeating to him what had been said. The man nodded gravely and replied in a tempered tone that even the two English men could not mistake.

'Tell them that my men have surrendered to the British. We are the enemies of Moscow, of the Communists and Tito. Our fight has not been with the British or the Americans. We surrender to the British in this camp but will never surrender to the Russians and we will fight them to the last drop of our Cossack blood.' His dark eyes flashed as they interrogated those of his visitors and with a forced smile and a final salute, dropped his withering gaze, turned sharply and strode back to his tented quarters.

Anna took a backward glance at the man and was fascinated by him. The stuff of legend and films, she mused.

They left the camp and drove for three hours on the empty road, past Spital and were halted by a road block. In front were several British and American army vehicles and dwarfing them, a battle-scarred Red Army tank. A British Red Cap came to their car and informed them the Soviet tank crew had orders not to let them pass. In the fields and scattered houses they witnessed Russian soldiers shooting livestock and breaking into the houses, as most of the rural community had either fled or, like the remaining handful stood by helplessly, mute witness to the destruction.

'What do you reckon, Mac?' said the colonel.

'Mmm,' came the reply as Macmillan rubbed his chin. 'Bit of a stand-off, if you ask me. They've got more armour than we have around here and the way the Soviets see it, possession is nine tenths of the law. It's our fault really for letting them get ahead of us. We stuck to the Yalta agreement but they just drove their tanks right through it. Look what happened in Berlin. They beat us to it, yet we crossed the Rhine weeks ago. Could have been in Berlin a week before them but no, we played the game by the rules and waited. Eisenhower was warned by Churchill but he wouldn't listen and now we have the same here.' Anna listened and reasoned that Mac must be some sort of diplomat seconded to the army and seemed to know his ground, but at this moment in time, made no decisions. The Red Cap returned, shaking his head.

'Looks like they'll not let you through, sir. Suggest, sir, you return to base, as things might turn nasty round here.'

'Yes, I quite agree, sergeant,' said the colonel. 'Okay driver, back to camp at the double.' The lance corporal nodded and with a deft three-point turn headed back towards Lienz and their company HQ.

Once back it was Macmillan that went straight to a telephone and contacted London, whilst the colonel wrote his report. Anna overheard the names of General McCreery and Archer mentioned, then a Major Davis and Generals Shkuro, Krasnow, Domanow then Pannwitz. The latter seemed familiar but then it was not her business. Macmillan replaced the receiver and immediately asked the switchboard operator to put him through to Klagenfurt, and to speak urgently to General Keightley.

Being a lull in activities, Anna was now free to do as she pleased and was ecstatic when she was requested to go to the pay office and collect her occupation money. She signed for her US dollars and pounds sterling and was informed that that was for expenses. Her pay would be at the end of the month.

'Better than I thought,' she mused.

On a chair an English newspaper several days old drew her attention. Anna stifled a cry as she opened up the folded paper and saw the picture and headlines about a camp named Auschwitz, somewhere in Poland. Here were stacked row upon row the bodies of naked men, women and children. She gazed at a photo of the crematorium ovens and the mountainous piles of shoes, glasses, hair and clothing of the thousands who had met with an untimely end. The headlines screamed at the Nazi butchery of innocents and went on to list the names of those Germans caught and executed on the spot by some of the inmates that had saved the last of their strength for vengeance and retribution.

Another article then caught her eye. 'American sergeant goes berserk, blasts 300 Nazi guards at Dachau Death Camp.' Anna's heart froze as she thought about Helmut and the fur coats, their contents and their unfortunate owners. Horrified, she went on to read an American soldier, having seen the emaciated inmates, the piles of rotting corpses and the well-nourished SS guards, rounded up some of these and shot them. It was believed other Americans also assisted in the carnage.

The article went on to say the size of the camp was staggering – a thousand acres with incriminating photographs of barbed wire partitions, piles of human ashes, mountains of shoes, together with bales of human hair and boxes of industrial soap, of doubtful origins?

A large fortress-like hill stood in the middle and this was the place that now housed the Gestapo and SS war criminals that were being interrogated and sent for trial. Her blood ran cold as she examined the pictures in detail. She had had no idea, even though she had been only a few miles from the place and thought of Helmut again. He and Willi *must* have known but had said nothing. Totally confused and troubled by her conscience, she passed the lounge and bar where officers were gathering for the evening's entertainment and went quietly to her room.

The next day, after breakfast she was called into the colonel's office. She went along as soon as she had seen Eddi off to his kindergarten. The door's inscription read 'Col Fergus McDuff'. She knocked on the door, and entered.

'Ah yes, good morning Mrs Bauer – sorry, Anna, please be seated.' She sat in front of his red leather-topped writing desk and watched as he shuffled his papers into some semblance of order. 'Yes, here it is. Good news and not so good about your husband.' He glanced at the wired message and with a congenial expression handed it across to her.

Anna took a deep breath as her laden heart beating with a gamut of emotions was about to burst. She had for so long lived for this moment but now was afraid to know the truth. With a sense of fear and apprehension, began to read the document.

FAO Col. F. McDuff = BAOO + LIENZ + Austria / your enquiry 14.05.45 +

Kapitänleutnant Franz Eduart Bauer + CO U-888 + Last Base Lorient France +

Sailed 08.06.44 + No U-classification + Destination + Japan + Routeing unknown +

Sighting + Unconfirmed + 25.08.44 + Mauritius + End +++

She read, then re-read the message and with eyes brimming with tears handed it back.

'So, what do you make of it, sir?' she said, dabbing her cheeks with a handkerchief.

'Well, Anna, it's as I said, it could be good or bad news. But because it doesn't mention any contact with our boys, or the other allied navies in the area, I would say that he is still somewhere out there. Possibly he made it to Japan and as you know, we are still in conflict with the Japs. Sorry I can't be of any more help to you.' He reached for his briar pipe and ceremoniously stoked and lit up to envelop her in passing clouds of Navy Shag. 'However,' he continued with satisfaction, 'I will keep you posted as soon as I hear anything from naval intelligence as they still have to compile a mass of incoming data.' Anna thanked him and was about to leave the room, when he called her back.

'Oh, by the way, my dear, I forgot to thank you. You did a splendid job with old Genghis yesterday.'

'Genghis?' she queried with a frown.

'Ha! sorry, my dear. That old sultan Girej chap. We nicknamed him Genghis – you know that Mongolian chap that sacked half of Europe. Awfully funny, eh, what?' Anna gave a wan smile and nodded in a semblance of understanding as the whole thing was lost on her, especially the way the British made their jokes. It always was a puzzle to Germans like herself.

For the next few days, nothing much happened. Anna sat around, studied reports on the Cossacks and drank Brazilian blend coffee. She was happy about her husband, as he had not been reported as missing in action.

'I know he's out there somewhere,' she kept saying to herself and with a woman's intuition knew they would find him.

For the Americans and the British the question about the Russian land-grabbing tactics was still under intense discussion. Yalta-agreed boundaries were re-drawn and the Americans had to concede part of the captured German territory north of the Bohemian Forrest. Multi-Zones of occupation were agreed upon for Berlin and Vienna, but a ring of steel had now surrounded all of the nine Russian-conquered territories, which now included the town of Judenburg some 110 miles from Lienz. It had been tentatively agreed, over open gun-sights – the Red Army would not cross the bridge of the river Mur to the west.

As the sun rose higher and the days grew warmer, the plight of the Cossack POWs became desperate. News had filtered through they were to be sent back to Russia. Also, that one of their respected commanders, a German from Silesia, General Pannwitz and his XV Cossack Cavalry was soon to swell their ranks. The British at Lienz were left with the problem of trying to negotiate an agreeable and humanitarian settlement and had repeatedly requested the Cossacks be allowed to stay in the west. Stalin however stood his ground and held the Western Allies to the Yalta agreement whereby all those Russians that took up arms against him must be handed back. This included the Cossacks and all Russian POWs, in German camps.

By late May all negotiations had failed and on a balmy summer's day, Y Company of the Argyle regiment found themselves rounding up the leaders of the Cossack bands in order to repatriate them with their comrades across the bridge at Judenburg. Guns and sabres that had not been surrendered now came to the fore. The scene turned ugly as British soldiers held the unfortunates at bay with rifles, batons and fixed bayonets.

Anna was immediately sent for and a major by name of Davis informed her she must talk with Girej and an Ataman called General Shkuro. She was to relay the request that senior officers were to travel in British transports for a meeting and to be returned later. Anna knew the full story, but went with him to the camp and the Sultan's marquee.

Already a large unruly crowd had gathered clamouring for news and threatening to break out of the camp as British soldiers stood uncompromisingly on guard around its perimeter. Major Davis and Anna were let through and were followed inside by several Cossack officers still wearing their German army tunics. Anna held up her hand to quieten them and called for silence. To her amazement, it worked.

'Kameraden,' she said, 'please listen to what Major Davis has to say.' Davis handed her a document she had already studied on her way to the camp. Anna swallowed hard as the smell of unwashed bodies mixed with the pungent effluvia of horse assailed her nostrils. Clearing her throat and with a voice tinged with Prussian authority, began her address.

'I have been asked to explain to you in Deutsch what is on offer and that which has been agreed by the British and Americans. For this we require all high ranking officers to attend a special meeting at Spital. You are to leave any weapons here at the camp before boarding the transports.'

In an instant a deafening uproar split the humid air at the mention of further dis-arming. Voices were raised as suspicions were aroused. Again she held up her hand for calm and asked them to listen.

'In your absence, extra food will be issued by the British for your men and all families.' Anna paused as the suspicious murmurs continued. And with an engaging smile added, 'and also for the horses.' It had an immediate effect and broke the ice as hardened fighters grinned and nodded. Reluctantly the officers agreed to the meeting and stilled their men. Major Davis, wearing a suspicious frown took the document from her.

'What was that last bit, Anna?' he whispered. 'What did you say to those headmen to make them change their minds?'

Holding his questioning gaze she said calmly, 'I told them they can all join your army.' With that and a sense of Teutonic humour she walked back to the car, as the major stood pondering and scratching his chin.

One Ataman led by example as he knew full well that their fate had been sealed and placed his side arm and sabre on the table. Other officers followed and moved out to board the transports.

The Cossacks crowding round the marquee were calmed by their officers and told about the extra rations as, one by one, the lorries left the compound to the accompanying wails of wives and children. Major Davis and a sergeant major nicknamed Big Jock and Anna brought up the rear. Some thirty miles later as they by-passed Spital, a hue and cry arose but the lorries sped on. Under guard and gunpoint, they reached their final destination, the small bridge at Judenburg.

Here all prisoners were off-loaded as the transports were forbidden by the Red guards to cross the bridge. With howls of rage at the British, the Cossack officers were unceremoniously handed over to the waiting Russians and their NKVD interrogators. Big Jock was ordered to turn the car and head back to HQ as Anna looked back, horrified, realising she had had a hand in their betrayal.

It was the next morning, after a restless night of guilt and soul searching she was summoned to join McDuff and Major Davis for breakfast. It was explained to her what had happened was regrettable, but that was war. Also, there was another agreement other than Yalta and it concerned the Russians also handing back allied POWs which had been freed by them from the hands of the Germans. They explained to her that after all, the Cossacks were the enemy and had to be treated as such.

Before she could comment as to her role, McDuff handed her a piece of paper. Anna excused herself to catch some fresh air as she recognised the blue oval British Admiralty insignia. Once outside, she sat on the old schoolhouse steps to bask in the morning sunshine and opened the already unsealed dispatch.

RESTRICTED

29 May 1945 To HQ commanding officer. 8th Argyle and Sutherland-Y Company ⊦

From Admiralty Report following your request of U-Boat CO Kapitänleutnant Franz Bauer + His whereabouts at this time unknown +

U number unknown + previous command U-888 + Suspect voyage to Japan +

Possible casualty Far East arena + U- Boats surrendered Indian Ocean / Arabian Sea + Possibly with Japanese fleet + Some U-Boats still to surrender + Dutch and American records cannot verify at this time + End

She read the communiqué several times over, but it revealed nothing, it did not state or confirm anything. Lost in the fog of war as, apparently, U-Booten were still at sea. 'Aha, ja that was positive,' she said to herself. 'You're out there somewhere Franz,' she said in a comforting whisper. 'I know you are. Please, Heilige Mutter, bring him back to me.' Once again, she examined the wired document as a dew drop tear fell to stain and fade out his name as, all around in the flowering grass the crickets chirped their laughter.

***

Corporal Gordon gave a polite cough as he approached from behind. 'Tae colonel needs yer, Ma'am. He'll be oot in a wee while.' Anna turned to thank him as she saw the man approaching.

'There you are, Anna. I've been looking for you. Good news, I trust?' Anna stood and answered with a shrug as she wiped away a remaining tear. She was grateful to him and did not wish to be rude but that business from yesterday and now the communiqué had affected her badly.

'Yes, thank you, sir,' she replied, having composed herself with a sniff into her handkerchief.

'Have to tell you Anna, we need your help as we have some very unpleasant business to attend to.' He handed her a document. 'You can read it in the car. The Sergeant Major is waiting out front.'

'Thank you, sir,' she replied. 'Just let me get my things.'

Going to her room she changed into a khaki shirt, skirt and tie. Minutes later, Big Jock and Anna were driven to the Peggetz camp. They were in the van of a convoy of canvas-topped Bedford lorries which for her was already an omen in itself.

The saloon halted at the gates as the lorries swept past a ring of grim-faced soldiers with rifles and fixed bayonets stationed around the perimeter. Except for the keening of the women and the cries of children there was a silence from the Cossacks that stood around the Ataman's Marquee.

Major Davis was already there with them as the saloon was waved in to join him. As the car came to a halt, Anna noticed a smart-looking German officer standing with the major. The odd thing was he wore a similar hat as the Cossack Ataman. Anna was beckoned to join Davis and was immediately introduced to the officer.

'Anna, this is General Helmuth von Pannwitz. He is the German Ataman of the Fifteenth Cossack Cavalry Corps and highly respected by all Cossacks. I hope you don't mind but I have already managed to convey your position with us.'

Anna met von Pannwitz's steely gaze and felt foolish now dressed in a British army uniform. His features seemed Slavic to her but dismissed it as he immediately put her at ease with an engaging smile and offered his hand.

'So what can you tell me Anna?' he said. 'I see you have brought your transportation with you.' The smile faded and his broad features turned into a calculating mask. Caught off guard, her cheeks flushed with embarrassment as it was not her forte to communicate with such high-ranking officers and turned to the major for advice.

'Tell him nothing, Anna,' said Davis under his breath. 'Get the officers here to listen to you and read the document. It's official and they know it.'

'Yes, sir,' she replied. Saying 'sir', made her feel official and it regained her confidence as, at the same time the Cossacks well understood the British honorific acknowledgement. Sultan Girej and his officers looked on as Anna cleared her throat and began.

'To all Cossacks at Peggetz camp, you are to be repatriated to your homeland as agreed between the Allies and Marshal Stalin.' From outside there was uproar as inside the canvas walls the remaining officers shook their heads in disbelief. 'You and your families will be able to travel back to your homelands with the Soviet army to assist you.' Again uproar as curses and shouts of betrayal rent the air. Amidst the furore, it was the Sultan who now spoke as he raised his hand for silence.

'Frau Anna,' he addressed her in halting German. 'Ask your major where are all my officers from yesterday, are they still at this meeting?' His suspicious eyes and encompassing nod flustered her. This was not supposed to happen. It was not in her notes and she was now visibly out of her depth. Quickly she conversed with Davis who told her what to say in order not to let matters get out of hand.

'Herr Sultan,' she said, nervously clearing her throat. 'They're at another camp at Spital and awaiting the arrival of their men from this camp.' The veteran soldier shook his head, however proof was another matter as Von Pannwitz stood listening and said nothing. He stared at her and could not comprehend why she, a German officer's wife was dressed in a British army uniform and going along with this spiel.

Now with a raised voice, Anna continued as she read from the document. 'You will all have to take your families and return to the Soviets who will re-settle you as agreed at Yalta. And, as the remaining senior officers, you will be asked to take the commanding role to form the vanguard of the exodus from this camp.'

Howls of impotent rage and anger rent the air as from outside, some thirty thousand voices took up the cry. Conjecture and fear took hold, together with angry shouts for action as fists were raised at her and Major Davis standing resolutely by her side. A booming Scottish voice rang out as Big Jock elbowed his way through, followed closely by a squad of soldiers with fixed bayonets.

'If the blighters come one step closer, sir, and with your permission, I will order my men to open fire,' said the CSM.

Colonel Davis, his face ashen stood his ground and shook his head, signalling with his hand for the old Sultan to do something. With a reluctant nod the man casually reached for his pistol and raising it, fired once to drill a 9mm hole through the top canvas of the marquee. A hush fell over the whole camp at the sound of the shot and a loud murmur arose from outside as silence reigned within.

'Frau Bauer,' he addressed her again. 'Tell your major here that as the remaining officers we will do as we are asked. However, let the world know that as soldiers we surrendered to the British. That our fight was to free our homeland along with the Lithuanians, Latvians, Estonians and Ukrainians of the Russian yoke. We are all here, just see for yourself and we never harmed any of you. We are not Russians and now you betray us. We, who surrendered to you are now to be marched to our deaths.' Anna translated as the old Cossack said his piece.

Sultan Girej then addressed his officers and told them to prepare for the journey back to Russia. 'We will have to trust our enemy, trust his word as Herr Roosevelt and Herr Churchill have given theirs.' The astonished hush was immediately drowned in a howling sea of dissent and angry voices, both from inside and out of the great tent. Girej raised his pistol and sent another bullet through the canvas as hush returned once more.

'Kameraden!' he continued. 'In order to show good faith, Frau Anna will come with us so that your men and your families can follow. She will accompany the British officers, who will negotiate with the Soviets for the best terms under the agreement.' Anna was speechless at first, but rapidly explained to Davis and Big Jock what had just transpired.

'The cunning old fox,' muttered Davis. 'If we back down his men will smell a bigger rat and we'll have a riot on our hands. But if we let Anna and ourselves go with their officers, he will have a civilian witness at the other end. Clever old bastard, eh, what?'

'We can't let the lady go, sir,' said Big Jock. 'It's got nothing to do with her. She's a civilian and we'll have to clear it with the diplomats for us to get involved as we can't just enter their zone.'

'Quite so, Sergeant Major,' replied Davis, 'but we'll play their game. We have to hand them over, by force if necessary. But if we send Anna along for part of the way, then at least they will follow with their womenfolk. I don't like it any more than you do but that's for the diplomats to decide. They've gotten us into this mess, let them deal with it.' He turned to Anna. 'Would you help us out here,

Anna?' he said in a loud whisper. 'As you can see, we're in a bit of a bind.' Anna gazed at him with incredulity. Was he out of his mind?

Davis saw her misgivings. 'But, of course,' he added, 'the British Army will guarantee your safety, at all times.'

As the Sultan and his officers watched and waited, Anna's mind was made up. Having seen the appalling state of the camp, together with the plight of its people, especially the women and children, she had to do something positive. Also there was her husband to think of. She still needed more information and they had, after all, guaranteed her safety and well-being.

'I will try to help, sir,' said Anna reassuringly. 'I'll go with them to their destination as in a way; they are my people, too...'

From a distance the first shots rang out. Immediately the tent cleared and once outside they watched in horror to see, at the camp's perimeter, Cossacks shooting their mounts and turning the guns on themselves in swift self-execution. Women and children screamed as the spasmodic firing continued along with the pathetic whinnying of the dying beasts.

As the sounds reverberated throughout the camp, hardened soldiers from opposing sides looked on with tear-filled eyes. It was amongst this distress and confusion that Big Jock ushered the major and Anna back into their car as by now the soldiers were loading the lorries. Rifle butts and bayonet points were used to cram the unfortunates into the transports. Those who tried to escape were beaten and slung back onto the lorries. Anna was horrified to see men hanging themselves from nearby trees, whilst others threw themselves and their children into the fast-flowing river.

The car was about to leave when a radio message from HQ crackled in the driver's headphones. The corporal wrote it down and handed the chit to the major, at a glance Anna recognized the name Pannwitz, as the driver started the engine. With the Argyles clearing the way they passed through the main gate and waited.

Chapter Thirty-Eight

BALALAIKA

After a four-hour journey through the Tyrolean countryside they eventually arrived at a small valley town. Here, at the middle of the Judenburg bridge was the border and to the east the Russian zone of occupied Austria. The convoy of distressed humanity halted at the British checkpoint and the sentries waved them through. However, the Russian guards on seeing the British transports halted the convoy.

Cautiously the staff car drove towards the checkpoint and stopped. The CSM presented his papers, this time written in Cyrillic script. To his utter amazement the Russian guards with their PP submachine guns slung over their shoulders, examined the documentura, unfortunately holding the papers upside down. They began shaking their heads vigorously.

'Nyet, Uj-ti Uj-ti!' they shouted and gesticulated that he should leave, depart. Big Jock pointed at the lorries, but it had no effect.

'It-ti Na-zaht!' they shouted as the CSM walked back to the car. He asked Anna and the Major to accompany him. He explained what had transpired and that the young soldiers were totally illiterate.

'They were informed we were coming and it's all in Cyrillic,' said Davis in annoyance. 'We sent them one load, what's wrong with the blighters?'

'Perhaps they speak German, sir?' said Big Jock. 'Everybody else seems to around here.' Anna stifled a laugh at the big man's sense of humour as she and Davis left the car and walked back towards the Russian checkpoint. By this time, a Red Army officer had appeared and the CSM once again handed him the document of repatriation.

'Da, da,' he said somewhat triumphantly. 'Fascisti Kossaka,' he explained to the guards. He went inside the red and white painted hut and, cranking a handle, spoke rapidly into a field telephone. After several minutes a jeep with the Soviet red star on its bonnet and doors skidded to a halt and two high-ranking officers with their peaked caps and red bands climbed out.

'Sprechen Sie Deutsch,' said the taller of the two, whose dark hair and high cheek bones indicated his Slavic roots, whilst the other man was stocky and more of the peasant farmer type, with a moonface and cunning blue eyes.

'Ja,' said Anna and stepping forward, 'I speak German. I am the interpreter. This is Major Davis and his Company Sergeant Major of the British Argyle regiment.'

'Kah-ro-shij,' replied the tall officer with a satisfied smile. 'We have been expecting you and the traitors. You can lead your transports behind that row of trees and tell them all to get out.' He indicated with a wave to where several groups of Soviet soldiers were standing, casually smoking and watching events.

'You mean we drive through your checkpoint?' said Anna.

'Jawohl, you can lead the way. Once offloaded, you can go back for the next load.' Anna nodded and explained to the major what had been said.

'I don't like it,' said Davis. 'Driving into their territory after all those negotiations, but I suppose we'd better comply. I cannot see any harm in that as we cannot just off-load them here. What do you say, Sergeant Major?'

'Bit tricky decision, sir. But if the Cossacks see us pulling out early, they might cause a problem, sir.'

'Yes quite, Sergeant Major, exactly as I thought. Tell him, Frau Bauer, we will comply with his request.' Anna turned back to the two Russians to explain what had been said. With the paperwork signed the stocky man said something in Russian at which the two burst out laughing. Anna, casting a glance in their direction, was sure it appertained to her.

Big Jock waved to his driver and to the rest of the convoy as the barrier was raised and the lorries followed the staff car as they made their way past the checkpoint and into the Soviet zone.

Subdued Cossacks peered out from behind the canvas awnings to view their welcoming comrades and surroundings. The lorries ground to a halt a few hundred yards distant and to everyone's amazement there were tables loaded with food along with bedding and railway coaches ready to be boarded. The prisoners were ordered to disembark and each handed a blanket and told to help themselves from the table.

After an hour the lorries, now empty, began their journey back to Lienz and the Peggetz camp. Major Davis, pleased with the smooth transfer thanked the Russians who replied with wide grins and asked him to bring back the others as soon as logistics would permit. To show support they brought one of the German-speaking Cossacks and explained that he should go back with them to assist with the others from the camp.

'Sounds reasonable,' said Davis after Anna explained it to him, meanwhile Big Jock took a wary glance in the direction of the now empty tables and the train, still waiting as the Cossacks and their families disappeared from sight.

By twelve o'clock the following day, the transports had once again been loaded and a bedraggled mass of humanity left their friends, horses and belongings to start their journey into Russian captivity. With the returned Cossack officer relating how well they had been received, the loading was made that much easier.

To speed up the transfer, separate convoys of humanity were taken to a nearby station and transported by rail to the abandoned iron works in that town. With the lorries loaded, once again Anna travelled in the car, this time only with the CSM, a corporal driver and two soldiers armed with Lanchesters. Ninety loaded trucks followed with a jeep and three armed guards bringing up the rear.

This time they drove over the bridge and through the Soviet check-point where they halted at the designated clearing. The Cossacks and their officers had gone as the train, this time with goods wagons attached stood waiting. The tables were bare as Russian soldiers gave orders for them all to disembark and to be marched behind the wagons. Once clear, a Soviet officer waved the transports away and brusquely told the CSM to bring the next load.

'Looks like the tea party finished early,' said Big Jock as he climbed into the car.

'Mmm, I wonder where the others are?' said Anna. 'Seems awfully quiet around here.' The staff car brought up the rear and as they passed through the Russian check-point Jock's head suddenly spun round as he gazed through the oval back window.

'Listen! Did you hear that? Sounds like gunfire.'

'I thought it was the train, sir,' said one of the guards, 'but did you see those Russkies? They looked like a tough bunch to me. Been through a few fire fights, I bet.'

'I'm not surprised,' said the CSM. 'They had a hell of a time fighting those fanatical Nazi bleeders of the Waffen SS. Lost several million men, they did.'

'What's going to happen to those Cossacks, sir?' asked the driver.

'Well son, they're going to send them back to Mother Russia and make them dig beetroots for Stalin's Borscht, I guess. Teach 'em a lesson to behave, yer ken laddie.'

Anna sat in the back of the car with the two guards, listening to their banter as the evening shadows lengthened and lamps appeared from the wooden houses high up the alpine slopes. She was pleased how the day had gone but now had other things on her mind as she thought about Franz and what else she could do to find him. As the staff car pulled into company HQ, Anna swore blind she had just seen General Von Pannwitz leaving the building under escort.

***

Days later the camp was all but cleared as all that remained were the Sultan, his family and several fierce-looking guards with weather-beaten faces and upturned moustaches to match. They had been allowed to keep their side arms and sabres as a sign of respect but as things stood, would very soon be relieved of them. All that remained was a blot on the landscape where a mass of humanity had gambled and lost their fight to live in the West.

Dead horses, their bodies bloated, lay where they had fallen, their shattered skulls attracting hordes of flies, together with scavenging crows that fought noisily among themselves to pick at eyes and soft underbellies. Their once fearsome riders lying beside them, united in death and respectfully covered with canvas or horse blankets until the Tommy squaddies could lay them to rest.

Mounds of earth depicted graves of Cossacks who had decided that Siberia was not an option and in many cases, these included whole families, children and their grandparents, entombed as one. Now only the tents remained as zephyrs stirred the limp summer leaves and loose canvas flapped idly in the heat. Many of the tents had their sides slashed open, like gaping wounds they bore witness to children's toys, abandoned and scattered from where their playful owners had been forcibly removed.

Outside the camp, in the light air the telegraph wires hummed their strain of summer, as the sun beat down from an azure sky. Abandoned dogs lay idle with lolling tongues, as they panted in the pine wood's shade.

It was to be Anna's last visit to the camp and she was glad this whole repatriation business was coming to an end. Taxing it was to say the least, both for her and the soldiers who carried out the orders. But news was once again filtering through that thousands of the German Osttruppen, the main bulk of the Caucasus army had been released by the French and Americans. They were free to live in the West and had joined the refugees and homeless souls which

315

drifted, like an incoming tide of humanity across Europe's stricken plain. Ironically it was the BBC that had broadcast the news but somehow failed to mention the human tragedy that was unfolding here at Peggetz Camp and Judenburg.

As the staff car and another drew up outside the Sultan's HQ goats and sheep scattered, stared and bleated as two Bedfords followed. With firm politeness the soldiers escorted the remaining womenfolk to the transports along with their children, cooking pots and personal belongings and indicating for their Cossack guards to follow. They still wore their field-grey uniforms but had taken the precaution of removing all insignia of unit and rank.

Big Jock and a lieutenant stood outside the marquee to wait as Major Davis, along with Macmillan and Sultan Girej left the Grand Marquee for the last time. As if on parade, the Sultan inspected his escort and gazed grimly at the two lorries and his car which stood waiting, with its engine running.

Slowly the old man turned and facing his tent drew his sabre. The long blade glinted menacingly as, with two swift strokes he severed the leading guide-ropes of his tented HQ. Majestically and without a sound the marquee swayed and slowly folded to fall in on itself as the stanchions collapsed. With a satisfied grunt he replaced the trusty blade and with ramrod composure, which even Big Jock admired, turned his back on his last command and strode purposefully towards the waiting car. A corporal held open the door; Sultan Girej drew his sabre and with a benign nod approached Major Davis to surrender his weapon. The major shook his head, turned and climbing into his staff car gave orders for the driver to return to HQ.

As Girej's car passed through the gates, the two British sentries shouldered arms in salute to the old man who acknowledged with a curt nod and battle-weary eyes brimming with tears. The view from the back of the lorries which followed was that of a camp abandoned to the animals, with goats and sheep wandering aimlessly and hundreds of hens scratching and clucking over the barren soil.

They drove in silence, passing columns of refugees with their carts and bundles, all heading in the opposite direction. It told its own story as the three vehicles headed east along the Alpine road. On reaching the Judenburg bridge and British checkpoint they were waved through – however once again the staff car was stopped by the Russians and asked for their papers. This time recognising the British Army notepaper, the soldiers walked back to check the lorries. The ritual accomplished, the pole was raised and the vehicles passed through, only to be halted again by a senior officer who greeted them with indifference and demanded in German the final documents of transfer and repatriation.

Anna translated to the army lieutenant sitting with the driver what was required and the officer handed them the appropriate documentation. Duplicates were signed and countersigned. Finally the deed was done, with thirty-five thousand souls handed back by road and rail. The lorries were once again instructed to drive towards the railway wagons and again the tables were bare. Sultan Girej's guards, their families and scanty belongings were rapidly offloaded, the lorries checked and sent back to join up with the staff car. As for himself, Girej was stripped of his sabre and pistol then marched unceremoniously by two flanking guards towards a log cabin.

As the convoy turned and headed back towards the checkpoints one of the Soviet officers, a major, stepped out in front of the car and held up his hand. The driver hit the brakes and cursed under his breath as the officer approached, pointing a podgy finger at Anna seated at the back. The CSM wound down the window and met the Russian's glaring gaze. '*Deutsch, Fascisti! Raus, Raus!*' the major shouted.

Immediately a cluster of Red Army soldiers surrounded the car as the officer pulled open the rear door and indicated for Anna to get out. Tense seconds passed, nobody moved until the lieutenant, taking the initiative, casually got out from his seat and slammed Anna's door shut. As nobody spoke English, he remonstrated with the Russian major by using the old colonial ploy that if the natives don't understand, shout louder.

After several attempts at trying to explain Anna was with him and a British army interpreter he gave up, gesticulated with a wave for the major and his men to get out of the way, before getting back into the car.

'Step on it, corporal'! he ordered the driver and indicated with his hand for all to see. As the car leapt forward the soldiers scattered, but those ahead at the checkpoint stood their ground and fired. With reflex action the corporal hit the brakes, discretion being the better part of valour when faced with battle-hardened men firing submachine guns.

With wheels locked and a cloud of dust, the Hillman skidded to a halt on the hard baked track. Luckily for its occupants, the guards had fired over the car as a soldier with a gun in hand pulled open the rear door. Once again the Russian major shouted for Anna to get out. At the same time, Big Jock opened his door from the other side and with guns pointing at him walked behind the car and confronted the Russian officer. He straightened up to a full head and shoulders over the Russian and pointed and tapped at his British Army insignia and regimental badge.

'Nietsky Raus, comrade, British army, yer ken?' And spoke in slow and deliberate tones, pointing at the occupants inside the car. 'Angliskij. Angliskij, all of us.'

'*Niet Angliskij! Nemetsky – Fascisti!*' shouted the enraged officer and elbowed him away as he indicated to one of his men to get Anna out. Guns were levelled at Big Jock's midriff as the scene became uglier by the minute. With a pistol now pointing at her head, a soldier reached inside the car and grabbing her arm pulled Anna screaming from the safety of the vehicle.

'Shall we open fire sir?' asked the lance corporal sitting in the back, quietly addressing the lieutenant, at the same time releasing the safety catch on his Lanchester.

'No corporal, hold your fire,' ordered the officer and sat watching powerless as Anna was dragged away by two soldiers.

'Please, Jock, don't let them do this to me!' she pleaded as the big man stood there helpless and incandescent with rage as the soldiers continued to nudge him at gun point. With Anna now being taken across the clearing to their guardroom, the major indicated for the CSM to get back into the car. Jock stood there dumbfounded, not believing what was happening before his very eyes as the soldiers pointed and indicated direction with their guns.

'*Davai! Davai!*' they shouted and pointed towards the bridge.

'Better get back inside, Sergeant Major,' said the lieutenant. 'We'll sort this out back at HQ.'

'Yes, sir,' replied Jock, realising how completely powerless they were when faced with such odds. He turned, checked himself and called out after her. 'I'll be back for you, Anna. We'll get it sorted, lass,' but his words were lost on the wind as it soughed through the pines and the guardroom door slammed firmly shut behind her.

As the sound of the departing car and transports faded Anna was beckoned to sit in front of a table as two NKVD officers of Stalin's secret police examined a file in front of them. By now her mind was again in turmoil as in such a short space of time her life had once again changed from one of reasonable stability to that of anxiety and trauma. Trauma as she thought about Eddi, he would be on his own with strangers, so to speak. Then there were the stories she had heard about the Russians which only added to her fears about her own safety and that of never seeing her son again. The fear for her son blotted her mind to everything that was happening around her as she held a handkerchief to her face to hide her desperation, self-pity and stifle a flood of anxious tears.

It was only after a while that she noticed the old Sultan. He sat quietly in an adjoining room smoking and just staring at the wall in front of him. The cabin door opened as two soldiers entered and left with the old man, who nodded at Anna in passing with glazed, unseeing eyes. The policemen lit cigarettes and talked among themselves as Anna was reminded about another time and another place, where the same type of people had used similar tactics. Then, the uniforms were black, but now they were an olive green. Same dog, different fleas, she mused, and knew through experience what lay ahead.

The silence was suddenly shattered by women's screams from somewhere in the distance followed by the sound of a single shot. The NKVD men eyed each other with mutual satisfaction but said nothing. Picking up the documents they began with the self-same patter that was typical of such sycophants of the state.

'You are Anna Bauer?' said one and speaking fluent German but wielding a heavy Krakow accent. Anna sat stone-faced and refused to answer. She'd heard it all before and knew they already had her details. It was just a game. It was their way of intimidating her and besides, she had been wrongfully arrested − if that was the correct term for her unlawful apprehension.

'Frau Bauer, we are holding you as we have information that you were wanted by the Gestapo for questioning as a British agent. Also, we have information that your husband is a submarine captain and is involved with building a special bomb. Perhaps you can you tell us something more about all this?'

Anna's mind reeled in horror. What's all this? Gott im Himmel, they've somehow got hold of Gestapo records. They must know all about me and Gruber and what do they know about Franz? She stared at the two men as she tried to envisage her husband building bombs. What on earth was going on? Heavy footfalls beyond the door paused the interrogation and the door swung open to reveal the major. The two NKVD men shook their heads in a negative way and vacated the room as Anna tried to follow what was going on. In broken German the major introduced himself.

'Guten Tag, I'm Major Yuri Konstantin,' he said and held out a podgy hand. 'And you are Anna Bauer, I am given to understand, ja?' Anna side-glanced him and still nursing her eyes with her handkerchief, stared woodenly at the bare table. 'I see you are upset,' he continued. 'Those policemen are unkultura, as we say. They have no manners.' Pulling up a chair he sat down opposite her and continued. 'Frau Bauer, I would like you to work for us, just like you did for the British. We need people like you as interpreters as we have to work with our allies, ja? And of course you are free with us too,' he added as an afterthought.

'If I am free then let me go,' snapped Anna angrily. 'I have a young boy who needs me.' A wan smile crossed his face and he nodded solemnly.

'You may go, but not back to the British. I will see about the boy. Tomorrow we will go to Vienna as the war is over here, now that we have them all back.' He indicated with a jerk of his thumb in the direction of the pine trees and the railway terminal.

'Wien?' cried Anna. 'Nein, Herr Major, I'm not going to Vienna. I'm a German civilian and you have no reason to hold me. Kindly let me go.'

'German yes, but the wife of a U-Boot captain who went on a special mission I am given to understand and associated herself with the British army.' Anna froze; how on earth did he know that? I've only been here for an hour and they know everything about me. 'Herr Major, I cannot answer any of your questions. I just want to go back to my son. Please let me go.'

'You can call me Yuri,' said the major, 'and I will call you Anna if you like as we will be working together, ja? Gut?'

'*Nein!*' Anna shouted and thumped the table with a fist '*It is Nicht gut!* The British will come for me and I shall wait here until they do. They said so, that is your ja, gut!' Yuri smiled at her naiveté and shook his head in mock desperation, as obviously this woman had no understanding of what was happening around her, and that included the British.

'Well suit yourself,' he replied. 'We will wait for them and if they don't come tomorrow you will follow us to Vienna.' A knock on the door interrupted their conversation as a soldier entered bearing a silver tray with coffee and poppy seed strudel. 'Good man, Ivanovitch,' said Yuri. 'Now Anna, be our guest.'

The young lad grinned at her. His high cheekbones and almond eyes cheerfully depicting his ancestry. Anna was quite taken by his youthful and tanned features as it was the first time she had been greeted by such a person. What amazed her even more was the lad, who seemed not a day over seventeen, had several watches strapped on his arm. They drank their coffee in silence as Yuri glanced over the documents left by the NKVD then buried his face in a dog-eared copy of *Pravda*.

As agonising minutes ticked by, Anna toyed with her cake. Yuri sat smoking and gazing out of the window, occasionally humming a tune. It annoyed her as it was 'Das Volga Lied', the same song that her countrymen had sung as they sat on the banks of that river, secure in the belief that Stalingrad would fall. As the minutes turned into hours, only the cuckoo clock with its mellow chimes and the bird's responsive calls broke the smouldering silence.

As time went by the shadows began to lengthen and still no sign of the British. With the onset of night came the crunch of wheels on gravel as a jeep sped to a halt. Having given her the benefit of the doubt and time to weigh up and come to terms with her situation, Yuri broke the silence and explained that the vehicle would take them to a nearby house.

Anna shook her head in disbelief and resignation and turned her thoughts to Eddi. He would be frightened at not being with her, even though he had made friends with many of the British children and their parents. To him they were strangers, especially as none of the children understood his language

'Please follow me,' said Yuri. 'This is my jeep. Don't worry, everything will be good, you will see.'

Anna had no option but to follow and climb into the jeep and join the two guards riding shotgun. They were quite cheery towards her, which was at odds with what she had been led to believe, besides having no choice – she needed desperately to freshen up as Mother Nature was calling.

As darkness fell they set off along the rutted track, which then crossed a single railway line. As the jeep slowed, Anna met a sight that would remain with her for the rest of her days. In a reflex reaction she hand-shielded her mouth, as there in the glare of the headlights, stood several wagons and beside them a mound of corpses. She recognised the uniforms as German, the bodies being none other than the Cossacks which only hours before she had assisted in transporting to this place. To one side lay the body of an Ataman, along with his family, both young and old.

The horror and its implications nauseated her as she feared for her own safety being held captive by these butchers and a witness to their crime. So it was true after all, she told herself, all those rumours in the camp and the reason for the suicides and the shots they'd heard the other day. Here in the glare of the headlights lay the bodies and the evidence.

Anna, still in shock at what she had seen was soon brought back to her own situation as the jeep turned onto a metalled road, gathered speed and passed a convoy of Red Army lorries and tanks holed up for the night.

Minutes later they turned into a farmyard with soldiers standing idly around a tank and several other vehicles. On seeing the major, they straightened up and now had something worthwhile to talk about as they watched Anna alight from the jeep. Their loud frivolous comments and low whistles were soon nipped in the bud as one of her escorts leapt out and put them in the picture.

Major Yuri led the way for Anna to follow across the yard and into the house. Anna noticed at a glance that the place was bereft of its owners as Red Army soldiers were everywhere. Once inside Yuri placed his cap on the kitchen table and turning to Anna greeted her with a broad grin and an open-handed gesture of welcome.

'Make yourself at home, Anna,' he said cordially. 'This is your house for the night. I will get you some coffee, ja?'

'Major Yuri,' said Anna raising her voice. 'I thank you for your kindness and hospitality but I must protest that I have been wrongfully detained and request that you take me back to the British zone in order that I might be with my son.' She met his amused gaze, which irritated her as she reasoned he was playing games with her.

'Ja, Anna – I may call you that, ja?' he said scratching the back of his head. 'I was just coming to that.' He nodded to an orderly who opened a door behind her.

Anna turned and was surprised to see a pleasant-faced woman in a dark blue uniform who, with twinkling eyes met Anna's startled gaze.

'Hello Anna,' said the middle-aged woman standing in the doorway and beckoning to another woman of similar age and style behind her. Together they entered the dimly lit kitchen. Anna's eyes opened wide in disbelief at the jaw-dropping sight, as there behind the first and in front of the second woman, stood Eddi. A dam of grateful tears burst in an instant as she rushed towards him and fell to her knees to embrace him. Her joy was complete as she forgot all else as she hugged and kissed her little boy.

'Mama, Mama, look,' he said, trying to coyly brush off the attention and to show her his wooden toy train, not quite understanding what all the fuss was about.

'Ja, Eddi, it's very nice,' said Anna brushing the hair from his eyes as he waved his toy with its little red star on the front. Yuri kept well clear and observed the happy family reunion; however, deep inside it left him cold.

She glanced up to thank the two women. It was then that she noticed, through a veil of happy tears the emblem of the British Red Cross.

'Danke, danke… oh sorry, thank you, I mean. How can I ever thank you?'

'Mrs Bauer, my name is Kate Chesterton,' said the first woman. 'And this is my colleague, Mary Robins.' Anna nodded at her two Samaritans with their blue-rinse coiffures and held out her hand in greeting. 'We were requested by the Russians to help – on humanitarian grounds. We brought you your things as well, my dear, which the regiment packed at short notice. The British and Russian Consulates in Vienna have been made aware of the situation and are trying to sort it out. To get you back, that is. But please be aware, these are difficult times and they have to follow the proper procedures through diplomatic channels.'

'Procedures!' Anna snapped, as she stood to remonstrate with them and angrily dabbing her eyes. 'These people,' she continued but lowering her voice, 'they didn't follow procedures. They don't know the meaning of the word. Tell him to let me go immediately as he has no right to hold me. The war is over and I just would like to go home; please tell him.' They nodded more in sympathy than anything else, as Anna likened them to caring mothers rather than being part of a pseudo military styled welfare group.

'Yes, Anna, we understand,' continued Kate in a soothing tone. 'But these are difficult times and we are not a political movement and have no authority over such matters. Here, in this place you are a long way from any diplomacy. Rest assured my dear, the Red Cross will do everything in its power to get you back to your home as the regiment is up in arms about the whole incident. I am allowed to inform you of that. Please try to be patient and we'll get you out. Meanwhile we have a Red Cross parcel for you, to help you along. Don't worry Mrs Bauer, we'll get this misunderstanding sorted, after all, they are our allies.'

Anna nodded but with differing thoughts as Mary came forward with a small cardboard box depicting a Red Cross logo and lettering.

CANADIAN RED CROSS.
PRISONER OF WAR. FOOD PARCEL.
FOR DISTRIBUTION THROUGH
INTERNATIONAL RED CROSS COMMITTEE

'Thank you so much,' said Anna gratefully as Yuri, standing by the sink eyed the box suspiciously. 'I'm sorry I spoke to you like that, please forgive me. It's just that I'm not thinking straight. This war has had a devastating effect on me and I have not found my husband. Please, you must help me...' she pleaded before bursting into uncontrollable sobs. Mary came to her aid and placed a comforting arm on shaking shoulders.

'Don't upset yourself Anna, you have your little boy back and we will help you. It just takes time.' Anna, with the aid of her handkerchief composed herself as the two women checked their shoulder bags and made to leave.

'We have to go now Anna,' said Kate. 'Our train will be here shortly, but I'm sure the major here will look after you and keep you safe. You know what we mean?' Their eyes met in mutual understanding of the unspoken word as they cordially shook hands.

'I shall be relying on you to state my plight with the powers that be, yes?' said Anna.

'Yes Anna, rest assured. Just do as they ask and no harm will come to you. Seems they just would like to throw a little weight around, that's all. So, goodbye for now.'

'Dasvidaniya,' said Yuri shaking their hand and courteously showed them to their car as a Russian jeep escort stood waiting. Yuri gave instructions to the driver and the two guards to ensure their safety.

As he came back into the house he sensed Anna's discontent – after all, he himself would have felt the same under the circumstances but then that's not how it was. Had he not just won the war and obtained prized *kultura* female company?

'Please follow me, Anna,' he said politely. 'I will show you to your room, da.'

Without waiting for a reply he took her leather case, letting her carry the Red Cross parcel and led the way up the stairs. Opening a door off the landing he went into a spacious bedroom with a double bed and washstand in one corner.

'A nice room for you Anna. I hope you'll be comfortable here.' He placed her case by the bed and made for the door. Turning, and with a Cheshire cat grin said '*Nochi*,' and closed the door.

***

Suddenly, after a long weary day, Anna was alone. Mentally and physically exhausted she methodically gave Eddi a quick wash and wipe. The water from the jug was cold, but it had to do. A glazed white pot stood under the bed which served for both their needs and undressing her son, got him into bed.

Anna went out onto the landing, but found only a tap with an ancient half-moon, enamelled bowl. She tried the tap – the water ran cold and alpine clear. Filling the pitcher she returned to her room and carried out her ablutions. Towelling herself down she was ready to sleep for a week but not before utilising the comfort station under the bed.

A knock on her door roused her – gentle at first, then louder. She checked her watch, seven-thirty and the light of day was beyond the curtains. Anna slipped from the bed and still in her nightdress, cautiously answered the door.

'Ja, bitte?' called out Anna. A faint female voice replied in the local dialect. Anna unlocked the door and peered onto the landing. Her senses reeled; there stood a young girl in a dirndl costume with a tearstained face and precariously holding a wooden tray.

'Please, come in,' said Anna and locked the door behind her. 'It looks like breakfast, ja?' she said uneasily as the girl placed the tray onto a small table by the window. She was about to leave when Anna called her back.

'Please, you can join me. My little boy is still asleep.'

'Danke,' she replied and stood staring aimlessly out of the window. She's just a child, perhaps fourteen, mused Anna. Better see what all the tears are about.

'My name's Anna,' she began, 'and that's Eddi my son.' The girl nodded with a wan smile that died on her lips. 'Here, come and sit with me,' said Anna and patted the bed. 'Bring the tray and we can have breakfast together, ja?' The girl joined her as Anna took the tray and handed her a slice of cake.

'My name's Gretel and this is my parents' room,' she said in a barely audible whisper. Anna glanced at her features, a little on the chubby side for her age, but this was a farming community and most folks around here had a sound disposition.

'I'm sorry about the room Gretel, but they gave it to me last night.'

'I know.' She replied with a blank stare at the floor.

'So, where are your parents?' Anna probed, trying to sound as casual as she could. 'Are they somewhere else in the house? Are they alright?'

'Yes,' came her whispered reply and burst into tears. Her long chestnut hair hid her face as she leant forward, her shoulders shaking with every sob. Anna placed a protective arm on her shoulder and soothingly asked her what had upset her.

'They came here three days ago, the Russki; they just drove into the farmyard and stormed into the house. They took my mother and me and, and...' Gretel stopped as she let out a stifled scream, her whole body shaking. With great sobs she re-lived the memory as Anna hugged her close and could only imagine what had taken place.

'It's all right, Gretel,' she whispered. 'You can tell me. Let it all out and tell me, it will make you feel better. Just take your time. Here, take this.'

'Danke,' sobbed the girl as she took the proffered handkerchief and placed her mug of cocoa on the floor. 'They rushed in and took us both downstairs into the kitchen. Mutti tried to protect me with a knife but they hit her with a rifle butt then did terrible things to us both...' Her body shook as she began to sob once more and turning to Anna flung her arms round her. 'Please Frau Anna, help me. I'm still bleeding and I haven't seen my Mutti since.'

Appalled at the revelation she let Gretel cry on her shoulder as the poor girl had no one else to turn to. It will do her good, Anna mused and thinking what was to be done here. However, she realised she could hardly help herself, as they were at the mercy of the Red Army. She wondered where her father was, where is he in all this? She would ask once the girl had composed herself.

'Gretel come over here with me and we'll have a look at you.' Anna took her by the hand and led her to the washstand. She still had water in the basin and used that to wash the girl's hands and face. It soothed her face and made her feel better as Anna gently held the cold flannel to Gretel's eyes. 'Now that feels better, so let's have another look, ja?'

Gretel answered with a submissive nod as Anna lifted the dirndl dress to find a dishcloth soaked in blood inside her once white underwear. Gently Anna eased her panties down and with Gretel assisting with her dress Anna began to wipe and dab the affected area. Once clean she was relieved to see there was no further internal bleeding but noticed several deep scratches to her inner thighs and waist.

Placing the bowl to the floor, Anna left Gretel to wash herself as she searched several cabinets and found what she was looking for. Cautiously diluting the iodine she applied it around the girl's lower region and using her mother's panties and towel got Gretel dressed.

'That feels better, Gretel, ja? Now, you can join Eddi and get yourself some rest.' The girl nodded and painfully made her way across to the bed.

Anna stood by the window and gazed out at the Alpine scenery of pine forests and towering mountains while below her and in stark contrast stood a T34 tank and several Red Army vehicles. Anna gathered her thoughts as she watched two eagles soaring high over the valley.

They're so free and here I am a prisoner once again, she mused. Why did the Russians kidnap me? They could have taken me before as I had been there several times. Was it because all the Cossacks had been handed over and I'm a German? Are the British really as innocent as they make out to be? Ja, just look what happened to the Cossacks and the Yugoslavs in Klagenfurt – weren't they handed over by the British too? They washed their hands of everything but by the same token they treated me well, really looked after me. This Russki, Yuri, he's also looking after me. Why is everyone always trying to look after me? And Franz, what's happened to him? This damned war is over and he might be in Aachen now, or is he in Japan, still fighting? How on earth do all these people know about him and this special bomb?

Then there's this house the whole area. Why did the Americans and the British let the Russkies have all this territory? The eagles had gone and left Anna with her thoughts gazing at the serenity of the pines and snow-capped mountains beyond.

She snapped out of her melancholy as movement down in the yard disturbed her thoughts. Several soldiers with tanned complexions and almond eyes were busy checking their vehicles. They had similar features as many of the Cossacks she had seen at the camp, it was puzzling? Mulling over this latest conundrum, a loud knock on the door startled her. She crossed the room and cautiously opened it. Yuri in dress uniform presented himself.

'Guten Morgen, Frau Bauer, I trust you slept well?' Anna did not reply as he gazed and admired her figure. She avoided eye contact and stepping back let him into the room while quickly putting on her dressing gown. Removing his cap he took a cursory glance at the bed with its two occupants. However he said nothing but moved to stand by the window, hands and cap behind his back.

'You can come down for breakfast. You are safe here with us,' he said, turning to face her.

'Ha! Safe!' snapped Anna, clutching her dressing gown tightly about her. 'What about her?' she said crossly and pointed at the bed. 'You tell *her* that.' Yuri nodded without expression.

'Unfortunately, she's a victim of circumstances,' and with an irritable and dismissive shrug added, 'aren't we all?'

'She's just a child,' Anna replied angrily. 'What about her mother and…' Yuri held up his hand.

'Anna please, I can tell you horrendous stories about what happened in Russia to my wife and children. Suffice to say, I watched them die. Never try to moralise with me, and please, let's not fight, the war is over; just keep the peace, ja?' Stung by his remarks and revelation she was suddenly lost for words as she sat down on the bed and Eddi, awake now, began to rub his eyes.

'Am I to be paid as an interpreter or will the police arrest me once more?' Yuri never bargained for that as a shadow of unease passed over his features. Anna detected the surprise and annoyance in his expression as he avoided her questioning gaze.

'That's not for me to say,' he replied, 'but of course the Red Army will take care of everything. Have no fear Anna; we will treat you well and better than the British.' With a satisfied smirk at his diplomacy he lit up a cigarette and offered it to her. She shook her head but his evasive answer and uneasy demeanour needed no explanations, the man could not be trusted.

'I have told the police you will be my interpreter and they have accepted that, especially as we will be in our own zone in Vienna.'

'Vienna, I don't want to go to Vienna…' She paused as another thought crossed her mind. 'Ja, Herr Major, what about my husband?' She waited for his reaction but Yuri's face remained a mask. 'He will be released and not know where I am. Who will tell him?'

He mulled it over and casually stubbed out his cigarette on the window sill. 'Anna,' he said benignly. 'I'm a soldier and I speak as a soldier. I don't wish to alarm you but what makes you so sure he survived the war? Our records show that most of the U-Bootmen never returned. Their sacrifice was enormous for such a small group. You must have heard about the statistics. We all have, ja?'

'The British and Americans have very good records,' replied Anna. 'They have no record of him being a casualty.'

'We destroyed U-boats too, you know… Perhaps we did not inform them. He might be a prisoner of war in one of our camps? What was the number of his boat?'

Gott im Himmel! It had never crossed her mind and made sense now that he had mentioned it. It was always the British and the Americans that did the damage at sea and in the air, while the Russkies would take the land. How stupid of me not to think of it any other way. Or was it Goebels that had put it into their minds, conditioned us to believe the Russians were a sub-species of humanity, to be despised, conquered and suppressed? But then the British never mentioned it either?

'I don't know. He never mentioned it,' she replied, quite taken aback by his revelations. 'However, you said that he had gone on a special mission – or was that from your police?'

'Makes no difference,' he said, with a sweeping hand gesture. 'I will try to find out for you. I will make enquiries once we get to Vienna. They'll have all the answers there.' It was now her turn to be caught off guard. Here was her abductor, willing to help her find her husband when, only a short while ago, he had threatened to send her to Siberia. Now he was extending an olive branch. Anna felt foolish and cast an apologetic smile in his direction.

'Thank you, Herr Major, I'm sorry I have no information about his boat.'

'We do have some information,' continued Yuri, 'but it is not up to date. The police which held you know he was in France on a scientific project. I can tell you in secret Anna, just between you and me, that he was working with scientists in Berlin. We captured some of them and their documents.' Confused, she glanced in his direction and re-assessed his integrity as he was now telling her official secrets. Once again, it contradicted her feelings about the man. Yuri saw her consternation and knew he was beginning to gain her confidence.

'Now, changing the subject Anna, I will get a doctor for the girl.'

Was she hearing this right? First he was offering to help her solve the riddle of Franz, and now he was going out of his way to help the girl. What's he playing at? Yuri stood watching her as he lit another cigarette, pleased with himself at seeing her confusion.

Eddi needed the toilet; Anna obliged making a mental note that it will have to be emptied later. Yuri stood gazing out of the window smoking his foul-smelling tobacco and watched as his men rotated the turret to service their battle-scarred tank.

'Strange people,' he said, breaking the silence and indicating with his cigarette. 'Youngsters, hardly eighteen and a long way from Mongolia.'

Anna said nothing; as these were probably the culprits that had raped Gretel and her mother. But their being Mongolians solved the puzzle of the eyes. It was all very confusing as she fussed with the bed. Lieber Herrgott, I just want to go home was all she could think of as a knock on the door startled them both.

'*Vajdi-ti*!' he called and stubbed his cigarette. The door swung open and a soldier appeared carrying a small cardboard suitcase. He spoke with Yuri in a language that Anna did not recognise and obediently put the case down by her feet. He glanced at her and smiled with soft, almond eyes. His face was a tanned, smiling mask with high cheekbones and a ruddy complexion that spoke of a harsh existence, in open and windswept places.

On seeing the girl the smile faded as he hurriedly made for the door. Anna recognised the case as the one the British had given to Eddi. It was for toys they had given him. How thoughtful of them she mused, but realised with alarm they would not go to all this trouble if they were really intent on rescuing her. Her spirits sank as realisation dawned that she was here to stay.

***

'So now you have all of your belongings, soon we will leave for Vienna,' said Yuri. 'Better check the case to see if everything is there.'

Anna nodded with a sigh of resignation as she placed the case on the bed, while Eddi gazed, wide-eyed in anticipation at seeing his toys once more. On top she found a few of his clothes together with a jumble of toys and several books depicting Humpty Dumpty, Three Little Pigs and other nursery rhymes. Trust the British, mused Anna with a smile. They seem to like children.

Tucked into one side was an envelope. It had been opened and clumsily sealed. Anna extracted the letter as Yuri looked-on in wry amusement as he already knew its content and to Anna's annoyance, lit up another Soviet stinker. He offered one to her from a silver case, marked with a swastika but Anna shook her head as she concentrated on the letter with the friendly red emblem of the British Red Cross.

BRITISH RED CROSS

Dear Frau Bauer,   Lienz

                                                    24.07.45

We are pleased to be able to forward the remainder of your belongings and those of your son, Eddi. We would also like to inform you that your circumstances have been made known to the

Russian and British consulates in Vienna. Unfortunately, as you are not a British citizen, there is only a limited amount that the British consulate can do in order to alleviate your current circumstances.

Further, with regard to your husband, Franz Bauer, we can only inform you at this time that he sailed from Lorient, France on a special mission to the East. We are pleased to inform you at this time that his name does not appear on any British or American casualty returns.

Yours sincerely,

K. Chesterton

Kate Chesterton (British Red Cross)

'Good news, I trust,' said Yuri as she read the letter several times over, as any news about Franz was what kept her sane and motivated. She met his wily gaze and guessed that he and his cronies had already seen the letter and knew its content.

'Ja, from my friends, the British,' she answered in a dismissive tone. She was annoyed at him and all things Russian now that the British could do nothing for her. 'Please, Herr Major, if you don't mind, I would like to get dressed and sort out my things.'

'Da, da, but of course, Anna,' he said apologetically, 'and please, Frau Anna, call me Yuri when we are together like this, in private, ja?' Anna ignored the request as he made for the door. 'Don't unpack too much, as we will be leaving soon,' he said with a retrospective grin.

Anna, sitting on the bed nodded and wished for him to disappear. She just wanted to be left on her own and to think about her future and what she could do about it, if anything. As the door closed, she read the letter once more and thought about her missing husband. If the British say he went to the East then the Russkies were not involved, that must be right she reasoned and the major can take a running jump.

Yuri descended the stairs, pleased with himself and how his future would change with Anna as an interpreter, and perhaps even more? He looked upon their meeting and conversation like horse-breaking – using a whip in one hand and an apple in the other. Now he had exactly what he needed to gain recognition and to raise himself in the ranks, to join the Soviet elite, the power makers and those that got to keep the spoils of war. He had made friends with comrade Khrushchev on the battlefield and, as farming stock, they ploughed the same furrow.

Dressed in a black British siren suit, she went down for breakfast where Yuri was already helping himself to buttered rolls, marmalade and coffee – luxury items for the majority of Austrians who were still plagued with their roasted acorn and burnt barley extracts. Yuri played host by filling both their cups and lit up with another obnoxious Russian Woodbine.

'Perhaps you could type up a translation for me once you have finished, Anna? It's only a one-page transcript.' He handed her a document as she nodded, more in resignation than agreement, as the choice was translate or a freezing Gulag in Siberia.

'It's a document stating the British have now handed over all of the Osttruppen of Colonel von Pannwitz's Sotni troops,' explained Yuri. Anna, confused glanced over the top of the paper.

'Sotni? What on earth is a Sotni?'

'Bah!' exclaimed Yuri, banging the table with a fist. 'They're just groups of bandits on horseback and in fascisti uniform. You had them in your camp. We have them back now as traitors. Carry on, what else do they say?'

Anna began translating the document out loud. 'It says the Soviet government is now responsible for them, as agreed at Yalta, between the three powers. Goes on to say that General von Pannwitz is not a Nazi and is not wanted for war crimes. He's a German officer and should be treated as such, that's all.'

'Ha, German, indeed,' said Yuri angrily. 'In my book he's Polish and him and his Cossack misfits have caused me to lose several thousand men. We shall certainly treat him and his friends accordingly.' He leant across the table, took the paper and glanced at the familiar names with a satisfied grunt before handing it back. 'When you have typed it up, hand the translation to Vladimir in there.' He pointed to a closed door. 'He's our radio man and will send it on to Vienna and Moscow in German, as not many understand English. I think I shall be the first to inform them about that Ataman von Pannwitz. We have him locked up, together with his top henchmen down at the old steel works. Thank you, Anna, for that.' She threw him a wan smile but her mind was racing, trying to think of a way of escaping from the clutches of this vain, glorious man and his Soviet colleagues.

'Jawohl, Herr Major,' she replied. 'I will type it up later, as first I have to see to my son and the girl.'

'But of course,' he said and waved a dismissive hand. 'If you need anything, please let me know!'

Back in the room, Eddi was sitting on the floor close to the bed, where Gretel was still asleep. 'Who is the lady in our bed?' he asked as Anna handed him a banana. She showed him how to peel the fruit, as they were not available before now, and it was the first one that he had ever seen, courtesy of the Red Army.

'That's a girl and she's not very well, my dear, she needs her rest so try not to make any noise.' Eddi nodded as he carried on munching and asked whether he was going to kindergarten.

'Nein, not today, as we are going on a long journey,' replied Anna. 'You will see the Riesenrad in Wien – that's a big Ferris wheel, and we will go to the top. Then we'll see the nice Blue Danube, you'll like that.' He nodded, as if he already knew all about it.

'I need the toilet, Mutti,' he said. So do I, mused Anna. Draping a towel over their china comfort ware, they went down the stairs and outside to the small wooden construction that stood away from the house.

To her chagrin the soldiers stopped their banter as all eyes turned in her direction. They conversed in low tones and with intermittent guffaws, chuckles and laughter followed Anna with their gaze as she self-consciously made it to the door and the sanctuary beyond. It was a simple affair and challenging for small children as, with a board across and a cement pit below she held on to Eddi until he had finished. The paper was Russian newsprint and she caught up on the news of the fall of Berlin with a Soviet soldier planting his flag on top of the Reichstag building.

With nature relieved and clutching Eddi in one hand and the empty convenience in the other she once again encountered the chastening gauntlet of whistles, suggestive cat-calls and sniggers as they passed.

For the rest of the day her time was spent typing and translating and, true to his word, a doctor arrived who treated Gretel, he being a friend of the family. He said she would recover but the mental scars and trauma would take longer to heal.

He related he'd recently treated her father as a patient as the soldiers had beaten him with rifle butts. He'd tried to protect his family but with only one arm he did not stand a chance. He had been wounded a few months ago fighting in Italy and now this, but again, he was lucky they hadn't shot him. Had they been older troops the doctor was convinced they would have done.

Then there was their 16-year-old son, he continued. He had been wounded trying to stop Russian tanks with a Panzer Faust unit. He and his indoctrinated Hitler Youth group had been rounded up by the Russians close by in an apple orchard; their anti-tank gun had jammed and they were now under guard in the local hospital suffering from concussion and steel splinters after a shell decimated their makeshift bunker. Horrified, Anna cast her mind back to what Heinrich had said and feared.

'Sounds like they need their mothers not Russian guards,' said Anna after the doctor had finished his story. 'Perhaps I can help? I will ask the major and see what he can do.' The doctor cast her an inquisitive glance as nobody around the village had such influence, if any, over the Russians.

'Well it would help to keep the family together,' he replied. 'The mother was also treated by me and is frantic about her children.' He glanced over his shoulder. 'She's hiding down in my cellar,' he whispered. 'They don't bother searching my house as I'm treating some of them.'

'What, they're wounded?' she said with a frown. 'The war's been over for nearly two months.'

The old man evaded the question and indicated a hypodermic action to his buttocks.

'Ach so,' said Anna as realisation dawned. 'Serves them right.'

The doctor casually smiled at her reproof as he stood and picked up his bag from the kitchen table.

'By the way,' he said, 'why are you here, you're from Köln, judging by your accent?' Anna nodded and with a tedious sigh, related her problem.

'Ja, it's a long story but this major here has more or less blackmailed me into working for him, as their police took me for questioning whilst I was working for the British.

'Ach so,' said the doctor, noting her trim figure and nodding wisely with a tug at his white goatee beard. 'Sounds to me like you're his prisoner and it's only the British who know you're here? Be careful Frau Bauer. You realise Vienna, Budapest and Prague are all Soviet territory now. They've got the lot, including this part of Styria.'

'I don't care what they've got, as long as I can go home. Once in Vienna I will go to the British consul as they are responsible for me, being they employed me.

'Well Frau Bauer, I wish you luck. Nice meeting you. Auf Wiedersehen.' Donning his Tyrolean hat he climbed into his pony and trap transport and with a click of his tongue disappeared down the winding lane.

***

In another room, Yuri and his fellow officers were noisily engaged in an afternoon binge. Seeing her by the door he invited her to join them but Anna declined, feigning a headache. Yuri came out into the kitchen and informed her there had been a change of plan – they would now be leaving tomorrow.

At six that evening Anna and Eddi went for their meal as Gretel decided to stay in her room. She said she felt better but still looked the worse from her ordeal. It was as the doctor had said – it would take a long time for the mental scars to heal.

Downstairs the Russians were in a jovial mood and, as Anna entered, quickly made room for her and the boy. Perhaps it was high spirits but Anna was surprised at their hospitality towards her. These people were not quite how they had been portrayed and branded by Hitler, as uncultured and sub-humans. The table was served by a young steward who loaded her plate to capacity with steaming dumplings, roast pork and chopped red cabbage. They certainly know how to eat, mused Anna as she assisted Eddi with his plate, who soon pushed the dreaded cabbage to one side.

Moments later a jeep screeched to a halt in the yard. Doors slammed and a tall broad-shouldered man entered. He was missing an arm and sported two black eyes and a cut cheek. Behind him was a teenage lad with a bandaged shoulder. Yuri beamed at Anna and gestured with his fork. 'You have visitors Anna.' Feeling responsible she pushed her meal aside and went to greet them. 'I have given instructions for one of my officers to leave his room and the farmer can move in there.'

She nodded her thanks as the man bemused by events, glanced from one to the other and tried to gauge what was going on in his house. As for the other officers they hardly gave him a second glance and carried on with their meal. Anna excused herself and took Eddie and the walking wounded back to her room.

Father and daughter were now joyously united as they hugged each other, with tears of relief in each other's eyes. Gretel having perked up explained about Anna, as the farmer could not express enough thanks and gratitude at what she had done for them. Anna related what the doctor had told her and all being well, with the Russians out of the house they could all be a family once more.

Once again, he thanked her profoundly and said she would always be welcome there at any time, day or night.

'Just ask for Werner, Werner Wienner,' he said, 'that's my name and this is my son, Josef.'

'We are lucky to be alive,' said Josef. 'They could have shot us all, like they did in Vienna. Any resistance…' and pointed a finger pistol to his head, 'and bang!

'Trouble was,' continued Werner, 'in Vienna they put up a lot of resistance and the Russkies wanted the place before the Amis got there. Pride and Stalin's greed got a lot of them killed. After that, they took it out on the civilians.'

Standing by the window, she and Werner looked on as below the soldiers had lit a log fire as more transports arrived, bringing soldiers, many of them women.

'Those swine down there,' said Werner, 'I could kill them for what they've done to my family. I ask you, do we deserve to be treated like this?'

Anna declined to comment as he glared venomously from the bedroom window. She could have enlightened him about both sides and their atrocities as quoted in the English newspapers, of Auschwitz, Belsen and Dachau. Let him vent his anger she mused, as eventually enlightenment will follow, and diplomatically kept her own counsel. As twilight descended into night the chink of glasses, singing, clapping and music from an accordion drifted on the still night air.

'Damned heathens,' grunted the farmer in disgust at their antics and angrily joined Gretel on the bed. Anna stood fascinated as she observed the soldiers with arms linked across each other's shoulders and letting off steam – dancing and kicking out in rhythm to the sounds of Kalinka as they moved in a circle round the blazing fire.

'I will be away from here tomorrow,' she said, 'so you will have your bedroom back. If you like, Gretel can stay with me until then.' Father and daughter both nodded their thanks as a bang on the door cut their conversation. With another bang the door swung open and Yuri entered carrying a bottle, several glasses and a smile that would envy a Cheshire cat.

'Zdrastvujte comrades,' he beamed. 'I would like you all to drink with me as no doubt you have seen our little party downstairs.' He made for the window and gazed down at his men below. 'You must make allowances. They are happy not just to have won the war but to have survived. We won but many lost their lives doing it.' Werner moved to confront him but Anna shook her head to warn him off.

'Ja, Herr Major,' Anna cut in. 'That would be nice. We understand.' He handed them a glass and played the congenial host, by way of courtesy and expense of the evicted Nazi Gauleiter and his well-stocked cellar.

'Gesundheit comrades, we are all friends now, da?' Werner and Anna raised their glasses and went through the motions of humouring the man who had obviously had a good day with his colleagues. He downed his wine and helped himself to a refill. 'Your arm,' he said, turning to the farmer, 'where did you lose that, Kursk?' Werner met his inebriated gaze and shook his head.

'Nein Herr Major, Italien,' he said and raised the stump of his upper arm.

'Good tovarich, then you did not fight us – we are friends. Tomorrow…' He paused, trying to steady himself. 'Tomorrow as I am a farmer myself you can have your farm back, Da, tovarich?' There was another staggering pause and refilling his glass he beckoned for Anna to join him at the window. 'They're good men, look at them. You like the dancing?'

Werner left them, quite overcome by it all as he shook his head and sat back down on the bed with his son and daughter. He was glad to hear the Russians were moving out and now thanks to this woman, like the Good Samaritan of old, his son had been released from the threat of a prison camp and deportation.

'Ja, they're good,' said Anna standing beside the tottering major who had his glass in one hand and the empty bottle in the other. She had seen similar dances at the Peggetz camp, only this crowd were leaping over the flames with ever-increasing bravado. The female soldiers however were gathered round a wireless, with some of them doing what seemed to Anna a cross between a polka and a Glen Miller boogie. With the sounds of 'Kalinka' and the 'Song of the Volga Boatmen' in his ears, Yuri swayed towards the door. With a salutary wave and the bottle raised high, he staggered out of the room.

'Danke Anna, for all you've done for me. For us all,' said Werner, his eyes brimming with tears and reflecting his gratitude. 'I don't know your business but this man is obviously trying to impress you. He seems to have a lot of sway and influence. Be careful my dear, and try to get away from him as soon as you can.'

'You don't have to thank me,' she replied. 'I did what had to be done, any mother would do the same, and the major, I think I can handle him.' She stifled a yawn. 'Sorry, I'm feeling a little tired, it's been a long day.' Werner got off the bed and nodded at Josef as they made for the door.

'Sorry about that Anna,' said Werner. 'Get some rest, you too Gretel. I'll see you all in the morning. I must go and attend to my cows and see what's left of the herd. Gute Nacht.'

'Gute Nacht,' chimed Anna and Gretel as father and son left and closed the door behind them.

Anna slept late into the morning. When she awoke, Gretel was already up and standing by the window, gazing down at her erstwhile tormentors. The youngsters stood in small groups, chatting and smoking with the odd burst of humour while others sat cleaning their weapons. Transports were being loaded with military stores cached in the barn as Werner and his son looked on, helpless as their hens and pigs were rounded up.

Anna joined her to greet the day before going down for breakfast and coming back with a tray for them all. They sat by the window, Eddi eagerly watching the soldiers as Anna spoke soothingly to Gretel as they sat gazing at events. With a knock on the door Yuri entered in full uniform, with epaulettes and the high-peaked officer's cap.

'Guten Morgen, ladies. I trust you slept well?' He removed his cap as he joined them and received a curt nod from Anna, who was combing Gretel's hair.

'Ja, Danke,' she replied. 'What time are we leaving?' Yuri peered down into the yard to watch his men loading the lorry that was his and destined for Vienna. With screeching cries and squawks it was now the turn of the hens as several soldiers unceremoniously tied them, to hang by their legs off the back of the tailboard.

'As soon as you can be ready,' he said. 'Let's say one hour.' He checked his watch. 'Say nine-thirty. We should make Vienna by five as the roads are still cratered in places. You and the boy will travel in the second jeep, he will like that.' Anna nodded. She had always wanted to see Vienna but not this way – not with the Red Army as her means of transportation and a Russian major as tour guide.

'Ja Danke, Herr Major, I'll be ready. It will only take me a few minutes to pack.'

'Anna, please,' he said with a sigh. 'You may call me Yuri in situations like this. We have to be friends as we are working together. Of course, in front of my men that would be different but now, I will let you pack and will see you at nine-thirty, da?' Without waiting for a reply, he turned and left.

As soon as he had gone, Gretel flung her arms round Anna. Wiping her tears, Anna explained she had arranged for her to meet her mother and she should try to forget about her brutal attackers as they will soon be gone. Once more she attended to the girl and noted with satisfaction all was well and with the aid of the medication her wounds were healing.

A knock sounded at the door and a soldier entered. With his grey moustache and aquiline nose it distinguished him from his younger comrades. He asked to carry Anna's suitcase and noted the girl and her distress. He met Anna's gaze as he lifted the case and, as an act of contrition for those responsible, sombrely shook his head and made for the door. Amid a flood of tears Gretel said her goodbyes.

'Just watch us from your window, Gretel, we'll wave to you. Once they have all gone, go down to join your father and brother. You will all be together as a family once more and your mother will join you later.' Anna kissed her forehead and with a final conscience-stricken hug, left Gretel to cry despairingly in the empty room.

They climbed into the back of the jeep as the convoy started out of the yard. Werner came across and shook her hand and pointed at his hens hanging in distress from the lorry in front. Anna shrugged her indifference as this for her was a minor detail amid the trauma of the last few days and pointed up to the window where Gretel was waving farewell.

'Better go to her right away,' she said. 'Try to get her with her mother as soon as you can. Perhaps we'll meet again, Auf Wiedersehen.' With a final wave the jeep set off, turned into the lane and followed the convoy heading for Graz and Wien.

Chapter Thirty-Nine

VIENNA

First impressions count as the city was not what she had expected, even allowing for the many military vehicles on the streets. To her the buildings seemed dull, their structures monotonous except for the fine architecture of the religious and official buildings. Bombs had damaged roads, railway yards and entire housing blocks and the once busy streets were empty, their cobbles lying in churned-up heaps, gouged and cratered by the passage of tanks and tracked vehicles.

Soldiers, dressed in olive tunics, britches and well-dubbined boots stood in groups on street corners with Balalaika machine pistols slung at ease and at a rake across their shoulders, and Red Army tanks and transports stood strategically positioned at crossings and bridges.

Soon the convoy was stopped by an American and later by a British checkpoint as they passed through the zone-divided city. This rankled with the Soviets as they had to yield this same territory which only weeks before had so tenaciously fought over and died for. Seeing the British uniforms and their cheerful faces Anna felt like crying out to them for help and assistance but the thought perished, stillborn, as the checkpoints were a mere formality and were waved through without let or hindrance. In retrospect, it was only the plight of the hens which caused comments of derision and cruelty accompanied by chuckles as by now the birds looked a sorry sight, trying to right their necks and being devoid of their plumage.

They passed the bomb-damaged Westbahnhof with its locomotives and carriages, burnt and rusting where they stood, along with tangled and twisted lines that now led to nowhere. Avoiding craters, they picked their way towards the city centre, heading down towards the Danube and the heart of the Russian zone. Anna recognised some transports as British, and soldiers standing in groups, casually smoking, with their familiar Lee Enfields slung idly from their shoulders. If this is Vienna, she mused, then there's not much to sing about.

340

Being close to the river the damage was severe as the main target had been the old, steel-structured Reichsbrücke that crossed the Danube linking the rural east of the city. It stood, miraculously undamaged and now renamed as Red Army Bridge. Here the streets had hardly been cleared as olive green T34s stood in a line along the river and further along, tanks stood at crossroads as the Red Army waited and the Western allies procrastinated with Stalin and his demands.

Civilians were noted by their absence. If anyone, it was middle-aged men that dared venture out into the streets, carrying leather bags filled with items of barter.

The convoy came to rest at a hotel not far from the bridge and near to the giant Ferris wheel of the Prater amusement park. Over the roof tops Anna caught a glimpse of the spire of St Stephen's Cathedral which, damaged, was also miraculously still standing.

An Imperial hotel bellhop took her bags as the lift was out of order. Anna and Eddi followed him up several flights of exceptionally wide stairs. With his little legs and negotiating the high steps, Eddi was soon tired and out of breath. Anna waited while he caught up as he laboured and panted his way to the fifth floor.

The bellboy showed her into a spacious suite as more bags and suitcases arrived behind them. Alone once more, Anna gazed at her surroundings; to see the trappings and splendour of a bygone age. She went to inspect the two bedrooms with their large mirrors in heavy ornate frames and the study with a mahogany and marble-topped credenza and accompanying bureau to match. A grandmother clock in its walnut case chimed melodiously, as a clock from beyond the rooftops was faintly heard to strike the hour of six. The Maria Therese chandeliers were of gilded metal, twenty-five electric candles radiated a soft brilliance to be diffused and scattered in miniature rainbows through an abundance of pear-shaped droplets of Austrian crystal.

Impressed by the ostentatious opulence and imperial surroundings, Anna sensed with trepidation that Yuri, by the signs of the items of luggage would be staying in the same suite. That might not bode well for the future, she mused as she settled with Eddi into the larger bedroom supporting two single beds.

Tired as she was, Anna allowed herself a look from the secondary-glazed windows to gaze across the shattered rooftops of the old city. Her mind drifted to her plight as she viewed the pigeons vying for space on the rooftops. Her thoughts turned to Franz, was he really in Japan, or a POW somewhere with the Allies?

Then this Yuri major, how long might he keep her here? Surely there must be many Russians that speak both English and German? It was all very puzzling as here she was, a married woman with a son and now sharing a luxury suite with a Russki officer?

As the sun began to hide below the rooftops Anna sat wearily on her bed, resigned for the moment to her fate of being a working guest of the Red Army. A knock at the door brought her back to reality as a room-boy entered, carrying a tray with silverware and monogrammed napkins of the Imperial Hotel.

'Your soup madam, courtesy of the Major,' said the lad in a lilting Viennese accent as he served them slices of crusty brown bread and soup from a silver tureen. 'Sorry we have no butter. It seems to have disappeared,' he added diplomatically. Anna thanked him and was amused by his accent and pictured Mozart and Schubert sitting in rooms like these, speaking with the same soft accent of her own Teutonic language.

After that, it was a much-needed bath for them both. Eddi played with the nailbrush, pretending it was his papa's boat, which prompted him to ask when his papa was coming to see him. He needs his father now that he is growing, mused Anna, especially as he often asked whether the picture on the photograph was really his papa. It cut her to the core as all she could ever say was that he would be coming home soon.

After putting him to bed, she ran more water into the Kaiser-sized bath and relaxed in its luxurious embrace and joined the league of great bath-time visionaries, as she planned ahead for the morrow. Consulate first, explain her plight to them, get a visa to cross into the British sector and home to her house in Aachen. It sounded simple enough and was not too much to ask, she mused, as she towelled herself dry. A full-length mirror reflected her still shapely figure as she examined herself. Apart from slight stretch marks she was pleased she still had the figure men admired. Only her features showed the strain she had suffered during the past year as faint lines creased her brow and the first threads of silver reflected to mock her as she examined the healing wound from Gruber's gun.

By this time night had fallen, and Anna drew the embroidered curtains but not before peering inquisitively into the street below. Soldiers on duty still stood at street corners, whilst others chatted to girls by lamplight before disappearing into the friendly shadows of the gas-lit streets. Looks like business as usual for some, she mused as she turned out the light to settle into the luxury of a feather bed.

It was in the early hours that she was disturbed; perhaps it was the hall clock as it chimed the hour but closing her eyes she felt the pressure on her body and the stale reek of tobacco and wine. Instinctively she tried to scream as a podgy hand clamped her mouth. 'Lyu-bóv-nik, lyu-bóv-nik,' came a voice she recognised as Yuri's rasping brogue. 'Listen… Anna,' he slurred. 'You're mine, mine you understand, gut, da?' Removing his hand he planted slobbering kisses on her mouth as Anna struggled under his weight. Her mind racing, if she cried out who would hear, or even care? And it would waken Eddi in the dark and he might harm the child?

He was strong and used his weight to force himself onto her. Her mind froze as he pulled and ripped her embroidered dress and forced her thighs apart – with several drunken thrusts, Anna felt a stab of pain as he entered her unyielding body. Mercifully it was over quicker than it had begun as Yuri soon lay snoring; his body slumped across her and the bed.

With effort she prised herself free and ran a hot bath to cleanse herself from the evil that had befallen her. With tears of helpless rage, fear, anxiety and revenge she washed his filth from her body and dressing into her siren suit, joined Eddi in his bed. Thankfully he was still fast asleep, oblivious of his mother's ordeal.

Anna lay there in pain and staring at the ceiling repeated the word rape, over and over again. Her thoughts turned to Gretel as only hours before she had assisted and calmed her fears but now it had happened to her. Even as an adult, it still hurt and now, she too was bleeding. Silent tears of pain and self-pity crept past her cheeks to settle and moisten her pillow as thoughts turned to flight, to escape the clutches of this drunken beast and drab, bomb-scarred Vienna. Her thoughts turned to Franz, what would he say and do? Would he still want me after this she mused as the hall clock harmoniously chimed the hour of five?

***

Anna awoke with a start, it was daylight and realised she had been asleep as glancing across the room saw Yuri had gone. However her ordeal came flooding back as it hurt her to move and the whole incident, like a bad dream came flooding back. But dreams fade from the memory once night becomes day but the memory remained and stepping to the bathroom, it hurt even more.

With a laden heart she reasoned she was now his prisoner as apart from leaping out of the window, she could do nothing. Who would care? A death like that would be tragic but among the millions who had already died, it would be but a statistic and she had her child to think of.

By late morning, Anna was hungry, even though she had no appetite and Eddi needed his breakfast. Again it hurt to negotiate the stairs but she made the effort. Room service could have provided the same but the telephones were out of order. Once in the foyer Anna could not help but notice the buxom woman with high cheekbones and flared nostrils that tagged on, none too discreetly, behind her. Anna sat at an empty table but was surrounded by Russian officers and local civilians, the latter in ill-fitting, baggy suits reminding her of the American gangster movies.

An elderly waiter came to serve them their late breakfast of bread rolls, marmalade and an accompanying chocolate drink. Anna discreetly caught the waiter's eye and asked him the directions to the Russian or British Consulates. The man took a furtive glance round the room and pretended not to hear as her buxom shadow edged closer, to examine a potted palm in minute detail.

Their meal over, Anna handed in her room key and was surprised as the woman behind the desk suddenly remarked in a loud voice, 'Ja Frau Bauer, room number twenty-one. Here, I will write it down for you and the street.' She scribbled it on a piece of paper and then handed it to her.

Anna embarrassed by the woman's ostentatious manner took the proffered note and noticed several other addresses. Once outside she ostensibly checked her purse and, slipping the note inside, paused long enough to see the names of two streets, one marked '20 Siebenbrunnenfeld Gasse' and the word 'Russki'.

Anna and Eddi walked in the sunshine and took a horse-drawn cab to the Margareten district of Vienna, the cabbie was amazed as she pressed a one dollar note in his hand. She soon found the street and a black-stencilled sign of the Komandantura that issued the Russian identity passes and visas.

Anna produced her British ID card to the two burly guards who examined and discussed it in detail and pointed at the official stamp of the British Crown. They let her pass with a sweeping hand gesture, 'Davai! Davai!' they called out, as they waved her through.

Once inside, Anna joined the queue of local people who waited for their cases to be heard. The man next to her struck up a conversation, telling her that he had had his bicycle stolen by the sentry down by the bridge. He needed it back for his work as he had to travel several miles a day. He was eventually called in to state his complaint. Minutes later, a raised Russian voice was heard, the door opened abruptly and he came back out – with an ornamental ashtray from the base of a cut 88mm shell casing hurtling past his ear.

'*Russki sal-daht nix sabrali!*' screamed a voice, as an orderly indicated to Anna that she was next. She walked in bemused and unnerved by the incident as by the looks of things complaints here seemed to land on deaf ears. The orderly came in behind her and discreetly replaced the brass ornament. The official heard her story and asked her to produce her British ID.

After careful examination and making notes, he handed it back and picked up a phone and conversed for several minutes. 'Da, da spasiba,' he finally said and replaced the handset. With a broad smile he opened a drawer at his desk and produced a buff card. Copying from his notes he filled in the card and stamped it with his name stamp, '*I.V. Peschek'* and with a broad grin handed it to her across the desk.

Delighted Anna examined her visa only to find that it was written in Cyrillic. At a nod from the colonel the interpreter who sat to one side explained to her the visa applied to anywhere within the Soviet-occupied territories, except Berlin. It was as good as, if not better than the British as they, the Russians, possessed more territory. Her joy was short-lived as she realised it would be impossible for her to get out of the Russian zone in Vienna.

'Ja, Danke,' said Anna despondently, trying hard not to show her feelings or sound ungrateful. It was nice to have the visa but it was a visa to nowhere as far as she was concerned. 'I can visit Germany, then?'

'Yes, you may,' replied the official, 'but you are not allowed to cross any borders. You will need a special pass for that issued by the NKVD, as many investigations are still ongoing between our allies in the matter of war criminals. It is understandable, ja?'

'War criminals, but you know who I am,' she said with disgust. 'The British too, I'm a civilian.'

'Yes, you are now, Frau Bauer,' replied the man, 'but we have to check all records. We have been handed documents by our allies and have also found many things in Hitler's bunker. We know of some involvement of a Captain Franz Bauer and the Japanese – with whom I might add, we are still at war.'

Unbelievably she heard her husband's name once more and immediately her hopes were raised, as this was the second time something like this had cropped up. He must be somewhere other than France, England or Germany, as her mind raced back to May. Hitler had shot himself on the fourth day, so Franz was probably still alive then, otherwise his death would have been documented and found. It was ironic that of all people the Russians knew more about him than most and if she had not come here to Vienna, she might never have known. Perhaps things do happen for a reason, mused Anna as the two officials noted her change of attitude.

'So, you have information about my husband?' The two men conversed with each other.

'We understand that you speak good English,' said Peschek through his interpreter. 'Major Yuri speaks highly of you. We need someone to help us with the searches for war criminals as the British have sent us many documents. If you can see us in two weeks we might have more news.'

What? She reflected. The swine is everywhere – no wonder I received my visa. Diplomatically Anna composed herself and nodded in agreement. She would have to wait for news and at the same time translate for Yuri. How she was going to sort things out after last night she had not decided but fleeing the city was impossible as the Russians had a tight grip on anything that moved and Yuri seemed to be quite popular around here.

'I'll come and see you next week, Herr Peschek, thank you.' He nodded politely as the orderly beckoned the next unfortunate to enter.

They walked a short distance in the sunshine and finding a bench Anna had to rest as her body, still tender, made walking a strain, she sat and pondered her next move. Eddi, meanwhile found a spent cartridge case and amused himself as not too far away, plant woman from the hotel kept her eye on them.

Somehow she had to get away from Vienna and go home but with Franz in mind the Russkies were her best bet so she would have to play along with them. Translations for information she mused, but the spectre of Yuri kept coming back. If he had done it once, no doubt he will to do it again. She was concerned as Yuri must have informed the Kommandantura about her as before, she had no papers, yet quite suddenly she had access to half of Europe. Communist Europe, she reminded herself. It seemed she was between a rock and a hard place as all roads led back to the hotel and Yuri, who could do as he pleased. Another niggling thought crossed her mind; what did people do about money now that

346

Hitler's Reichsmark had joined forces with the Dodo? How did the locals buy their food?

It was the sound of engines which distracted her as several lorries with open sides and troops sitting on benches approached at speed. The local horse-drawn traffic scattered as the soldiers, in high spirits jeered their drivers. In an instant they shifted their focus on Anna as with a broadside of wolf-whistles, gestures of depravity and a load of Slavic grins they sped past. With an inward smile she welcomed their youthful antics as it assisted to assuage the events of the night and to recharge her flattened batteries of femininity.

Not wishing to return to the hotel they strolled away from the main road and towards the old part of the city. She looked-on as Russians loaded shop window glass into vehicles, their owners enraged and powerless to act, while bystanders stared in dismay and disbelief.

'Thieving Russkies!' they ranted but Anna neither condoned nor condemned it as by now she knew the other side of the story. Perhaps two wrongs never would make it right but to the victor the spoils, and with Russian towns and cities in ruins and factories decimated they would need every lintel and pane of glass they could lay their Soviet hands on.

She paused with Eddi at St Stephen's Cathedral. Its roof had been damaged by blast and incendiaries, leaving the huge historic bells lying shattered like pieces of pottery on the flagstone floor. Workmen, the faithful, together with priests and nuns were busy clearing the rubble whilst beneath them, in the confines of the catacombs, lay the grinning earthly remains of the victims from the Plague.

Anna stood there for a while and holding Eddi's hand pondered at the devastation and how Almighty God could let this happen. She reasoned that perhaps all the people around her, herself included, were guilty. All of us, she mused, we assisted – no, collaborated with Hitler for a greater Germany and former glory of the Reich but then we never bargained for any of this. That's not what it said on the Nuremberg Rally tin.

They walked along the narrow cobbled streets towards the Graben, where a few horse-drawn cabs were providing transportation. She asked to be taken back to the hotel as Eddi was by this time beginning to plod and drag his feet. It was pleasant to be driving through the streets of the old city, on top of which the horse-drawn ride was an exhilarating experience for them both.

Anna would have appreciated it more given a different time and not having to dread her return to the hotel and that drunken bear Yuri.

Assisting Eddie, Anna gained her apartment and on opening the door noted with anger that Yuri was already there.

'Anna,' he said benignly. 'You're back. I was getting concerned about you. Did you have a nice day?' She said nothing and went to her room. She was about to close her door when he followed her. 'Yes, sorry,' he continued. 'I meant to give you some money,' and held out a fistful of dollars.

'You can keep your filthy money, Herr Major and don't treat me like a whore!' Anna screamed. *'And get out of my room, better still, get me another room!'* He stood there with a little boy lost expression, still holding the notes as Anna glowered at him and Eddi hid behind a Kaiser chair. With an open arm gesture Yuri shook his head.

'Nein, it's not possible, the city is a mess and places like this are hard to come by. Please Anna, I am sorry about last night. I think I had too much wine and we Russians are not used to that sort of drink. It will not happen again, da. I swear it as my head has been splitting all day, never again.' Anna narrowed her gaze to look him straight in the eye.

'Why can't I go home? Back to Germany?' she snapped.

'Look Anna,' he replied, with a pained expression; 'the NKVD wanted you for questioning and mentioned your husband's involvement in a special bomb. I saved you from that and I hear the Kommandantura are trying to help you find him.' Ach so, he knows all about my day, Anna mused. News travels fast in the Soviet jungle.

'It could even mean you ending up at NKVD HQ in Moscow,' he continued. 'Then it would be very difficult for you to get back. I told them you're working for me. Because of that they will leave you alone and make enquiries elsewhere. Give it time and they'll forget all about it.' He shrugged and gave an unconvincing smile as he made for the door. 'I need to get some water and an Aspirin. Please, I will come back.'

She closed the door and sat on the bed and pondered her situation as once again she was at the mercy of others. She was trapped in this place with a Russian who had, only hours before abused her and thought little of the incident, whereas in his country he would be killed for less. What's more, the threat remained she reasoned as the door suddenly opened.

'Here are some documents,' he said coming back to the room. 'They're important and need to be translated and typed up. I'm sure you can type, ja?'

'And if I refuse?' She challenged him with a cold stare.

'Stop playing games Anna,' he said wagging a podgy finger. 'We can make this work together or you go back to the police. That's not a threat, that's a promise and there's a possibility I, or anybody else will never hear from you again. Now let's not fall out with each other, ja?' She glared at him and angrily snatched the papers from his outstretched hand.

'I'll do these for you but as soon as I get my pass I'll be away from here. You've no right to keep me like this. Now, if you don't mind, I would like to be left alone.'

'But of course Anna, please take your time,' he said patronisingly. 'Once we Russians are established here perhaps you'll change your mind. Things could go well for you.' She gave him a milk-curdling look. Was that a smirk on his peasant features as he turned to leave the room? The phone rang, making her jump. It's not supposed to be working she reminded herself as she picked up the receiver.

'Guten Abend,' said a tinny voice. 'We are testing the telephone, can you hear me?'

That's handy, she mused. Now I won't have to see their bumpkin faces anymore.

'Ja, I can hear you. Kindly tell room service to call me back, danke.' Minutes later, she ordered a meal for them both and ran a bath to get Eddi off to bed. Later, as the outside door clicked shut Anna locked her door and settled down to read through the document with its Royal Air Force logo and letter heading.

She was dumbfounded by its content as she read about the brutal murder of fifty RAF aircrew at the hands of their captors. It was a request from the RAF police to assist in tracking down the persons who were named and held responsible, many of them now residing in Russian-occupied territories or in Soviet POW camps. She read how the POWs had escaped through a mass breakout at Stalag Luft lll, how they were hunted down, shot in cold blood and cremated at various places throughout Germany. Two of the Nazi officers were alleged to be Austrians.

As she wrote down a draft of the translation she felt conscious-stricken that serving officers from her country had apparently carried out Hitler's ruthless orders. It went on to say that all those so far arrested had confessed to being involved but blamed others for the killings and they were only carrying out Hitler's orders. So, once again, it's true, Anna reasoned, and it's not allied propaganda now as the culprits are admitting their guilt in order to save their necks. Always blame the orders, being their maxim. She read through a list of names and noted that Yuri had already underscored several, Post and Zacharias being two and written something in Russian alongside with Peschek's name appearing at the bottom. Peschek, so the plot thickens, she mused as she transcribed the translation.

Anna slept late and felt better. Yuri had gone she noticed as they went down to breakfast. Several high-ranking officers sat having coffee and the conversation seemed to falter as Anna and Eddi entered the room. Anna felt herself grow hot as she sensed the comments being made were about her and selected a table as far from them as space would allow. The local waiters too seemed distant, as what they must be thinking was not hard to guess. So, once again I'm in a no win situation, she reminded herself as a waiter poured out a cup of the local fig blended coffee.

Deciding to finish the document she returned to the apartment and went into Yuri's room for the typewriter. Her attention was drawn to a pile of documents as from out of the pile was the edge of a dog-eared photograph. Curiosity being a female trait she marked the spot with a pencil and pulled out the photo. Immediately she recognised Yuri wearing an army captain's uniform. Beside him stood a dark-haired, pleasant looking woman holding a small child with another, a girl of about eight years– standing in front. On the back was some faded writing and in Cyrillic. So, Anna mused, this must be him with his wife and children and recalled what he'd said to her at the farm, and if he was telling the truth these people really are dead and probably why they're stuffed in his files.

She replaced the photo with unease at having pried into his life and wondered what he must think of her and her boy. Was he taking some sort of revenge? She pondered the question as the mental and physical hurt was still there from that night – mental scars she would never forgive or forget.

A week had passed and Yuri had hardly used the room as he explained he was needed for manoeuvres. He had left her with some occupation money and mentioned the local currency would soon be the new Schilling. It made her feel cheap, like a kept woman and mistress. But then his wife is dead, she reasoned. Was this to be her lot? To be paid for services rendered, typing and otherwise?

With the balmy August weather Anna went for walks with Eddi, now five and in need of proper schooling and the company of other children. She took him round the permitted parts of the city for walks in the outdoor classroom, to show him the historic buildings and the statues of Mozart and Schubert and down to the defunct Prater fairground and zoo. A notice had been placed by the Ferris wheel to say that the motor had gone missing – and Peppi the elephant had died of trauma and fright from the bombs.

A week later, a shoestring tram service began to run and at a Konditorei they began to sell cakes and ice cream. Anna had called again at the Kommandantura but there was no news about Franz. She felt they were not really trying as it was not in their interests and speculated that Yuri had vetoed it, anyway.

During the second week as they sat in the Konditorei with their ice creams, news came that a special bomb had been dropped on Japan. That over one hundred thousand people had been killed and their homes wiped off the face of the earth. Anna tried to get more information however all the owner could tell her was that it was a massive device, an uranium bomb dropped by the Americans. So, once again the Russkies had got it right, Anna mused, there was a special bomb.

That night Yuri arrived back and told her the bomb was made from atoms and splitting them to cause the explosion but that's all he knew. He kept himself to himself as Anna did his translations and typing. Again he paid her in US dollars and told her it would be easier to change to local currency once it was in circulation. In the mornings and at night it was just a cordial greeting of 'Guten Morgen' and 'Gute Nacht' between them. Time had healed the hurt but the memory of the assault still lingered and if he had contrasting reasons to keep her, the more she could not trust him.

***

One mid-August afternoon Yuri knocked on her bedroom door and walked in with a grin as wide as the Urals.

'Anna, I have good news! They've given me the rank of Colonel, thanks to your translations, we can celebrate, da?' Anna froze and eyed him with a suspicious frown as this did not bode well for her, being reminded of his last drinking bout and its consequences.

'We have two celebrations, as we have also declared war on Japan. Already our troops are well into Manchuria, Russia will be great once more. My promotion was linked with the fighting in Czechoslovakia, Hungary and here in Vienna, and to the work you have done for me. I should really have been given the rank of lieutenant-colonel; however comrade Khrushchev waived that for me.'

'I suppose I had better congratulate you,' she said coolly, at the same time thinking about Japan and whether Franz was over there. Yuri, still hovering pulled some papers from his uniform pocket.

'Look Anna, I have tickets for a show tonight. We can celebrate, ja?' He waved them at her enthusiastically. *Ouch*, mused Anna, I can't get out of this one.

'Ja, that's good,' she said more enthusiastically than she had intended. It was better to go along with such things than fight them and with his promotion he would be better placed to get her away from the NKVD. 'So, what time do we leave?'

'Say eight o'clock,' he replied with a questioning grin. Anna nodded as he turned and nearly tripped over himself as he left the room.

She put on a long evening dress that Yuri had provided and using the electric heating tongs, put waves in her hair. She swept her hair up at the front and let the remainder fall to her shoulders.

They left the hotel with a Red Army chauffeur driving a black Mercedes, still marked with the outlines of a swastika on its doors. Anna sat Eddi in the middle, who acted as a convenient buffer as they sped along.

She had passed by it many times, but now the Russian Buryat Theatre was open and the guests were assembling. They were led to a round table with a large reserved notice leaning against a vase in which were several red roses. Anna allowed herself a glass of wine as the musicians started to tune up and play on accordions and balalaika instruments. Soldiers appeared on the stage and began to sing and harmonise with songs of old Russia. To loud applause a group of Magyar Gypsies played with characteristic sobbing violins, to end with a rousing Chardaz that had the mixed military audience of officers and men clapping and stomping their boots.

With the wine flowing Yuri, in his new uniform was a transformed man as the choir entertained them with Kalinka, followed by a rousing chorus of The Volga Boatmen. Several officers came across to congratulate him on his promotion and in turn kiss Anna's hand. She allowed her glass to be re-filled and as the evening wore on was surprised to find she actually enjoyed the show. But all this had been a prelude to the highlight of the evening as friendly Cossacks with belted tunics and loose riding breeches appeared together with girls in uniform skirts and red boots; to dance, twirl and perform highflying leaps in traditional style. A more spectacular and vibrant show had not been seen in the old city since the day the Ottoman Empire set up camp outside its walls.

Eddi by this time was asleep, a victim of rich Viennese cakes and fizzy drinks. A minder had made him a bed of army coats and sat to look after him. As the grand finale approached, a local flower girl was besieged with demands for roses which were immediately flung at the dancers to descend in a kaleidoscope of colours and carpet the stage.

Once the noise had subsided and the final curtain fell, Yuri beckoned for Karoline the flower girl to join him with a glass of wine and taking the remaining roses from her basket presented them to Anna. Comrade Peschek came on the scene bringing a bottle of Champagne. Filling their glasses he offered Yuri a toast and congratulations. He nodded at Anna as if they were old acquaintances which, after much chinking of glasses caused her further unease as she felt herself being slowly drawn into Yuri's web of friends.

They left the Buryat with a stout minder woman carrying Eddi and Anna followed, a little unsteady and carrying a bunch of red roses. Yuri and his friends sat talking as Anna was chauffeured back to the hotel and with effort made it back to her room. She thanked the woman who, after carrying Eddi up the stairs was blowing like a carthorse. Slumping over the banister she recovered enough to accept the money that Anna pressed into her hand.

She got Eddi to bed, put her flowers in a water-filled bowl and slipping into a nightdress fell into bed. She lay there pleasantly woozy but happy at having had an enjoyable and most entertaining evening. As the welcoming mantle of sleep descended she heard Yuri return, his heavy footsteps approaching and to stop at her door; with a sigh of relief she heard him carry on to his room and the comforting sound of his closing door.

Yuri sat down at his bureau and from its bottom drawer pulled out a glass and a bottle. He reached for the round tin and extracted a cigarette and with a flick of his Zippo, lit up. With passing clouds of Virginia tobacco he poured himself a generous measure of the potato spirit and settled to casually stretch his feet on the bureau's top. He sat and pondered his day; his promotion and the evening with his pretty Zhèhn-shchi-na. After a while he extracted the dog-eared photograph from the pile of paperwork and gazed longingly at his wife standing there next to him, his young daughter and his baby son. He finished his drink, removed his uniform and turned out the light.

He felt her move once he touched her as he eased his body onto the bed and lay there, his naked thigh touching hers. Leisurely he positioned himself as Anna moved a sleep laden arm across her body. His breathing became laboured as he lifted her garment and juggled to support his weight. Anna uttered a dream-laden moan and stirred as Yuri eased himself into the soft folds of her slumbering body.

Disturbed and like an uncurling dream she felt the intrusion as he began to press his body down. It was that waking moment, when confusion reigns as prowling nightmares relinquish their hold that she lay, exposed and covered by him. With wine dulling her senses Anna remained passive and biting her lip to shield her pain as blood and judgement co-mingled with her silent, salty tears. Only the lame feeling of his efforts and the sound of his laboured breathing made her even more aware of the hopelessness of her situation. *But then how long can this go on?* Her tortured mind screamed. *How long must you endure this ignominy and physical abuse?* Soon it was over for them both, as he grunted something unintelligible and she felt his hostile seed enter her body.

Breathing heavily, Yuri rolled to lie down beside her as the nauseating odour of his tobacco and vodka-laden breath permeated the room. Once again, Anna performed her cleansing ritual as she immersed herself in the soothing embrace of her bath.

With the bathroom door ajar, Yuri's snores filled the room which served to harden her resolve to break out and escape to the British zone just one kilometre distant. She had already noticed most of the Soviet sentries at the checkpoints were illiterate young men from ethnic backgrounds who did not include education as vital to their survival and goat-herding existence. With her British and Russian papers, she would play the mother and child card and bluff her way through. At worst, she would only be turned back but there were many checkpoints and it only needed one sentry with a hangover to let her through.

It was late when she awoke. Eddi was sitting beside her looking at his book. She sat upright and noted with satisfaction that Yuri had gone. They went down for breakfast and to her chagrin, he was there. Their eyes met and he sheepishly dropped his gaze but asked her to join him and the other officers. Unable to refuse as all tables were occupied she sat with him. Anna finished her coffee and assisted her son with his breakfast as Yuri leant towards her and said casually, 'We're leaving.'

Anna cast him a questioning frown, puzzled about the 'we' business.

'I have to go to Budapest,' he said with a shrug. Hungary she mused, that's good, now's my chance for freedom.

'So how long will you be away?' He smiled at her sudden interest.

'When I said we, Anna, I meant you and I. We have to meet a man called Tito and some British and American people and I need an interpreter.' Again she noticed the fate accompli smile and on seeing her frustration added, 'of course, you can bring the boy along too, he will like that.'

'Tito?' said Anna, searching for an answer and a way out. 'I thought he was a bandit, why see him?' Yuri and his three officer colleagues burst out laughing at her naiveté.

'Perhaps to you, but a bandit to us never,' replied Yuri. 'He's a partisan and helped us all to win the war. Now he's the leader of Yugoslavia and we're all going to talk to him. It's the Americans; they want to give the Sudentland back to Germany. Perhaps you've heard that Tito wants part of Austria too; Carinthia to be exact. We have to have a meeting, da?' His colleagues nodded as Anna shook her head, as it meant nothing to her and she had bigger fish to fry. She met his gaze and asked him bluntly.

'If I agree to go with you Yuri…' She paused, it was the first time she had used his name and it was not lost on him either. 'Then can I go home? I have to go back to my home and Eddi here has to start his schooling.' Yuri's peasant face creased into a reassuring smile and nodded his head in appreciation as his colleagues listened, amused at their sparring.

'Da, Anna, this will be the last time. As I am a colonel they need me to do this. Then of course we can all go home.' He sat and beamed and waited for her reaction. It was what she had been waiting for and felt elated. So her self-sacrifice had not been in vain as there was now light at the end of the Soviet tunnel. She smiled her thanks and appreciation and decided to do her best, to meet him halfway even if it meant another humiliating midnight ordeal. The end would justify the means.

'How long are we expected to stay in Budapest?' He met her questioning gaze, shrugged and conspired in Russian with his colleagues.

'Just days Anna, only a few days for a conference.' He smiled and nodded reassuringly and pulled out a gold cigarette case, complete with a diamond encrusted swastika and offered it round before lighting up. 'Anyway you will like Hungary, Budapest is similar to Vienna, you really will like it.' Pleased with himself he casually blew smoke at the chandelier and ordered more of the fig-blended coffee.

'Then we come back here and you'll let me have my pass and travel papers, ja?'

He nodded at her request. 'But of course Anna, Mikhail here will have them all waiting. He deals with such matters.' He indicated with a thumb at his colleague who politely beamed in her direction. 'He will get onto it right away – after breakfast of course.' However the young lieutenant twitched his moustache, uneasy at being singled out and acted like a cornered hare about to bolt.

'Thank you lieutenant, that would make me very happy,' said Anna as the officer rose from the table and excused himself.

'Sorry to spring this on you at short notice,' continued Yuri. 'Can you pack just a few things, we have to travel light and the room here is still ours. We have to leave right away, twelve o'clock at the latest and please bring the typewriter.' It was a bolt from the blue but there again she did not have any choice in the matter. After all, had she not agreed?

'Well, we'd better get ourselves ready then,' she said with a resigned shrug and beckoned to Eddi. 'Come along, we're going to see the big river Danube. You'll like that.' He pulled a resigned face as he followed her for the climb back up those arduous stairs.

At twelve their transport was waiting as Anna entered the foyer. Mikhail approached her and produced a document that needed her signature. Anna's frown turned to elation as she recognised the British Army note paper and the visa authorising her and her child to enter the British zone. She was requested to sign the document and was informed by the officer that it will have to be countersigned by the Komandantura, her 'friend' comrade Peschek.

Anna eagerly signed and noted they already had a picture of her pinned to it. These people really are efficient she mused, as she recognised her Buryat roses in the background. Yuri was busy organising the loading of several leather cases as the bellhop took hers and in a matter of minutes they were on their way. They passed the airfield which was still not operational and on to the Westbahnhof where a skeleton rail service was in operation.

The train ran across the Danube and along lines that were still under repair and passed the burnt-out shell of the paint factory and its scattered railway wagons lying at crazy angles down a steep embankment. At the Hungarian border they disembarked as the damage was severe and from there a Mercedes staff car still with its faint swastika emblem took them on a lengthy detour until they arrived in the darkened city. From what she could see the place had been badly mauled from artillery duels and hand-to-hand fighting but apart from that, the city of Budapest was of the same drab character as Vienna. Only olive-clad soldiers occupied the streets and soon they stopped at an army barracks complete with an expansive parade ground.

Anna was given her own room which she shared with Eddi. It had not long since been the abode of a German officer as his name and rank were still on the door. Quite ironic she thought as she entered the room. So, it's from my fellow countryman she mused – wonder what happened to him?

As a precaution she double-locked the door and being tired got Eddi and herself off to bed. I feel safer here than in that hotel, she reasoned as she turned out the paraffin lamp and was soon catching up on lost sleep.

In the morning Anna found her way to the kitchens and a cafeteria-style messing. Helping herself to rye bread, marmalade and coffee she made her way across to a long table with bench seats where both men and women of differing ranks messed together. They courteously made room for the newcomers as Anna noted she was the only person in civilian dress. Some spoke good German whilst others were local and she wondered how many of them had changed sides once the Red Army appeared knocking at the gates. At least they accepted her being there and with Eddi by her side it made her presence acceptable.

Minutes later Colonel Yuri entered and sat down opposite to Anna. The conversation round the table turned to whispers as Yuri asked Anna if she had slept well. He outranked them all and soon they were left to themselves. Yuri ate quietly and was by no means his usual self. Anna sensed something was bothering him but put it down to the loneliness of command.

'So, what time do we get to see this Tito man?' Anna asked, breaking the silence. He glanced at her and rocked his head before swallowing hard.

'I've been informed of a change of plan,' he replied. 'We have to fly out from here to Prague. It's to avoid a clash with partisans. Marshal Tito does not want to be embarrassed by his old friends.' With knitted brows she searched his face in disbelief.

'Prague? That's Czechoslovakia,' she queried with a hint of suspicion in her tone. 'Are you certain about all this?'

'Da, Anna, da,' he reassured her. 'We are going to fly. It's quicker and safer to fly around here and will shorten our stay.' With a deep sigh of frustration, she accepted it as plausible. Anything to make her stay shorter and get away from these Soviet-impregnated backwaters.

'What time are we leaving?' she asked.

'Within the hour. Pack your things and meet me outside. The transport will take us straight to the airport. Sorry about this Anna. When we get back I will make it up to you, and young Eddie, I promise.' Standing to leave he rubbed the boy's cheek and with an endearing smile excused himself.

Pack! thought Anna, he's out of his tree. What have I got to pack? Just my toothbrush.

Within the hour they were once more on their way. This time the car was Italian. By its faded insignia she could tell it was a leftover from their 8th Army, with sumptuous leather seats and a gearbox that whined in several mournful octaves as they slowed to negotiate the mounds of rubble in the streets.

The stale breath of war still lingered as squads of German prisoners with long-handled shovels and weary, ashen faces were laboriously clearing the streets under the vigilant gaze of their Soviet guards. For Anna it was disheartening as she tried not to look at the emaciated figures that were once the cream of General Horthy's 22nd SS Division. For her it was too close to home as her mind turned to her husband, he too could be somewhere out there and receiving the same treatment.

The prisoners stopped and stared, their faces gaunt with dark hollow eyes as they let the Soviet officer and his family pass and Anna discreetly keeping her gaze in her lap. At the airport it was Eddi who raised her spirits at the sight of so many aircraft which thrilled the young boy. He tugged at her hand and pointed excitedly in every direction. Anna's hopes rose even higher as she noticed the roundels of several British planes, together with the white stars and stripes of an American bomber. So they are here after all, she mused and admonishing herself, having doubted what Yuri had said in Vienna.

Minutes later they found themselves whisked off across the apron by a jeep with Red Army markings and joined several other military personnel already boarding a DC3 transport. Anna climbed along the steep angle of the cabin floor and seated herself, with Eddi by her side in the crude bucket seat. With a whine of electric motors followed by several coughs, first one engine then the other roared into life and they were soon taxiing along the peri-track towards the main runway.

Yuri sat in the aisle seat opposite and kept himself busy by reading sporadically from a document and nervously toying with his watch. Flying nerves, mused Anna as she side-glanced him.

With a roar of its the twin engines the aircraft gathered speed, its tail lifting to a more comfortable angle before taking to the air in a stomach-lifting lurch. Once airborne the sunlight blinked through the ports and settled to rest on its starboard side as the aircraft scribed an arc over the city and levelled out towards its destination. Anna and Eddi peered with excitement down at the twin city of Buda and Pest rolling by beneath them with the Danube snaking its way under the ancient bridges and reflecting its silver ribbon in the morning light. Scattered cotton wool clouds swept past, briefly masking the numerous green domes, now toy-size and rapidly receding from sight.

As she pointed out more of the landmarks to her son, a feeling of doubt began to creep into her mind as the sun remained to starboard when it should have been, if anything, astern. By all accounts and from her yachting experience they were still heading in a northerly direction. After a while she leant across the aisle and tapped Yuri's arm.

'We seem to be heading north,' she said in a raised and quizzical voice as the aircraft droned on and someone behind mentioned the Carpathian Mountains. For a moment he stared expressionless into the seat in front of him but meeting her troubled gaze, nodded in agreement.

'Da, Anna, we are going home,' he replied.

'Home?' Anna queried. 'What home? What about the meeting?'

He met her wide-eyed gaze and with a supercilious smile, said casually, 'Cancelled my dear, at the last moment. As I said, we are going home.'

Anna stared at him as he leant away from her and pointed to a vast line of vehicles far below. 'Tanks Anna, tell your son they are all Red Army tanks.'

'We don't care about your stupid tanks Yuri,' Anna hissed. 'Where are you taking us?'

'Home Anna, home to our little mother Russia,' he replied. 'We're all going home, for us the war is over.'

'You can't do this to me,' she said angrily. 'What about my son? What about him?' Heads turned as her raised voice could clearly be heard over the drone of the engines. Yuri nodded dispassionately as Anna fumed and burst into heart-rending sobs.

'Listen Anna,' he said purposefully and reaching across to hold her arm. 'Listen to me. Your husband never returned. You must face the fact that he died in the war and his boat was never found. We will start a new life together – you, me and the boy, da? It will be good for us. We will all forget about our recent differences and make a fresh start. Mother Russia will be good to us and she needs people like you. I will be good to you too Anna, I promise.'

She wiped her eyes with a sleeve and met his gaze and was sickened by what she saw in his calculating, piglet eyes. He would use her as before and God only knows where she would end up. Then, am I a widow, like he says, she pondered?

Anna gritted her teeth until it hurt. He can't do this to me, was all she could think of as the towns and villages below thinned out to give way to woodlands and the expansive Pripet marshes of the Ukraine.

With Eddi asleep, a sea of self-pity swept over her. How did she ever let herself get into this mess? But then how could she complain as she had agreed to go with him and gain her release, but he lied and who would listen? She slumped back in her seat as tears of anger, abandonment and betrayal meandered past wan cheeks. She bit her lip in vexation at her ever trusting a Russian, him of all people and the British, how they had used her but worst of all, her own people and what they had done. As the plane droned on she composed herself and resorted to running a motherly hand through Eddi's hair. Awake now and oblivious of his mother's plight he gazed happily out of his window to watch the decimated city of Lvov slipping by at a distance on the starboard wing.

Chapter Forty

STALIN'S GUESTS

Minsk, a large Russian city, lay decimated by the acts of a German army which had acted in two phases. The first was the Wehrmacht's victorious raping and plundering as it blitzed its way towards Moscow; then came the surrender at Stalingrad and the onset of the second phase, namely defeat coupled with ignominious retreat. Here vast areas of Russia were razed and reduced to rubble some three years after Barbarossa's dawn.

With peace restored, Russia set itself on a vast programme of rebuilding the nation and here it was that Colonel Yuri Konstantin found himself chosen to be part of Stalin's five-year plan. He had been granted extended leave and privileges to salvage and rebuild his home, together with the village which was there before the Nazi onslaught. Being of farming stock he was considered by Moscow to be the ideal candidate for re-establishing the task of food production in his district and was subsequently placed in a position as military overseer to that of the local commune and the peasants that worked the land.

All seeds and materials had to be sanctioned by him together with the accounting of expenditure and the resulting harvest. He also had to ensure the peasants did not hoard food or livestock that was the property of the communist state. But the plan was labour-intensive and with the loss of some twenty-five million of its people Stalin was short of this human commodity. The shortfall was soon augmented by the retention of some three million prisoners of war from the Axis countries and partisans which did not meet with Stalin's political point of view.

With the Colonel's theatre of war changed to that of an agricultural mode and combining a war on want with the collective gathering of the harvest, here it was amid this scenario that his plane touched down at Minsk in a broiling summer afternoon of 1945. As the aircraft taxied along the renovated peri-track, Yuri gazed out in consternation at the sight of the bombed-out buildings. Shell holes were numerous and the burnt-out skeletons of planes littered the surrounding military airfield. He noted with satisfaction a smart line of Soviet Dak fighters and in the background the abandoned aircraft of the Nazi war machine.

As the plane came to a halt an army jeep was there to meet him. Anna said nothing as she negotiated the makeshift wooden steps and shepherded her son into the vehicle. From there they continued on the short journey into the city.

After threading its way past heaps of rubble the jeep stopped with a dusty screech outside an ancient looking, three-storey building. It had been painted a mustard colour which was now faded and pockmarked with numerous shrapnel and bullet holes. Yuri jumped out and held the door for her and the boy but leaving her to carry her hastily packed travelling bag. Anna, weary from the effects of travel and mentally drained by events, noted the building was devoid of glass in its windows. The overbearing smell of cabbage as she entered the building was all she could stand but unknown to her, this was just the beginning.

Carrying her scant belongings she followed Yuri but to her consternation he had disappeared to leave her standing in a large hallway. Sounds from children at play came from many of the rooms, punctuated by bawling babies vying for attention. The wooden staircase was bare of any covering and paint peeled off the walls and ceiling. Youngsters with ill-fitting clothes, their faces tearstained and smudged began to gather round as Anna stood and waited. They jostled, elbowing each other with curiosity, some sniffing with runny noses and wiping themselves with bare arms as Eddie clung to her, confused and frightened. A door opened and for once she felt relieved to see him as Yuri reappeared from one side of the staircase.

'Anna!' he called and beckoned with a wave. 'Come, meet my sister and aunts.' Reluctantly she followed him into a room and on seeing them, cringed at their bulk. They advanced line astern like dreadnought battleships, their multi-coloured headscarves like bunting at a Kiel regatta. She gave them an endearing smile and offered her hand in the uncertainty of the moment as Yuri, beaming from ear to ear, announced their names. With arms like lumberjacks each handshake resulted in near dislocation as Katja, Natasha and Yuri's sister, Ludmilla, offered their welcomes with an enthusiastic shake of their callused, ham-sized mitts.

'Zdravstvuyte Anna,' they called out and beamed. Their large flat faces and matching noses were creased in weathered smiles as they stood gazing at this 'undernourished' creature from another world.

With the formalities dispensed Yuri beckoned for Anna to follow Natasha who, despite her size was quite agile as she mounted the stairs. At the first landing they halted. Anna noticed the daubed-over slogans and swastikas of its previous occupants as Natasha, now wheezing with effort, indicated to an open door.

'This is your room Anna. It's the best in the house,' she said proudly in halting German. Anna gave her a ghost of a smile as she thanked her but her mind froze as she glanced at the sparse furniture and peeling wallpaper. South-facing, sunlight flooded the room to reveal the double bed that dominated the bedroom and an ancient wardrobe in the corner with a mirror at its front, broken and repaired with brown paper sticking tape. An old rocking chair with a pronounced list was the only other piece of furniture which graced the room.

Natasha looked-on, bemused at her bewilderment and pointing to the communal toilet situated on the landing and left Anna to collect her thoughts and unpack. With a laden heart Anna sat on the unmade bed and hugging Eddi held his head to her bosom as tears of angst and despair mingled to moisten his hair.

Minutes later Yuri strode into the room with the older boys carrying his bags.

'So, we're home Anna, all this is ours.' He swept his hand in a grand gesture to emphasise the point, as the children at the door stood and looked-on with curiosity and awe. 'It-ti! It-ti!' he barked, as they fled with screams of laughter and delight.

'You had no right to bring me here, I demand to be taken back,' said Anna, lifting her tearstained face.

'You are mine Anna,' he growled. 'I told you in Vienna that you were mine. You did not object. Am I right?'

He strode to the door and slammed it shut. Anna said nothing as she recalled the drunken incident.

'When you are ready and have made the bed,' he continued, 'you can go down to the kitchen and help out with the meal. You have to make yourself welcome and useful, da? Natasha will look after you as she had a husband who taught her German and was a teacher before they killed him at Stalingrad.'

'Eddi,' said Anna, fearing more to come. 'Go and look out of the window and watch the children playing.' He left her as Anna, eyes brimming with tears, gazed pleadingly at Yuri. 'Please Yuri,' she begged, 'you cannot do this to us. We don't belong here. Take me back to Vienna and I will stay with you there, I promise.'

'*Nyet, you will stay with me here!*' he shouted, as the blood rose and spoke in his cheeks. 'We will rebuild Little Mother and you will help me do it.' He glared at her insolence as he recalled her countrymen destroying his village only kilometres distant. 'This is my country and the likes of you will help to rebuild it. As soon as the materials arrive and my Dacha is ready, we will move back to the village. Once there we'll have a good collective farming life. Until then go down to the kitchen and say Guten Tag to the Babushkas and learn Russian, and what's more be thankful that I will look after you and the boy.'

He stood glaring at her as Anna, in total disbelief at his sudden outburst and change of manner, could only gaze at him in astonishment and angst at his Jekyll and Hyde transformation and the disclosure of things to come. Yuri lit a cigarette and waited as Anna, through a veil of iron tears resolved to battle for her freedom. Without a second glance at Yuri she removed the blankets, all grey and still bearing the Wehrmacht insignia and began to make the bed. He left the room in silence as Anna found her siren suit, changed and wiping her spent tears took Eddi's hand and went to join the others downstairs.

Children can be cruel and kind. As they saw Eddi with his mother some came towards him and two girls took his hand and beckoned for him to come outside to join them. He shook his head but Anna bent and whispered words of encouragement; gently but firmly the children, all excited at the newcomer, took him to play with them.

Anna followed her nose and the overpowering odour of cabbage and soon found the open door of the kitchen. Several women were seated round a sturdy oblong table, whilst Natasha, standing, was busy skinning rabbits. Anna stopped by the door as they waved and beckoned for her to enter. One woman rose to give Anna her seat at the same time leaning across the table to fill a cup from a brass Samovar. Anna nodded her thanks as she was handed the questionable liquid. Another woman passed a jar which Anna understood to be molasses. They indicated for her to put it into her cup.

'Tchai, tchai,' they chorused and smiled their denture-challenged welcome.

'It's tea, Anna and sugar beet extract,' said Natasha as she methodically stuffed the rabbit skins from a pile of old newspapers. 'It might be too strong for you but you'll get used to it.' Anna nodded and thanked them as the old women carried on to discuss the newcomer with the others and kept pointing at her chain and crucifix. Plucking up courage they came closer and to touch it, one even tried to kiss it as they all crossed themselves repeatedly as Natasha explained religion was not allowed in modern Russia.

'We have comrade Stalin and the Party,' she said, shaking her head and ramming the last of the paper into the hide. 'It's for the winter,' she explained. 'We make gloves, hats and muffs.' Anna nodded politely. At least they were friendly but wondered what would happen to her now she was totally dependent on her benefactor, Yuri.

That evening they had Borsht. It was soup made with slices of beetroot and onions but enhanced with pieces of rabbit. It was eaten with thick slices of rye bread which was mercifully familiar to her and Eddi. During the meal the women told her that soon they would all have to help with the harvest and they expected things to get better after that. Anna had heard about Russian farming methods and knew from pre-war days how unproductive their methods were. Now, she mused, I'm about to find out – first hand.

After the meal she helped to wash the children's faces. There were no teeth to clean as toothbrushes and paste were luxuries and not to hand. She felt guilty as the children watched Eddi clean his and mimicked his actions with their fingers. After that she went to her room. Natasha had made a bunk bed ready for Eddi – he would sleep with five others in a room on the same floor. Eddi cried but his newfound friends crowded round and soothed him in their own way, and with Anna holding his hand he was soon asleep. To her relief Yuri did not come home that night. However, as a precaution against the unexpected, she slept in her siren suit which was just as well as there were mosquitoes and the window was a gaping hole with just an ill-fitting curtain.

He was absent for the whole week and the women, through Natasha, explained he had gone to oversee the delivery of materials. They informed her about his past and his family. How the Panzer crew had raped his wife before shooting her, along with the children.

She poured tea for the women who handed round cigarettes that were strong-smelling and alien to her senses.

'The whole village was rounded up,' Natasha continued and breaking into the vernacular from time to time to keep the others in the conversation. 'Many of the youngsters were sent to work in Germany as slave labour until they could work no more and ended up in camps to die. It all came out after our army liberated the first camp. A few who survived returned to tell the tale.'

Anna felt horrified, guilty by association and embarrassed by the actions of her countrymen. She could only say how sorry she was on behalf of the decent folk of Germany but in the back of her mind she remembered her own ordeal. Then it struck her. Was this Yuri's revenge? Could this be the real reason for my being here? Was it pay-back time?

'You'll see them walking around here, all meschugge,' and pointing to her forehead made a circular motion. 'They walk about aimlessly and cannot come to terms with their newfound freedom. They're crazy and do stupid things. They collect everything they can find and hoard it until they can no longer move in their rooms, meschugge, the lot of them.' Anna could only shake her head in sympathy and wondered from where Natasha got that familiar Yiddish adjective. The women all nodded in agreement as they sat in the kitchen and elderly neighbours who had joined them wept openly.

Back in her room Anna peered into the gathering dusk. She recalled events of what the women had mentioned and was puzzled why Yuri had deceived her by bringing her here. Am I a substitute for his late wife, she wondered? But then why me, a German? Surely that would be like rubbing salt into his wounds and would remind him of the old enemy.

She was distracted by a group of older children that were still at play below. They shouted at her and made rude noises. She waved her hand and they waved back and screeched with delight as several fluttering bats were to be seen, jinking and circling in the gloom.

She turned the whole thing over again and again in her mind. Did he need to punish someone for her countrymen's past misdeeds? But then why her, a woman with a child? Had he not conquered with his troops and occupied his enemy's lands? On the other hand, she reasoned with a self-indulgent smile, I have yet to see a woman around here with a figure like mine. Was that to be the truth of the matter and the reason for my being here? Does size matter after all? How am I ever going to find out?

The high-pitched buzz of a mosquito interrupted her thinking. It hovered close, sensing its evening meal. Anna drew the curtain and lay down on the bed with her latest possession, a Wehrmacht phrase book of the Russian language. 'Zdravstvuyte' it began. A greeting, 'Hallo...'

366

Yuri turned up a few days later, still in uniform and with a squad of soldiers who parked their Wehrmacht Mercedes transports outside the building. He had brought a lorry-load of food parcels with US Army markings, along with used mechanical parts and panes of glass. After offloading the glass he left, but not before informing Anna that he would return in another week. Materials, he told her were now arriving by rail and he was going to supervise the rebuilding of his village. It suited her as she had no desire to be with him, especially in these cramped and communal quarters where privacy was not included in the five-year plan.

Apart from Eddi's black eye, where he'd been hit by the boys playing Russki and Fascisti, things went smoothly as Anna was left to her own devices. She helped out where she could and was on friendly terms with all of the babushkas who came in for Tchai, and a chat.

***

'You seem to be settled now, I hear,' said Yuri one day, as he walked into the building and saw Anna wielding a broom. He indicated for her to follow him to the kitchen. He spoke to the others there, who all nodded with wide grins.

'We are going to move, Anna. You will like your new house, our very own Dacha.' He produced a plain bottle and poured himself a hefty drink. 'Here's to us, Anna.' He raised his glass and in two gulps, downed the eye-watering spirit. 'Gooseberry vodka,' he said with an accompanying belch. 'Home made and over-proof,' and re-charged his glass.

'I'm not what you want me to be,' said Anna eyeing the bottle suspiciously. 'This is not my country, how can I be settled?'

The others, through Natasha were kept informed as Yuri offered them the rest of the drink. Natasha told Anna they had already packed their bags but would not be leaving until the morning.

'We will be neighbours,' she said with an encouraging smile, as Yuri fetched more bottles and with outsiders gathering round the party soon got into swing. After a while Anna excused herself as they began to sing their interminable patriotic songs and once again related, with great animation their heroic stories of the war.

Once again fearing the worst, Anna changed from her dress into her siren suit and lay down to sleep as the din from the kitchen carried on into the night. Sometime in the early hours she heard

Yuri enter the room. He staggered around until finally crashing into the bed and falling in an inebriated heap beside her.

It was late afternoon when they began to move house. Yuri said nothing as he and the others nursed their hangovers and loaded the transports that had stood waiting since dawn. A black Horch staff car arrived, its long bonnet concealing the eight cylinders and the power that lurked beneath. Its plush interior of walnut panelling blended well with the burgundy leather seats still depicting the Swastika emblem of its erstwhile owners. Anna, with Eddi on her lap sat in the back and was joined by Yuri's sister and two aunts. With the car's top down and Yuri sitting in triumph like an historic Roman general, the convoy of three transports set off for their destination some two miles distant.

For the small community it was a day of great occasion as they left the suburbs and proceeded at a tangent onto an un-metalled road which led out into the countryside. For Anna it was just another day of even greater uncertainty as, surrounded by people of a simple culture and in an alien land, she felt she was on a steep and thorny road which at every turn led further into the unknown. Happy at first to be away from her oppressive communal surroundings she became concerned as now here was just open countryside with nothing but dirt roads, distant forests and vast fields that stretched to the limitless horizon.

She was free, Yuri had said. Free to do whatever she wanted to do. But it was the freedom of her chains; the freedom with nothing left to lose and included a field of beetroots ready for the harvest. Anna pondered on that as the once gleaming Horch was soon covered in a thick blanket of brown dust.

Passing fields of sunflowers, maize and potatoes, Anna was suddenly jolted from her melancholy as upon rounding a woodland the village came into view and there in the fields she saw them. Hundreds of men in Wehrmacht uniforms, with a smattering of Red Army guards standing by the roadside, the latter smartening up as they recognised the staff car and their Colonel.

Katja elbowed her and pointed with a grin. 'Nemetsky – Fascisti; robotney, robotney, da?'

Anna nodded in polite understanding and noted how wretched they appeared, with some not wearing boots but rags tied round their feet.

'They're working here on the farms,' explained Natasha. 'They'll never go home as comrade Stalin has ordered it. We are so short of manpower and have to use them.'

'Serve them right,' said Katja as she heard the mention of Stalin and knew exactly what Natasha was referring to. 'Tell her they butchered our menfolk so we cannot have husbands and children. Look! Just look at the devastation.'

As the car slowed Anna saw the scale of destruction as nothing remained of the old village of some two hundred houses. There were just the remains of burnt-out shells, scorched timbers and twisted pieces of corrugated metal.

Negotiating a bend they arrived at the 'new build' village and its houses. They were chalet-type bungalows, all of timber construction with corrugated iron roofs. Wehrmacht prisoners were working on their construction as nearby stood a compound with some twenty wooden huts and surrounded, in turn, by barbed wire. That must be their Stalag, mused Anna. At least I shall have company.

The convoy came to a halt alongside a larger dwelling with a paddock to the rear. Natasha pointed towards a pinewood nearby.

'That's where they buried them,' she said, 'the villagers, including Yuri's wife and children.' She crossed herself, her eyes brimming with tears as Anna gazed at a sparsely-covered mound with its border of blue flowers.

She glanced once more at the prisoners and tried to comprehend the bizarre situation which confronted her. She could not make amends for what had been done, but neither could those unfortunate young men held captive and who, perhaps like her, would never see their homeland again. But in mitigation she did see the local's point of view as there were few young men about. Revenge was sweet, especially served cold as it was here.

She thought about the early days of the Russian campaign, with Germany victories and the BBC reporting the atrocities committed by the soldiers, which Goebbels dismissed as nothing but English propaganda. Russia had suffered and now it's our turn, she mused. We're the scapegoats here.

Once out of the car, Yuri (with great pride) showed Anna her new home.

'You'll like it here Anna, you and the boy will have all the freedom you ever wanted. We shall have horses and I will teach him to ride like a true Cossack.' With a sweep of his hand he told her that he would be in charge of all that she could see, including the prisoners, who would work the land and build up the village. 'Come, I will show you our new house, our Dacha. I give it to you Anna, as a present from Mother Russia.'

To her mind the whole thing was absurd. She was given all this but did not want to be any part of it. She hated him and his backward country and just wanted to go home. Once inside Anna compared it to a glorified garden shed with partitions and windows and a back door that led out to the paddock. The kitchen was part of the living room and there was no running water. On inspection the outside toilet was as basic and rudimentary as that encountered in the Tyrol. Even down to the ubiquitous copies of *Pravda* hanging conveniently at arm's length and a round-wooden lid to cover the pit and contents below.

Several horses peered out from their stables as Anna followed Yuri back into the house. He pointed to another room to where a double-sized bed dominated the master bedroom. Eddi's was in a smaller room leading off to the side, with four small bunk beds. Seems the horses have got it better than me, she mused. At least they have their own room. Suddenly a chilling thought took hold; Gott im Himmel, four bunk beds, so that's his game. He thinks he's going to be the stallion round here, the filthy Schweinehund!

Her mind in turmoil she tried her best to suppress her thoughts and directed the soldiers as they offloaded the kitchen contents and cases into the Dacha. She noticed the two aunts and sister were given the Dacha next door with a stretch of garden between. They were ecstatic with their new possession, courtesy of the state and 'oohed' and 'aahed' as they dragged in their bundles of clothing and pieces of broken furniture. It was not lost on Anna how simple and grateful for small mercies these people really were. Whatever must have got into my fellow countrymen to commit such atrocities, she mused? Had they all gone meschugge after eating the local mushrooms? What was the explanation?

Anna was familiar with the wood-burning stove and after all, they would need a meal. She set to her task as mother hen and started to make herself at home in the kitchen. With an engaging smile, Anna inveigled the young soldiers to fetch her a watering can of drinking water.

'Va-dah! Va-dah,' she said, making herself understood and looked-on as a soldier went to the paddock to operate an ancient hand pump. Lighting the fire, the small range began to shed heat as the pungent smell of burning pine logs permeated the room.

Yuri for his part was not idle. Having recovered from last night's binge he had backed one of the lorries up to an outhouse in the paddock and was busy with his men unloading supplies. Mostly dry-food, as diverse as American SPAM, olive-grey tins of U-Boot rations, Canadian wellingtons with a 'Gutta Percha' trade mark, together with a large quantity of British Red Cross parcels that somehow hadn't made it to their intended destination. (Anna was to find out later that it was the Germans that had hoarded them and the Russians had taken possession as they overran the Nazi POW camps. A case of finders, keepers.)

Some prisoners were ordered to assist and carry items into the house. At close quarters she saw how badly their uniforms fitted as many were in tatters and the men all suffered from lack of nourishment. They hardly spoke with anyone or spared her a second glance as with stubble beards and gaunt, resigned faces, they methodically toiled under the wary gaze of the trigger-fingered guards. Four men struggled with an ornate mahogany writing desk, complete with its eagle and swastika embellishment as one grunted at her. 'Wo hin?' Then nearly dropped dead as Anna pointing to a corner said calmly; 'Dort, in der ecke, bitte!'

It spread like wildfire that the newcomer, 'Die Frau' as they now called her, is German. It made their day and cheered up their miserable lives, if only for a moment.

Anna guessed most of them were in their twenties and early thirties and with a motherly instinct she would have loved to help, but discretion rather than foolish acts held sway. The last thing she wanted was to compromise both them and herself in front of Yuri and his suspicious guards.

They sat down for their first meal. Anna had made coffee and salami sandwiches and at the same time preparing an evening meal for later. Yuri informed her that he had been placed in charge of 25,000 POWs in the surrounding area, which included the building of an airfield capable of handling the new heavy bomber that Russia was yet to build. He went on to explain Stalin had surreptitiously withheld the release of an American B-29 Superfortress bomber that had landed in the East after a raid on Japan. It was only handed back after all of its parts had been logged and photographed as this type of aircraft was way ahead of any Soviet state-of-the-art technology.

'We'll have the means to deliver the special bomb right on their doorsteps,' Yuri said, banging his fist on the table. 'We are already building a bomb like the Americans used. Russia will be great once more and not be dictated to by the West.'

'I thought you were all allies?' Anna cut in, sarcastically.

'Up to a point, my dear, but now we must show Britain and America who can build the greatest empire. All of occupied Europe and lands to the east shall be ours!' He took a gulp of coffee, 'and it will all be Soviet and Red,' he added with a satisfied grunt.

Anna did not comment. To her the whole Hitler war was for nothing and now, by all accounts it was starting all over again. Same dog but different fleas, she mused. Franz had said the same to her all those years ago. Germany had to challenge Britain's navy, build bigger ships, modernise. Where was he and all those ships now? Disgusted with events, she excused herself and took Eddi to his room.

Night had fallen by the time the last of the lorries were offloaded and a peaceful hush descended on the fledgling community. Anna had prepared supper and now for the first time the three of them sat facing each other across the kitchen table. She had found a yellow gingham cloth and placed a vase with several yellow roses in the middle. Anna had made an effort and had it not been for the absurdity of her situation it would have matched any close-knit family meal.

It was the first time for her to be alone with him in Russia and now, for all intents and purposes she would be his wife – his Zhynáh as she heard him mention by others. He had played his cards well she mused, as she served up her bread dumplings and horse-meat stew.

Vegetables were not to hand except in tins and Yuri had decreed that all of the tinned goods must be kept for use in winter and handed out to the community as and when the need arose. For fresh meat the soldiers would bring whatever game there was to be had, which invariably meant more of the horse delicacy and the occasional rabbit stew. Anna had made a meal by name only, this to assuage their hunger and to feed herself and her boy as her heart was absent in creating a loving meal in the circumstances. They ate in silence, except for Anna assisting Eddi in cutting up the leathery chunks of horsemeat that graced his plate.

With the meal over, Yuri lit up and Anna cleared the table. As the silence became unbearable between them, she finally spoke up from the sink.

'Why did you pick on me? Why not a Russian woman? God only knows there's a surplus of them from what I've seen.' He pondered the question as he reached back to the sideboard for a glass and bottle. Anna dried her hands on her apron and sat down across the table from him and waited for an answer. After pouring a drink of gooseberry vodka, he raised his glass in benign salute.

'It's quite simple Anna, I liked you the first time I saw you with those British soldiers, and of course you spoke the language. Like you I speak two languages but not English. In my country as anywhere else, knowledge is power, especially after a war where everyone is juggling for positions of high authority, as is now the case here in Russia. I needed someone to help me with the language of the occupation forces in Austria. When you came along I wanted it to be you, as you are a pretty woman and appealed to me.'

Anna felt a flush to her cheeks and dropped her questioning gaze. Yuri knew his last remark had struck a chord – but as with all of the opposite sex, a little flattery can get a fellow a long way.

'Without knowing it,' he continued, 'you assisted me in my promotion for the translations you did. Remember those British airmen? Well, they have already caught more of the Nazis that murdered them. Then as an officer's wife, you know how the Western mind works – in a military sense that is. That's another asset and important to me.'

He refilled his glass as Anna stared at the tablecloth and tugging mindlessly at her wedding ring So I'm pretty she mused, and he likes me and I'm useful as I speak English. There's got to be something else, and there's those bunk-beds – he's stalling.

'Anna,' he went on, 'I know that I acted underhand and I'm sorry but all is fair in love and war and I needed you. Look Anna,' he said in a pleading tone. 'Together we can have a good life with little Mother Russia, just be patient. As soon as the airfield is finished, I'll be given a high position in Moscow, comrades Bulganin and Khrushchev have said so.' He nodded to emphasise the point and lit another cigarette. 'Then look at Germany,' he indicated with a sweep of his hand. 'It's destroyed, kaput, flattened. I know I should not say it but your husband will not return, believe me.'

That remark touched a nerve, as weeks of pent-up fury now exploded. With a clatter, the chair flew across the room as Anna leapt up and screamed at him.

'*You have no right to say such things!* If you think that I am going to be your intellectual German tart, you have another think coming. Show me poof that my husband is dead and I might think differently. Until then, just shut up and leave me alone!' She banged her fist on the table and the vase went flying as Anna stormed towards the bedroom door.

'And another thing,' she said, turning towards him with a wagging a finger. 'Don't think that I'm staying in this shack one minute longer than I have to. You can keep your Dacha and little Mother Russia all to your goddamned self!'

Angrily she banged the door, making the timber structure shake as Yuri, quite unperturbed refilled his glass. Minutes later he pulled out a pile of scorched blueprints from his attaché case and began to study plans of the V2 rocket and its mobile launching system.

Hours later, having stayed with Eddi she came back to the kitchen. She swept past him and in a frosty manner told him she was going outside for some fresh air.

'Be careful,' he said as he topped up his glass. 'There might be wolves.'

'Wolves, what here?'

'Da, great big timber wolves that eat little girls,' he said with a chuckle, pleased with his joke. He's got a stupid sense of humour, she mused, as she opened the front door and stepped out into the welcoming night air.

'Wolves rubbish!' she muttered, but all the same cast a wary glance towards the whispering pines bathed in the peaceful brilliance of the harvest moon.

The sudden sound and cough of an engine disturbed her thoughts. She heard several men's voices, while the light of a torch stabbed the darkness a short distance to her side. Again she heard the voices, distinct and German, then the cough and whine of an engine as it fired and faltered. She made out a lorry standing by a low building and decided to investigate as she knew it could only be the POWs and what's more, she needed better company than Yuri's.

Anna approached the building and was stopped in her tracks as a challenging voice rang out.

'Stoy!' And a torch beam stabbed her face. Shocked and blinded by the light, Anna stood there as the guard, recognising the Colonel's woman, turned off the light and melted back into the night. The silhouette of a man loomed at the door and behind him a candle flickered, accompanied by several guttural voices.

'Guten Abend,' said Anna to the complete surprise of the four men dressed in Luftwaffe fatigues.

'Guten Abend,' came a stunned reply as behind him the engine coughed, whined and burst into life. A lamp from the ceiling slowly glowed yellow, increasing in brilliance as the Bosch generator picked up speed. In the harsh tungsten light, gaunt, inquisitive faces peered out to where she stood and from the surrounding houses came shouts of acclaim and joy. Light bulbs glowed from the Dachas as candles and paraffin lamps were extinguished and Yuri's community, by the courtesy of a Nazi field generator found themselves catapulted into the twentieth century.

'I'm Anna,' she said, coming forward and holding out her hand. One tall airman shook her hand, as the others waved and smiled with oil-stained faces.

'My name's Heinz,' said the airman. 'And that's Manfred, Karl, and Gunter over there.'

'Please don't let me disturb you,' said Anna as she gave them a welcoming smile and acknowledging wave.

'Nein, nein,' said Heinz. 'We've just finished and you now have light.' Anna nodded her appreciation as the others came forward and stood in a little group. They all began to speak at once, excited at seeing another one of their own and a woman at that. They eagerly wanted to know why she was here and was she really his wife? And the boy, he did not appear to be Yuri's?

'Perhaps I'm a guest of Stalin, like you,' she said with a Mona Lisa smile. It was the first time for a long while since they had heard each other laugh, even if at their own expense. Then they were eager to find out what was happening in Germany and she explained the terrible hardships which everyone had suffered.

'What about prisoners?' one asked. 'Are they being released?'

She told them the allies were still holding thousands of prisoners. They were even educating them – de-Nazifying them, to join the new order of things. She mentioned Belsen and camps like Auschwitz and how all German prisoners were made to see films of the terrible events which occurred at these places. They could not believe it themselves and dismissed it as Anna pointed at the mound by the forest, to which they just shrugged their shoulders.

'Army and the SS,' murmured Gunter. 'They can't put that on our doorstep.'

They asked about the new weapons, about the V2 rockets. What happened with all the 'Wunderwaffen'? What went wrong? Anna shrugged and changed the subject.

'So, when are you going to be released?' she asked.

Grimly they shook their heads as Gunter, the youngest in his early twenties, spat on the ground. 'Never,' he said solemnly. 'Stalin will keep us forever. We'll all perish here.'

'They won't bury us,' chipped in Manfred, who seemed to be the eldest – in his thirties, she assumed, with his greying hair and stubble. 'They'll just work us into the ground.'

'The problem is, they won't communicate with us and we have no one from the outside world that seems to care,' said Heinz. 'They get us to work for nothing and keep us on starvation rations and now we have to help them rebuild. It will take years, even with all this stuff coming from us back home.' To emphasise the point, he jerked his thumb towards the machinery humming in the background.

The guard, having finished his cigarette, emerged from the shadows. Pointed at them and then at the generator,

'Robotney, robotney. Arbeit, schnell schnell!' he demanded with a wave of his machine pistol.

'Da, da,' replied Heinz and pointed at his watch, indicating five minutes with his fingers. He handed the guard a cigarette, who immediately forgot all about the work as with camaraderie, they all lit up.

'They always want us to work,' Heinz explained. 'Can't let us be seen taking a break, otherwise their officers will punish them. We're waiting for our supply of petrol, as our machines don't start too well on their poor grade.'

As he spoke the rumble of a motorbike was heard in the distance; minutes later a BMW combination roared into view. The guard quickly stamped on his cigarette as a Red Army lieutenant stepped from the sidecar and spoke sternly with the youngster. Once more he moved away from the prisoners to keep his distance as the Soviet officer ordered Ernst to drive him and a truck back to Minsk. Ernst disconnected the battery jump leads which had been used for starting the generator and excused himself to Anna. He leapt into the truck and sped off back towards the city.

'This is Rolf, our rear gunner,' said Heinz as Anna shook hands with the smiling teenager. 'We get the high grade petrol from the old Luftwaffe planes and mix it with the Red Army stuff.'

'Ach so,' said Anna as the others removed several Jerry cans and filled up the fuel tank by the side of the building. 'I had better get inside, it's getting late,' she said. 'Nice meeting you all. Gute Nacht.'

'Gute Nacht,' they chimed and gazed after her and her feminine curves.

Chapter Forty-One

MOTHER NATURE INTERVENES

Once back indoors and with an electric light in each room, it felt a little more civilised, albeit the lamps glowed bare without shades. Yuri had not bothered to turn off the paraffin lamp and had crashed out next to his empty bottle. A spent cigarette lay in an abandoned cocoon of ash, having burnt its way through part of the V2 plans and Anna's new tablecloth. With a snort of disgust Anna left him there and turned out the lights. Still in her siren suit she went to her bed.

She lay there feeling hot and shivery as thoughts and events of the day flooded her mind. Then there was Franz, was he really dead? Does Yuri know more than he wants me to know? Still feeling shivery she now had a headache and put it down to a chill from being outside. Covering herself with the duvet and still thinking about Franz and happier times – was soon asleep.

It was in the early hours that she felt him. Yuri lay beside her with a heavy arm draped across her waist. Anna prised herself loose, removed her siren suit and went for a drink of water. She checked Eddi in his room and lay back down on the edge of her bed. This can only get worse, she reflected as Yuri, mercifully deep in the hallucinatory realms of Bacchus, snored into his pillow.

By the time he was awake Anna had prepared breakfast of soft-boiled eggs and rye bread 'soldiers' that her son liked. Without saying much and still suffering from the effects of the home brew Yuri left the house as his transport to the airfield was waiting. Anna felt better now and not so shivery but still her headache weighed on her mind. Sipping her tea and gazing at the burnt tablecloth she made up her mind to escape as this, to her, was nothing but an open prison with her as an inmate for life.

Seeing a guard passing the front window she offered him a cup. He thanked her and asked for a cigarette. Anna held a hushing finger to her lips as she handed him a whole tin of fifty from Yuri's cache. The man's eyes nearly left their sockets as he gazed at the tin of Players. Furtively he glanced up and down the road, took the proffered cigarettes and to Anna's surprise, kissed her hand. I've gained a friend she mused as an hour later she left the house, leaving Eddi drawing from a story book.

The guards acknowledged her and nodded in a friendly manner as she crossed the compound to talk to more of the prisoners working on the other new builds. She needed information in order to make her escape and was soon getting a mass of feedback from men that themselves had sought flight. During the afternoon she made an excursion back to the generator house and spoke to Heinz of her intent and plan to break free.

'I'll go as soon as he's left for work,' she said. 'Catch the train from Minsk to Moscow. He would not expect me to go so far north. Once there, I'll throw myself to the mercy of the British Embassy, as they were responsible for getting me into this mess in the first place. What do you think?'

Heinz stood and thought for a moment, lifting his forage cap to scratch his head.

'Sounds good enough to me,' said another voice. It was Gunter, busy wiping a dipstick. 'As a woman they probably won't question you. Make yourself look a little more like the locals though, a little more round at the edges, ja?' He imitated a babushka shape as Anna smiled sheepishly and they all laughed.

'Ja, I never thought of that,' she replied. 'I think you're right.'

'If you can't beat them, join them,' said Heinz. 'A couple of pillows in the right place should do the trick.' He patted his chest and posterior. The two men chuckled at their own wit as Anna stood and watched them have their fun.

'I think I get the idea,' she said after a while. 'But really, what do you think?'

Back to reality, they nodded their approval. 'What about money and identity?' said Heinz.

'I'll sell cigarettes and coffee to the guards,' she replied. 'I'm sure they'll oblige me with a few roubles. For a travel document I already have one from Vienna. It covers all of Russia and the occupied lands beyond. Gut, ja?'

'Sounds good to me,' said Heinz as he dug a hand into his tunic and pulled out a wallet. 'Here, take this. It will help you get started,' and handed her some local currency. 'This will get you to Moscow and a return ticket. You can pay me back some other time.'

'Danke vielmals, Heinz,' said Anna and smiled her appreciation. 'Let's say four tins of cigarettes, some coffee and chocolate.' He

378

nodded. 'Oh, and by the way,' she added as she turned to leave, 'I think it will be a single.'

That night Yuri came home at seven and his meal was there waiting. 'I was tired last night, Anna. I celebrated my first night back at my village. Please forgive me.'

'You could have set the house alight,' she scolded and carried on at the sink.

'I would like you to spend some time with me, Anna,' he continued. 'Learn Russian. It will be good for us both, da?'

'Niet da,' Anna mused, handing him a bottle and glass.

'Ha, Anna,' he laughed. 'It looks like you make a good Russian wife after all,' and gave her a pat on her bottom with a Cheshire cat grin. Anna shot him a cold stare – in your dreams, she mused, and excused herself, explaining she had caught a chill as her headache had returned. 'You get some rest Anna,' he said as he poured himself a drink. 'I must go and visit some friends. They arrived today and were part of the old community. Don't wait up, as I might be late.'

'Ja Yuri, I understand,' she replied. 'Have a nice time.' I hope you drink yourself under the table, she mused, as the front door closed behind him.

She spent some time with Eddi who lay down beside her and began to read the alphabet in English and German. Later she put him to bed and not feeling well, retired early.

In the small hours and not sleeping too well she heard a noise as Yuri entered the room.

'Anna!' he called in a loud whisper. 'I'm home.'

Wide awake now she turned, alarmed and filled with apprehension as she heard him removing his uniform. He joined her as this time he was reasonably sober. With only a nightdress on she was an easy victim as he moved his bulk to cover her. To resist was futile as with several misguided attempts, he entered her body. Anna lay there passive and choked back her tears with a desire to scream and hit out. Once again she bit her lip to mask the pain of his wanton assault and physical degradation of her body as she submitted to his primeval instincts and that of his bear-hugging embrace.

Mercifully her ordeal was brief as she felt his warm release. He lay there like a stranded whale as Anna extricated herself from his snoring bulk. She lay there crying silently into her pillow. She could kill herself now, she thought. Use his pistol and shoot the swine and herself as there it was hanging on the chair. However she had Eddi to think of. I'm leaving today, she promised herself. Not a day longer with this perfidious pig.

As the living nightmare faded into an innocent dawn, she was up early. Yuri awoke to the sound of her retching in the kitchen. After having dressed in his uniform he brewed up some cold tea. He handed her a slice of bread with a thick spread of marmalade but she ignored him. Taking the hint he left the house. Anna meanwhile sat at the table with butterflies in her stomach, as realisation dawned her monthly period was weeks overdue.

***

For Yuri it was time to celebrate as he informed all and sundry in the local community about the event. However for Anna, pregnant with his child it was a catastrophe beyond comprehension. Women, total strangers came to her Dacha to congratulate her as Anna put on a brave face and slowly came to terms with her situation. She would have cut and run as soon as she found out but did not feel up to it at the time. Now it was too late as people made a point of seeing if the German woman, Yuri's 'Zhynáh' was keeping well and her absence would immediately have come to light.

If nothing else, it was a blessing in disguise as she did not allow Yuri with his impassionate manners to molest her any more. No doubt he would assuage his drunken passions elsewhere, Anna surmised but that was the least of her concerns.

As news travels fast in the jungle it was several days later that she met Heinz and told him what he already knew. The prisoners felt for her and did not say too much about it, at least not to her face. Under the circumstances it put everyone in an awkward situation as they knew she did not want this child; however, a mother-to-be is still a mother-to-be and nature tends to bond mothers in her own special way.

'Perhaps it was just as well I did not buy my ticket, as I might have needed the return after all,' Anna said, as several of the airmen chuckled at her ironic sense of humour. 'I'll shelve my plans until later but in the meantime, I'm learning Russian. Who knows, it might come in handy one day?'

'Da Anna,' said Gunter. 'Good for you. We've already done that as we have plans too you know.'

Anna gave him an endearing smile. 'I hope your plans don't end up like mine,' she replied with a chuckle. 'Just be careful, Gunter.

380

Pa-nyaht?' and patted her tummy. Heinz cracked up at that, as Gunter stared at the woman in utter amazement.

As the weeks went by the leaves on the birches mellowed with the accompanying bleach of autumn. Then came the rains, turning the roads and fields into a quagmire of churned-up mud. For the prisoners it was a hardship beyond compare as they still had not lifted all of the potatoes and other root crops and Stalin was waiting for his bonanza, post-war harvest festival. Machines and horses became bogged down and the men in the fields had no protection against the elements. Many became ill and died of pneumonia. By mid-November the first flurries of snow arrived and the roads froze into solid ruts as the Arctic winds picked up to herald the onset of the harsh Russian winter.

Anna kept herself to herself as much as she could. Yuri would feel her bump from time to time but that was his limits. Natasha called with the others and they would sit and drink tea as Anna picked up the language and began to understand their train of thought. They did not feel sorry for the prisoners as they too had suffered and still spoke about it every day. They would never forgive or forget their own ordeal at the hands of those – guilty by association, Luftwaffe POWs.

For everyone's entertainment Yuri had procured a five-valve Sobel wireless set and once he was out she would try and tune in to the BBC which was still transmitting on extra power. She discovered German prisoners were now coming back from Canada and the USA, only to be sent to open prisons in the UK. She learnt more about the terrible bomb which had been used in Japan, killing thousands of civilians from a thing called radiation. That a U-Boot had travelled sixty-six days, mostly submerged and tied up in Argentina on 17 August. It set her heart racing, but the news about that was scant.

She heard how obstructed mail for the POWs was getting through and the Red Cross was trying to place broken families with relatives. Many German prisoners had opted to stay in the UK or return to Canada as they had nothing left to go home to.

The latest news was now about Berlin. The Russians had made a ring of steel around the city making it difficult for the allies to reach the city. Talk of war was once more in the air. Sometimes the programme was jammed, so there were days when she could not listen and would concentrate on Eddi and teach him to read and write.

As the temperature dropped to minus 40 Celsius, loud cracks echoed in the stillness of the night as the intense cold split trees like matchwood but the work on the airfield continued. POWs died every day and were laid out to be buried once the thaw came but the work carried on regardless.

By Christmas Anna was well into her fourth month. She made a tree for Eddi to which Yuri turned a blind eye. Although not a Christian he celebrated with her anyway, in his own way with a copious amount of the local brew. Invariably they led almost separate lives as he was gone for most of the day and sometimes did not come home at all.

Anna with the aid of her bump was able to conceal tins of food as she did her Good Samaritan trips out to the generator shed or the stables. The airmen shared what she gave them amongst the hundreds of prisoners and they were truly grateful to their pregnant angel of mercy. The guards received their share from the vast stockpile, mainly cigarettes and sugar and kept schtum about Anna's fraternising with the prisoners.

Time passed and by late February the winter began to release its grip on the land and a steady thaw began. Once again the local roads became impassable to all but the military and Anna stayed indoors for most of the time. March saw the first snowdrops in her front garden and bulbs began to sprout from the unfettered soil as her baby began to kick in earnest – and announce its desire to come into the world. In the sky the sound of birds on the wing brought her out of the house as the sunshine bathed the land with its warm rays. She looked-on, as geese honked joyously as they winged their way north to their breeding grounds in V formation.

As the days grew longer Anna busied herself with knitting and chatting to the local people who were now her friends. She said nothing to them about her future plans as they remained the same, baby and all. Later, as the ground permitted the prisoners were put to work back in the fields, while others erected the poles to carry the telephone wires to the village. Of course the system was not for everyone but as communists they were all equal, but some were more equal than others. It was therefore no coincidence that Yuri and the local People's Commissar received their phones first.

Anna could now speak conversational Russian and understood a lot that was said as Yuri, oblivious of this fact, spoke freely on the phone to his superiors and underlings, both at the airbase and elsewhere. She gleaned the extended runway was near to completion and a prototype of the American copy would soon be ready for trials.

Days later she heard Moscow was combing the POW camps for any technicians that were involved in the V2 rocket programme, or had any involvement with the A-Bomb. All prisoners were to be screened – anyone so connected would be given their release from the camps and work alongside their Soviet counterparts.

Anna managed to relay this to Heinz and the others who immediately set to work on a fast-track programme of technical re-education as many could qualify as V2 rocket scientists and technicians. Anna was able to lend them the V-2 plans from Yuri's desk, just to make a copy and return them within the hour. One week later she dropped a bombshell in their midst with the news half of the camp was to be moved to some place in the Urals, something about mining the much-needed Uranium.

'Uranium,' said Gunter. 'That's the stuff they used to make the atomic bomb.'

'Never mind the bomb,' said Heinz thinking out loud, 'What about us? The Urals is the back of beyond and not too warm either. That's our death sentence, I can tell you.'

'Any idea when we're likely to go?' asked Manfred as he knocked out his pipe.

'He might have mentioned it,' replied Anna, 'but I did not understand some of it. Just the gist of it, sorry.'

Manfred nodded, shrugged and continued to stuff his pipe.

The screening commenced and eighty of the 'lucky ones' (as they were termed) were whisked off to somewhere near Moscow. Heinz had stayed, Manfred told Anna, as he had other plans but at least those eighty would now be fed and clothed with a good chance of getting home one day.

As spring gave way to an early summer the first four-engined bomber with its capacity to strike America landed on the new runway. One day later, on 23 May, Anna surrounded by fussing babushkas with calloused but experienced hands, gave birth to a girl.

At a stroke her life once again changed. Eddi had a sister and for all intents and purposes Yuri and Anna were now a family. With that in mind Anna was caught in a paradox that would have taxed the Wisdom of Solomon. For here she was, cradling her beautiful baby with its curls of chestnut hair and blue eyes but which alas, had wantonly been conceived in grief and hate.

As she gazed down at her little Katrina, Anna had flashbacks of that night in Vienna where he had so crudely forced himself upon her. She would never forget this innocent child was the product of such abuse. She loathed and hated him even as the father of her child and would gladly have seen him dead, out of her life forever but for the moment, it was just wishful thinking. With tears of indecision welling in her eyes, nature made amends as Anna tenderly put Katrina to her breast and as of time immemorial the motherly bond was sealed.

Yuri came home elated, swaying and reeking of drink and was allowed by the babushkas to hold the baby before hitting the bottle once more. At least this time he had a reasonable excuse as others joined him in the celebration of the first-born in the new village.

Anna lay in her bed as the celebrations went on into the night and wondered what would happen to her now. How could she ever go back to her homeland like this? Even if she did, without Franz who would support her? I've got no one, she mused, I'm alone, perhaps she should stay here after all, she reasoned? And his parents in Dresden, ja of course they would help and I could stay with them. But Franz, even if he did return, what would he think about playing father to a bastard Russki child? Tired and exhausted Anna, in lonely grief, cried herself to sleep as her baby lay beside her, cradled in a Moses basket made of woven birches, courtesy of the POWs.

September came and the prisoners were still there as a new directive from Stalin stipulated that more food had to be grown and harvested. However after the initial harvest they would all be sent off to other camps. As the fields of nodding sunflowers ripened Anna took walks with her baby and Eddi. She had been given a pram by the women of the community which now boasted forty Dachas and a bus service to the city, albeit at irregular intervals as petrol was still a scarce commodity.

On hot days Anna went by the path to the woodland as it was cool in the shade. She would pass the mound with its solitary metal icon where the cornflowers grew and blossomed. Further along were a row of fifty wooden crosses, dated 1941. Yuri had mentioned it and so had Natasha. It was Yuri's handiwork that fateful day as he levelled his Ack-Ack gun and shot up the personnel carriers. Now all were at peace as they slumbered in the earth, the brief victors and their unfortunate victims.

With the aid of the pram Anna wheeled various items to the prisoners and passed on information from the radio and Yuri's telephone conversations.

Heinz had informed her the men would be making a mass breakout. They accepted the risk of shooting and recapture but if they went to Siberia they would die anyway as no one ever returned from the Gulags, especially Germans.

Their plan was simple as Heinz had explained. Several lorries would head towards Vilnius, some 100 miles west – it was the shortest route to the Latvian coast. They would leave a false trail along that route for the Russkies to follow, as the men in those transports would be invalids and not capable of work. Five hundred others would head west, to Vilnius by a different route. Another group would head south, towards Pinsk and eventually Poland. There were still many thousands of Folksdeutsche there and language would not be a problem. Provided transports were to be commandeered along with several of their own, left over from the war. These, as far as the Russians were concerned were kaput, but that was their secret. Again some transports were to be abandoned on a false trail and the escaping lorries double back on themselves as they headed south.

'It's a long shot Anna,' said Heinz, 'but we're desperate. We have to do something to make the outside world aware of our plight.' Anna nodded and agreed as even the newscasts had now dropped the subject of POWs – except in the Far East, where Japan's soldiers were still fighting in isolated pockets on various islands, not knowing the war had ended. 'We will tie up the guards but try not to harm them, not take any weapons as in a firefight we could never win. Besides,' he allowed himself a chuckle, 'we don't want to alienate them.'

Anna admired him for his sense of humour, even at times like these.

'If you like,' he continued, 'you can come with us but we have to know beforehand as I know you have your own plan. We just need to know when Yuri and the Commissar are not around.'

'It sounds like a good idea; I'll let you know as soon as I've found out their movements. I'll talk to you later, ja?' Heinz nodded in reply, as Anna with a happy heart returned to her Dacha.

So, that's it, she mused, they're going, but she still had Katrina to think of. How else could she get away? It played on her mind as she prepared the evening meal.

I'll take the bus to Minsk, she decided. Go to the railway station and find out the times and prices for trains to Moscow. She would talk to Yuri and ask if she could go there in the morning, take the children for a check-up with a doctor. That was her plan but if it failed she'll join the prisoners as a contingency. For once Anna found herself waiting eagerly for him to come home.

He arrived with an army colleague and by the smell they had had a few drinks along the way. Yuri introduced Ivan as his army friend and she recognised him immediately as he had stayed in Vienna, at their hotel. Anna served them both a meal and joined them as Ivan spoke a corrupted form of German having spent a year in Vienna. After dinner she excused herself to feed the baby but handed them a bottle and glasses, as was the custom.

As she fed Katrina with the bedroom door ajar she could hear as their banter and laughter turned to loud conversation. She heard her name mentioned and listened as best she could with her limited understanding of the language. She learnt to her satisfaction that it was as she had surmised; the Soviet authorities had no knowledge of her being here. He had abducted her in collusion with others, this man Ivan included. Her husband was mentioned as Anna, still holding the baby to her breast listened intently behind the door.

They laughed as Yuri told his friend how everyone was in fear of him in the district – all except the NKVD, but they were not around for most of the time. He explained how everyone took Anna to be his zhynáh. They simply accepted it and the local priests kept a low profile as they assumed her to be his wife and would never ask questions. He could have them arrested at any time so they were allowed to keep their flock, the old and the dying, as long as they did not interfere with him.

'They can keep their icons and Black Madonnas under their beds,' he said. 'I know some even marry in secret. Candles and incense, give me vodka any day!' They laughed heartily as Yuri pulled the cork on another bottle.

In vino veritas, mused Anna as the jigsaw began to fall into place. So, he has an Achilles heel after all. One word to the NKVD about my abduction and the hoarding around here and he would be seeing Siberia from his cell in the basement of the Lubyanka.

Armed with this latest information Anna decided to go ahead and catch the bus. I'll mention it to Natasha over our morning coffee, she mused.

Satisfied with her plan she lay Katrina down, kissed Eddi goodnight and turned out her light. I won't need to worry about him tonight, she reasoned, as the chink of glasses and the men's drunken banter carried on into the night. However as an afterthought she slipped into her siren suit as the last thing she needed was an accident...

Morning came and Yuri was late going to the base. He had crashed out beside her and was now in the grip of his customary hangover. Anna gave him black coffee and managed to get him off and out of her way as his driver paced up and down outside. Later, with Natasha and Katja round for morning coffee and slices of Anna's poppy seed strudel, they told her about the bus and its route. That afternoon Anna, Eddi and Katrina caught the bus into the city.

***

The Warsaw express pulled in at 8.20 that evening and came to a clanking halt amidst a cloud of smoke and hissing steam. At this late hour there were few people about, except the alighting passengers and others that were there to greet them.

Looking for the non-existent transportation, a slim, tall man with several days' stubble asked for directions to the air base. He carried a small black case and once on the right road, managed to get a lift from a passing transport.

At the main gate he spoke in halting Russian with the guard and produced his photo identity and work permit which was stamped with the Polish double-headed eagle and authorised by the Russian authorities in Warsaw. He asked the whereabouts of Colonel Konstantin's office, explaining he had been sent to work on special equipment and his train had been delayed. He opened the case and pointed out the various drawings, components and test instruments. The guard picked up the phone and cranking a handle managed to speak to an official in Yuri's office. He relayed the information from the man's papers as Doktor Boris Rusedski. Replacing the receiver, the guard told him to come back in the morning as the Colonel had left the base.

'Bal'sho'ye spasiba, comrade. I'll see him later,' said the scientist. 'I'll go back to Minsk and freshen up.' Self-consciously rubbing his stubbled chin he pulled out a battered cigarette case and offered the guard a black Russian cigarette. The choice tobacco was a luxury and the man's features lit up with surprise and delight. 'I need a lift back into town,' said the scientist. 'Perhaps I can visit the Colonel in the morning, does he live local?'

'Da, Comrade Dok-tar, It's the new village, not far from Minsk,' and pointed in the general direction back down the road.

'Spasiba comrade, dasvidaniya,' said the scientist as he stamped and crushed his half-smoked cigarette and waved down a transport that was just leaving.

***

Next day Anna was jittery. She would speak with Heinz as she had been into town and found out all she needed to know. However, she was frightened and needed his advice and support. Should she take the pram on the bus and station? How much to charge for cigarettes whilst not arousing suspicion, as she needed more roubles? In theory it was easy but actually doing it was a different ball game. She realised past words and bravado were cheap, as here she was alone and with two very dependent children.

She was about to go out, leaving Eddi to mind his sister when a knock on the door startled her. It was too early for the women to come calling. Cautiously she peered from the window to see a man in a dark grey suit that had seen better days and a brimmed hat to match. He looks the official type, mused Anna with alarm, and with a pang of déjà vous, was reminded of Gruber, the Gestapo agent. She presumed he was one of Yuri's men as he carried a black case and seemed familiar. He knocked again, but louder this time.

Anna opened the door and momentarily dazzled by the morning sun squinted as the silhouette with a courteous raise of its hat introduced itself. The guard had seen him too as he passed by, glancing at them both and carried on towards the generator shed. Replacing his hat the man in a soft and familiar voice, said quietly, 'Anna?'

Chapter Forty-Two

LAST TRAIN

He caught her before she almost fainted in his arms and kicked the door shut behind him. Her whole body trembled with surprise, joy and relief as time stood still for them both and they clung to each other for an eternity. Warm, passionate tears ran down her face as he held her in his arms once more.

'It's over, sweetheart,' he whispered, 'I've found you at last.'

'Franz! Oh Franz!' she cried. 'How I missed you. Everyone thought you had been lost with your boat but I never gave up hope.' Removing his hat he hugged her once more as she placed her arms around his neck and pressed herself to him.

'Anna,' he said tenderly and kissed away her tears. 'I'm taking you home.' She nodded as she clung to him but knew she had to tell him. Reluctantly she released him and with undue modesty wiped her eyes on her sleeve. She had so much to say to him but most of all there was the baby. What irony she reasoned; having waited and worried about him for all this time – time, like a thief in the night had changed everything – she had to tell him.

He stood sensing her anguish as she moved away from him.

'Franz, bitte I have to tell you something,' she said as she stood by the table patting her cheeks with a handkerchief. He gazed at her expectantly and noted her outmoded dress, and her face, without make-up, troubled and lined. However notwithstanding, she was how he had remembered her and the girl he had married. Perhaps it was the boy he reasoned, something must have happened to him.

'Eddi? Where's the boy?' he asked with a frown and a hint of caution in his voice.

'He's fine Franz, he's with the ba...' Anna felt lost, with a howl and a flood of tears she threw herself back into his arms. Lifting her head to meet his gaze and with a heavy heart, said quietly, 'Franz, please leave us. You don't understand, I'm so happy to see you but now you must go. Please Franz, just go.'

He held her as her body shook with heartrending sobs at the stigma and shame of the baby by another man.

'What is it, Anna?' he whispered and gently stroked her hair. 'Tell me, sweetheart. If you like, we can leave right now. Pack a few things and we're away. Just a change with my plan.' Stifling her tears, she shook her head.

'Franz, I have to tell you something,' and dabbing her cheeks continued. 'I have a baby.' It was an electrifying moment for them both as the die of uncertainty was cast. He released her and Anna sat down at the table. He met her wide-eyed gaze as expectant tears could not extinguish the sense and gnawing fire in her heart and mind. 'He forced himself Franz, he's a strong man. Please my love, go now. Just go.'

Confused, his mind maimed by circumstances never envisaged was in turmoil as Anna, so happy to see him again now sobbed inconsolably into her handkerchief.

He stood bewildered. This is not happening to me, it can't be, he mused but recalled the horrendous stories of the Soviets' rape and plunder of their conquests. Now he was witness to it, only this time it was his wife. What a blind fool I've been, he reflected as time's wide wings held sway for them both.

Anna, still dabbing her eyes gazed at him as if seeing him for the first time. This was the man, *her* man and his character was on the rack and about to be sorely tested.

Franz remained standing, frozen to the spot – like Rodin's statue, as an inner voice reminded him of another time and place. Of her heady perfume and those soft, willing lips, their passionate embrace as the embers emitted their comforting glow. It was a moment of truth as the irony of the situation hit home. Ja, he reflected, my act was wanton and primitive, whereas he knew with his distressed wife sitting there before him, it would have been the exact opposite, a living nightmare, with its ensuing consequences to match.

He reflected on events which had brought him here. How, after his release as a POW by the British he had gone home to Aachen and found his house, a bomb-site. How the British Red Cross had Anna's records and case history, including the name of a Red Army major. Once in Vienna and with the assistance of the Imperial Hotel staff and a two hundred dollar kick-back to the clerk in Peschek's office, he was able to obtain the whereabouts of his wife's abductor.

***

Their eyes met in marital bond, Anna's red and pleading; his, an aspect of remorse and pity. Trying not to show his guilt, he went to her on bended knee and took her hand. 'Anna, it doesn't matter,' he said gently. 'I can understand. I want you to know that I've come here to rescue my family and not as a judge. I'm not leaving without you. I know part of the story but you can tell me later. You're my wife and I love you, the baby comes too.'

Anna remained seated and placed his hand on her tearstained cheek. Throughout her pregnancy she had pondered the question and now, beyond the shadows of her wildest dreams her burden was lifted. Lovingly she cradled his head in her arms and hugged him to her breast.

'You're a wonderful, wonderful man, Franz Bauer,' she whispered. 'Danke, Danke, my love for understanding,' and put her face against his, nuzzling his hair and kissing him repeatedly. 'I'll always love you and dreamt of this moment. Bitte Franz, take me away from this awful place.'

He stood slowly, his hair damp from grateful tears and stooped to kiss her trembling lips.

'I want you to know I have also envisaged this moment, I love you as ever before and have searched all over Europe to find you. Tomorrow my darling we'll be away from this place. I've got rail tickets and we'll take the last train from here as it's always packed with workers and families going home. We'll head up the line towards Moscow; they will not suspect that and then travel west, to Riga and the coast. Also there's something about a troop train in the afternoon and no passenger trains. Please wait one more day and we'll make good our escape, ja?' Anna nodded and dabbed her face as Franz stood gazing round the room. 'Where's Eddi, can I see him as my bus will be here soon?'

'Ja, but of course, just wait a moment as I have to explain to him you're here. He only has an old photo of you. I'll tell him that his daddy has left his ship and come to see him. He'll like that.'

Franz nodded and fished in his pocket. Seconds later a boy's face peered from behind the bedroom door. Franz went down on bended knee and called his name. With Anna behind him whispering words of encouragement, Eddi saw his father for the first time as a grown lad. Hesitantly, he came towards him as Franz opened his hand to reveal a clockwork bus.

'Hallo Eddi,' said his father in his familiar tone. 'Look I've brought you a present all the way from England.' Bashfully Eddi took the toy and examined it as Franz opened his other hand. 'Here, look Eddi, you've forgotten the key. I'll show you how it works.'

Franz held out his hand as Eddi unsure, handed it back. He inserted the key as Eddi watched him wind up the spring and set the bus down. With a whirring noise it gathered speed across the wooden boards. He laughed with delight and picked it up as he took the key from his father's outstretched hand. Franz winked at Anna, who still could not believe he was real and they were a family once more.

'Ja, and the baby?' said Franz with a mischievous grin. Anna took his hand and led him to Eddi's room where Katrina was asleep. 'It's a girl,' he said with delight. 'Why didn't you say?'

'You never asked,' she replied with mock disdain and a friendly dig at his ribs. 'Her name's Katrina Bauer, I trust you like her?' She sensed his approval and kissed his cheek.

'I like all girls,' he said with a wink. 'Now let me go before I miss my bus,' and patted her bottom. She liked that and responded with a smile as it reminded her of old times. 'Remember, I'll come tomorrow afternoon as soon as the coast is clear. Do you have any identity?'

'Ja, I have my visa.'

'Ja gut, then we can travel together although I brought one for you and Eddi does not need one. I'm travelling as a scientist working on V2 rockets. I know a little about them as they were on my boat. It's enough to get by and fool the Russkies.' Anna nodded and was reminded of what Yuri had said about rockets.

'Better go,' she urged, 'otherwise they'll shoot you and ask questions later. Don't worry, I shall be ready tomorrow.' She went to the sink and splashed water on her face as Franz assisted Eddi with his toy. Anna tidied her hair and applied the remnants of her precious lipstick.

'There, how do I look?' He gazed at her as a lump came to his throat. She's as pretty as ever, he reminded himself and smiled his appreciation.

'You look wonderful sweetheart, any more of this and I shall be in trouble.' Her lips parted in a radiant smile as Anna, for the first time in years, felt like a real woman once more.

A horn sounded in the distance and Franz made for the door. 'I'll be on my way and tell that man Yuri that you're going into town to do some shopping. Or better, say you need to see the doctor, dentist, anything like that. My bus comes here at three o'clock, runs to the next village and returns at around five-fifteen. We'll all travel on that, ja?'

'Jawohl, I know the time table, now please just go and remember, I love you.' So saying, she rushed over to him and kissed him as the bus rounded the last bend in a cloud of dust. Quickly she closed the door behind him and peering in the broken mirror, reluctantly wiped away all traces of her rose-red lips.

Anna was elated and never so happy as now as she picked up Eddi and kissed and hugged him until he wriggled free. 'Your daddy is home! What do you think of that?'

'He gave me an autobus, Mama. Will he come again?' Typical boy, she reasoned.

'Of course, but we have to be schtum, ja?' He nodded as Anna made a mental note to hide the toy. She made coffee and brushing her hair felt like a teenager in love for the first time.

She sipped her drink and wondered about the next day, will it all go to plan? What if Yuri came home early? She agreed with Franz's plan but it was Yuri that worried her as someone might have seen Franz. People around here inform on each other, it's the system. As long as they did not put two and two together, Yuri would assume she had run away. He could not complain to the authorities as he had no jurisdiction over her and it would expose him as well. It seemed simple enough as that was her original plan before the baby. Then there was the news from the BBC, there was discord between the allies about Berlin and the other zones. The Russians were sending troops and tanks.

Franz would have some way of making it back home once out of Russia, she surmised. However I speak a little of the language, which would help. Suddenly she hit upon an idea; she could assist after all…

Yuri came home earlier than usual and seemed agitated and annoyed.

'You had a visitor?' he asked bluntly. Anna felt a flush to her face but tried to hide it as she busied herself at the sink.

'Ja, Yuri, he said he was looking for you. It seems that you sent for him. I tried to get rid of him but he kept on talking. Then he wanted to wait for you. I gave him some tea then asked him to leave.'

'*Shto, tchai…*!? Are you mad, woman? What did he want? Who sent him? I must know immediately?' And banged his fist on the table. Anna turned and glared at him as their eyes locked in mutual mistrust.

'I told you, he came looking for you as you had sent for him. Something to do with a rocket, as he is a scientist. I thought you wanted people like that?' She kept herself moving, as the last thing she wanted was a confrontation. She poured hot water from the samovar and handed him his tea. He seemed calmer now.

'Then why didn't you phone me?' he demanded. 'We have a phone. You should have called me immediately.'

'*Phone!*' She spat out the word. 'Since when have you allowed me to use the phone? Then who should I call, comrade Stalin? Even you have problems with your operators. Don't they cut you off, or give you the wrong department? Answer me that?'

Yuri stared glumly into his cup as Anna sighed with relief. She'd won the battle but then the war was still raging. 'Anyway, you'll see him tomorrow, he'll be at the air-base and has some drawings for you. Blueprints, ja? That's what he told me.' He swallowed her story and perked up at that, but still had the bit between his teeth.

'The gate guard sent him here and you sent him back? Did he look like an official or police? Are they spying on me?' Where is he staying tonight, did he say?'

Anna shook her head as she refilled his cup. So that's it, she mused. He's worried they might find his stash of Red Cross parcels.

'Well he could be an official, Yuri. One never knows around here, does one?' she said with a wagging finger to emphasise her point. Got you, you swine, she mused. Taste some of your own medicine. 'Oh yes, he said he had booked a room at the railway workers' home.'

Yuri was not happy or satisfied about the whole issue with this sudden stranger in his midst and smelled trouble. He grunted something about women as he went to the sideboard for a glass and bottle of gooseberry spirit. With an old copy of *Pravda* on the table he sat chain-smoking, thinking and glancing at the paper but his mind was elsewhere as he settled to watch her prepare the evening meal. He admired her full hips and trim figure along with her cleavage as she leant across to lay the table. He would try his hand with her again. Tonight she'll be mine, he mused, da, I'll make us a son.

To his surprise, Anna joined him and sat opposite as she brought a glass and helped herself from the bottle.

'I've decided to join you. Misery needs company,' she said with a smile. Caught off guard, Anna topped up his glass before he could utter a word. She lifted her glass to him and they chinked glasses as Yuri's pleasure and desire went into overdrive. How splendid of her to join me, he mused, what a great night I'm going to have with her.

In a better mood he tapped the paper and pushed it across to her. Immediately she recognised the picture. The text was in Cyrillic, but she knew enough letters and there was a picture of him in full Ataman dress.

'It's that fascist Cossack,' said Yuri as he topped up his glass. 'Pannwitz, it says here he's been tried for war crimes in Moscow. Found guilty and going to be executed.'

'Ochin 'zhal,' she replied with a shrug and excused herself as water was boiling on the stove. Nice timing, she mused as she tipped her glass into the sink and replaced its content with water. She thought about General Von Pannwitz and was saddened by the news, but dismissed it as she had other things on her mind.

'Da, ochin 'zhal!' he said with a chuckle as his capture had assisted in his promotion. He was also happy she had applied herself with a few catch phrases of his language. 'We'll be rid of them tomorrow,' he continued, as he re-filled his glass and finished the bottle.

'Who? Rid of who?' Anna asked, as a chill travelled down her spine. What's he talking about?

'Those flea-ridden prisoners,' he replied. 'I'm shipping them out to Moscow. We can then have the place to ourselves and be a quiet village as before.' Yuri lit another cigarette and relaxed with his feet on a chair. 'We can keep about fifty for the stables and wagons, but the rest can go.'

'That's good,' said Anna, her mind racing. Gott im Himmel, I have to tell Gunter and the others,

'Supper in five minutes and stop smoking, the smell is making me ill. Open the window or something.' Yuri stubbed out his cigarette, not wishing to upset her, tonight of all nights. Why, she was even warming to him.

'Da Anna, I'll open the window, smells good. What is it?'

'Ukha, fish soup with vodka, you like that and Hungarian goulash, your favourite,' she said, putting her meal onto a plate and with a determined smile, tipped half a bottle of his best Smirnoff into the rest of the stew.

Minutes later, his soup was on the table. Anna busied herself and occasionally glanced in his direction as he finished with a slurp. Yuri nodded congenially as the influence of the soup and his drinks started to take hold. With an endearing smile she removed his bowl and placed their main course on the table. Like any good zhynáh she produced another bottle and poured out a drink for herself and some for Yuri as she sat down to join him. She toyed with her meal as Yuri wolfed his down with satisfied grunts.

'Tastes a bit spicy but nicely flavoured, is there any more?'

'I think I put in too much paprika,' she replied, going back to the stove with his plate and her drink. With relish she tipped it into the remaining goulash before ladling out another serving and once again, filling her glass with water.

'I have to feed the baby. Shall I get her to sit with us?' said Anna, placing his plate on the table.

'Da, da,' he replied with a slur, as he emptied his glass and emitting a resounding belch. 'Excellent, Anna. Prima, what a good cook you are!'

Carrying the baby she sat herself down, stifling a smile at the compliment and at her culinary expertise. Tantalisingly Anna produced a generous breast to feed Katrina. Yuri, aroused by the sight and her joining him with a drink, happily refilled his glass.

Finishing his meal he went with a lurch to use the phone and spoke with a loud inebriated voice about the organising of the transports and the time of the train which would take the POWs to their new camp. The word Kolyma was mentioned several times, however Anna, having put Katrina to bed, sat listening in the bedroom.

Her mind was in turmoil as she had to get word to the prisoners. Putting caution to the wind she went back to the sideboard and brought out another bottle. Yuri, with another belch banged the receiver down and came back to join her at the table. Anna refilled his glass and put a half measure in hers.

'It's your favourite,' she said. 'Gooseberry vodka, Prosit gesundheit,' and raised her glass. Unsteadily he attempted to join her, but abandoned the attempt. 'I heard you say Kolyma,' she continued. 'What's that?'

'Kolyma, my little dyevoshka,' he slurred, 'is gold. They're all going scratching for gold.'

'But I thought they were going to Siberia?'

He rocked unsteadily on his chair as the doctored goulash took hold, however he managed to light his cigarette at the fourth attempt. 'It's way out in the east,' he replied. 'It's the same wilderness, who cares a damn about them, anyway?' He took another slug of the potent brew as Anna excused herself, to check on the baby.

'Yuri, be careful,' she said, coming back and seeing the burning cigarette lying by the ashtray. 'You're burning the tablecloth again.'

'Da, da,' he managed to slur and patted her bottom affectionately. 'You're a pretty woman, Anna. Shall we go to bed?'

'Ja, later Yuri, I just have to clean up and I need some fresh air, I won't be long.'

'Da,' he replied with a hiccup, 'my stomach's on fire.'

'You had too much to eat,' she replied. 'I keep telling you that.' Methodically she cleared the table, topping up his glass as she finished. After a while she stole out of the back door. He won't have me tonight, she promised herself, or any other night as she made her way to the generator hut. In the stillness of the night she heard Yuri's inebriated singing.

Outside the hut she recognised the familiar forms of the airmen and their guard as their glowing cigarettes hovered like fireflies to pierce the night. She smiled at the guard and indicated with a mime about Yuri's drinking. He nodded, amused as the strains of 'Ey ukhnem, Ey ukhnem, Yeshcho razik, yesch da raz' drifted on the night air.

'Hallo Anna, see you're having a concert tonight,' said Heinz with a chuckle.

Gunter swore under his breath as his spanner slipped and barked his skin. He raised himself from his tinkering with the BMW combination and wiped his hands with an oil-stained rag.

'It's that scheiss Russki benzin,' he muttered. With a grin he said, 'Guten abend Anna, sounds like you've been driven out of house and home.'

Anna gave him a wan smile, as such humorous banter was for another time. She flicked her eyes at Heinz and away from the guard. Quickly she repeated what Yuri had said and told him about Franz. Heinz nodded, as they had seen the stranger and now it all became clear.

He stood for a moment, sucking his teeth and lifting his forage cap scratched his head as he contemplated their next move. Kolyma, he calculated, that's about three thousand miles from here, in the eastern wastelands. No way, Herr Colonel! We're getting out of here.

'I'm glad he survived,' he replied. 'He must have balls like planets to come here and get you back. Excuse the language.' Anna smiled, amused at the audacious compliment.

'He's an exceptional man Heinz, he'll take us all back, the baby too.'

'Sounds good, but how?'

'By train and he's got a work permit. He's now a rocket scientist.' Heinz raised his brows. So that's the ploy, he mused. Beat them at their own game. Nice one, Franz.

'What are you going to do now?' asked Anna?'

He lit a cigarette and pondered the question. 'Strange, as we wondered why all those transports were arriving,' he replied. 'So that's it, nothing's changed. We'll just bring it all forward. Tomorrow we'll all make our move. Halls und Beinbruch, as they say.'

'They'll do more than break a leg if they catch you,' said Anna shaking her head, and sensing trouble.

'Nein, we're technicians and cheap labour,' replied Heinz. 'They need us. They've sent all the deadwood home, along with the wounded, made them look good on the newsreels. Stalin will keep us here until we drop. Tell your man if he wants to, he can join us. But I'm sure he has his own plan.'

He paused and surveyed the scene. 'We'll use all of the transports so they can't follow. Then abandon them along the way. Karl over there's a mechanic.' He spoke loudly for all to hear, with a nod in the man's direction. 'Worked in a garage, so he's good at wrecking engines.' Gunter and others allowed themselves a nervous laugh as their desperate planning was becoming critical.

'We'll drain the oil and water,' said Heinz, and run the engines, so they'll have to find new transports. Tell your man we've decided to head for Pinsk and the Pripet Marshes, the Russki used the swamp to ambush us in '42 and left their marsh boards and hide-outs behind. We know from information that they're still there. It's the biggest swamp in Europe and a good place to hide until the dust settles. It's less than two hundred kilometres from here and we can make it under cover of darkness. We're convinced that it's the last place they'll look for us.' There was a murmur and nods of approval from the small gathering, just as Gunter's temperamental engine sprang into life.

'Again, tell your man about our plan in case he needs to join us,' continued Heinz. 'We'll cut the phone wires – it will stop them raising the alarm for several hours, and help Franz, I imagine.' Anna pulled a face and thought it might just have the opposite effect.

'Ja, gut Heinz, I wish you all the best and hope you can all make it. Once we get home, I'll inform the authorities about what's going on here in Russia. Someone has to listen. Hals und Beinbruch as you say, but I'd better get back to see how the Colonel is getting on. I spiked his goulash and had to use his best bottle of Smirnoff, but I'm worth it, ja?' she added with a chuckle.

'Really?' said Heinz with a grin. 'He'll be like a bull in a china shop come tomorrow, and such a busy day ahead of him as well.'

'Serves him right,' voiced Gunter. 'It's about time the authorities took him to task. He acts like Genghis Kahn around here, they're all afraid of him, you know.' Heinz nodded in mute agreement, as that included them all. Yuri could have them all shot with no questions asked.

'Right Anna,' said Heinz. 'I wish you well as I have to get organised. If you don't hear from me before, then all is well. We'll disarm the guards and lock them up. There's only a few and they've all become complacent.' He flicked his eyes to the one standing and watching Gunter with the bike. 'However from what you say, Yuri will have a sore head by the morning. Get him away as soon as you can and we'll cut the wires during the afternoon break.'

'Ja, Heinz,' she replied. 'I cannot shake your hand, but Auf Wiedersehen. Good luck to you all. I'll get him out of the house as soon as I can, as the last thing we need is for Franz to bump into our Russian bear.'

As if he'd overheard them, the guard suddenly showed interest. With a nod of farewell, Heinz went to join Gunter and began to offload several Jerry cans from the sidecar as Anna went back to the house.

Yuri was lying legs akimbo on the bed, which was more or less what she had expected, except that he was naked. For some reason (which Anna could not understand herself) she felt sorry for him inasmuch as she was partly, if not wholly to blame for him being in this state. However the consequences of him being sober would have been too much to bear, she reminded herself, as she went to join Eddi and the baby in their room.

That morning she woke early and fed the baby so little Katrina would not wake and cry. The last thing she needed was her Russian bear staggering about and making amorous demands on her, which could prove her undoing. By six o'clock Anna had finished and with the baby in one arm, set the table and waited for him to surface. There was no hurry, just act normal, she told herself and get him out of the house without arousing undue suspicions. That was her plan.

By seven, Anna checked the bedroom to find him still stretched out, with his mouth open like a stranded carp. For the sake of decency she put a blanket over him and opened the window to allow the alcoholic haze to disperse. She made coffee and poured some for herself. Not to take any chances, she poured a good measure of Smirnoff in the remainder.

Finally he was awake as the sounds and vibrations of several more transports shook the house.

Hearing a noise Anna poured the coffee and went to see what Yuri was doing.

'Good morning, what happened to you last night?' she said cheerfully, handing him his coffee as he sat on the bed. He looked terrible and felt it.

'Spasiba,' he growled as with an unsteady hand he reached for the drink.

'I don't feel too well myself Yuri,' she said. 'I think I'll go into town to see the doctor. Maybe it was the meat – that horse stuff never seems fresh to me.'

'My head,' was all he could say. 'Any of those Aspirinski left?' Anna went and got him two tablets and another mug of the laced coffee with an extra helping of sugar.

'Here, Yuri, drink up, it will make you feel better.'

'Shto eta, it tastes horrible?' he muttered as he sipped his drink and made an all-out effort to pull his trousers on.

'It's coffee, I made it especially for you, and the way you like it. Black, with lots of sugar.' Got you again, she mused. It's payback time.

'What's the time, is my transport here?' Anna checked her watch.

'Eight thirty-five and your breakfast is on the table, but the driver has not turned up. More coffee Yuri?

'Da, spasiba.' Yuri nodded his head, which made him wince. He took the coffee and dragged himself to the sink. Splashing cold water on his face, he peered in the mirror as an alien face stared back, with blood-shot eyes that resembled a road map. He cringed and went to the table, where Anna had dutifully prepared his bread and marmalade, together with two more Aspirins and laced coffee.

'Can't eat anything,' he muttered. 'Have to go, I need fresh air.' He took his jacket as a car horn sounded. 'He's here, dasvidaniya,' he muttered and staggered from the house.

Once in the car Yuri shielded his eyes from the sun, at the same time leaning his head to one side to catch the salubrious breeze. He felt sick as the car jerked along the un-metalled road, and his head felt like the devil himself was driving a wedge the size of Mother Russia into his skull.

Meanwhile, elated at her culinary expertise, Anna packed a few needful things into a canvas shopping bag, which was the usual thing women here carried. She made breakfast, dumped Yuri's coffee and poured the fresh into a thermos flask. With Eddi by her side, she explained they would be going on a long journey and his daddy would be looking after them. Eddi nodded, quite unfazed by it all and carried on playing with his bus as he finished his cocoa and munched his potato bread.

Having packed there was nothing else to do but wait anxiously for Franz to turn up. All the same, she was worried and had that empty feeling in her stomach, just like times before when in the hands of the Gestapo. She watched the clock as the minute hand crept slowly towards the hour and its pendulum seemed to be making more noise than usual. The hours dragged by, each one getting longer as suddenly the phone rang. Its shrilling tone shattering the silence and making her jump as her heart beat loud and fast.

'Ja?' she said cautiously, trying to sound as calm as she could, as nobody ever rang during the day. A gruff Russian voice asked for Colonel Konstantin. Anna understood reasonably well, but decided to play dumb.

'Niet pa-nyáht, Nemetsky,' she said quietly, as the caller slammed down the receiver.

So, Yuri's gone AWOL, she reasoned and it was best to play dumb with the authorities than to start a conversation in Russian, as she was certain it had been the air base calling. Her anxiety mounted as once again the seconds ticked by. Was Yuri perhaps coming back here? She glanced at the clock, which showed two-forty. It was time to make more coffee, as she was too nervous and worried to eat.

She made Eddi his semolina and managed to sit still long enough to feed the baby, when suddenly the sound of a shot rang out. Quickly, Anna put Katrina to bed and told Eddi to keep away from the windows and cautiously peered out from the back door into the paddock. Several hundred men were running and shouting in German. Transports were loading and moving off and the telephone wires had been cut, snaking to earth beside their poles.

The community of villagers stood and watched as the guards, minus their uniforms and their hands tied behind their backs, were being herded towards the generator room. After that, it was the villagers' turn as they were rounded up at gunpoint and, with the horses freed, forced into the empty stables and the doors securely fastened. Anna found herself as the only person left free in the village and with a pounding heart sensed there would be trouble ahead.

401

With all that was happening, she never heard the soft footfalls and a voice from behind that made her jump.

'Anna!' She whirled round and seeing the familiar figure threw herself at him, wrapping her arms round his waist and hugging him as if there was no tomorrow.

'Franz, I'm so glad you're back,' she said in an excited whisper. 'Where have you been? How did you get here?'

'I got a lift on one of the transports,' replied Franz. 'Showed them Yuri's address and the man brought me here. Simple, ja?' Anna released him and pointed at the remaining transports, which were pulling out and taking some of the trussed-up guards with them.

'Ja, I figured it out for myself as soon as I got here,' he said. 'They grabbed my driver and commandeered his lorry.' He chuckled as he continued, 'They were about to take me too, but I told them in good healthy German who I was. You should have seen their faces.'

'I told them last night about you, news spreads quickly around here. So, what shall we do, go with them?'

Franz shook his head. 'Nein, it would be too risky. Some of them will no doubt make it, but others won't be so lucky. We'll head back into Minsk, use a couple of horses and hitch them to a wagon. Our train leaves in about three hours, after the transporter. Where's Yuri?'

'I don't know,' she replied. 'He left here with the mother of all hangovers. Some official called for him but now they've cut the wires I think we had better leave. Get away from here before news gets out and the shooting starts.' Franz nodded and gritted his teeth. Damn them, he thought. Today of all days, they have to do this to me.

By five o'clock all but a handful of men were left as Franz checked his watch and decided to make his move.

'Get your bags, Anna, we're leaving. Just give me a few minutes to hitch up the wagon.'

'I can help, I know how to do it,' and indicated towards the paddock. He frowned and shot her a questioning glance as Anna, smiling assurance was about to join him when frantic banging on the front door made them both freeze.

'It can't be Yuri,' said Anna shaking her head. 'He never knocks, I'll check it out.' She hurried through the kitchen and glancing out of the front window, saw it was Heinz. Quickly she opened the door. Heinz shot inside and slammed the door closed.

'There's a car coming,' he said, 'a jeep. Looks like trouble. All of the transports have left except mine. It won't start and we're now cannibalising one of the wrecks to get it going. There's just myself and twenty others left. We'll wait to see who it is. Can I go out here?' He was already on his way and brushing past Franz, shook his hand. 'Name's Heinz, nice to meet you.'

'I'll go with him,' said Franz. 'We'll stay close and see who it is. Leave the door ajar.' Anna nodded, her heart about to burst as the two men hurried out into the paddock. Minutes later the jeep came to a halt; a door banged and with a gear-wrenching three-point-turn, it sped back along the dusty road.

Yuri, still the worse for wear and nursing his hangover stepped inside the house and immediately slumped down onto the nearest chair.

'Va-dà, devushka, get me some water,' he pleaded.

'Ja, Yuri, just relax, you don't look too good,' and wondered where he'd been? So far so good, he obviously knows nothing about the escape. She poured a glass from the sink watering can and handed it to him. Eddi came into the room and Anna quickly put a hushing finger to her lips and indicated for him to go outside.

Wide-eyed and not understanding all the adult goings on he walked past Franz and Heinz and climbed onto the wagon. Franz met his gaze and put his finger to his lips as the youngster nodded, and with a grin, copied his father.

'You're home early, is it your head?' Anna said and sounding as innocent as she could but her mind was racing. 'Perhaps you'd better go and lie down and I'll make you some nice, strong coffee.'

'Da, spasiba, I don't feel well. I'll just have a lie down as the station will call me as soon as the train arrives. We have a change of plan. I have to move the prisoners at night, orders from Moscow. Did anyone call for me?' Anna froze; what to tell him?

'Nein, all quiet here, I was going into town but had a headache all day.'

Yuri grunted with satisfaction as he made his way to the bedroom, removing his pistol and jacket. '*Anna!*' He suddenly called out. Her heart skipped a beat, as Yuri slumped down on the bed. 'Why are the horses out?' Her mind racing, she thought about a logical answer.

'The prisoners, they're cleaning out the stables. New straw and hay has arrived,' she called back from the kitchen. He muttered something as she returned and handed him his coffee, sweet with extra sugar and a liberal shot of comrade Smirnoff.

Seeing him 'comfortable' she immediately went out to relay the information to Franz and Heinz, especially about the delayed POW train. Franz gritted his teeth as the situation looked grim. Even if they left now, they would not make it in time and with Yuri here and awake, she dare not leave. There was now the option of the morning train, however they could not afford to wait around at the station, or in the city, as the mass breakout would soon be discovered and the hue and cry would be on.

'You have to come with us,' said Heinz. 'It's your only chance. As soon as we get the lorry fixed, we leave. We have to change a timing chain, but after that we're away.'

Muffled shouts, banging on doors and women's screeches for help could be heard coming from the locked-up villagers as Anna quickly tuned in to Soviet marching songs on the radio. Heinz considered tying Yuri up, but left that as an option whilst his mechanics sweated and toiled with spanners. Anxiously the others waited, talking quietly amongst themselves, chain-smoking and cursing their luck. Gunter mentioned something about the waiting train and no POWs, however he was not aware that luckily for them, they were to be moved at night.

Gunter started the generator just as the last bus arrived with several villagers; the driver waited for passengers and with a puzzled frown he eventually put the old bus in gear and set off to the next village. Heinz watched from the paddock while others quickly rounded up the five newcomers and locked them in a stable. 'If anyone else comes Anna, try to turn them away, stay calm, we're nearly ready. She nodded and with mounting tension, waited anxiously by the sink.

As twilight fell, a jeep arrived with two soldiers. They knocked on the door, which Anna answered. They asked to speak to the Colonel, as the phone was not working. They had orders to take him back to his HQ, in Minsk. Anna's mind went into overdrive as they mentioned something about a train and the German prisoners. She explained in her best Russian that the Colonel had gone with the Commissar, to sort out a problem at the airfield. They said and indicated they had orders to wait.

Not wanting them to wander about outside she indicated for them to come in, as he would be back soon. She offered them tea and cake and put a tin of Players on the table and asked them to talk quietly, as the baby was asleep. They nodded at that, grinning in appreciation as Anna fetched two glasses and served them a drink.

Gunter arrived at the back door and informed Heinz, Franz and the round-up gang that the transport was ready. Heinz pointed through the half open door at the new arrivals, Gunter, grim faced nodded, 'What now?' he asked with a frown.

'Get going,' Heinz said with a wave, 'but cut the engine. We'll push it past the house. We'll use the other plan, the one we discussed last night, as it's too late for anything else.'

'Jawohl, I'll tell the others,' said Gunter with a determined smile, and hurried away.

'And don't forget – take all of the Jerry cans,' said Heinz in a loud whisper. At hearing their voices Anna, frightened and confused, came to the back door as their simple escape plan, of only yesterday was rapidly unravelling. Heinz quickly came to meet her as the radio played and the muffled shouts of the locked-up villagers were getting louder.

'Anna, you go and draw the curtains and leave them with the bottle, said Heinz, trying to stay calm as not to alarm her. Pass the baby out through the bedroom window and make an excuse to go outside. Schnell, let's make a move. Any trouble from them, get them outside, say it's one of the horses. We'll gag and tie them up. If Yuri comes out we'll do the same, but he might be armed so we'll have to be careful. Any shooting and the game's up. Hals und Beinbruch, here we go!'

'Just as well,' said Franz with a chuckle as he came to assist. 'We take any more and we'll have half of the Red Army tied up. Maybe we should have done it this way in forty-one.'

Anna, peering through the door, shot him a nervous glance. How can he joke at a time like this? she mused, but admired him for being so cool as she went to draw the kitchen curtains.

Trying hard to act normal, she played hostess to the two youngsters, poured out more tea and told them to help themselves to cigarettes and left the bottle of vodka on the table. Best not to make it too obvious, she reasoned. Anna left them as they lit up and closing the bedroom door quietly behind her checked on Yuri as she stole past and into Eddi's room. She made a mental note; Yuri was not snoring, which did not bode well. With Katrina asleep she passed the baby and her bag out of the bedroom window into the waiting arms of her husband.

Anna came back into the kitchen, closed the bedroom door and putting a finger to her lips smiled at the soldiers in passing. She turned down the radio and as calmly as she could, walked out the back door and closed it behind her.

Heinz was talking rapidly to Franz as they walked at a pace towards the generator hut. Anna, clutching her baby, followed with

Eddi trotting by her side. They watched the POWs as they pushed the lorry round the corner and past the house. She was confused. How are we going to leave now? She wondered as, seconds later, she saw them all clamber inside and the transport pull away.

'Schnell! Schnell!' Franz indicated to her and the side car as they rounded the hut. 'Get inside and lie down. I'll pass the baby, Eddi, you too. Lie down beside Mama.'

Heinz handed Franz a German tunic and forage cap and with Anna and the baby tucked inside, left Eddi lying squeezed in beside her and covered with a Wehrmacht blanket. With several empty Jerry cans piled on top the two men pushed the combination towards the house.

It was then that they saw another vehicle, with headlights blazing, coming towards them. Still they carried on pushing until they were well past the house and with one deft kick, Heinz started the machine as Franz leapt onto the pillion and they thundered in pursuit of the others.

As the combo roared past the jeep, both rider and driver glanced at each other. Blinded momentarily by headlights, it was not easy to distinguish the occupants of the jeep, but Heinz recognised the characteristic flat epaulettes of a Soviet lieutenant and knew speed was now of the essence.

They caught up with the lorry outside Minsk, took the lead and branched off towards the west. Meanwhile back at the Dacha, the jeep screeched to a halt as two rounded and flat-nosed faces peered in bemusement from the window, and before the lieutenant could knock, they had opened the door.

Seconds later, Yuri, eyes blinking staggered into the room as the soldiers, with great animation, were still requesting the lieutenant to keep his voice down because of the baby. Yuri called for Anna as he flung open the back door. It was then that they heard the commotion and muted cries coming from the stables...

***

The station was far from busy as Yuri's jeep screeched to a halt and the soldiers piled out. He questioned an old man with a pony and trap taxi, then pumped the man in the ticket office for information about a German woman with two children.

'Da, comrade Colonel,' replied the clerk in a puzzled tone. 'I've seen lots of women with children, but the train for Vilnius does not leave until the early morning, we are still waiting for the prisoners, their train is still here and pointed to a siding. I was informed of a change of plan, comrade Colonel'

'What about other trains?' Yuri bellowed through the tiny window with its narrow bars.

'Da, comrade Colonel, the train for Riga left a few minutes ago. Now the one for the POWs is coming in.'

'Riga, that's north-west,' said Yuri, more to himself than to the bemused clerk. 'What's the first stop?'

'Vilnius, comrade Colonel. I can call them for you and keep the train there.'

'Da, da,' he said, nodding vigorously. 'Stop that train!'

'*Comrade Colonel!*' came a shout, as the lieutenant ran towards him. 'The lorry and the combination took the airbase road to the coast. It goes to Vilnius, and then splits for Riga, Klaipeda and Kaliningrad. I'll radio on ahead as our bases there still have no telephones.'

Yuri mulled it over for a moment. Did Anna take the train, or was she with the lorry, as the two soldiers, who Anna had entertained, had related that she was still in the Dacha, minutes before he had emerged from his room? In any case, once they caught up with Anna, the proverbial cat would be out of the bag but then, he had no choice. He would blag it out with the NKVD and nodded his approval.

'*Da, davai, davai!*' he shouted and gesticulating with a wave. '*Use the radio!*' However a disturbing shadow crossed his mind. What about all the other transports? Where the devil are all those prisoners? Which road did *they* take? The tied up guards could only say that it sounded like they went on the western road, towards the next village. He had already sent some of his men in that direction and they found several lorries with only sick POWs. Cold sweat began to trickle from under his cap as he wiped his face with a sleeve and the enormity of the breakout and its consequences began to dawn on him. Once Stalin finds out, he'll put me on the rack, he reminded himself. Round them all up and it might not be so bad. However his thoughts lay with Anna and his baby, Katrina. That German whore, had she not tricked and deceived me? He would get even with her, he promised himself.

'I've been too lenient with that bitch,' he muttered as he sat in the jeep beside the lieutenant and hurtling along the Vilnius road as the babushka's words and their wagging tongues now came to haunt him.

Be careful, Yuri, they had cautioned. She's a pretty woman, but devious. Like an apple, all rosy and red but inside it's rotten. She's not for you. What a fool I've been, he reasoned, as the jeep sped on.

'*We must catch them!*' he shouted above the noise of the engine 'Call the airbase, lieutenant. Tell them we need some men with rifles and get my staff car ready. That Horch can go twice as fast as this thing.'

In the back a soldier called up the base on the walkie talkie and arranged for the car, and men with rifles and to ensure that the other bases in the locality had been notified. With the dragnet in operation Moscow would soon be informed and half the Red Army will soon be camped on Yuri's doorstep. With that in mind Yuri hammered the jeep towards the airfield and the lieutenant, with the pedal hard to the floor, speculated that Comrade Stalin would not be amused, as he took a side-glance at his beleaguered senior officer.

Chapter Forty-Three

RACE AGAINST TIME

Night had fallen by the time Heinz turned off the main road into the airbase and stopped by the barrier. The guard recognised him but not the Feldwebel riding pillion. However, he accepted it as another benzin run as he strolled to check out the sidecar. Heinz kept blipping the throttle as the soldier, on seeing the usual Jerry cans, started to raise the pole.

Anna, lying uncomfortably on her side spoke personally to God, as Eddi lay cramped beside her and assisted in cradling his sister. Disturbed from her slumbers and hungry, her cries were drowned by the revving engine and the merciful clatter of its loose tappets.

With the barrier raised they were through and sped past the hangars to stop, as always, by the control tower. Heinz signed the book in order to proceed onto the airfield. He handed the disinterested youngster several cigarettes and proceeded towards the line of redundant Luftwaffe aircraft.

Although the airfield was closed, there were still a handful of personnel to be seen in the control tower. It was normal routine for them to see the single beam of the bike as it trundled along the new peri track, and stop on the apron and for the men to be filling their Jerry cans.

Heinz passed under the noses of several aircraft and stopped by a Heinkel 111 which stood close to the end of the line and was easily identified by its twin engines and 'greenhouse' nose cupola. He switched off the headlight and cast a watchful eye along the road, some three hundred yards distant. Franz began throwing out the empty cans and took the baby as Anna and Eddi scrambled from the cramped side-car.

'Here they come,' said Heinz as headlights appeared from the road and the transport carried on beyond the fence. 'Let's hope they make it through the gate.' With tension mounting he swung open a side door of the old bomber. 'There are seat belts, so clip them on for yourself and the boy,' he advised Anna as Franz assister her to climb up into the aircraft.

With Anna onboard Heinz switched the headlight back on and told Franz to busy himself by walking around with the cans.

'Try and stay visible and occupied,' he called as he climbed into the aircraft and made his way forward into the cockpit. He sat down in the co-pilot's seat and flicked the main triple battery power switch to 'Auf'.

Meanwhile at the main gate the guard was in the throes of changing watches as Gunter drew up with his lorry. He leant out the cab and addressed them in fluent Russian and explained he was following on behind the others with a load of empty petrol cans and some stores for the base.

The guard peered at him in the dim light and across the cab at the other man dozing and leaning against the door. He was about to wave him on when his wide-awake relief asked to see into the back. Gunter felt the icy fingers of fear touch his soul as he jumped down from the cab. He followed the guard, with his heart in his boots and untied one flap of canvas to reveal a stack of food parcels and a dark outline of Jerry cans. Further back, a tarpaulin covered the eighteen men who lay prone, packed like sardines, waiting for Stalin's tin opener.

'Anything for us?' said the old soldier rubbing his flat nose. Gunter, with an inward sigh of relief, handed him one of the boxes.

'Spasiba, comrade,' and took it back to his hut, indicating with a grin for his colleague to lift the pole. Gunter leapt back into the cab and gunning the engine, eased out the clutch. He rounded the hangars and headed for the control tower and stopped to off load and sign the book. This time he opened the back and pulled out several of the boxes and told the sentry they were to be stored here in the tower.

'Orders from Colonel Konstantin,' he said with a shrug. The soldier nodded, leant his rifle against the wall and with the assistance of the co-driver began to shift the boxes to the stair casing. Once off-loaded Gunter calmly signed the book, stepped back into the cab and began to drive along the peri-track towards the light across the other side of the runway.

Franz reported to Heinz that the lorry was through and heading their way. Heinz shouted an acknowledgement and immediately began to flick more switches. Eerily, the tiny cockpit lights began to glow in their familiar reds and purples as he turned their dimmers down. The turn and slip indicator shuddered, unsteady at first, as did the compass as their respective gyros began to hum and stabilise.

Fuel pumps and hydraulic motors whined and a cursory glance at the fuel gauges indicated – over half full.

Heinz heard the screech of brakes, followed by the sound of men's excited voices, some cursing as they leapt from the lorry and in their haste missing their footing as they scrambled up the aircraft's ladder and into the belly of the plane.

There was a frantic shout from Franz as he pushed the combination away from the plane.

'*They're coming, Heinz, they're on the road!*'

'They don't know we're here,' he calmly called back. 'Better get inside, Franz, and shut that door.' Gunter handed Franz a chart as he made his way forward and took the pilot's seat.

Franz watched as several jeeps sped past and headed towards Vilnius, but one slowed and turned into the base.

'*Have you seen any transports going past?*' Yuri shouted at the guard.

'Niet, comrade Colonel. I've only been on watch a few minutes and only one lorry has come in here.'

'One lorry? What lorry?' he demanded. 'Were there any Nemetsky fascisti? Did you see?' He glared at the trembling man who was trying his best to hide the box by pushing it out of sight with his foot.

'Only two comrade Colonel, they had food parcels and petrol cans.'

'*Food parcels! Where? Which way did they go?*' screamed Yuri. The man pointed in the direction of the hangars and control tower, as the lieutenant slammed the jeep into gear and crashed it through the wooden barrier.

***

Gunter was once more the eager Luftwaffe pilot as he checked his instruments. He was once again taken back, back to flying his long range Condor over British convoys and reporting to Berlin of their routeing. Then the spectre of Stalingrad loomed, with the vision of snow and flames after the Soviet Yak fighter strafed and riddled his lumbering Junker transport. The engines enveloped in flames as the aircraft plunged to earth. He recalled how the snow and trees had saved him, as it absorbed the impact. How he had recovered from burns and fought with the others until Von Paulus's surrender. The vision faded as Heinz tapped his shoulder.

'Alles klar!' he called; 'hydraulics on line, undercarriage two greens and locked.'

411

'Here we go,' said Gunter. 'Let's hope I've done my homework,' and activated the port engine starter switch. Lights dimmed as the propeller began to turn, slowly at first then spin, but the engine did not fire. He eased back on the throttle and tried again, but still it failed to start.

'*Gott im Himmel!*' yelled Heinz. '*Schnell! Schnell!* Try the starboard. Get that running.'

Sweat accumulated on Gunter's brow as he methodically switched on the starboard magneto switch and pressed the button to prime the engine. Again the lights dimmed as the ageing batteries surrendered their last spark of life. Agonising seconds passed as the blades began to turn then spin. With a sudden cough and a roar, the Mercedes 601 engine burst into life. From the rear of the plane and above the noise of the engine, came the muted cry of 'hurrahs' as Gunter released the brakes and they began to roll off the apron and onto the peri-track.

Gunter flicked more switches as the generator cut in and the lights brightened. He noted the red safety catches on the gun switches were in place, but knew the plane had been disarmed. Prior to all this, and days before, it had also been agreed there was to be no shooting – a precaution in case the escape failed. He noted another red safety cap marked with faded lettering, but dismissed it. He hit the twin landing lights switch as the aircraft, now clearly visible, rumbled on towards the runway.

Gunter opened up the starboard engine and tried the port engine once more. It fired and coughed several times but did not start.

'Hals und Beinbruch,' he said wiping the sweat from his eyes. 'We go on one.'

Heinz, wide-eyed, side-glanced him but said nothing. From his text books he knew it could not be done, although they were only carrying a quarter of the aircraft's capacity in weight. For him the only comforting thought was the runway had been extended. From the vast expanse of cockpit glass, he pointed to Heinz as two large headlights appeared at the control tower, turning sharply to stab the night in their direction.

'Looks like Yuri's come to see us off,' said Gunter with a determined grin as he spun the aircraft onto the refurbished runway and opened the throttle for maximum thrust.

Lights went on in the control tower as Gunter nursed the controls and the converted bomber began to gather speed. From the cockpit's port side, they saw the headlights of other vehicles and the tell-tale stabbing flashes of gunfire as the old bomber lumbered down the runway.

'Everybody down on the floor!' yelled Gunter as bullets found their mark and holes appeared in the fuselage.

Yuri, having abandoned the jeep, now had the Horch on the runway and, Al Capone-style both he and his men were shooting from the windows and running boards as the powerful engine howled in protest and the car gathered speed.

With the starboard engine on maximum boost, Gunter sped down the runway and muttered for divine intervention it would be long enough to give him the required air-speed. With the ground speed increasing to fifty knots, the tail wheel lifted giving the aircraft more speed but he decided to wait until the last yard of concrete before he rotated the controls to lift the plane.

Suddenly the landing lights lost the runway and the rumbling sound of wheels on concrete ceased as the Heinkel lifted with a stomach wrenching jerk and became airborne. Heinz hit the undercarriage up selector and as the wheels nestled in their bay, the air-speed increased and the two green lights extinguished. In the glare of the landing lights Gunter's eyes widened with alarm as he saw the nearby tree tops looming towards him. Heinz waited for the impact as in his peripheral vision he saw Gunter reached for the red protective cover on the control column.

'*Achtung! Hang on!*' shouted Gunter and flipping the cover open, pressed the button. With the sound of a sizable detonation the aircraft lurched drunkenly to port. Gunter wrestled with the controls as the increased thrust pushed him and Heinz back into their seats. From behind came the sound of shouts and men's curses; however all other noise was suddenly drowned by the roar of the twin booster rockets as they propelled the aircraft with 2200 pounds of extra thrust.

Gunter clung to the controls and watched with relief and satisfaction as the tree tops swooped by beneath him, clearing them by inches as the plane clawed for height and roared with a comet's streak into the night sky. Cries of jubilation and hearty cheers arose from the rear as the pilot eased the plane into level flight. With the rockets spent he jettisoned their twin pods and satisfied beckoned for Heinz to take the controls. Heinz tried the port engine; it ran for a while then stopped, however it did give them extra height.

'Looks like my homework paid off,' said Gunter 'I kept this plane until last when collecting fuel and the batteries I used to bring them to the hangar for charging. Told them we were using them for our village generator. Even put extras, new local ones onboard. Very obliging people, the Russkies.'

'What about the rockets?' queried Heinz. 'I knew some of our planes had them, but they were not successful. In fact they were downright dangerous as they tended to force the plane off course one way or the other. It was a bit of a lottery, whichever way one went.' Gunter grinned and nodded in agreement.

'Ja, you're right. I knew about this type of aircraft as they carried extra bomb loads or supplies with the aid of the rocket-assisted take-off. They even made some with a twin fuselage, had five engines, however they proved to be unreliable; they had four rockets and were temperamental, like ours. Did you see me fight with that bank to port? I was waiting for it.'

'You might have told me, you rogue,' said Heinz with a grin. 'Scared the living daylights out of me and them back there. But how did you know they were going to work?'

'I didn't! I knew they were fitted and on my last inspection knew they were still serviceable. After all it's only a glorified firework. Light the blue touch paper and wait for something to happen, ja?'

'Guess you're right. How far do you think we'll get?' said Heinz, glancing at the fuel gauges and tried to start the port engine once more.

'If the engine lasts, we should make it across the Polish border, or head further north-west and ditch in the sea,' replied Gunter. 'We're not carrying any great load and I don't think they'll send up fighters until daybreak. We'll be home by then.'

Franz made his way forward and tapped Gunter on the shoulder.

'I would like to convey everyone's thanks from back there,' he said. 'Especially mine. Even if we don't make it, no one can say we didn't try. What's our chances?'

'Well, Franz,' replied Gunter, 'thanks for that. Tell them the stewardess will come round with coffee and Cognac biscuits in a short while.'

They chuckled at that and cracked a few jokes about Yuri trying to explain to Stalin why his prisoners were no longer there to dig his beetroots and potatoes. It helped to relieve the tension and took their minds off their immediate plight. 'By the way, anybody hurt back there, from the bullets I mean, said Gunter?'

'Nein,' said Franz, 'we're all good, just a few ventilation holes.'

Ja, gut,' said Gunter, 'these planes have a steel sheathed underbelly, stops us all getting shot up from the ground. By the way, how's our course?'

'That's the lights of Baranavicy to port, said Franz, checking his chart. 'Keep heading towards the north-west, we're on course with the wind in our favour.'

'We can't go to Berlin as the Russkies have a ring of steel around that place,' continued Gunter. 'So, with the wind from the east, we have a good chance of making it along the coast and south towards Hamburg. That's the British zone and about seven hundred miles the route we're taking.'

'I take it we have enough fuel?' asked Franz.

'Ja, ja,' Heinz assured him. 'This plane usually carries a full load of two tons with ammunition and bombs, so we only have half of that weight. With full tanks we can fly just over one thousand miles. Only snag is, we are using fuel at a greater rate as the starboard engine is on maximum power, and flying at this low altitude doesn't help. We'll head towards the coast, pass well to the south of Vilnius and towards Horodna, Koszalin and the coast. Head west along the coast and try for Hamburg. Any problems with the landing gear and I'll try and ditch in the sea. Chances are, some friendly ship will pick us up.'

Gunter tried once more with the feathered port engine and managed to get it to cough into life. Again, a cheer arose as the plane gathered height and speed; however, minutes later it cut out again. Gunter guessed it was fuel starvation and set to in creating a vacuum in the system before trying again. It worked, as the engine sprang into life and they carried on, hedge-hopping on a wing and a prayer as the temperamental port engine was coaxed into life.

Franz with his experience as a navigator guided the pilots using the out of date chart and his knowledge of the stars as the gyro compass might have errors. Soon they past the lights of Lida to starboard as they continued towards Horodna and the Baltic coast.

No one slept that night, with the exception of Eddi and the baby. Franz sat with Anna, who rested her head on his shoulder, happy to be with him as he tried to allay her fears. 'Once we're over the water,' he explained, 'we should be safe.'

She nudged and reminded him that she was never much good at swimming. He kissed her cheek and gave her a special hug. 'I lost you once,' he said, 'and will not let it happen again. This time it's all or nothing. Besides, there are several inflatable rafts on this thing.'

She smiled for his concern but said nothing as fate had, of late, dealt her a poor hand. Perhaps this time it would be different, she mused as she listened to the sound of the struggling port engine, cuddled her baby and tried unsuccessfully to obliterate the terrible happenings of the past two years.

***

It was just after dawn that an astonished duty air traffic controller at Fühlsbuttel airdrome rubbed his sleepy eyes as he could have sworn that a Nazi bomber, complete with Swastika insignia, had just roared past his control tower. Swiftly he trained his binoculars and alerted the base as the aircraft circled and with a waggle of its wings, began its one-engined approach.

He reached for the Very pistol and fired a green flare, at the same time alerting the ground crews. Alarm bells shrilled as a single crash tender was on hand and scrambled along with an ambulance.

In the cockpit Gunter lined himself up with the runway having gauged the wind direction from the sock on the tower and glancing at his co-pilot gave a nod. Heinz selected the undercarriage control. Hydraulic motors hummed but to their intense dismay only one wheel of the landing gear came down. Beads of perspiration ran down Heinz's face as he tried repeatedly to activate the starboard undercarriage.

'Everyone brace themselves!' Gunter called out. 'I'm going to shake it down!'

With one wheel down and locked Gunter brought the aircraft down hard on the port wheel. With a spine-shattering jolt the old bomber hit the runway and came airborne once more as Heinz sat glued to his gauges and undercarriage indicator lamps. As the hydraulic motors whined, Heinz gave a satisfied grunt.

'Two greens,' he called out in jubilation as the starboard undercarriage locked into position.

Circling once more Gunter lined himself up with the runway and eased back on the engine and struggled to keep the aircraft's nose up as the air speed diminished. With a screech of tortured rubber the aircraft touched down on one wheel, teetered and settled back onto both as the crash tender sped in hot pursuit. Gunter stopped the plane at the end of the runway as 'Snowdrops' of the RAF military police came on the scene. Franz lowered a ladder and assisted Anna down onto 'free' German soil. The others assisted in handing down the baby and Eddi followed.

As the re-united family stood and waited for the rest to join them, Franz took his wife in his arms and held her tight. Anna, holding her baby burst into tears of relief and pent-up emotion, daring not to believe her long and torturous ordeal was at an end.

They all assembled as they vacated the aircraft, Gunter, followed by Heinz came to the door and were greeted with three hearty cheers. The two pilots waved and grinned, having defied the odds by sheer pluck and courage. More RAF personnel arrived and began to question the malnourished men, along with several WAAF nurses who came to the aid of Anna, baby Katrina and young Eddi.

She stood with Eddi and holding her baby, waved her thanks to those two brave and daring airmen as Franz, standing by her side, placed a protective arm around her.

'Welcome home, darling,' he whispered as Anna, her eyes brimming with joyful tears turned towards him and smiling happily lifted her head to be kissed.

THE END

GLOSSARY

French

Amour	Love, of
Au revoir	Goodbye, interjection
Avec glace	With ice
Bonhomie	Good natured friendliness
Bonne chance	Good luck
Bonsoir	Good evening
Bosche	Of a head shape, derogatory term for Germans
Bouteille	Bottle
Bon voyage	Good voyage, (Lit.)
C'est bon	It's good, that's good
C'est la guerre	Such is war
C'est la vie	Such is life
Café del Mare	'Café of the sea', (French cafés sell alcohol)
Certainement	Certainly
Château	Castle type of building
Cognac	Brandy, from Cognac region
Fait accompli	Something already done, finished
Filles de joie	Prostitute
Gauloise	French cigarette, strong tasting/smelling tobacco
Je t'aime	I love you
L'amour	Love, of
Le rendez-vous	Meeting
Mademoiselle	Girl, Miss
Ma chérie	My darling, my dear, (affectionate) (fem)
Maquis	French resistance fighters, bandits, terrorists?
Merci	Thanks
Messieurs	Gentlemen
Ma chére	My dear
Mon ami	My friend
Mon chére Mon chéri	My dear (m) My dear (est) For the man you like/love
Mon Dieu	My God
Mon petit chou	My little cabbage. (French endearment)
Non	No
Que voulez vous boire	What would you like to drink

419

Qui	Yes
Rouge	Red, colour
S'il vous plaît	If you please
Tête-a-tête	Head to head (Lit.) Conversation
Touché	To be touched, making a point. Fencing, a point scored
Une	One
Une affair de passion	A passionate affair
Vert	Green, colour
Vin	Wine

German

Abwehr	Defence organisation, counter-intelligence
Ach Nicht das kaffe Haus	Oh, not the coffee house Lit. (Pub, Inn)
Ach	Expression, like Oh. Ah, emphasis – good or bad
Achtung	Alert, take note, watch-out
Alles Klar	All clear (expression)
Amis	Americans, (slang)
Amt	Department, etc
Angst	Anxiety, feeling of. Feeling of fright
Anschluss	Annexation
Arbeit	Work
Auf	On, as in turn on, open, as in a door
Aufwiedersehen	Goodbye. (See you again, Lit.)
Bahnhof	Railway station
Benzin	Petrol
Bestätigung	Affirmation, acknowledgement
Beton	Concrete
Bitte hilfe uns	Please help us
Bitte	Please
Das Volga Lied	The Volga song (Lit.) (F. Lehár, Merry Widow)
Danke vielmals	Thank you very much
Der	of, the
Deutsch	German
Die Hund	The dogs (Der Hund, singular)
Die Hunds Franzosen	The French dogs
Die Russen	The Russians
Dom	Dome, spire
Domstrasse	Dome-street
Dort in der ecke	Over, in the corner
Dünkirchen	Dunkirk
Ein flieger	An aeroplane
Ein Kapitän	A captain
Ein	One, numeral. Also A, as an indefinite article
Eine Judin	A Jewess
Elf Uhr Dreizig	Eleven-thirty. Time
Erlösung	Deliverance
Ersatz	Coffee made from roasted wheat, acorns, (Replacement Lit.)

Fangrost	Bomb trap made of close spaced, inverted U shaped beams
Feldmarschall	Field marshal
Feldwebel	Sergeant, military term, rank
Franzosen	French
Frau	Mrs (woman, lady, etc)
Fräulein	Young woman, single girl
Frau Holle	Sorceress Grimm's Fairy Tales
Fuat	Gone, left. Alpine Dialect
Führer	Leader
Gauleiter	Nazi party district leader, provincial governor
Geburstort	Place of birth
Geburtsbecheinigung	Birth certificate
Geburtstag	Date of birth
Gefreiter	Private soldier
Geheim	Secret
Gestapo	German secret police. (Geheime Staats Polizei)
Gesundheit	Health, 'Your health'.
Gott im Himmel	God in heaven
Grosse	Big
Gruppenführer	(Military term,) Group leader (SS)
Gut, Guten	Good
Gute nacht	Good night
Guten Abend	Good evening (greeting)
Guten Tag meine Herren	Good day gentlemen
Guten Tag	Good day
Hals und Beinbruch	Break a leg. (Neck and leg break, Lit.)
Hauptman	Captain (army) (Lit. Head man)
Haus	House
Heil Hitler	Hail Hitler (Similar to Hail Caesar)
Heilige Mutter	Holy Mother
Heimwehr	Home Guard
Herr	Mr (also the German Army,)
Herrgott	God
Hilfe	Help
Hitler Mädchen	Hitler young girls group (Girl Guides?)
Hochachtungsvoll	With high regards (Yours sincerely)
Hochadmiral	High Admiral (Lit.) Rank of General
Hochdeutsch	High German (Lit.) Of a language
Hund	Dog

Ich nur klein	I only little, Lit. (Pidgin German)
Ivan	A Russian. Slang.
Ja	Yes
Jawohl	Emphatic yes. Yes sir (Military)
Jude	Jew
Judenfrage	Jewish question (Lit.)
	(WW II, Zeitgeist question)
Kaleu'nt	Kapitänleutnant Abrv.
	Kaleu'nt or Kaleu as spoken by crew
Kalt	Cold
Kapitänleutnant	Captain lieutenant (Lt. Cmdr.)
Kaplan	Chaplain
Kaput	Broken, ruined, not functioning.
	(Prob. Old French)
Keine angst	Have no fear
Kind	Child
Kirche	Church
Klosett	WC, closet, toilet
Kommen Sie mit uns	You, Come with us
Kopf	Head
Kriegsmarine	Navy (War navy Lit.)
Kriegsschiff	War ship
Kristalnacht	Crystal night
Küche	Kitchen
Leutnant	Lieutenant
Lieber Jesus	Dear Jesus
Luftschutz	Air raid shelter
Luftwaffe	Air force (Lit. Air weapon)
Mach schnell	Make it quick, hurry up
Mach's (Mach Es)	Make it
Mein arsch	My Posterior, arse
Mein Gott	My God
Mein Kind	My child
Mein Mann	My husband. (Lit. My man)
Meldung	Report, announcement
Milch	Milk
Montag	Monday
Mutter	Mother
Mutti	Mummy
Naumen	Name (vernacular, dialect)
Na	No, slang

Ne, ja wie geht's?	No, yes, how's it going. Lit. (Idiomatic Bavarian, Austrian)
Namen und Stand des Vaters	Name and profession of father
Naxos	Early 10cm radar detection device
Obergefreiter	Corpora; military term, rank
Oberleutnant zur See	Lt. Commander
Oberstleutnant	Lt. Cmdr. Or similar. Naval rank
Obersturmbannführer	Similar to Lt. Colonel (Leader of a 'storm troop' Lit.) SS
Oberst	Abbreviation of Obersturmbannführer
Offizier	Officer
Ort	District
Ost truppen	Eastern troops (Lit.) German troops from Soviet lands
PAK	Panzer Abwehr Kannone, Anti-tank gun
Panzerfaust	Anti-tank gun. PAK Abrv. (Panzer (tank) fist, Lit)
Partisanen	Partisan (s) Guerrilla movement
Polizei Amt	Police station
Prost Gesundheit	A toast, (drinking term) Cheers, good health
Raus	Out, Get out
Reich's Geheim	Top secret, of the country
Reichsführer	Leader of the SS (Leader of the Reich, Lit.
Richtig	Right, correct
San'	Are. Alpine Dialect (German, sind)
Scheiss their hosen	Crap their pants
Scheisse	Crap
Schmuck	Jewellery
Scheister	Defecating person
Schnell	Fast, quick
Schnellbooten	'S' Boats. MTB's. (Fast boats, Lit.)
Schokolade	Chocolate
Schtum	Stay silent, not say a word (Lit. dumb)
Schwarzblut	Black blood (Lit.)
Schwarzen	Black persons
Schwein	Swine, pig
Schweinehunde	Swine dog, (Lit Plural with the 'e') (stinker, bad person)

Servus	Encompassing greeting, used in Austria, Hungary. Bavaria
Sie Kommen	They're coming
Sie sprechen Deutsch	You speak German
Sonder	Special
Sonder Geheim	Top secret
Sonder Meldung	Special, extra-ordinary, report
Sowie	see also, (a conjugation) as, 'and also'
Stein (s)	Beer glasses
Steuermann	Helmsman (Lit. steer man)
TELEFON ABTEILUNG	Telephone exchange (PBX)
Tag	Day
Todt	Name of an organisation, (civil engs.) Fritz Todt, founder
Totalverlust	Total loss
U-Boot	Submarine, (German) (Unterseeboot)
Uhr	O'clock, (Lit. clock)
Um	Around, about.
Unterseebooten	Submarines (Undersea boats (Lit.)
Vater Unser	Our Father. (Lord's Prayer, New Testament)
Vielen Dank	Many thanks
Volkischer Beobachter	Newspaper, of the Nazi party, (Folk Observer, Lit)
Volksdeutsche	German nationals, of that district
Vor und Geburtsname	Fore and Birth-name of mother (Lit.) der Mutter
Was zum Teufel	What the hell (What the devil, Lit.)
Wehrmacht	Armed forces
Weihnachtsmann	Santa Claus
Weizen	Wheat, corn
Wie Geht's	How's it going
Wiederschaun	Goodbye, colloquialism, Austrian, Bavarian.(See you again,)
Wiedersehen	(Shortened, Auf Wiedersehen,) goodbye
Weihnachtsmann	St. Nicholas, Santa
Wirtzhaus	Pub, Inn
Wo hin?	Where to?
Wunderwaffen	Wonder Weapons (Lit.) (Latest technology weapons.)
Zeit	Time

Zeitgeist	Spirit of the time (Ghost of the time, Time Ghost, Lit.)
Zeitzünder	Time-bomb
Zigeuner	Gypsy

Japanese

Geisha	Professional female, artistic female, trained to socially entertain men
Hai	Yes
Iie	No
Ipon	In judo, full point
Judogi	Judo suit
Konnichiwa	Good afternoon
O Hayo gozai-masu	Good morning
O Soto- Gari	Major judo hip-throw
Same	Shark
San	Mr, Ms, Miss, Mrs, (after a name)
Sayonara	Goodbye
Yoroshii	Very well, affirmative

Russian

Angliskij	English
Bal-shoye Spasiba	Thank you very much
Boshe Moi	My God
Bystza	Quick
Da	Yes
Dacha	House, wooden type
Dasvidaniya	Goodbye
Davai	Go ahead
Ey ukhnem	Yo- heave -oh
Devushka	Girl or young woman
Dok-tar	Doctor (in chemistry)
Dvoitchka	Woman
It-ti	Go
Isba	Log Cabin/chalet
Karoshij	Good
Kultura	Cultured
Lyubóvnik	Love, lover, (darling)
Maht vodnya	Our mother
Maht	Mother
Meschugge	Crazy (from Yiddish)
Na-zaht	Go back
Nemetsky	German
Niet	No
Niet pa-nyáht	Not understand
NKVD	Peoples' Commissariat for Internal Affairs (Special Police)
No-chi	G'night
Ochin zhal	That's too bad
Pa-nyáht	Understand
Pravda	Right/newspaper
Robotney	Work, to
Sabrali	Steal, pinch
Sal-daht	Soldier
Shto eta	What's this
Shto	What
Stoy	Stop
Tchai	Tea
Va-dah	Water
Vajdi-ti	Enter
Volga V. Maht Ri-kah.	Volga V. (River V. our mother)

Zhèhn-shchi-na	Woman
Zdravstvuyte	Hello, Hi
Zhynáh	Wife

Miscellaneous

Barbarossa	Code name for invasion of Russia (Barbary pirate (Lit. red beard))
Cable length	200 metres, (Nautical)
Cow's death	Old Norse, to die in bed, not in battle
Mae Vest	Film Star, her figure giving title to a life jacket (When inflated?)
U-Numbers	Used at build. Emblems used for non-recognition/identity
Hold one's thumb	Lucky, like crossing fingers. (German/Austrian etc.)

Volga Boatmen   Song of bargemen pulling boats
Along a tow-path in 1800's

Yo-heave oh, Yo-heave-oh,
Ey ukhnem, rpt.   One more time and yet, one more
Yeshcho razik, yeshch da raz   Rpt.
Rpt.

www.ingramcontent.com/pod-product-compliance
Lightning Source LLC
Chambersburg PA
CBHW050121030726
47505CB00007B/1975